ALL COME TO DUST

Bryony Rheam was born in Kadoma, Zimbabwe. Her debut novel *This September Sun* won Best First Book Award in 2010 and reached Number 1 on Amazon Kindle. She has also published a range of short stories in anthologies. In 2014, she won an international competition to write a chapter of an Agatha Christie novel. She has attended the Ake Book and Arts festival in Abeokuta, Nigeria and Africa Utopia at the Southbank Centre in London. Rheam is a recipient of the 2018 Miles Morland Writing scholarship. She is an English teacher at Girls' College and lives in Bulawayo with her partner and their two children.

ALL COME TO DUST

Bryony Rheam

amaBooks

PARTHIAN

Parthian, Cardigan SA43 1ED www.parthianbooks.com
amaBooks, Crug Bychan, Cardigan, SA43 1PU amabooksbyo.blogspot.com
First published in 2021
© Bryony Rheam 2021
ISBN 978-1-913640-02-6 paperback
ISBN 978-1-913640-03-3 ebook
Edited by Jane Morris
Cover images: Dreamstime and Unsplash
Cover design: Syncopated Pandemonium
Typeset by Elaine Sharples
Printed by 4Edge Limited
Published with the financial support of the Books Council of Wales
British Library Cataloguing in Publication Data
A cataloguing record for this book is available from the British Library.

For my mother

Chapter One

It was three o'clock in the afternoon, Bulawayo time. A cyclist ambled down the road, his bike tilting gently to one side as he peddled round the corner. The weak winter sun was already beginning to wane, leaving shadowed places cool and dark. The cat at 274 Clark Road moved idly two steps up onto the warmed verandah floor, lazily chasing the sun as best he could manage. Inside the house, Marcia Pullman put the finishing touches to the mushroom vol-au-vents and stood back with a strained look of critical pride. It would have to do, she thought, with a resigned shake of her head.

The fresh mushrooms had cost a great deal of money, and it was a pity no one really appreciated the amount of time she put into these events and all the expense. She couldn't help but remember the meeting at Brenda's the previous month. Janet and Brenda had shared the costs, but even then they couldn't come up with anything good. Pizza. Of course, Janet had maintained it was homemade, but Marcia was quite certain she had seen the Pizza Inn boxes in the kitchen. Anyway, it showed the limits of both Janet's and Brenda's imagination and skill, even if it was homemade. People could say what they wanted about the modern world and how progress and change were necessary, but Marcia knew the way things were done – and should always be done – and it was a crying shame that more people didn't. Nor had she ever accepted the argument that things had changed in Zimbabwe and one had to 'make do'. Her blood would almost turn cold when she saw ladies trying to make something presentable out of Marie biscuits and Marmite. And they couldn't even use proper butter, but margarine instead. Cheap brands, too. It just wasn't acceptable, whatever people said about inflation and shortages and how they didn't have the money any more.

'Oh, Marcia,' she could just imagine Janet saying in that

1

silly schoolgirl voice of hers, 'You do do everything *so* well. You put the rest of us to shame.' And then the titters of agreement from the other women as they marvelled at her table settings: the way she arranged a plumage of purple voile to spill out from a crystal vase, just as though it were a waterfall, or the way she scattered rose petals over the tablecloth in such a way that it all looked *so natural*. All the other women whispered to each other, 'Isn't she clever? It's different every time we come here.'

Marcia blew through her nose as she arranged a little shredded lettuce on the sandwiches. Her hand trembled slightly and a few pieces fell onto the table. Her head thumped with the urgency of a migraine and she swayed a little and put out her hand to steady herself. She took two aspirin from a bottle and decided to go and have a lie down. Her legs were tired from all the standing she'd been doing. She hadn't just done snacks for book club, she'd also made her famous scones with homemade strawberry jam for tea. Janet was coming round in an hour to do a quick stocktake of all the books. Stupid time, really, she had thought, but Janet said it was the only time that afternoon she could leave her elderly mother – and said she'd check the books more quickly as they were laid out on the table. Of course, Marcia had told her she'd be far too busy to help with the books, and it was Janet's job anyway as she was Secretary and really Marcia had to draw the line somewhere at what were her duties and what were Janet's. She couldn't do *everything*. Heavens, no! There was all the crockery and cutlery to lay out and she had to make sure that all the tablecloths were clean.

Marcia poured herself a glass of water from a jug in the fridge. Dorcas, of course, was useless. She had seemed intelligent and capable at first and Marcia had had great plans for the girl. They had already had one near catastrophe due to that big stain that she hadn't said a word about. She'd just folded the tablecloth away! And then they'd had to make do with the pale lemon instead, which was quite unfortunate considering the colour of the napkins. There had also been a question over some food that went missing before last week's bridge evening – vol-au-vents, cheese straws, sausage rolls, that sort of thing – and Marcia felt she just couldn't have Dorcas help with the food in future. She had questioned her about it, of course, even threatened to call in the police, but Dorcas had denied everything, suggesting the cat may have jumped up and eaten them. Really, the stories these people came up with! Mind you, she could write a book on domestics. They just weren't the same any more. They wanted everything: cell phones, makeup, high heels and they thought they got all that by clicking their fingers and demanding more. Well, Marcia just wasn't going to have it. She'd given Dorcas a warning: 'Once more and you're out,' and Dorcas had bowed her head silently and nodded.

The importance of good linen wouldn't occur to Janet, thought Marcia, remembering what she had produced at the last meeting. Her tablecloths were quite threadbare and she tried to cover the holes and stains with plates of food, but frankly, Marcia despaired, how much food could you put on a table? Heavy with tiredness, she stumbled as she walked down the corridor, reaching out for the wall and knocking a picture out of place as she did so. Water splashed out of her glass, but she didn't seem to notice.

'Damn sooes,' she said aloud. 'Sooes.' She stopped, breathless, and tried to think of the word. Her mouth felt heavy and unwieldy. The morning's incident had obviously had more of an effect on her than she had imagined it would.

She would just have a little lie down. She slipped off her shoes, giving them a slight shake as she did so and slowly swung her stout, stocking-clad legs onto the bed. 'Just an hour,' she said aloud to herself, but even as she said it, the words deserted her and she struggled to call them back. What was it she was thinking? What had she just said?

She reached down to the foot of the bed and pulled up the red travelling rug, laying it across her legs. Her last thought before her eyelids closed was that she must remind Dorcas to use a bit of fabric softener when she washed the blankets.

3

At four o'clock, Janet Peters buzzed the intercom outside the gate. No one answered. She buzzed again. Still no one answered. She tried the gate. It was a heavy green metal gate that slid open on rollers. If Marcia was home, it was generally unlocked as it was now. She walked up the drive and knocked at the front door.

'Cooo-eee,' she called, putting her hand up above her eyes as she peered through the window panel at the side of the door. 'Mar-ci-aaa.' Janet tried the door, but it was locked.

'That's strange,' she said aloud. 'There should be someone here.' She tried again, but there was no answer. She went round to the back, but was equally unsuccessful. There didn't seem to be anyone in the house at all. She took her cell phone out of her bag and dialled Marcia's number. An irritating fake American voice told her that the cell phone she was trying to reach was not available, please try again later. It was unusual for Marcia to have her phone switched off. Where was Dorcas? Where was the gardener? She went round to the servants' quarters, behind a wall at the back of the house. They seemed all shut up, too.

She was just coming back round the side of the wall when she met Dorcas, carrying a large plastic shopping bag from Game that looked full of clothes. She wasn't wearing her uniform; in fact, she looked quite carefree in a floral cotton dress and pumps. She was smiling, swinging the bag a little as she walked and hummed. She stopped as soon as she saw Janet. Her smile disappeared and she seemed to pull her languid limbs together as though Janet had just called her to attention.

'Hello, Dorcas,' said Janet, brightly. 'Where is everyone? Where's the madam?'

'Madam is inside,' said Dorcas flatly, pointing half-heartedly to the house.

'Well, she's not answering. Have you just arrived?'

Dorcas nodded.

Janet looked down at the bag in Dorcas's hand. 'You've been out shopping?'

Dorcas immediately became defensive. It was as though a shutter fell across her face, rendering it expressionless, except for her mouth for she kept pulling her lips in and pursing them, as though ready for confrontation.

'Madam gave me the afternoon off.'

'Really? But today's book club?'

Dorcas shrugged.

'She didn't need your help?'

Dorcas shook her head.

'Not for laying out the table or washing cups and saucers?'

Dorcas shrugged again and rolled her eyes slightly, as though to suggest there was nothing out of the usual about this and that Janet was overreacting.

'Where's Malakai?'

'Fired.'

'Fired? Why? When?'

'Last week. He cleaned madam's car with Vim.'

'Oh dear. I'm sure it was a mistake.'

Dorcas kept quiet, waiting to be dismissed.

'Well, I really wonder where she is. Her car's here and I don't think she is likely to have walked anywhere.' Janet couldn't imagine Marcia being the walking type. She drove everywhere, and if she didn't drive, she 'sent' for things or sent someone to deliver things. Varicose veins, she had once told Janet, were the bane of her life. Janet had tried to tell her about an article she had read which claimed that exercise was good for varicose veins, but Marcia had dismissed it with a wave of a profiterole-full hand and what could have been a laugh, but what could also have been a sneer.

'Janet, *dear*, I really don't know where you get these notions half the time.'

'It was *Reader's Digest*–' Janet had begun, but Marcia had cut her off with another half-laugh, half-sneer, as though that explained it all.

'Perhaps I'm overreacting,' said Janet, more to herself than to Dorcas. 'Perhaps she has just popped out somewhere.' Her eyes met Dorcas's, which seemed to mock her for thinking

5

that Marcia was the type to run out of something at the last minute. Surely everyone knew that with her everything had been prepared hours beforehand. Janet must have seen her extensive shopping lists and had she ever seen Marcia in a tizz because she didn't have enough sugar or had run out of eggs? Her pantry was like a small shop and was always kept well-stocked. Of all people, Janet should know how much effort went into Marcia's preparation for book club, and that it just wasn't like her to decide that now was the time to pop out quickly.

'Have you got a key?' asked Janet, holding out her hand.

Dorcas looked at her with a mixture of suspicion and hostility. She pulled her bag closer.

'Dorcas, have you got a key?' Janet pronounced each word more slowly and deliberately than she had the first time. She felt slightly irritated as the young woman didn't seem to share her concern for her employer's whereabouts.

Dorcas hesitated, as though wondering whether or not to make a run for the gate, but then sighed and opened her handbag. She brought out a large old-fashioned purse with a twist clasp and clicked it open. From it, she took out a single key on a key ring and held it out to Janet.

'Thank you. I'll just see what's going on. There must be some logical explanation.' Her face furrowed into an anxious frown. 'Perhaps someone has come to fetch her?' She stared at Dorcas, hoping for some sort of confirmation from this person who stared blankly back at her. 'Perhaps there has been an emergency? Maybe Mr Pullman has been taken ill at work and someone has come to tell her and taken her to him at the hospital?' She stopped, her hand over her mouth. 'Perhaps something terrible has happened!'

Dorcas didn't say a word, but moved her feet impatiently as if to suggest the interrogation was over. Then she turned wordlessly back to the staff quarters and walked away. Janet hurried over to the back door and slipped the key in the lock. It turned easily and she entered.

'Marcia? Marr-ciaa?' she called as she went through the

hallway into the kitchen. Everything looked very spick and span, except for a small pile of washing-up at the sink, which made Janet look twice. The only thing Marcia ever washed herself was the cut-glass crystal, but she wasn't the type to let dishes collect at the sink. It just didn't make sense why Dorcas had been given the afternoon off.

She went into the lounge, which was usually busy on book club day with Dorcas polishing anything and everything that could be polished and the gardener sweeping the verandah that ran along the length of the house. In the summer months, book club was held there, the books arranged on a large wooden table (covered with a suitable tablecloth, of course), but in the winter, Marcia had everything indoors, usually with a large fire in the grate and flasks of coffee and cocoa as well as the wine.

Janet looked around. Besides a table that had been brought in to lay the books on (which hadn't even been covered with a cloth at this late stage) and the boxes of books, which had been placed under it, there was no sign that book club was imminent. It occurred to Janet that there was something peaceful about the room that she hadn't noticed before. It was something to do with the way all the colours blended: the reds and browns of the beautiful Persian rugs on the floor and the deep mahogany of the furniture. They were all antiques, of course. There was that glow to them, the deep knowing air of age and of wealth. Janet half thought she'd like to lie down on one of the rugs to see what wealth felt like, but the thought of what Marcia would say if she walked in and found her prostrate on the carpet, a Persian one at that, brought her back to reality and she turned out of the lounge and treaded softly down the corridor.

'Marr-cii-aa, oh, Marr-cii-aa!' She was reminded of those thrillers where the protagonist calls through the house, 'Is that you, John?' or whatever the name happens to be and, despite receiving no answer, on and on they continue until invariably they end up in the basement or the attic where some terrible fate awaits them. 'If it is John, he'd answer, for

7

goodness sake,' she remembered shouting at the television the last time she'd watched such a film, curled up on the couch and hiding behind a cushion. Marcia would definitely answer, Janet thought. More than that, she would appear, shaking her head, slightly irritated, and saying something like, 'You don't have to keep calling me, Janet. I was just in the bedroom. You do sound like a fishwife sometimes.'

The floorboards creaked a little and Janet noticed that a picture at the far end of the passageway, nearest to Marcia's bedroom, was askew. She began to feel slightly afraid as she approached the bedroom door. She lifted her right hand to knock and pressed her ear closer to the door to see if she could hear anything. It was quiet. She felt like a child outside the head teacher's door, knowing that, if she entered without knocking, she'd be in even more trouble than she already was; and yet she could be in as much trouble for entering at all.

Janet knocked gently and listened again. She half hoped to hear the rustle of clothes, or footsteps on the floor, or the creak of the bedsprings, but there was nothing. She took a deep breath, bit her lip and turned the door handle. 'Haven't you done anything yet?' she imagined Marcia snapping. 'Come on! Chop, chop, girl!' She was ready; she could take it, she thought.

Marcia Pullman lay on her bed seemingly asleep, a small red rug lay across her legs and on the bedside table next to her was a half-full glass of water. If it weren't for the silver letter opener sticking out of her chest and the small bud of crimson that bloomed from where the blade went in, there was nothing whatsoever out of the ordinary about the scene. Janet crept towards the body with a horrified fascination. She felt her bag slip from her shoulder as she turned and ran from the room.

Dorcas, who was just then turning on the kitchen tap, jumped as she heard Janet scream.

'Murder!' she cried, stumbling down the passageway. 'Murder!'

Chapter Two

Chief Inspector Edmund Dube sat at his desk in Central Police Station and tried to focus on the work in front of him. It was Monday afternoon: he usually liked Mondays, but today he felt frustrated. He was filling in a report form, or at least trying to do so. The 'S' and the 'R' were missing from the police station's only serviceable typewriter, an anomaly that may not have worried the average police officer, but one that irritated Chief Inspector Edmund Dube beyond belief. As a young constable new to the force, he had initially regarded the presence of typewriters (there had been five at the time he joined) with a certain degree of relish, looking forward to using them with great anticipation. He had imagined inserting a sheet of crisp white paper, the feeling of a purposeful task ahead; the effortless movement of his hands across the keyboard – no mistakes, of course – and the sense of completion as he removed the document, the flourish of a signature: everything in order.

It hadn't taken him long to realise that things weren't going to be like that at all. He was assigned to filling in charge sheets on cheap grey newsprint, which invariably tore as he tried to extricate them from the ancient jaws of failing Imperials and rusting Olympias. There was little glamour to filling in details about drunken driving or speeding offences, but still he felt it must be done. Order must be kept, and he was the only officer willing to plod through miles of overdue paperwork and put it all in place.

As Chief Inspector, such petty jobs were ostensibly below him: he was supposed to be out fighting crime, having meetings with local dignitaries to reassure them of the police's continued devotion to keeping the people of Bulawayo safe and sound, and organizing the police force so that it ran smoothly and efficiently. Again, reality was something quite different. He had never been an authoritative enough figure at the police station; he was well aware of that. His voice wasn't quite loud enough and his stature, he was short and slim, did nothing to earn him respect amongst both new recruits and old hands, many of whom were taller, and fatter, than he. At times he felt his lack of confidence ooze out of him as he spoke and even he wondered why he got the promotion.

He could never seem to engender much enthusiasm in the force. At one time, he had attended the daily muster parades, which ended with him giving a quote for the day, words intended to inspire and elevate. For a while, this had worked, but then he lost his hold somewhat by quoting lines from *The Saint*, most of which had gone over everybody's head. 'All of us want to do our jobs well. We want to be heroes, to be saints,' he had once addressed them. 'You have to be a very good, and usually very dead person to become a saint. And more importantly, you need to work three miracles. Now, get to work.' His remarks had been greeted with a collective mix of suspicion and confusion. 'You want us dead?' came a voice from the second row followed by a short burst of laughter.

If he had stopped after the first two attempts, he might have regained his footing, but, determined to educate the force on the wisdom of Lesley Charteris, he had persevered, meeting only dwindling enthusiasm and growing boredom. Shakespeare would have been a better bet, even if no one had understood what he was trying to say, and the Bible was always a winner: 'Genesis 5 tells us...' or 'And so as Job teaches us...' but Edmund had sought a higher truth, and failed.

A further result was that, with a half-hearted force beneath him, he had found it difficult to convince the local dignitaries of any sense of commitment from the police. In fact, he couldn't help but think they thought him a liar. It wasn't that he was a big talker, making grandiose promises he would never be able to fulfil, and he certainly never asked for back-handers or anything of the kind. It was his soft, quiet voice that tended to trail off, leaving sentences incomplete, and the way he looked down when he talked, his hands folded in front of him apologetically.

In all probability, Edmund was right about his suitability for the position he occupied. But it wasn't necessarily that he was the wrong person for the job; he was in the wrong place at the wrong time and the more he worked there, the more he came to realise this. Policing in Zimbabwe was very different to what he had thought it would be. It had started with his reading books at school, relics of the permanently sun-filled 1950s when mothers wore flowery dresses and didn't go to work and fathers wore bowler hats and seemed to be in a constant state of getting the train to London. While he was away, Constable Copper could always be relied on to keep the home fires burning. He was tall, sensible and approachable. He climbed trees and rescued cats, he took lost children home to Mother and he always offered timely advice about crossing the road.

As Edmund grew up, this image was dented a little by the crime novels he read in which the policeman was always an idiot and the last to work anything out. The private investigator was much more able and dashing a figure. The bane of the police world, he proved his superior intelligence through a variety of means, often adopting rather less conventional methods of detection than simple interviews and form filling. His was a life of fast car chases, dangerous gun battles and beautiful femmes fatale. Somehow, however, Edmund had retained his respect for PC Copper. The life of the private detective had attracted him, but the life of the constable was his; it's what felt right. He had longed to be part of his reading book world, part of a world that worked; in which all conflicts were resolved – cats returned to their owners, children to their parents and everyone slept soundly in their beds at night. That was the policeman's job and why he was much more the superhero than the private investigator who thrived on chaos.

How long ago was it that he stopped believing in his job? Longer than the typewriter ribbon running out? Longer than the wait for new office supplies, continuously delayed by the lack of financial resources? Or was it when they received their orders to round up and terrorise 'the great unwashed', to beat them and torture them and destroy all they had to their names? He still had the dreams. He still passed people on the street he thought he recognised from that time. He still expected that one day, perhaps while standing in the kitchen or lying in bed, he would receive what he believed was due to him and he could not protect himself from that. And so he hid himself in paperwork and routine and, although he no longer believed in his job in the same way he had when he started, he still got a sense of enjoyment from it. Somehow he was putting a little piece of the world to rights, feeling it spin a little slower as he typed ploddingly on.

This afternoon was like any afternoon. A week ago, he had asked Constable Banda to get the last six months of traffic offences up-to-date, but Constable Banda had then mysteriously disappeared and, by the time he had returned with a rather vague story of having to check the curio vendors at City Hall all had licences, Edmund had decided to tackle the work himself. There was something curiously relaxing about the mundaneness of paperwork that he appreciated. He glanced over at the book on the side of his desk: *Being in Control: A Practical Guide to Self Confidence*. The first step concerned organisation. An organised mind is a confident mind.

There was a soft knock at the door and a constable put his head round the corner. Edmund didn't look up. It was probably a request for tea from the storeroom to which he had the key. Now it was winter, they seemed to expect two cups a day rather than the customary one. He prepared himself to refuse the request. Lately, he had discovered that not looking up and merely shaking his head once while carrying on with his work seemed to do the trick and he wasn't asked again. Looking up involved a type of engagement that inevitably led to him handing over the key.

The head disappeared again and the door was about to shut when Edmund said, 'Yes?'

'I'm looking for Khumalo.'

'I'm looking for Khumalo, *sir*,' corrected Edmund, looking up.

There was a pause. The officer let go of the handle and the door swung open in an insolent arch.

'I'm looking for Khumalo, *sir*.' The voice was flat and bored.

'Why?'

'There is an emergency. They are looking for him.'

Edmund continued to concentrate on his typewriter. '*They?*' he asked, his voice that of a schoolteacher who has detected a mistake in the book of a pupil and wishes to make a lesson of it. 'Who are *they*, Mpofu, eh? Be specific. How many times have I told you?'

Mpofu lowered his eyes in apology, but seemed a little irritated at the same time. 'He is needed at the front desk. There is an emergency.'

'Yes, you said,' replied Edmund with weary resignation. 'He's not here. I'll come.' He stopped typing and took a deep breath, his eyes still fixed on the keyboard. He hated leaving a job halfway through, but thought he'd probably be back in a few minutes, once he'd issued another round of pens or staples or whatever it was that was needed so urgently and disappeared so quickly.

He leaned forward and tipped up his chair so that he could lift it backwards without scraping the floor, a habit he had learned at school. When he entered the reception area, he was confronted with a scene of mild chaos. A policeman was arguing with two vendors whose wares he had confiscated. The offending bags of naartjies lay on the reception counter, the hand of the policeman resting firmly on them. The vendors stood before him, one of them with his hands behind his back looked alarmingly juvenile as he twisted the fingers of each hand in a nervous fidget. Both men had a hangdog look with the sad eyes and the droopy

13

features of people who expect trouble and strife as naturally as others expect the sun to rise each morning. The policeman in question was enjoying a bit of psychological torture with them, repeatedly asking where they had got the naartjies and to whom they expected to sell them.

At the end of the counter was a man in his early forties. He was slightly overweight and his straight brown hair was just that little bit too long. It was a hairstyle best described as a mullet, one that was long considered old-fashioned in other parts of the world (and one of the few unlikely to ever be resurrected with a return of eighties fashion), but one that was still reasonably acceptable amongst Bulawayo's white population, never really known for their adherence to current Western fashion trends. He wore a pair of baggy jeans that were too long, the bottoms frayed from being walked on constantly, and a red tartan shirt with the sleeves rolled up and the tail hanging out. His whole being bore a look of frustrated endurance as he spoke slowly and deliberately to the officer taking his particulars.

'I was *not* speeding. You cannot tell me I was speeding when there are no speed restriction signs along that road. I tell you–'

The officer cut him off. 'Okay. It's okay.' He smiled.

The man's form relaxed and he stood back from the counter in surprise.

'You can go to jail instead,' continued the officer. 'It's your choice.'

Used to such scenes, Edmund's eyes glanced over the pair without much interest. He found the duty officer holding the phone between his ear and shoulder and writing at the same time. Edmund noted how many times the officer had to repeat a question and how many times he asked for something to be spelt and how slowly the man wrote.

'An emergency, obviously,' he couldn't help mutter as he came up behind him. Edmund waited until he had put down the phone before asking: 'Yes, what is it? We haven't any more black pens at the moment. If it's a black pen you're after, you'll have to get your own. I keep telling you all to conserve what we have.' He could never quite understand the preference for black pens over blue. The latter were consumed in great quantities at the start of each school term when stationery had to be found, but this usually died down after the first month back. From then on, it was black pens that were in great demand, as though they elevated one's status above the norm.

'There has been a murder,' said the duty officer, ignoring Edmund's comment.

Edmund felt a slight surge of excitement, but his face didn't change. 'Whereabouts?'

'Suburbs,' replied the officer quickly, obviously bursting to tell someone the news. 'An ikhiwa woman... I mean a white lady,' he corrected himself as he caught Edmund's disapproving look. 'She has been stabbed to death in her bed... the gardener is missing... and...' he started to read from the form in front of him.

'Thank you, Bhebhe,' said Edmund, a warning in his voice. 'There is no need to tell the whole police station the details. And let's make no assumptions, shall we? I hardly think you are the Prosecutor-General.'

Bhebhe's mouth snapped shut, but a smile played around his lips and Edmund couldn't help feeling that he was a bit of a joke in the young officer's eyes. He could imagine him telling his friends about it later on: 'And he says to *me*, "I hardly think you are the Prosecutor-General! Hah! This man!"'

Edmund took the form out of Bhebhe's hands, glancing at it with a practised look of disdain, as though the contents were of no particular interest to him. His initial interest in the case, which had flickered like a tiny flame, had fizzled out as soon as mention was made of the gardener. A white woman dead, her gardener missing – it looked like an open and shut case. She had probably threatened to fire him over some minor theft, or perhaps he had come to work drunk, or spoken cheekily to her and he had lost his temper and

15

stabbed her with the closest thing to hand. He had run away, but the police would find him and that would be it. Case closed. Edmund looked about him.

'I'll need a couple of men. What's the gardener's name?'

The officer shrugged. 'She didn't say.'

Edmund felt his temper rise. 'She? And who is *she*, hmm? The cat's mother?'

Bhebhe looked at Edmund in amazement. He hadn't mentioned a cat – what was he on about now? 'The woman who phoned,' he replied, 'didn't say what the gardener's name is.'

'But did you ask?' Edmund almost shouted in exasperation. 'Ask and it shall be given unto you! You ask for pens and for tea and for pay rises, but you can't ask for a potential murderer's name! What are you paid for?' With that, he strode out of the police station and down the front steps. He came to an abrupt stop at the bottom when he realised he didn't have any transport. The one and only working police vehicle was being used that day by Sibanda, or Sibanda and Friends as Edmund more commonly called him. Edmund was sure he used the police vehicle as a taxi service, but had never been able to prove this conclusively, mostly because if Sibanda had the vehicle, it meant that Edmund didn't, which made following him difficult.

Edmund put his hands in his pockets and let out a great sigh, leaning backwards as he did so. It wouldn't do to go back inside the station, where no doubt they were all waiting for him to reappear feeling more than a little sheepish. He looked down at the sheet of paper with the details of the murdered woman's address and thought he could probably get a tshova and be there pretty quickly: Suburbs was very close to the centre of town. But white people, he knew, thought very little of the police force and arriving without police transport would just increase their disdain – and who could blame them really? Would you trust that the perpetrator of such a heinous crime would be caught by a police force that shared one vehicle and couldn't even maintain their bicycle fleet?

At that point, the man who had been inside complaining of an unfair charge of speeding came hurtling down the steps like an untidy whirlwind, muttering something about Human Rights and the state of the government. He stopped when he saw Edmund, thinking perhaps that he would have another unfair charge laid against him: being rude to police officers or speaking badly of the Law. The man went to open his car and Edmund had a sudden brainwave. Pulling himself straight and adjusting his hat, he went over to him.

'Good afternoon.'

The man looked at him with suspicion. He pursed his lips as though he was about to say something but decided against it. 'Good afternoon,' he muttered, turning the key in the lock and lifting the handle.

'I'm sorry you are Mr...?'

The look of suspicion deepened. 'Martin. Craig Martin.'

Edmund cleared his throat. He had been about to ask very politely for a lift, but at the last minute thought some authority was probably needed. His request was somewhat shaky. 'Mr Martin, I... er... I need to borrow your vehicle.'

'Borrow it? Haven't you got your own?' He looked around as though he expected to see a fleet of police cars lined up somewhere.

Edmund was increasingly aware of the fact that he needed transport urgently and he was loath to go back inside the station. He took a deep breath and said as confidently as possible: 'I may have to commandeer your vehicle if you do not comply with the wishes of the police.' His voice was soft and lacked the required firmness. He wished he could take the words back and say them again.

The man, who was about to get in the car, stopped and gave a forced, sardonic laugh. 'Hah! Brilliant!' He shook his head. 'Look, why don't I just give you guys my car? I mean, you've just given me a fine that's going to pretty well bankrupt me, so why don't you just take it?' He collapsed into the driver's seat, crumpled in despair.

Edmund's eyes turned to the car. It was a fawn coloured

Renault 4, the type that used to be popular as a taxi before the Hyundais and Honda Fits moved in. For a brief moment he was transported back to his childhood and he was a little boy excited at the prospect of a ride in Mr MacDougal's car.

'What year is it? '75?'

It was obvious Craig Martin didn't like Edmund's question. His eyes narrowed and his mouth turned down angrily. He drew in breath sharply and tapped on the steering wheel in hard staccato. To Edmund's surprise, he then closed his eyes and appeared to count to ten under his breath. Then he exhaled and said, 'Where do you need to go?' His voice was low and resigned, edged slightly with sarcasm. 'Perhaps I can give you a lift if it's not too far out of my way.'

'Suburbs. Clark Road,' said Edmund, who was already making his way to the passenger side of the car. The man nodded and reached over to unlock the door from inside. Edmund felt a tingle of excitement as he got in and looked over to the dashboard.

'This is a wonderful car,' he said to Craig, who didn't answer, but eyed Edmund with a suspicious glance. 'How long have you had it?'

'Ten years,' said Craig, shifting the car into reverse. 'Now do you know which end of Clark Road it is? It would save us some time.'

'No,' said Edmund, 'but I imagine it's towards the museum end.'

'A break-in?'

'A murder.'

Edmund heard Craig draw breath slightly and accelerate a little.

'It's a pity you don't have one of those flashing lights we could slap on the top of the car,' he said. Edmund noticed he was relaxing a bit.

'Yes, I know what you mean. Like they have in the movies.' Those cars were the special cars, the ones that looked like your average sedan, but could be so easily converted into something far more sophisticated and out of the ordinary just by throwing a light on top. *You thought I was just your everyday person going about his everyday business, but what I do is top secret, it's important. I solve crimes, I fight criminals, I put the world to rights.*

'Would you mind waiting a while?' Edmund asked Craig as he opened the door and got out in a hurry. 'I'm not sure how long I'll be. I'll let you know if it's going to be a while.' He was pleased when Craig agreed, although he saw him hesitate a moment.

Edmund rang the buzzer on the intercom.

'Hello?' It was a woman's voice.

'Chief Inspector Edmund Dube, CID,' replied Edmund, flicking a piece of cotton off his jacket and drawing his shoulders back.

'Wait a minute.'

Expecting the gate to open immediately, Edmund was surprised to hear footsteps approach. The gate slid back enough for a head to peer round.

A maid, a tall thin young woman with a very bored look on her face, proceeded to talk to the air above his right shoulder. Yes, this was the Pullmans' house. Yes, they were expecting the police to arrive. But she didn't move; instead she looked at him as she might a chance passer-by.

'Can I come in?' Edmund asked, wishing his voice carried more authority.

She looked him up and down and then pushed the gate open wider. He followed her up the drive to the back door. Inside the kitchen, Edmund found an odd assortment of people. A slightly hysterical woman, with faded red hair that stood up from her head in a fuzzy halo, was crying softly in a chair. Before her on the table was a half-finished cup of tea and a couple of biscuits. Opposite her sat a large, but not fat, man with bulbous features and hair protruding through the top of his shirt. Edmund noticed he was wearing a short-sleeved shirt despite the chill in the late afternoon air and guessed him to be a hunter by his short shorts and brown leather boots. The maid returned to the sink, where she slowly dried some glasses. In all the time that he was there, she didn't look at Edmund once.

'Come on, Dorcas, man! Bring those glasses over here! Bloody hell, what's a man got to do to get a drink around here?' He looked up at Edmund with a scornful look on his face and added, 'Pull yourself together, Janet. The cowboys have arrived.'

Edmund nodded apologetically at the three.

'Mr Pullman?' he said, extending his hand to the man who waited a couple of seconds before taking it in a grip so strong, Edmund thought he must have broken at least half a dozen bones.

'I might be,' was his answer. 'And you are?'

Edmund noticed Mr Pullman's accent had changed and he was speaking to him in the way in which he might speak to someone whose knowledge of English was limited. Someone from the rural areas perhaps, not someone at his level.

'Chief Inspector Dube,' said Edmund, holding his hand behind his back and trying to get some feeling back.

'Where's Khumalo?'

'He is busy. I am here to investigate this terrible crime.'

Mr Pullman's eyes narrowed as he looked Edmund up and down.

'I'm sorry to hear about your wife,' Edmund stammered, looking from Mr Pullman to the woman at the table to the maid.

The man continued to stare at Edmund for a few seconds before replying: 'Are you? What's it to you, hey? Another white person dead. You should be glad. Celebrate. Another one down – how many more to go?'

Quite taken aback, Edmund was lost for words. When they did come, he found himself making little sense. 'I need to have to ask a few questions... and have to see the scene of the crime.' He stopped and tried to rearrange his words. 'I'd like to see the scene of the crime first please.'

A sob exploded from the other side of the table as the red-haired woman put her head in her hands and cried more hysterically.

'Struth!' said the man, getting up. 'I'll take you. Don't go putting those glasses away, Dorcas. This way,' he said to Edmund. 'And chop, chop. I don't want you guys hanging around my house any longer than you need to.'

They were just walking out of the room when the maid gave a scream. Edmund turned and saw her throw open the window and push her face right up to the burglar bars in an effort to look out.

'What the hell...' began Mr Pullman, his face reddening in anger, but Dorcas ignored him completely and ran out of the kitchen door, closely followed by Edmund.

'Catch! Catch that man!' she shouted. 'That's the one! Catch him!'

The man in question was Craig Martin.

Chapter Three

Edmund gave chase, of sorts, after Craig Martin. Running after a moving car isn't always easy, even if the car in question is a 1975 Renault 4 – but it did start first time. Edmund was perturbed, but not overly concerned. It was unlikely that Craig Martin would have given him a lift had he been involved in the murder, unless he had done it deliberately and used the opportunity to make sure his tracks were covered and that he had not left any incriminating evidence. When Dorcas had recognised him, he had panicked and run away. It was a possibility, but anyone who scared that quickly would be easily tracked down.

Standing at the top of the kitchen steps, he had a strong sense of déjà vu. It was not the scene of the two earnest policemen chasing the retreating figure of Craig Martin, but the place that was familiar: the view from the top step, the long flank of drive, the high green wall separating the yard from the neighbours'. There was a feeling, too, like a rushing sound behind him. Edmund turned and looked to the side and the feeling disappeared.

When Edmund re-entered the kitchen, Mr Pullman was standing in the doorway to the hall, waiting for him. Dorcas was nowhere to be seen.

'Who was that guy?' growled Pullman. 'What the hell was he doing here?'

Edmund hesitated, not wanting to tell him that Craig had given him a lift to the house as he didn't have his own transport. 'That's what I need to speak to your maid about.'

'Dorcas says he's white.'

'That's correct.'

Mr Pullman looked momentarily stumped. Edmund wondered if he weren't of the thinking that no white man could commit a murder.

He twisted his notebook in his hands.

'Well... er... I need to speak to Dorcas right away.'

His words fell on deaf ears.

'You can sort that out in your own time. This way to the body,' said Mr Pullman, pulling his shorts up with the air of a hotel proprietor showing a guest the way to the best suite his facility could offer. Craig Martin appeared to have been forgotten.

Edmund had the strange feeling again as he entered the hallway that he had been there before... except that it was different, a different room. He shook his head to rid himself of the feeling and opened his eyes to find Pullman watching him.

It was with some trepidation that Edmund walked down the passage to the bedroom. One thing he had never got used to was the sight of a dead body. The door to the bedroom was open and the body lay as it had been found: straight down the bed with hands at her sides. A red rug was pulled up over the legs and what looked like a long, thin knife stuck out of the left side of the chest. A small flower of red surrounded it. The eyes were closed and there was no sign of a struggle.

Edmund looked quizzically at the body. He placed Marcia Pullman in her mid-fifties; like her husband, she was large, but not fat. Stout was the word. Her light brown hair had a slightly red tinge to it. 'Dyed,' thought Edmund, noticing the darker roots.

'Hasn't bled much,' he said, staring down at the knife. He heard a snort behind him and turned to see Mr Pullman rolling his eyes at him.

'What d'you want? Blood and guts, eh?'

'Not at all, sir,' said Edmund, turning back to the body. 'But usually a knife wound to the heart would result in huge blood loss.' He heard Mr Pullman snort again and wondered if he'd been mistaken in thinking it a snort of contempt; perhaps it was a snort of misery. 'I'm sorry,' he continued, 'this must be very hard for you. You don't have to be here, Mr Pullman.'

Mr Pullman shrugged and looked away. 'One dead body's the same as another,' he said, rather cryptically.

Edmund thought it best to let the comment go unheeded. Instead he said, 'Did your wife always sleep like this? I mean, in this position?'

There was another snort and shake of the head.

'It just doesn't look very natural,' Edmund quickly tried to explain himself. He was beginning to feel a distinct sense of threat from Mr Pullman. He didn't like the way the man stood behind him rather than at his side.

'Who knows what natural is?'

Edmund looked around the room briefly, taking in the fine furnishings. The cupboard was open and it looked like a couple of drawers had been rifled through. A large carved wooden chest at the foot of the bed was open and its contents were strewn across the carpet. Yet a handbag sat neatly on a chair, seemingly untouched. Edmund's eyes rested on the bedside table on the opposite side of the bed. It was empty of anything but a lamp. He looked back at the body lying down the middle of the bed. It occurred to him then that this was a single person's room.

'Is anything missing from the room?'

'Not that I know of.'

'You've checked? Money, jewellery–'

'Nope. Nothing's missing,' interrupted Mr Pullman, his voice edged with irritation.

'And the knife? Is it one of yours?'

'Nope. Not a knife. It's a letter opener. Never seen it before in my life.'

'Your gardener is missing? Could I have his name, please.'

'Missing! The bugger was fired. Malakai is his name. Malakai Ndimande.'

Edmund decided not to ask any more questions. He said, in as much of a matter of fact way as possible, 'Please make sure no one touches the body. It will have to be taken for a post-mortem.' Then, in an attempt to appear more official, he added: 'We will need to run some tests.'

'Tests!' Mr Pullman snorted. 'CSI Bulawayo. What a joke!'

If there was anything that Edmund liked, demanded even, it was order. He liked to go through things systematically, working backwards from the discovery of the crime.

'I will need to interview you, sir,' he said to Mr Pullman in as kindly a voice as he could muster. 'However, I would like to ask Mrs... '

'Peters.'

'Mrs Peters. I would like to ask Mrs Peters some questions first.'

Mr Pullman shrugged and pulled a face as though he had just been left out of a round of cards and was slightly nettled. 'Suits me, but I doubt you'll get anywhere with her tonight. The woman's a wreck. Can't string a sentence together.'

Edmund found Janet Peters still sitting at the kitchen table, her thin, bony hands gripping the whisky Mr Pullman had poured her. Her grey-blue eyes held a frightened look and every so often brimmed with tears.

'I have to ask you a few questions, Mrs Peters. I'm sorry, I know you are upset, but it is important I get the main facts correct.'

'Yes,' agreed Janet, dabbing her eyes with a handkerchief. 'Of course, Chief Inspector. Please, do ask me anything, anything at all.' Her voice wavered as she said the last words and she took a small swig of whisky to steady herself.

Edmund watched as she lowered the glass unsteadily to the table and wiped her eyes once more with the handkerchief. He placed her in her mid sixties. 'Nervous. Sad,' he thought, too and not just with the sadness of the moment.

'You came to the house at what time?' he asked, his voice soft in the coldness of the kitchen.

'At four. I was here on time.' She looked at him in anticipation of being reproached for being late.

'You were expected?'

'Yes, you see that's the strange thing, Chief Inspector.' Janet sat up a little straighter and became more animated. 'Marcia was expecting me at four and when I came I couldn't find anyone. It was as though everyone was out.'

Edmund looked sideways at her. 'Why was that unusual? She could have been a few minutes late. Perhaps she was out shopping.'

'Well, it was book club night.'

Edmund looked blank. 'Can you explain?' he asked. 'I'm not sure I understand.'

'Every month our book club meets to – you know – swap books. This month it's Marcia's turn... I mean – well, it *was*. I came over to help her and couldn't find anyone here. You see, Marcia took these things very seriously. She wouldn't have gone anywhere and she certainly wouldn't have given Dorcas the afternoon off. No, Dorcas would've been in cleaning and polishing and shining and scrubbing since six thirty in the morning. The gardener would've been trimming and pruning and cutting big bunches of flowers for the vases...'

'Yes, the gardener. What do you know of him?'

'Only that he doesn't work here anymore.'

'When did he leave?'

'About a week ago, according to Dorcas. I asked her this afternoon and she said he was fired. Cleaned Marcia's car with Vim.' Janet suddenly made a funny spluttering noise and Edmund looked anxiously at her, thinking she was in the throes of choking on something. It took him a few seconds to realise she was laughing.

'I'm sorry. Sorry, Inspector. *Chief* Inspector. It's all been too much of a shock.'

'I'm sure,' he agreed, 'and I won't be much longer. I just need to ask you some details about when you found the body. I know this must be hard for you.'

Her eyes welled up again and she took another sip of whisky.

'You arrived here at four o'clock.' Edmund's voice was gentle, encouraging. 'How did you get in? Surely the gate was locked?'

Janet opened her mouth and then closed it again.

'The gate was unlocked. It's not an electric gate. It used

to be, but it doesn't work properly any more. It's kept closed, but it's not locked if someone is at home. She – Marcia – didn't like me to ring the buzzer. She got irritated having to call someone to let me in. I wasn't, I suppose, special enough to warrant such treatment.'

Edmund was surprised. 'The gate was only locked if she was out?'

'Yes. I suppose she came home, hooted her horn and someone ran out to open it for her. There was always someone whatever time of the day or night.'

'So you found the gate closed, but unlocked?'

'That's correct. I went in and knocked on the door, but no one answered. I tried the door, but it was locked.'

'The gate was left unlocked but the front door was locked? Did she expect you to use the back door?'

'That was locked, too. I thought at first that Marcia must be out although it didn't make sense. I tried phoning her first but there was no answer. I then went to look for Dorcas – she has a key for the back door – but she wasn't there. I had just turned back towards the house when Dorcas arrived. She had obviously been out, which I was surprised about. She was carrying a plastic bag and she had her handbag with her – it looked as though she had just come back from shopping. I thought it was strange, of course. It was book club. Marcia would be giving orders left, right and centre and here was Dorcas in her glad rags.

'I asked her if she had a key and she gave it to me. She gave it to me and I opened the back door.'

'Why?'

'*Why?*'

'Well, do you usually panic when someone is not at home? She could've been out somewhere. Why go inside the house?'

Janet's cheeks went pink. 'You don't understand, Chief Inspector. Marcia Pullman did not go out on book club days. She didn't *need* to go out. She didn't *run out of things*. She was prepared – prepared for anything. Take a look at her pantry and her fridge. They are chock-a-block with food.

Marcia loved entertaining. She loved the limelight. Her functions were planned well in advance. She was *expecting* me! I would've had a phone call at least. Janet pick up this, Janet pick up that. That's if she had run out of anything, which she wouldn't have anyway. Her car was in the garage. All these things, Chief Inspector, suggested to me that *something was wrong.*' Her voice had reached a high pitch now and the words came tumbling out over each other in a tangled heap. 'I *knew* something was wrong. It was all too quiet – too *deserted*, that's the word. I went inside in case–'

'In case of what? Did you think something had happened to her?'

'I don't actually know,' she said, looking suddenly vacant. 'I expected her to come out of somewhere, hustling and bustling and shouting orders' – she gave a nervous laugh – 'like she always did. Marcia, always larger than life...' Janet stared down at the table, a strange crooked smile on her lips. 'But she was dead.'

Edmund didn't want Janet to revisit the murder scene too quickly as she was bound to get upset again and not remember any little details. He imagined rewinding her steps down the corridor and she walking backwards to the sitting room. 'Was there anything out of place? Did anything not seem right when you got inside the house?'

She thought for a second before answering. 'No, I don't think anything was. The books were in boxes under the table. It hadn't been laid, of course. That wasn't usual.'

Janet took a deep breath and began to calm.

There was a silence. Edmund waited for Janet to say something else, but she continued staring into a space ahead of her. He shifted in his chair and she moved, brought back to earth by the sound.

'You walked down the corridor...'

'Yes. Such a long corridor.'

'And everything was in order?'

'A picture... a picture was lopsided.'

'Which picture?'

'The one at the end of the corridor next to Marcia's room.'

'When you went into the room, can you tell me what you saw?'

'Marcia–'

Edmund's voice interrupted her gently. 'Can you tell me what the body looked like?'

Janet pulled herself straight in the chair and cleared her throat. 'She was lying on the bed like this' – Janet laid her arms straight alongside her body – 'and her eyes were open. I went closer and I saw... a... a letter opener! It was sticking out of her chest. There was blood...'

Edmund looked up from his notes with a silent nod. 'Thank you, Mrs Peters. Could you tell me, did you notice anything else in the room? Anything out of place maybe?'

He noticed Janet wavered a little at this question. 'Well, the drawers were open,' she said with a shake of her head. 'Like somebody had been through them. I had never been into her bedroom before, but I imagined everything would look neat and tidy. She, on the other hand, looked–'

'Neat and tidy?' prompted Edmund.

'Yes,' said Janet, as though she had realised something. 'Yes, that's exactly right. Neat and tidy. Unnatural, almost.' Her voice trailed off. 'I panicked,' she said, looking up at Edmund with a start. 'I ran out of the room. My bag slipped... but I didn't care. I ran.'

'And you?'

'Found Dorcas. She was just coming into the kitchen.'

'Ready for work?'

'I suppose so.'

'What did she do?'

'She came down the corridor with me. I didn't go in the room again, but she did. She came out looking deathly pale. It's the most emotion I've ever seen in her. She didn't scream or cry. She was much more composed than I was. Got on the phone right away.'

'To the police?'

Janet's brow furrowed as she tried to remember. 'She called someone else first, I think. I can't remember. She spoke in a very low voice. I think whoever it was gave her a number to ring. You know what it's like, Chief Inspector. You think the number is 999 because that's what you hear in films and on television. But it's not, is it? There are about five or six digits to remember. I couldn't possibly do it.'

'Dorcas reported the crime or did you?'

'She did. I couldn't speak. I was hysterical.' She looked apologetically at Edmund with a small self-effacing smile. 'I am useless at this sort of thing. Dorcas, on the other hand, just got on with the washing up!'

'The washing up?' Edmund looked across at the sink, which was spotlessly clear of anything.

'There wasn't a lot. A couple of glasses.'

'Glasses?'

'I noticed them when I came in. There were a couple of glasses and plates at the sink. I suppose they were from lunchtime when Nigel came home.'

Edmund pushed back his chair and went quickly over to the sink.

'Could you tell me which glasses?' He looked at the bare draining board with a sinking heart.

'Well, they weren't anything too special. Not what Marcia would call special anyhow. Her everyday is my special, if you know what I mean.'

Edmund nodded absently as he looked searchingly round the kitchen.

'You won't find them in here,' said Janet going towards the door. 'She keeps all the glasses in here.' She took him into the bar area, which was a little room between the dining room and the lounge. There was a faux cosiness to it generated by pictures of Victorian English country scenes and a line of toby jugs on a shelf. Mr Pullman sat there in a black leather chair tucked in near the bar, nursing a whisky. For a moment, Edmund thought he looked sad, but when their eyes met, Pullman looked away with a sneer.

'I've just remembered I have something to do,' he said as he heaved himself out of the chair. As he strode out of the room, whisky in hand, Edmund noticed he had left a piece of paper on the seat. He picked it up and examined it closely. It looked like a shopping list, except that each word was caged in by a box. Whisky, brandy, vodka, gin, red wine, white wine.

'That's his bar list,' said Janet, looking over Edmund's shoulder. 'He keeps a tight rein on what he's got.'

'Even at a time like this?'

Janet shrugged in a way that suggested that what Mr Pullman did was beyond her. 'Beer glasses and mugs in that cupboard, tumblers in here, shot glasses on the top shelf. You won't find wine glasses in here. They're kept in the dining room.' Janet navigated the bar area as though she were quite at home, thought Edmund. He had a sudden picture of her pouring cocktails, chatting flirtatiously as she pushed maraschino cherries onto cocktail sticks. A second later, she was herself again: small and thin and stooping slightly with her oversized jersey and silk scarf pulled closely around her as though she needed protection from more than the cold.

'Can you remember what type of glasses they were?' asked Edmund.

'I think they were tumblers. These ones,' she said, lifting a sample down and placing it in front of Edmund. 'Probably. I suppose you want them to run tests on. Find fingerprints and DNA?'

Edmund raised his eyebrows in ironic assent. He doubted the forensic department would know what to do if he handed them the glasses and asked them to run tests. Have a drink, probably. He hoped to glean some sort of feeling about the used crockery and glasses himself – a lipstick mark, perhaps, or an idea of what had been eaten and drunk.

'I'd like to know for sure which glasses were used. It's a great pity everything has been washed up. They may have provided some valuable evidence.'

'I'll call Dorcas,' said Janet. 'She'll be able to tell us.'

'Yes, thank you,' said Edmund, looking gloomily at the tumbler.

'Is it all right if I go afterwards? I'm sorry... it's all been a bit much for me. I just need to get home.'

'Yes. Yes, of course. I understand.'

Janet nodded her head in thanks but as she went out of the room he called out, 'Mrs Peters?'

'Yes.'

'I will need to ask you some more questions. Not this evening. Tomorrow morning? Could you leave your address? You will be at home?'

Janet paused while she twisted her handkerchief in her hands. She took a deep breath and nodded. 'Yes,' she said. 'I will be at home tomorrow.'

Edmund sat opposite Dorcas and took a good look at her while she spoke. She had a long, oblong-shaped face with large, rather sad eyes when she didn't let a veil of lack of interest in life cloud them. She kept her hair short and natural and there was something surprisingly pleasant about that, as though Edmund was suddenly reminded of what real beauty was. They were sitting in a little room next to the kitchen, which served as a laundry. There was a small kitchen table and two chairs inside, besides the washing machine, dryer and an ironing board.

'Madam lets me have my lunch in here, as long as I keep it clean,' she glanced at Edmund, 'which I do.'

Dorcas had not wanted to talk in the house, a sentiment that Edmund could quite understand. She had confirmed that she had washed two tumblers and two plates that afternoon and identified them as the top two plates in the stack on the kitchen shelf, but the two glasses had been used again by Madam Janet and the boss for their whisky.

'Dorcas,' Edmund began, flipping open a new page in his notebook and pulling his chair a little closer to the table. 'Miss Hlabangana.'

She didn't answer, but looked suspiciously at him.

32

Edmund guessed she wasn't used to being referred to as Miss Hlabangana, but he liked formality; it gave him boundaries.

'As you know, I am investigating a murder, the murder of your employer, Mrs Marcia Pullman,' he added rather superfluously, but he felt it was to good effect.

Dorcas nodded.

'Therefore, I need to know the truth.'

Dorcas inhaled sharply and was about to say something when Edmund put up his hand.

'I am just saying. I need the facts and I need the truth. Okay?'

Dorcas nodded, but looked away from him at a spot on the floor.

'Can you tell me what happened this afternoon?'

'I was out. I had the afternoon off. When I came back Madam Peters was already here. She wanted to know where Mrs Pullman was. I said I didn't know. Maybe she was in the house.' Dorcas shrugged.

'And then?'

She rolled her eyes and said, as though forced to state the obvious: 'And then I gave her my key for the back door and she went inside and she found the madam dead in the bedroom.' Dorcas's voice was flat and unemotional. It reminded Edmund of a child learning to read.

'Did you come in the house?'

'Yes, it was four o'clock. Madam told me to be back at four. I went into the kitchen and that's when Madam Peters came and told me the madam was dead.'

There was no mention of tears or screams or an hysterical Madam Peters. Dorcas, Edmund imagined, would be a terrible storyteller.

'So you phoned the police?'

'Yes.'

'You knew their number?'

'Madam has it up on the fridge. There is a list of emergency numbers.'

'Did you phone anyone else?'

Dorcas shifted in her chair. She shook her head.

'Mr Pullman, perhaps?'

'Yes. I called him.'

'What did he say?'

'He didn't answer. I left a message. I said he must phone me as it was an emergency.'

'He has your phone number?'

'Yes.'

'Why?'

'What do you mean?'

'Why does he have your phone number?'

Dorcas raised one shoulder in a half-shrug. 'Both Mr and Mrs Pullman have my number.'

'And then what did you do?'

Dorcas looked at him as though not entirely sure of what he was asking. 'I washed the dishes.'

'There were how many?'

Dorcas rolled her eyes in astonishment and looked at him as though he were mad.

Edmund couldn't help feeling a bit put out by all her eye rolling. 'For the record,' he insisted.

'There were two glasses and two side plates and a large plate.'

'What might Mrs Pullman have had for lunch?'

Dorcas shrugged. 'Sandwiches. If she had a visitor, she would make small sandwiches on a plate with some lettuce.' Dorcas made a gesture that suggested shredded lettuce sprinkled on top of sandwiches.

'And to drink?'

'Tea. Coffee.' Another shrug.

'In a glass? Would she have had wine?'

Dorcas smirked as though she knew something Edmund didn't. 'Not in a tumbler. She might have had water. She liked sparkling water.'

Edmund raised his eyebrows and wrote *sparkling water* in his notebook. 'You weren't here? You had the afternoon off?'

There was an almost imperceptible shift in her demeanour

at his question, a wariness. 'Madam said I could have the afternoon off. I had been working hard so I could go.'

'Madam Peters says that you should have been here preparing for book club in the evening?

Dorcas's mouth hardened at the corners. 'Madam wanted to do it herself. It wasn't difficult. The food was made and Madam Peters was coming to help. She only had to put the books out.'

'What about the cleaning? Shining, polishing. Madam Peters says Mrs Pullman was very fussy and wanted everything nice and tidy.'

'I did it yesterday.' Dorcas looked him straight in the eye and held his gaze. It was a definite battle of wits. Dorcas wasn't a usual maid. It was wrong, of course, to stereotype, but when you worked in this job for any length of time, you began to see people as types rather than as individuals. He couldn't decide whether Dorcas lacked emotion altogether or whether she kept all emotion tightly under control.

Edmund was the first to look away. He made a show of looking at his notes, tapping his pencil on the table as though to suggest pensive thought. 'How long have you worked here?' he asked after a long pause.

'Two years.'

'It's good here? You like it?'

She gave him a sideways glance. 'Yes.'

'No problems?'

'No.'

Edmund wrote *check previous convictions.*

'What about the gardener' – he looked at his notes – 'Malakai Ndimande?'

'He doesn't work here anymore.'

'Yes, yes, I know that,' said Edmund, his turn to be exasperated. 'What I am asking is if he made any threats against Mrs Pullman? Was he very angry over being dismissed?'

'You didn't ask that,' said Dorcas in a quiet voice, looking at the table.

'That is what I meant.'

'But it is not what you asked.'

'Let me start again then. Was Malakai Ndimande angry with the madam? Was he angry enough to come back and kill her?'

Dorcas shrugged. 'I don't know. I do not know what goes on in the mind of another person.'

Edmund sighed and snapped his notebook shut. 'Was he angry? In your opinion, was he angry?'

'No.'

'No? Good.'

She looked surprised.

'Why did you report him missing to the police?'

'I didn't!'

'You did. The information that was given to the police was that a woman was dead and her gardener missing. You are the one who made the report.'

'It was Madam Peters. She was standing next to me, saying things to me. I thought I must say them because she is the madam.'

'So you have no reason to believe that Malakai would have murdered Mrs Pullman?'

'No.'

'What about the other man? The man who ran away earlier?'

'The ikhiwa?'

Edmund nodded.

'He was the one who came into madam's office earlier today and caused a big scene.'

'Which office?'

'Top Notch.'

'Oh?' said Edmund, jotting the name down. 'What sort of business is that?'

'It is a recruitment agency. Madam runs it.'

'Ran it,' corrected Edmund and then felt bad for picking up on grammatical slips when a death had occurred. He saw no change in Dorcas's face; it was completely immovable. He cleared his throat and continued, 'What were you doing there? You are a domestic worker for this house aren't you?'

Just then he saw another flicker of emotion, like the one he had caught previously, the quickest of glances at him as if he was accusing her of something.

'The office cleaner is sick. Madam asked me to do some cleaning.'

'How long had you been doing this?'

'Doing what?' If he wasn't mistaken something angry had entered her being, turning the corners of her mouth down just enough so that she took on a slightly vampirish aspect.

'Cleaning the office.'

She relaxed and shrugged. 'A couple of days.'

Edmund wrote slowly in his notebook *a couple of days - check*. He didn't know why, but something about the story didn't ring true.

'But you were cleaning here yesterday you said?'

'For a couple of hours. Then madam said we were going to the office.'

'It was a sudden decision?'

Dorcas shrugged her characteristic shrug.

'And this man came in and...?'

'He said he was going to kill Mrs Pullman.'

'He said that?'

'Yes.'

'Exactly?' He noticed Dorcas shifted slightly in her seat.

She paused for half a second before confirming, 'Exactly.'

Edmund tried to give her what he felt was an interrogative stare. 'I need you to be absolutely certain that those are the words he *said*.'

She curled her bottom lip down and shrugged again. 'I think so.'

'Why did he threaten her? Do you know?'

Dorcas shrugged. She seemed to lack interest in the whole affair. 'He wasn't happy,' she hazarded as though Edmund had asked her a random quiz question. 'He came in and was

37

shouting at her and the other lady who works there. I don't know what the problem was.'

'How was Mrs Pullman afterwards?'

Dorcas frowned. Then she shrugged. Edmund's irritation over the eye rolling was replaced with greater irritation at her constant shrugging.

'I mean, was she upset? Did she phone the police? Her husband? Did she close the office for the day?

Dorcas looked at him as though he was mad. 'No. She told me to make some tea.'

'Did you work in the office the whole day?'

'No, just this morning. I told you, I had the afternoon off.'

'What about this afternoon? Where were you?'

'I went shopping.'

'Where?'

'The flea market on Fife Street.'

'Can anyone vouch for you?'

Dorcas looked puzzled. 'Vouch? What is this word?'

Edmund couldn't help feeling slightly superior as he explained the term. 'Can anyone say they saw you there this afternoon?'

She shrugged. 'I don't know. Some of the sellers maybe.'

'When did Mrs Pullman say you could have the afternoon off? Was it after this man coming in and making threats or was it beforehand?'

'Yesterday. She said I could have the afternoon off until four o'clock. Then I could work later this evening.'

'What time would you finish?'

'About nine o'clock in the evening. Mrs Pullman didn't like the washing up being left until the next day.'

'Did you come back to the house before going out to the market?'

'No, I went straight there from the office.'

'In your maid's uniform?'

Dorcas shifted very slightly, but kept her eyes on him. 'Yes.'

'One more question.' Edmund lowered his voice and

looked over his shoulder. 'Do the Pullmans... Did the Pullmans have separate bedrooms?'

'Yes.'

'For how long has this been the arrangement?'

'Ever since I started, it has been the same.'

'How would you describe relations between the two?'

'What?'

'Relations. Their relationship. Were they happy together would you say?'

'*I don't know!*' Dorcas clicked her tongue. 'Why are you asking me? You said one last question then you ask me ten more! Hah!'

Edmund thought again about the lunch dishes next to the sink.

'I wonder perhaps if there weren't an outside interest for Mrs Pullman?'

She stared at him, open-mouthed. 'What?'

'Forget I asked,' said Edmund, feeling more than a little embarrassed. 'But no children?'

She looked at him with deep suspicion. 'No.'

Edmund sat for a few minutes writing notes before telling Dorcas she could go. 'But I may have further questions,' he warned her. 'Don't go anywhere. Do you understand?' He hoped his voice had carried at least the idea of a warning. She stood up, but didn't move and he realised she was waiting for him to leave the room first.

'Good evening,' he said, as he went out of the door. He didn't notice there was a small step and he stumbled as he walked outside. When he looked back, Dorcas was in the doorway of the laundry, her large sad eyes watching him.

Inside the kitchen, Edmund stopped when he heard Nigel Pullman's voice. He pulled the door to behind him quietly and took a silent step towards the hallway. Edmund heard the voice disappear outside the front door, which slammed shut abruptly. About a minute later the door opened again and Nigel Pullman strode back inside, his face a twisted agony of hate.

Edmund took a deep breath and walked into the passageway.

'Mr Pullman,' he ventured with as much confidence as he could muster. His voice sounded small and thin and strained. He looked up at the stocky hulk of the white man with great hesitation. 'Can we talk?'

Chapter Four

'When did you last see your wife?' Edmund sat awkwardly on a bar stool just a little too high for him. He didn't like the sensation of his legs dangling beneath him for it gave him a strange feeling of being dangerously at sea with his anchor floating away from him in the darkness somewhere. He wished he'd taken his coat off before he sat down for it felt large and cumbersome on him, but he feared getting off the stool again as he doubted he could do it with any panache.

'This morning. I leave early. By six thirty I'm' – he made a whistling sound with his teeth and slid one hand over the other in a quick, fluid movement – 'outta here.' Seated across from Edmund behind the bar, Mr Pullman poured himself a large whisky and added some ice. 'Drink?' he asked, motioning with his glass.

'No... er, no thank you,' replied Edmund.

Mr Pullman looked at his watch, a huge, fat gold timepiece on his thick wrist. 'Still on duty, eh?'

'Actually, I don't drink,' replied Edmund, feeling at once very small and insignificant under the man's gaze.

'Religious. It figures.'

'No, no,' Edmund was quick to point out. 'Just never liked it.'

Mr Pullman squinted at him as though trying to work him out and took a large sip of his drink. Edmund felt it best to push on with the interview.

'And you came home for lunch?'

'Nope. Don't come home for lunch.'

'It appears someone came to the house for lunch. Do you know who that might have been?'

'Janet Peters?' hazarded Mr Pullman.

'No. She came at four o'clock. Is there anyone else you can think of?'

'Have a look in her diary. She wrote everything in there.'

'A diary?' Edmund's heart leapt. This was the stuff of novels. 'Could I see it, please. It might be very useful.'

'I'll get it for you,' he said but made no sign of moving. He was watching Edmund with an amused fascination.

'Did you speak to your wife at all during the day?'

'Don't think so.' Mr Pullman shrugged, his mouth pulling into an upside down bow. He had thick, rather purple lips, Edmund thought and he was momentarily reminded of a fat slab of fresh raw meat. 'She was busy. Book club. She had a lot to organise.'

Edmund considered telling him about the incident at the office, but had a strong feeling to keep the information to himself, at least for the moment. He wanted to talk to Craig Martin before Pullman had a chance to get his hands on him.

'Mrs Peters says it's unlikely that your wife would be here on her own when she had book club to organise, but there was no one else here this afternoon. No maid, no gardener?'

'Fired the gardener last week. Bugger tried to clean the car with Vim.'

'How did he take it?'

Another shrug. 'Who knows?' He sucked in his breath noisily. *'Who knows?'*

'He didn't make any sort of threat at all? Didn't want to go to the Labour Office and claim unfair dismissal?'

The lip curled up again, this time in a snarl.

'Nope. Wouldn't have won anyway. I know how to deal with those guys at Labour.'

'He wasn't replaced?'

'Not yet. My wife was picky. Wouldn't take any old rubbish.'

'Do you know where Malakai is now?'

'Nope.'

'What about the maid?' Edmund looked at his notepad. 'Dorcas Hlabangana? She wasn't here, I take it? Was that usual?'

For the first time, Mr Pullman paused and his eyes held a question.

He threw up his hands. 'Women. Never consistent. Maybe Marcia wanted to do things herself. I don't know. She was always complaining about Dorcas and how she never did things right.'

'Where were you this afternoon?'

'Me?' His eyes narrowed menacingly. 'I've been at work all afternoon.'

'Which is?'

'Pullman's Bespoke Safaris. Established 1988. "Your leisure is our pleasure".' He slapped imaginary quotation marks in the air with his thick, hairy fingers.

Edmund leaned forward a little and then wished he hadn't because he felt that unanchored feeling again as he swayed towards the bar top. 'And your wife ran a recruitment agency?'

'Correct.' Pullman was watching him hard.

'Was everything all right? Had she mentioned any problems?'

'Nope.'

'The man who was here earlier–'

'The guy who did a runner?'

Edmund nodded. 'Yes. Have you seen him before at all?'

'Didn't see the bugger, did I? I was sitting in the kitchen.'

Edmund felt stupid. Of course he hadn't seen Craig. He tried to recover some ground. 'Did your wife have any enemies? Anyone who disliked her enough to kill her?'

Mr Pullman laughed suddenly, a dark sarcastic laugh and Edmund, despite his heavy coat, shivered. Mr Pullman downed the dregs of his drink and wiped his mouth with the back of his hand. 'Nope,' he said, setting his glass down hard on the bar. 'No one. But I don't think it's the gardener – or ex-gardener. He would've coshed her on the back of the head or something. No, this was somebody else.'

'Do you have an alarm system? I notice you have panic buttons in some of the rooms.'

'Yup. Don't use them during the day though, do we?'

'You don't have an electric gate?'

'Hasn't worked for a couple of months. All the frigging power cuts killed it. Now it's manually operated – just slides open.'

'You are not afraid of someone breaking in?'

Pullman shrugged. 'At night we lock it with a padlock. And if we are both out.'

'Who opens the gate for you?'

Pullman stared contemptuously at Edmund. 'The gardener.'

'What about today? You don't have a gardener.'

'Dorcas.'

'Dorcas was out when your wife returned.'

'Marcia opened it then. What's the big deal?'

'She didn't lock it.'

Pullman shrugged and took a sip of his drink. 'She didn't expect trouble, did she? It's Monday afternoon for God's sake.'

'But she locked herself inside the house. Is that normal?'

'What do you mean *is that normal?*'

'Well, during the day, would it be normal for her to lock herself in the house – if she was going to have a lie down for example?'

The corners of his mouth turned down again as he shook his head. 'Dunno. I'm never here in the afternoon.'

It occurred to Edmund that Mr Pullman was one of the most unhelpful spouses he had ever met. Other men, and women, would be ranting by now, making all sorts of accusations and surmises.

'How many people have keys to the house besides you?'

Raising his eyes to the ceiling, Pullman appeared to count. 'One.'

'You and your wife?'

'Well done.'

'Dorcas?

'Dorcas has a back door key?'

'What about the gardener?'

'Why would the gardener need a bloody key, hey?'

'I'm just checking,' Edmund explained meekly. 'But he had a key to the gate?'

Pullman nodded his head slowly as though he were bored and looking for some way to get away from Edmund.

'Are any of the keys missing? I assume you have yours?'

'Correct.'

'Your wife's key?'

Pullman stared at Edmund as though he were a complete idiot.

'I'm sorry. It's tedious, but I need to confirm details.'

A nod of the head.

'And this key is now missing?'

'No. It's hanging up with her car keys.'

'I see. So she locked herself in because...?'

'I don't know. I suppose because she was going to lie down.'

'But she didn't lock the gate?'

Mr Pullman gave an irritated shrug. Edmund felt his time to question was rapidly running out. In a last bid at getting as much information as possible he said: 'I take it your wife's property is left to you?'

'What the hell are you suggesting?' Pullman turned on Edmund with an ugly snarl. 'You think I killed my wife? Yes, her money is left to me. That's because I'm her husband and her next of kin, bloody fool.'

A loud knocking at the door ended the interview.

'That'll be the doc,' said Pullman, easing himself around the corner of the bar, pulling up his shorts as he did so.

Edmund was both relieved to be excused from Mr Pullman's presence and surprised to see that it was the esteemed Dr Ndhlovu who had been summoned. Head of the pathology department in Bulawayo, he was a shrewd, elderly man whose enthusiasm for his job had grown in proportion to the number of years he had worked and, now that he should be retiring, he seemed set for another twenty years of examining dead bodies.

'Ah, *Chief Inspector* Dube,' he greeted Edmund effusively after Pullman excused himself to make a phone call. 'Long time no see.'

'Good evening, Dr Ndhlovu.'

'You are the only one here?' He looked around as though expecting to find someone hiding behind the door.

'Yes. Are you?'

'I have two assistants waiting in the car. Where is Khumalo?'

'I am in charge of the case.' Edmund felt the words stick in his throat.

Ndhlovu's eyebrows raised slightly and he glanced briefly at his watch. 'The body, please, Chief Inspector.'

Having a very slight frame meant that Dr Ndhlovu's trousers, of an invariably dark chocolate shade of brown, were kept up with a thin black plastic belt, wrapped one and a half times around his waist. His face bore an unsettling similarity to a skeleton, especially when he smiled or laughed, which had led to the predictable nickname of Dr Death. Edmund found Ndhlovu's enjoyment in his job both unnatural and morbid. He would have preferred the doctor to be a little more world-weary and cynical, perhaps even a little more aware of his own mortality. He hated the way the man greeted each case with a sense of awe for the murderer's ingenuity or ridicule for their lack of imagination, as though he were a teacher marking essays. But he was good, there was no doubt of that, and Edmund always had faith in his conclusions

'Uh-huh,' said the doctor, carefully putting on a pair of disposable gloves and smoothing them down over his wrists. He approached the body. 'I haven't had one of these for a very long time.' He smacked his lips together in ghoulish delight, his chin tilted in such a fashion as to suggest he were sampling a fine claret. 'A connoisseur of death,' thought Edmund, looking away as Ndhlovu inspected first the stab wound and then the eyes and hands of the dead Mrs Pullman.

'Rigor mortis just beginning to set in,' he said, letting the arm drop and then holding it up and dropping it again. 'Time of death within the last couple of hours. Would you mind calling Nigel, Chief. I'll need to ask him some questions.'

Edmund was surprised to hear Ndhlovu refer to Mr Pullman by his first name and annoyed with the way he called him Chief, but he didn't protest. Instead, he obediently followed orders and pushed aside a sense that it should be him giving them. Just outside the bar area, he stopped and listened. Pullman was on the phone again.

'Who is this guy, man? I thought you were going to send Khumalo? He's *where*? Well, tell him to come back immediately. What's the matter with you people?'

Edmund leant closer, listening carefully to all the harrumphs and mutters.

'You get your guys over here *now* or there's going to be hell to pay. You hear me?'

Edmund retreated back up the corridor to Mrs Pullman's room. What did Pullman mean? Who was he talking to? Edmund felt a flush of embarrassment. Had the man already made up his mind that Edmund was incompetent?

Edmund stood in a corner of the bedroom, watching Ndhlovu as he worked his way down the body, checking various organs by pushing and prodding. When he came to Mrs Pullman's legs, he looked enquiringly at the stockings, then reached up under her skirt and pulled them down. Edmund looked away again, embarrassed.

Ndhlovu examined her legs for a few minutes and then made some notes on a pad, his glasses slipping down his nose as he did so.

Edmund felt a presence behind him and turned his head quickly to see Nigel Pullman standing in the doorway, watching, a drink in one hand.

'Had your wife complained of feeling unwell recently?' Ndhlovu asked, looking over his glasses at the dead woman's husband.

He shook his head. 'Marcia? She had a bit of an upset stomach last week.'

'Last week when?'

'Friday. Well, Thursday night. She played bridge in the evening and woke up feeling unwell in the night. Blamed it on the snacks.'

'She went to the doctor?'

'Yip. She was at the quack's on Friday.'

'And she got better?'

'It was just a passing thing.'

Ndhlovu nodded his head. 'I take it you know she suffered from kidney problems.'

Pullman shook his head. 'Nope.'

'There is characteristic swelling of the ankles and puffy feet. Can you see?' he asked, holding up Marcia's right leg as though he were about to pass it over to Mr Pullman. Pullman picked up a chair and moved it next to his dead wife's bed.

'Thought it was gout.'

He let the leg drop and stood back, stroking his chin. 'She never mentioned painful, heavy legs? Did she have trouble with breathing at all?'

Nigel Pullman shrugged, pushing his lower lip up in a suggestion that he neither knew nor cared. 'She did have high blood pressure,' he said. 'We both do.'

'Headaches?' asked Ndhlovu, moving alongside Mrs Pullman's head. 'Did she ever complain about headaches?'

'Don't all women?' asked Pullman, giving Ndhlovu a knowing look.

Ndhlovu ran a finger along Marcia's face. 'See this, this white powdery stuff?' He showed Pullman his finger. 'This is called uremic frost. It is symptomatic of kidney failure. I am more than a hundred per cent sure this is what your wife died of. We'll take the body tonight. The results won't take too long to be confirmed.'

Edmund left Dr Ndhlovu and Nigel Pullman poring over Marcia's body and made his way to the kitchen. There was no one there. Edmund opened the pantry door and looked inside. It was noticeably well-stocked. He ran his eyes over the contents of the pantry: tins of smoked oysters and salmon, numerous packets of savoury biscuits, bottles of wine and specialist coffee seemed to take up an inordinate amount of space.

On two of the bottom shelves were trays covered in cloths. He drew the cloths back and found an assortment of snacks: the feast for the book club. He felt hungry just looking at them. One tray was laden with whole scones. The others were a mix of tiny sandwiches and things arranged on biscuits. He looked closer and then stood back and compared the two trays. One was more neatly arranged than the other and the snacks were arranged in a definite pattern: one mushroom vol-au-vent and then two savoury biscuits topped with cream cheese and oysters. The platter was edged with tiny sandwiches: one smoked salmon and cucumber and one cheese.

'Mushroom, biscuit, biscuit, mushroom, biscuit, biscuit on this tray.' He found himself saying, just under his breath. 'But on this tray,' he turned to the second, 'the pattern is different – and inconsistent. Mushroom, mushroom, biscuit. Mushroom, biscuit, biscuit. Biscuit, biscuit, *sandwich*. There is no order. No symmetry.'

Edmund pulled the cloths back over the trays and paused, his forehead furrowed slightly. A feeling had stirred in him that the disrupted pattern was important, but its significance eluded him. There was a small fridge in the pantry as well. He opened the door and found butter, more bottles of wine, white this time, some sauces in bottles, a punnet of mushrooms and five cartons of cream. He reached into the fridge and took out a small white container.

'Crème fraiche,' he read aloud and then jumped violently as a heavy hand came down on his shoulder. It was Mr Pullman. Edmund's first thought was that Mr Pullman suspected him of rifling through the pantry, but instead he seemed to be looking for something. He threw the cloths back on two of the trays and carried them out of the pantry with him.

'Bring a bottle of white wine,' he called back over his shoulder to Edmund. 'The sweet stuff.'

Still in shock from the unexpected advent of Mr Pullman, Edmund looked round wildly before realising that the wine was in the fridge in front of him, which was still open. He looked blankly at the labels and breathed a sigh of relief when he found a sweet white wine, closed the fridge and followed Mr Pullman into the bar area.

Ndhlovu was sitting on one of the black leather seats, his legs stretched out in front of him and looking quite at home, Edmund thought, watching him light his cigarette and blow out a haze of grey smoke in a rather careless manner that showed little regard for those he was with. Nigel Pullman couldn't have cared less, thought Edmund, watching the stocky man pull the cork out of the wine bottle with little trouble.

'Ah, you remembered,' said Ndhlovu as a large glass of white wine was placed in front of him. 'Sweet, I hope?'

'Like you said, I remembered,' said Pullman, pouring himself another whisky. 'Help yourself,' he added, slapping the two trays of snacks down on the table. 'I can't eat half the stuff. Nothing with wheat in it. Stokes the arthritis. Try the oysters. They are lekker.'

Edmund looked on appalled as the two men set into the trays of snacks. Ndhlovu had an unfortunate habit of talking whilst he was eating, which meant that anyone in his immediate vicinity could be hit by bits of vol-au-vent shrapnel. Pullman had an equally unappealing habit of sucking his entire fingers into his mouth one by one every so often to clean them off. Edmund backed away, disgusted.

'It's certainly a puzzling one,' spluttered Ndhlovu as Pullman refilled his glass. 'She was dead before she was stabbed.'

'Why,' Edmund's voice was small and dry. He cleared his throat and tried again. 'Why would somebody stab her if she was already dead?'

Pullman didn't respond, merely tilting his glass so that the chunks of ice knocked together.

'He didn't know she was dead. Thought she was asleep and took a stab at her.' Ndhlovu's head twitched from side to side like an inquisitive bird.

'Did your wife often sleep in the afternoon, Mr Pullman?' asked Edmund, turning to the man who looked straight past him when he answered.

'What's it to do with you?'

'It would help to know her routine,' said Edmund.

'Routine!' spluttered Ndhlovu, pieces of salmon sandwich flying out of his mouth. 'It was someone taking a chance. The gardener, I'd say. He knows the madam has gone for a rest. He creeps in the room and stabs her.'

'With what?'

'With what? With whatever he can find, man!'

'A letter opener that Mr Pullman says he doesn't recognise? If it was something she kept beside her bed, I'd understand, but if it does not belong to this house, then it means the intruder brought it with them.'

'A man never knows his own house,' was Ndhlovu's sage reply and Edmund noticed how Mr Pullman did not refute him. 'Women know everything: where they got it and who gave it to them and how long they've had it. Husbands don't know anything!' He cackled at what he obviously believed was a clarity of vision on his part.

Edmund sat silently for a few minutes. He didn't agree.

'The gardener doesn't work here anymore. Why would he come back a week after being fired, especially if he has a new job?'

Ndhlovu shook his head at Edmund as though the younger man had no idea of the intricacies of human nature. 'My friend, anger is a terrible burden. It is likely that he sat and planned and plotted and all the while his anger brewed.'

The gardener was always a suspect, but then so was the husband. Everyone knew that in Zimbabwe the police chose the nearest person to the victim and beat a confession out of them.

'What about the key? Why did he lock the door and how did he get the key back inside the house?'

'He had a duplicate. Easy enough to do.'

'But why lock the door?'

'Why not?' replied Ndhlovu. 'You are in danger of creating stereotypes, my boy. You are saying a gardener is not capable of this or that.'

'What's the point? He'd know the gate didn't work. In any case, Mr Pullman himself said that he doubted it was the gardener,' Edmund started, looking to the man for backup.

He was surprised to see Pullman shake his head. 'I'm allowed to change my mind.'

'There are other people to consider,' Edmund pursued.

'Perhaps,' agreed Ndhlovu with a slow nod of his head.

'It wasn't me if that's what you think,' said Pullman, his hand twitching ever so slightly so that the melting ice cubes clunked together.

'I didn't say it was,' laughed Ndhlovu, showing his rotten front teeth in a wide grin.

'I wasn't talking about you.' He looked straight at Edmund. 'Well, what *would* you say?' pursued Mr Pullman, looking back at Ndhlovu.

'I'd say she wasn't feeling well. She went to have a sleep and died. Kidney failure. Someone found her and took the opportunity to stab her.'

'But *why*?' insisted Edmund. 'If she's dead, why stab her?'

'Like I said, whoever it was thought she was asleep.'

'So you mean they *meant* to kill her? They think they have killed her?'

There was a pause while Ndlovu drank his wine, eyeing Edmund carefully over the rim of his glass.

'There'll be an autopsy, of course.' Edmund tried to make it sound more of a statement than a question.

Ndhlovu shrugged. 'Yup. And I am sure it will confirm what we already know.'

Ndhlovu knocked back the rest of his wine and looked at his watch. 'Nice wine,' he said, looking hopefully at the half full bottle on the bar counter. Nigel Pullman reached it down, shoved the cork in hard and handed it to him.

'For the road.'

'Nice snacks,' said Ndhlovu, turning his gaze to the nearly empty trays.

'Take them. Here!' He threw a packet of paper napkins at Ndhlovu and watched as the man piled the rest of the mushroom vol-au-vents into three of them and tied them each into a neat parcel.

'Could I have your wife's diary?' asked Edmund, standing up. It was impossible not to notice Mr Pullman and Ndhlovu shared a look over his head. Ndhlovu obviously gave the nod of assent as Pullman disappeared and returned with a heavy black book with gold leaf on the pages.

'You can see it, you can't have it,' he said, handing it over to Edmund with a sneer.

Edmund took it gingerly as though he were being handed a valuable Bible. He opened the book at where a thick piece of golden ribbon marked the day's appointments.

'One o'clock, S.P. S.P. is?'

'One of her friends, probably. I haven't a clue.'

Edmund closed his eyes in momentary frustration. Anyone would think Nigel Pullman had no interest at all in his wife's killer being caught.

Edmund looked back at the previous page and then flicked back through the used pages. 'Everyone else she's going to meet is given a name. Anne, Simone, Janet, Tristan. Could S.P. mean anything else? Plumbers? Skies Plumbers, maybe?'

'Skies Plumbers! What planet are you from?' snarled Mr Pullman, taking the diary back.

'I just thought... it would help to know... we could eliminate them from the investigation.'

'Eliminate them from the investigation!'

Edmund's heart went cold as Pullman's hand came down on his shoulder and the man pulled him close. 'You think you're in some sort of movie, don't you? Hey! You're in Bu-la-way-o. Now, good night.'

Edmund pulled away and made for the door. 'I may have to ask you some more questions, Mr Pullman,' he said, avoiding the man's eye. 'I'll find you at work if I do?'

Pullman stared at him a moment, something between a mixture of a smile and a snarl on his face.

As Edmund turned to go down the front path, he noticed that Ndhlovu hung back and a whispered conversation between the two men ensued. Catching his eye, Pullman closed the door. The gate was heavy to push open. He looked up. There was a small square at the top of the gate through which one could put their hand to take the padlock off, but it was not the easiest thing to manage. It was no wonder Mrs Pullman had not bothered to lock it. Not if she knew she would be called to open it soon by Janet.

Edmund set off down the road alone, quite glad of the cold night air. As he neared the intersection with the main road, car lights came round the corner at speed. Edmund stood back and glared. His expression changed when he saw it was a police car. It neither slowed nor stopped and he watched as it turned into the Pullmans' drive. He remembered Pullman's conversation on the phone. *Where's Khumalo?* The road descended into darkness again and Edmund was left with an overwhelming feeling that he was always on the edge, never in the middle of life. He breathed deeply and continued on his way back to the police station.

Chapter Five

1979

It was a beautifully clear day in January. The world basked in the aftermath of the storm's munificence. It had rained the whole night through and Edmund had lain close to his mother on the mattress as the rain hammered down on the tin roof, flinching every time the thunder cracked and the room momentarily lit up with lightning. The storm had eventually passed, although the rain continued steadily until, in the early hours of the next morning, it gradually lessened and then stopped altogether, leaving the world covered with a sheen of newness. It reminded Edmund of the hymn they sang in church. *Morning has broken, like the first morning.* He shook the rain from the gentle curves and dips of the canna lilies that grew in a long row outside the khaya and watched, fascinated, as single drops broke away and ran softly along the spine of the leaf and into the warm darkness of the plant below.

Edmund was splashing in puddles when his mother called him. He usually spent the mornings alone while she worked in the main house. He was always left with strict instructions as to what he could and could not eat, what to touch and what to leave well alone, what he could play with and what to stay away from. His mother abhorred any form of play that did not involve sitting quietly in a corner somewhere, an occupation that Edmund, at the age of seven, found extremely difficult to feel much enthusiasm for. She had said nothing about the rain or the puddles when she left, only reminding him not to play with matches or go anywhere near the paraffin lamp.

'Edmund!' she shouted 'Edmund! Your clothes!' It was not that Edmund had got his clothes dirty that was the source of her anger, but the fact that he wasn't wearing any at all. He had thought it a good idea to take everything off; he thought his mother would praise him for remembering his clothes above his excitement, so he couldn't understand why she now grabbed his left arm with one hand and brought her other hand down sharply on his bare bottom. He squealed in pain and indignation and pulled away from her angrily.

'It's all right,' said a voice. 'Leave the lad be. He's only a little boy. Just having some fun.'

The voice was a man's. Edmund looked up quickly to see Mr MacDougal standing a short distance away, watching the scene with humour. Edmund had seen Mr MacDougal before, but never here outside the servants' quarters. He usually saw only his head above the steering wheel as he drove in and out of the yard on his way to and from work. Sometimes he saw him trotting up the steps from the garden into the house; he had quite a spring in his walk, a lightness, and even though he dealt with criminals, wrongdoers and delinquents all day long, there was something about the way he walked that suggested indefatigable victory over them.

Edmund stood still. He was suddenly aware of his nakedness and placed his hands in front of him meekly.

'I am sorry, sir. I am so sorry,' began his mother, clenching his neck in a steel grip. To him, she whispered fiercely: 'Edmund, go and get dressed *now!*' He turned to go and she caught him again. 'And your face. Wash your face!'

Edmund scuttled into the khaya, dried himself with their one and only towel, a small blue one, and then lifted his clothes down from the back of the chair on which he had so carefully placed them. He rubbed his backside, feeling once again the pain of the slap. As it subsided, tears pricked at his eyes for now he felt the agony of his embarrassment more keenly. He washed his face with some water his mother kept in a bucket near the door, being careful to put the lid back on afterwards. Then he dried his face and, tucking his shirt in, walked slowly back outside to his mother and stood submissively beside her.

Mr MacDougal was still there. He looked at Edmund, a kindly expression on his face, one that Edmund would come to recognise as a particularly avuncular one reserved for him alone. Edmund's mother gripped him by the shoulders and pushed him in front of her. There was a momentary silence and then he felt a knuckle sharp in the middle of his back and she whispered with vehemence, 'Say good afternoon to Mr MacDougal, Edmund.'

'Good afternoon,' began Edmund, speaking to the man's knees.

'Good afternoon, *sir*,' corrected his mother. The knuckle twisted deeper.

'It's all right, Verna. That will do,' insisted Mr MacDougal. 'Edmund, come here.' He stretched out his hand, but Edmund didn't move. He looked up at his mother who stared hard at him and then gave him a sharp push. Edmund approached Mr MacDougal with trepidation. It was possible that his punishment was far from over; in fact, it may just be beginning.

'Edmund,' said Mr MacDougal, dropping to his haunches and putting his hand on the young boy's shoulder. 'How would you like to go to school?'

Edmund's face remained expressionless; only his eyes moved slowly.

'Mrs MacDougal and I would like to send you to school. To a good school, Edmund. A very good school.' There was another pause. 'Would you like that? Is that where you'd like to go?'

Edmund listened carefully to Mr MacDougal's words. He loved their sound, the way they rolled like honey off his tongue; the fullness of the 'r's; the way he pursed his lips to say the word 'school', how the word itself seemed to shiver with excitement.

'Edmund!' His mother's voice was harsh behind him. 'Say thank you, Edmund.'

Mr MacDougal pulled himself upright and put up his hand in protest. 'Don't worry the lad, Verna. It's a lot for him to take in all at once, isn't it, Edmund?'

Edmund managed a nod although he wasn't quite sure what Mr MacDougal meant.

'We're sending you to Sir Herbert Stanley Junior School,' he said the words as though expecting a reaction. Edmund nodded again. 'It's a good school. One of the best in Bulawayo. Things are changing, laddie. They're letting black... they're letting everyone in now. Education for all and you're one of the few to experience it ahead of others.'

'Edmund!' There was a note of pleading in his mother's voice.

The boy turned to look at her; her eyes were full of tears and she stood twisting her hands in a mixture of despair and happiness. He still wasn't sure what it was all about, this visit of Mr MacDougal's, and why he should be offered this opportunity to attend school and what the great changes ahead were, but it was far from his place to challenge his mother's employer.

'Thank you,' he said, turning back to Mr MacDougal, but catching his eye he looked away, down at his feet. 'Thank you very much, sir. Mr MacDougal.'

On the morning of Mrs Pullman's death, Craig Martin had woken up with a headache. 'Whisky,' he thought sadly as he lay back on his pillow, squeezing his forehead with his left hand. He hadn't meant to drink so much. He never did; it just happened somehow. One to dull the pain, another to be happy, a third to forget... and suddenly it was morning and the light was streaming in the window, the alarm clock was bleating and he had a headache. Babalas. That was the Rhodie expression, wasn't it? Although he had never considered himself a Rhodie. In fact, being a Rhodie was something he had failed at consistently in his life. Except for the haircut, there was little that defined him as part of that hardy, yet dwindling, minority race. He hadn't the lingo, or the swagger or the smokers' cough. He didn't wear short shorts or khaki and he didn't refer to small trucks as bakkies.

All of which made it difficult for him to understand the attitude he had been subjected to the night before. Of course, he should have known it all sounded too good to be true, but when Shantelle had phoned him and said she had what she called a 'prospective match' on the books and would he like to meet her, he had jumped at the chance.

Craig remembered the first time he had met Shantelle. She was a secretary in an office and had phoned about a repair job. He had stood on a ladder fixing a broken light fitting in her office while she had chatted away to him from behind a computer screen. The conversation had moved from the specifics of his job and all that it entailed to the dire economic situation in Zimbabwe, the government, the corrupt police force, comparisons of what he used to be able to afford in 1995 and what he could afford now and what he did in his spare time and that inevitably led on to some slightly more probing questions as to his marital status. It wasn't long before he was expounding all his woes in the relationship realm to her: the lack of attractive women in Bulawayo, gold-digging vamps who just wanted to be pampered and flattered rather than contribute to a meaningful relationship, and the proliferation of single mothers and divorcees, with the accompanying emotional baggage, which included shaven-headed, stocky thugs of ex-husbands wielding iron bars.

Shantelle had nodded sympathetically and made all the right clucking and tut-tutting noises at the right time and Craig quite enjoyed this unexpected opportunity to vent his troubles. As Shantelle handed him the payment for the job and he thanked her and was about to say goodbye, she asked him if he was busy on Friday night. At first he thought she may be interested in him and was about to ask him out. Despite being fairly flattered by this suggestion, he was also unnerved by it. Well-dressed and manicured, Shantelle was beyond Craig's expectations. He hesitated, but she saw his apprehension and cut in before he could say anything else.

'There's a party,' she said, handing him a business card. 'Friday night from seven thirty if you're not busy.'

He looked at the card and read: 'Mix 'n Match. Dating events for professionals.' He turned the card over and looked at Shantelle. 'What's this?'

'Just a little hobby of mine. I'm trying to start my own business, you know. I don't want to work here like *forever*. I like to put people together. We meet up, we have some fun and' – she looked coyly at him – 'sometimes you can get lucky.'

Craig was not convinced, but there was something attractive in the idea of meeting a whole lot of ladies who were there for the same reason that he was, and having his choices laid out in front of him was considerably more appealing than having to look for them himself. He had accepted the invitation and Shantelle had given him the details of where the next get-together was: in the grounds of a lodge in Hillside.

'White women don't really do this sort of thing,' she said. 'But if you're interested in black women, mixed-race women, perhaps, I can help you.' He had been a novelty at first, a white man in a sea of black ladies and he had enjoyed the attention greatly, feeling very much like Humphrey Bogart in *Casablanca* as he passed between tables, one hand in his jacket pocket, another clasping a glass of whisky.

Unfortunately, he was too much like Bogart's character, Rick: alone, aloof, apart. The problem, as Shantelle told him in a voice of concerned pity, as though he was struck with some awful disease, was that he was white. He remembered how she had closed her eyes and made that funny expression with her face that all his ex-girlfriends had done on breaking up with him. A cross between pity and constipation.

'You guys, you know, you've got to learn to loosen up a bit,' was her advice. She gave her shoulders a little shake as though to suggest he needed a bit of exercise. 'Just relax. But don't dance. Okay? White guys can't dance.'

Unfortunately, although the women he met were nice and

friendly and laughed almost too heartily at his jokes, there was something too shiny and polished about them as though they were just their looks and not much else existed beneath the farce of tight fitting clothing and shimmering eyeshadow. It would have been easy to have taken any of them home for the night, but he wanted more than that: someone a little cultured, with a good sense of humour, and hopefully fabulously good-looking (he was a man after all), but he was prepared to settle for 'nice' or 'not bad', such was his need for companionship. Yet, in all the time that he had been *on the books* of Mix 'n Match, about a year now, he had only ever succeeded in having three dates.

The first date he had messed up entirely, and it was one that he often looked back on with regret. It had ended appallingly with him getting drunk and trying to fondle her breasts in the car, while she tried to get out of the door. The next day, he had wanted to apologise, but didn't know how, the main problem being that he had forgotten her name. In fact, all he could remember from that evening was the sense of freshness and naivety about her, of untrammelled youth, as though she had just been beamed down onto the planet and hadn't had time to grow weary or disillusioned with it. How he had hated it.

Not that he only wanted to meet people who were weary and disillusioned with life; that couldn't be a lot of fun, either. It was just the way that she had greeted everything with a wide-eyed fascination, marvelling at the most irrelevant and mundane of things. There was something terrible, almost hideous about it. She was the sort of girl who'd watch a Nando's advert and then rush off to buy the latest promotion because there was twenty per cent extra free or their chips now came coated with cheese. There was nothing of the cynic in her: she was oblivious to the manipulation of advertisers and believed everything they said with utmost trust. In fact, she was like one of those Verimark adverts that irritated the life out of him on a regular basis. He could imagine her house was filled with Verimark gadgets: brooms that swept, dusted, washed and polished all at the same time and potato peelers with seven detachable blades. Cheese graters that sliced in fifteen different ways.

Ultimately, he knew, however, that it wasn't her lack of depth that had scared him, it was his own darkness, his own demons, and he felt he couldn't possibly have had a relationship with her, even if he hadn't messed things up, in case one day one of those little demons rushed out and stamped his hard, cruel little feet all over her and made her see what he saw. That's what made him afraid.

So although there was the occasional pang of regret for the way in which he had treated her – Coralee had, in fact, been her name – he consoled himself by thinking she had probably got away lightly with the botched grope in the car and he liked to think of her free and happy to meet someone equally effervescent about life and let them live in their very own Verimark world, comparing 'wonder' mops and corkscrews and the like.

But last night, last night was worse. Shantelle had phoned him rather excitedly at around three to say that she had a prospective 'client' for him to meet. Craig had winced at the use of the word 'client' with all it suggested of escort agencies and sex for sale, but heard Shantelle out nevertheless.

'Mmm,' was all he said at first, trying not to sound particularly interested. 'And her name is?'

'Jade,' came the reply and Craig winced again. Jade. Hard, green stone.

'Hmm, okay. And where does she work?'

'Well,' began Shantelle conspiratorially lowering her voice, 'I shouldn't tell you that, but' – she lowered her voice again and Craig had to press his ear hard to the phone in order to hear her – 'she works for an NGO. She's a *foreigner*. Here in Bulawayo. An NGO, hah?'

Craig rolled his eyes. What was it about everyone in this country that they were trying to get out? He could see Shantelle's train of thought. Meet woman from NGO, get married, go back to the UK or the US and get citizenship and a passport to a 'proper' country. Well, not a bad idea perhaps – if you wanted to get out. The trouble was that NGOs tended to be Scandinavian. Now he had nothing against Scandinavians per se, it's just when they became NGOs, they were weird: serious, stern people with one-track minds: getting Africa out of poverty. As though that could be achieved by one person; in one lifetime even. As if it were possible at all, ever.

They tended to be slim women with round faces and glasses and hair cut in blunt, straight bobs, a style that always gave the impression that they'd just hacked off their long locks in preparation for their great venture into Africa – or perhaps as some sort of penance for being Westerners with food and money and an education behind them. Sometimes they wore bandanas and always they wore sandals and chitenges of brightly coloured cloth and T-shirts with slogans such as 'One World, One Future' emblazoned on them (definitely nothing superfluous or funny or risqué). They read African novels – Marechera was a favourite – and they dated black men with dreadlocks, who were soft and sensitive and wistful looking and who painted meaningful pictures and had them exhibited at the Art Gallery or who wrote poetry that no one understood, but of which everyone said they could feel his pain and his loss. Sometimes they got married, these NGOs, to their Rasta men and went back to Norway or Sweden or Denmark, on the premise that their 'love' could not possibly 'grow' in a place as tortured as Zimbabwe. And so off they went back to their neat little lives in Stockholm and Copenhagen, glad to be earning a decent wage and even gladder still that they could spend it without guilt, leaving the burden of Africa behind.

Cynical? Probably. But Jade? Jade didn't sound Scandinavian. British maybe or American? Although suspicious of the NGO bit, he couldn't deny his interest was aroused and so, after a bit of umming and aahing, he finally agreed to meet her. He hoped he had sounded suitably nonchalant to Shantelle. He had tried to perfect a tone that was a mixture of laid back good humour and intelligence; he hoped to give the impression of a busy man with such a full timetable that it was unlikely he could see Jade within the next two weeks, unless one of his plans was cancelled of course. Unfortunately, Shantelle knew him too well and had already summed him up as a rather sad and lonely guy with not many options in a dull, generally uninteresting life. His attempt at nonchalance was interpreted as the hesitation of a pessimist and his hope to appear a busy man as the excuse of someone lacking in confidence.

'Come on, Craig,' she said to him at last, as he pretended to be looking at his diary and saying he would have to phone her back. 'Why don't you just meet her tonight? She looks nice, man. Just take her out for dinner somewhere, you know? Get to know her, talk...' Her voice trailed off suggestively.

'Dinner?' said Craig, almost breaking into a sweat at the thought of the expense.

'Yah, come on, man. All girls like to be wined and dined. Just take her out for dinner and... you know.'

Craig could imagine Shantelle twisting a strand of hair while she talked – and looked at the computer, of course. She seemed to be able to do everything and look at the computer at the same time. 'Multi-tasking,' he thought. Women were good at it, weren't they?

'I'm busy tonight...' he began again, well aware how his words lacked conviction.

'Just cancel,' insisted Shantelle. 'You can play tennis another night.'

'Squash,' Craig corrected her.

'OK, squash. Play tomorrow.'

'Well, it's not that easy,' Craig began. 'I've booked, you know.' He hoped he sounded put out, but he heard a noise, something like a cross between a yelp and a snort and a giggle and knew she was laughing at him.

'All right,' he said, finally agreeing and took Jade's number.

It wasn't a good start. Craig had hoped to take things in his stride this time. He had hoped that in pretending to feel laid-back, he would be. He had hoped that in not jumping at the first opportunity to meet someone in months, he himself would feel it wasn't a big deal and be able to handle the meeting in a confident manner. Now here he was – panicking. He had poured himself a large glass of whisky (no ice and not much water) while he got ready – well, while he chose between his only decent pairs of trousers, which happened to be a pair of jeans, and a pair of chinos with slightly worn patches in places (but which might not be seen in the relative dark of a restaurant).

The evening had not been a success right from the start. He knew as soon as he saw Jade sitting at the bar of Las Palmas he had chosen the wrong place to meet. He hadn't wanted to go expensive. Expensive in Bulawayo only meant he'd be doubly disappointed with the meal, for the idea of value for money was one that had died at least ten years ago. Since then, restaurants served what they liked and charged what they liked. Now and then, the odd person protested, but they were merely looked at with scorn; most people accepted paying exorbitant prices for unsatisfying food. Such is the way of Zimbabwe. Craig had long ago surmised that most restaurants served (or didn't serve, for it was customary for at least half the menu to be unavailable) the same thing. The only variable was how much one was prepared to pay for it.

Las Palmas wasn't exactly Chicken Inn, but nor was it Nesbitt Castle. The impression the original owners had tried to create was of somewhere in Mexico – the back wall was painted with cowboys, sombreros and cacti. Men with long, droopy moustaches and beautiful women with long, black sleek hair and long ruffled pink dresses, looking as though at any minute they would break into a dance.

Waiters in jeans and red T-shirts with the Las Palmas logo and ankle-length aprons with the strings tied two or three times round their waists took orders from customers who sat at small square tables with white cloths draped nearly to the floor. Each table was identical: there was a small arrangement of condiments (removed from their original plastic containers and put into slightly more gracious glass bottles) and a small brown plastic flower pot with a cactus in the middle of the table. Each place had a setting of one knife, fork and spoon. A paper napkin folded into a triangle was pushed under the prongs of each fork. 'Cheapskates,' thought Craig, who was scornful of paper napkins.

When the CD of Mexican Ranchera had done its loop a couple of times, the music changed to Céline Dion, which was played ad nauseam the rest of the evening. 'Very fitting,' thought Craig at one point. Eating dessert while the Titanic sinks for the fifth time. Yes, he thought on his way home, it was the wrong place. He knew it as soon as he saw her: her wide pale face with her long curly hair scraped back into a tight bun; the violet bandana with its pattern of tiny aquamarine flowers, the black top with the elbow length sleeves (probably the only smart item of clothing she had with her), the long skirt of shimmering emerald with tasselled fringe and the open leather pumps with bead motif. The chunky jewellery: a large white rock that served as a ring and a necklace of big blue stones with thin dark purple veins running through them. It was the jewellery that had been the first turn off. He didn't like chunky stuff. It was loud, over-confident, even brash, he thought. The ring was pure affectation and affectation was something he had little time for. The size, the colour and the fact that it must be quite unwieldy to wear all made him think that people with large rings wanted you to think of them as mystical, mysterious or exciting, but unless you are a character from a Tolkien novel, they remained affected and showy.

Later, he wondered if he shouldn't have just gone then. Said, 'Hello. Pleased to meet you, but I really don't think this is going to work out. I don't like your ring or that horrible chunky necklace. Goodbye.' If only life were as simple as that. It would have saved him money, and not only that, the agony of sitting out the evening, the feeling of utter panic and desperation when he got home. The need to drink... the headache the next day.

He was a disappointment, too. He could see that a mile away: the way her face visibly fell when she saw him, her eyes registering his hair, his rather red uneven skin tone and his race. No, maybe race was the wrong word to use. It wasn't that she was necessarily disappointed because he was white, but because he was what she termed, and what she was at pains to emphasise, a *white* Zimbabwean. Everything she asked him, and probably thought of him, was tempered by this fact. What had been the white Zimbabweans' response to the fact that the 2008 election results were delayed? How many white Zimbabweans had left the country? How did white Zimbabweans respond to the economic crisis? Every answer was received in exactly the same way: she pulled in her lips and tilted her head so that she appeared to look at him from an angle. And always her stare came to rest on his hair. There was something half-accusing, half... what was it? Interested? No, not interested, except perhaps in a morbidly fascinated way, as though she had someone to report to about the conversation – the truth about white Zimbabweans. 'Can you believe these people actually exist?' he imagined her confiding in a friend.

Craig often wondered what race he did belong to. His maternal grandparents had been Scottish and his paternal ones part of that now extinct minority race, the British Raj. He had once – a few years back when food had been very short and people carried money round in big bricks – tried to claim citizenship through his grandfather, but was turned down because he wasn't born on British soil. The man at the British High Commission had suggested he apply for an ancestry visa if he wanted to work in the UK, but he had made his mind up there and then that if the British didn't want him, he didn't want them. So he had stayed, as the dollar devalued and food disappeared off the shelves and friends left for greener pastures. Refusing to swallow his pride, he had sat out the crisis in Zimbabwe, mainly in the dark due to the power cuts, and often without water, money or the basics of life, and had emerged a little battered, a lot more cynical, but not that much thinner.

So he resented the tone of Jade's (he had an image of a sharp, green stone being jabbed into him) questioning. He resented the way she ran her eyes down the menu as though choosing one form of torture over another; the way she could pronounce the stupid Spanish dishes with the correct Spanish accent – in that irritating lisping manner; the way she recoiled when he asked if she'd like a drink as though he had suggested sex on the bonnet of his car, as if any suggestion of time spent with him in any way that didn't involve the asking of anthropological-type questions was somehow obscene.

It had all degenerated from there. He hadn't got drunk because he couldn't afford to. Now that Zimbabwe had changed to the US dollar, places like Las Palmas charged the same for a shot of whisky as they would have done for a bottle in the old days. It saved him from embarrassment, but instead he lapsed into a hard, bitter anger that in some ways was infinitely worse. He found himself spewing tirades of ugly resentment: the government, people who drove shiny, new cars, the Reserve Bank, the World Bank, people who thought they could change Zimbabwe through the vote, people who refused to belong to any political party... the list was endless. But as he sat and ranted the only person he really felt angry with was himself. He was lonely, pathetic and stupid. Yes, stupid. Stupid for agreeing to go on this stupid date. Stupid for listening to people like Shantelle. What else could you expect from someone who deliberately spelt their name incorrectly. Stupid for allowing things to get this far, for not knowing any other way to defend himself except through this bitter anger.

When he got home, he made up for his lack of alcohol by drinking most of a bottle of cheap whisky and so it was that he had woken up with a hangover. To add insult to injury, he had received a text message from Shantelle asking him how the evening had gone and informing him that she had put up her fees for organizing the date from $10 to $25. And so it also was that he had found himself in Shantelle's office late that morning. Shirt hanging out, hair greasy, and stinking of stale alcohol, how he had raged and spat and spewed and Shantelle had sat stiffly in her chair, looking down at her hands before jumping up and rushing into a back room. He had just been about to leave when the door opened again and a rather formidable character had appeared, rather like a ship in full steam. A middle-aged woman in a rather frumpy dress with thick white legs and the type of heels that reminded him of primary school teachers in age immemorial; short, square and black.

'Would you please mind leaving this office immediately or I shall be forced to call the authorities,' she barked, the top of her pale, creamy chest heaving slightly as it appeared above her dress.

Slightly taken aback, Craig turned for the door. 'Don't worry, I'm going,' he muttered. He started somewhere to feel that he wasn't quite within his rights to have done what he had and was just thinking it might be a good time to leave anyway. But when he got to the car, his mind changed again and he felt once more his old indignation. He was back up the stairs in no time and charging into the office again. Shantelle was seated weakly at her computer and looked up in great alarm as he bounded through the door. The old hag was suggesting they have a cup of tea. She turned to him with stony anger when he approached her.

'Out!' she ordered, pointing her finger in the direction of the door. 'Get out!'

But Craig wasn't having this, this being treated like a dog or some sort of social miscreant. At the same time, he was well aware that he was out of his depth and wasn't too sure of what to say. But it had to be something that ended the debacle that gave him power and them something to think about. He, too, raised his finger and brought it right up to the woman's face, which was now purple with rage.

'Watch out!' he said, as ominously as possible. 'I'll be back...' He faltered somewhat on these last words, trying desperately to avoid clichés such as 'be afraid, be very afraid'. Instead, he went for an action – he raised an imaginary gun to his head in warning and then turned on his heel and left, feeling a mixture of righteous indignation and yet somewhere, too, a feeling of shame at such appalling behaviour.

He spent the next few hours sleeping and woke with the sense of righteous indignation quite gone. It was only shame he felt now and he knew he had to put things right. In Craig's perhaps not very vast experience, women always appreciated flowers. He found himself at City Hall buying three, no four, bunches of roses – not red; he knew enough about the 'language' of flowers not to choose red – but was at a loss as to how to deliver them. He decided to do the delivery himself, but chickened out at the last moment and left them outside the office door with a note for Shantelle. Just as he was arranging the roses, he thought he heard a noise within the office and feared the door opening and someone finding him crouching outside. He quickly shoved them up against the wall and dashed down the stairs, jumping into his car. He sped off with unusual gusto for a Renault 4, and so it was that roughly four minutes later he was pulled over for speeding and hence Edmund met him at the police station.

The day, thought Craig, couldn't get worse. Was there anyone in the world with whom he would not have some sort of altercation that day? The speeding fine would cost a lot; at least one, perhaps two bottles of whisky depending on the quality and now here was this policeman wanting a lift and talking about his car as though he wanted it. The last thing Craig needed was for him to think he had been serious about the police taking his vehicle. He could have taken an aggressive approach and told the officer to get lost, but his speeding charge was still unresolved – he said he needed to go to the bank to withdraw the money – and he'd need to return to the police station in the near future. Although feeling very tense, Craig thought a slightly softer approach a better idea and so he had offered the policeman a lift. He expected by the time he dropped the police officer off, he would have made Craig an offer on the car, some ludicrously low amount, and be surprised when it wasn't jumped at.

He glanced over at the policeman who was gently running his hand along the dashboard. There was a slight smile on his lips as well, as though he were greeting an old friend. Craig shrugged. It was always the same. Everyone wanted something for nothing. And yet, there was something different about this man as well, something Craig couldn't quite put his finger on. Edmund – it was an unusual name.

'It's a pity you don't have one of those flashing lights we could slap on the top of the car,' he said, attempting a joke. He wondered if the policeman would take him seriously and was surprised when he smiled.

'Yes, I know what you mean. Like they have in the movies?'

For some reason, Craig was surprised to hear Edmund mention the movies. He supposed policemen must watch them just like anyone else. It was a pity they didn't pick up from them something of good governance and fair speeding fines. When he came to think of it though, most cop films showed the police chasing villains at the expense of the general public's safety or there were those good cop, bad cop films where the chief villain turned out to be the head of the police force. It didn't really help give policing a good image.

When the car pulled up at a house in Clark Road, Craig squinted at the name on the letter box on the gate: Pullman. He found his anger had dissipated somewhat, and his interest aroused in its place. He was quite glad then when Edmund asked if he wouldn't mind waiting, although he was sceptical of his claim to only be a few minutes. 'African time,' he thought, sarcastically.

Envisaging a long wait for the Chief Inspector, Craig decided to amble around the garden for a while. He walked up the verandah steps and peered in through the French windows at the living room inside. He stood quite still for a full minute before a slight feeling of panic overtook him and he had decided to go back to the car. 'Best to stay out of these things,' he thought, walking round the back of the house and past the kitchen. He could hear voices inside and wanted to move away as quickly and as quietly as possible. Suddenly, out of nowhere came the shrill voice of a woman. He turned to see a tall thin woman in a maid's uniform standing on the step to the kitchen.

'That's the one!' the woman shouted. 'Catch him!'

He carried on walking, not realising he was the object of the consternation until he was near the gate. Then he saw the officers turn and stare at him and in the split second before they gave chase, Craig Martin turned and pushed open the gate. He jumped in his car, praying to God it would start first time and careered off down the road.

Chapter Six

Janet had returned home on the evening of Marcia's death in a great state of shock. She let herself into the house quietly, not wanting to disturb her elderly mother with whom she lived. The house wasn't locked as the maid was still there, standing at the stove stirring a pot of sadza and talking softly to the baby strapped to her back with a bright blue chitenge adorned with pictures of Christ with droopy eyes and a sad mouth.

She turned in surprise to see Janet home early, for this was the one night every month when she worked overtime, making the old lady her supper and then watching ZBC for an hour or so while she waited for Janet to return home from book club. She looked slightly disappointed to see Janet come in the door.

'Book club was cancelled, Loveness.' Janet struggled to say the words; her chest was tight as though she had been running. 'Please, just carry on. I just need some time...' Her words trailed off as she went out of the kitchen and down the passage into the living room. Loveness looked after her, debating whether to see if the madam was all right or not and, deciding against it, shrugged her shoulders and carried on with her cooking. Madam was often a bit distracted and vague these days, even more so than the old lady.

At least the electricity was on. Janet couldn't have coped with getting home to a dark house after the afternoon's events. She put her bag and car keys down on a chair in the living room and pulled her red and orange silk scarf from around her neck, letting it drop on the chair too. She poured herself a drink from a nearly empty cut glass decanter that stood with two other empty ones on a tea trolley in the corner. She took a gulp and sank into a chair.

Marcia dead. It was too incredible to believe. People like

Marcia didn't die. They went on and on and on for years, ordering you here and there, picking holes in everything you did, never satisfied with any of your efforts. Marcia was someone who would have remained middle-aged forever. Janet had a sudden image of her thickset legs and the black court shoes with the square cut toes she invariably used to wear. Nobody ever saw Marcia in takkies or slops, not even sandals, and she always wore stockings of a very pale biscuit shade.

Janet shivered as she remembered Marcia lying on the bed, her shoes off and her stockinged feet sticking out of the blanket. She took another sip of the whisky, gripping the glass slightly as she held it out in front of her, half way to her chin.

Marcia dead. Well, that would change a few things, wouldn't it? The police would investigate, of course, not that she thought they were much good. It was unbelievable that such a tyrant, such a bully, could be felled so easily. She felt like a spectator in the crowd watching David take on Goliath must have felt, seeing the great giant crumple and fall, sending plumes of dust into the air.

The room was cold. The days when Janet could have afforded to have a heater on were long gone. In fact, Janet rarely sat in this room any more. There was a smaller room next door, which they still called the dining room although it hadn't been used as such for many years. The dining table was still there, but pushed up against the wall. Janet's sewing machine sat on top and the table was generally cluttered with sewing patterns and pieces of material. Squeezed in a corner were the television and two armchairs that had once belonged to a lounge suite. The arm and headrests were covered in oblong woollen crocheted pieces and a rug was appointed to each chair. Blue for Mum, red for Janet.

When electricity permitted, they turned on the TV to see what ZBC had on offer. Sometimes, just sometimes, you could be really surprised to find a real goodie, as Janet's mother called them, on ZBC. *Rising Damp*, *The Good Life*, *To the Manor Born*. Old, but still good, all these years later. None of that loud DSTV rubbish that everyone complained about. Sometimes, of course, there was nothing to watch except endless political drivel concerning comrade this and comrade that and The Party and The Fight Against Colonialism. On those evenings, they read their library books or their book club books (Janet always borrowed something for Mum) with their cup of tea. If Janet had a little more money than usual, they might have a very small whisky together or a cup of cocoa.

'Such pleasant evenings,' thought Janet, staring across the room blankly. Would they ever have a pleasant evening again? Would they be able to sit and read and not think of Marcia? Dead Marcia. Janet wondered where she was now. The body would be at the morgue. How Marcia would hate that. It would be dirty and cold; no plush carpets or rich red wines. No canapés. They might have to prod her and push her and squeeze her. Marcia hated being touched. Janet remembered a time her dog, Billy, an Alsatian, had died. Janet had been counting books and she had realised that she hadn't seen Billy since she'd arrived.

'Where's Billy, Marcia?'

'We had to have him put down,' Marcia answered, coming in from the kitchen and licking some cream off her finger. 'Yesterday afternoon.' She placed a plate of scones in front of Janet who looked at them with a kind of horror.

'Oh Marcia!' she exclaimed and threw her arms around her. 'Oh, I'm so sorry.'

Marcia writhed under Janet's grip and patted her gingerly on the back as though it were Janet who had just lost her dog.

'Yes, yes. Thank you, Janet. It's sad, but Nigel says he knows someone with an Alsatian stud up in Burnside and they might be able to replace him quite soon.'

Janet wondered if Marcia had any emotions. Had had. She tried not to think of all she hadn't liked about her. Never talk badly of the dead. Wasn't that the saying? It's something her father would have said. She imagined his quiet, calm voice: 'Don't think ill of the dead, Janet.' He would have some quote to add, some snippet of poetry from his vast knowledge. Death the great leveller, or something along those lines. Janet could hardly think. Thoughts swam in front of her: Marcia, her legs sticking out of the blanket, all the books that still needed to be counted, the letter opener in Marcia's chest, the washing up that hadn't been done, Dorcas and her long, sad face. The dog. Marcia's dead dog. The gardener.

She swayed a little and caught herself with a jolt. 'What an absolute waste of precious food,' she suddenly thought and gulped the remainder of the drink down and placed the glass back on the trolley. A small, faint voice called from another room and she picked up her bag and scarf and opened the door to the passageway. Her mother's room was at the end; she turned the handle with some trepidation and pushed the door open. An elderly lady was sitting in a chair in the corner by the window. She had been reading and a book lay open on her lap, which was covered with a blanket. She looked up over her glasses as Janet came in.

'Janet, dear,' she said, with some concern. 'I thought I heard someone. What on earth's the matter? Aren't you going to book club this evening?'

Janet paused, wondering what to tell her mother. She was elderly but tough, one of those 'salt of the earth' types whom it was common to refer to as 'a dying breed'. Janet had no compunction about telling her the news. She was unlikely to be horrified or suffer sleepless nights as a result; in fact, she was far more likely to be interested in it as though it were in a television murder series, like the ones she enjoyed watching. Sometimes Janet reckoned her mother fancied herself as a female Inspector Morse and had visions of driving round solving mysteries in a Jaguar with opera playing in the background.

Miss Marple wasn't quite her mother's style, or, rather, stylish enough, although she did have an annoying habit of talking to herself while watching television and every now and then giving a wry smile as though to say 'Well, you thought you had me fooled?'

Janet looked at her mother watching her. Her old grey cardigan was pulled across her stick-like shoulders and her trousers, where they protruded from under the blanket, were patched and worn, the fabric far too thin for the cold winter evening. Janet felt suddenly ashamed of her thoughts. Poor mum, poor old mum. Why shouldn't she indulge in detective-fuelled fantasies if it got her away from here, from the house in which she was increasingly confined?

'I have some shocking news, Mum,' she ventured at last and watched the old lady regard her intently, running her tongue lightly over her bottom lip. 'Marcia Pullman's been stabbed.' She blurted out the words and burst into tears at the same time. Janet clutched her mother's hand and tried to talk as she cried.

'Stabbed? Whatever do you mean?'

'Mum, she's dead! I... I didn't think she was the type.' She began to laugh now as well and eventually collapsed in a heap at her mother's feet. She felt like a child again and the soft touch of her mother's hand on her head was warm and comforting. It would all be all right as it always had been whenever she told her mother what was on her mind.

Her mother was talking, asking her questions and now and then nodding her head thoughtfully.

'A letter opener, you say? Really? How strange. Now if it was me, I'd be more likely to go in for a hatchet and chop her into small pieces and it would be outside. Spur of the moment stuff. Let's see, letter opener in the heart. Well, that's more likely the husband. Anger, perhaps? Years of suffering? Or maybe she's worth a mint. We'll have to wait until the will is read.' She nodded her head with determination and gave Janet's head another pat. Janet looked up at her in despair.

'Mum, this is not one of your murder mysteries. We're not playing a game of Cluedo – Miss Scarlet in the bedroom with a dagger. This is a *murder*, a real *murder*. Someone – Marcia – is dead!'

Her mother gave her a long, hard look.

'Yes, of course,' she said, without much conviction.

Janet took a deep breath and recounted her interview with the policeman.

'He asked me why I got the key and went into the house. I felt like a criminal, as though I had broken in.'

'The key... yes, of course.' Her mother looked as though she had forgotten something.

'You're doing your Miss Marple thing, aren't you? Trying to work out whodunit?'

Her mother snapped back into the present with a wry laugh. 'Just wondering why they would lock the door after them, that's all. Definitely *not* the gardener. Anyway, I am sure the police will get whoever it is.'

'Yes, we think like that, don't we?' said Janet, standing up and tucking her mother's blanket in round her. She stopped and stared at the blue tassels of the blanket dangling down. It was about a minute before she spoke. 'And then we'll all live happily ever after. I just wonder if that happens in real life.'

Her mother looked up sharply at Janet. 'What is it, dear? What's the matter?'

Janet sat on the edge of the coffee table and took her mother's hand in hers. 'You know what the police are like. There's no guarantee the murderer will be caught.'

'If only she had died a natural death. One wouldn't be compelled to feel any sorrow for her.'

Janet didn't answer; instead, she leaned over and turned down her mother's bedclothes. Her mother sat quietly as though wanting to say something, but deciding against it.

'Do you think we'll get everything back now?' she asked after a short silence.

'Some, maybe. I doubt we'll get all of it,' said Janet, moving to the door. 'Let's not think of that now. It's too much to take in all at once.'

The old lady nodded and looked away.

'Now, Mum, what would you like for supper?' Janet's voice assumed an authoritative tone. 'A bit of soup and toast?'

Chapter Seven

A figure stood at the window of number 272 Clark Road, watching the proceedings in his next door neighbours' garden with a detached interest. He had heard she was dead and he was glad. As long as it all went to the grave with her. He gave his whisky a little swirl and watched the amber liquid tremble in the glass. Police. They had come. Somehow he thought they wouldn't, known as they were for being incompetent. His house being slightly elevated and set back from his neighbours', he was allowed a slight vantage point and could view the driveway and part of the back garden quite clearly. He watched the policemen walk up the drive, one of them in one of those ridiculous trench coats, like something out of a 1940s movie.

He turned away and sat for a few moments in his favourite chair, alternately swirling the drink in his hand and sipping it. He stared off into space a little, wondering what would happen next. A collector of fine things, Roland Sherbourne's sitting room was a shrine to a bygone era. The furniture had belonged to his parents, both dead now: light blue chintz chairs and sofa, ball and claw coffee table with matching side tables, and a roll top writing desk. It was this object he now approached and fumbled through some papers. Despite having a laptop in the next room, Roland liked to think he was a man of letters. He blamed the postal service for the letter's demise over the past ten or so years. It was almost impossible to send a letter and feel any surety that it would reach its destination within two weeks. He had been forced more and more to rely on email, yet he despised doing so, keeping his laptop well-hidden and his writing desk very much in the foreground, a hope, perhaps, that one day things would return to normal.

Amongst his papers, he found a letter to his bank in

England. It was already in an envelope, the address written in Roland's small neat handwriting across the front. Taking a large pair of scissors out of the left hand drawer, he sat and methodically cut the envelope and its contents into long, thin strips, which in turn, he then cut into smaller and smaller squares until he couldn't cut them any smaller. He sat back in the chair and picked up the tiny pieces, letting them fall softly from his hand. Tears pricked at his eyes, but he wasn't going to cry. Not yet.

Later that night, when the police had gone from next door and the house had descended into quiet, he found himself looking across at it again. He assumed the husband – what was his name now? – was staying somewhere else. The maid he had seen walking quickly down the drive as though a ghost were at her heels. It was strange seeing it so dark. Even when the Pullmans went away, they left a multitude of security lights on. No one had had time to organise anything, he thought. Anyway, the house would be safe enough. News travels fast and superstition was such that no one was likely to break into a house where a woman had so recently been murdered.

He didn't want much to eat: his indigestion was playing up again. Instead, he ran a deep, hot bath and lay in it for close on an hour. It was one of his favourite pastimes, lying in the bath, especially in the winter. He had closed the door and let the room steam up, then he had poured himself a whisky and submerged himself in the delicious warm depth of the water. He rarely soaped himself until, right at the end when, with an almost guilty start, he quickly got himself clean. The best baths, though, were the ones in which he didn't wash. He didn't need to, he wasn't dirty. He wasn't dirty.

He lay in bed later, listening to the news on the radio. Somewhere across the other side of the world, a suicide bomber had killed 19 people, a ferry had capsized in Egypt and 47 were believed drowned, and some famous singer, of whom he had never heard, had died of a drug overdose. He switched off the radio and reached for the pen and notepad on his bedside table. It was already open on a long list of figures and it was to this list that Roland added the following: s. bomber – 19, ferry – 47, heroin overdose – 1. 67 people. He hated odd numbers, they left one feeling so strangely unbalanced. He added another figure: murder – 1. Yes, even numbers were so much more comforting and dependable.

Roland didn't sleep well that night. He hadn't slept well for a long time. Always fidgety and restless, his dreams were dark and, if not particularly frightening, unsettling still, and he generally awoke with a start, glad to see the morning light edging feebly through the curtains. He got out of bed and pushed his feet into his dark brown calf leather slippers at the side of the bed and wrapped his long, silky dressing gown round himself. It was cold, so he added a knitted cardigan to his apparel and went off to the kitchen to put the kettle on. He had, he reckoned, about five minutes before the power went off and, as he hated waking to the darkness, he made a point of rising before six.

Sometimes they were clever, mind you, these people at ZESA, who made you feel for weeks, months even, that you could rely on a certain timetable for power cuts. Not an official one, of course, those were all bunk in his opinion. No, the unofficial one. He had recorded the times the power went off and came on for a month and was not surprised to find there was method in their madness. He had been delighted – as though he had cracked a secret code. He knew, even if no one else in the whole of Zimbabwe did, that there was a pattern in the seemingly random switching on and switching off of power. And then they changed it, they changed the pattern and once more Roland's tiny world was plunged into chaos. Once more, he'd sit with his notebook, recording, deciphering until he had worked it out.

He was sitting with a steaming cup of tea in front of him and two pieces of toast and marmalade on a white plate next to his elbow when the electricity went off. He felt vaguely smug, thinking of all the households near him where that

81

collective 'oh' might be heard. He envisaged the harassed adults reaching gloomily for the portable gas stove, children not wanting to get up for school as it was cold and dark still and generators whirring into life. Roland's visions only ever included people like himself, people with what is nowadays called *disposable incomes*.

Roland's day began by following its usual routine: he ate his breakfast while listening to the news on his small battery-run radio. Wireless was the word he used. It suggested calm; the family seated round the wireless of an evening, tuned into the news while a clear, clipped voice informed them of the world's ills. No need for graphic pictures or the noise of gun battles, just the calmly detached voice. Radio? Radio had connotations of noise: pop music, loud and imposing, and the equally loud and imposing tone of a DJ with his constant interjections and suggestion that life was one continual merry-go-round.

His wireless, therefore, was constantly tuned into the World Service of the BBC and he switched it on approximately three times a day to hear the news. He enjoyed his breakfast news the most because it was new; later in the day the news became updates of what he had already heard. There was a certain relish to turning on and discovering what had happened while one slept, a feeling not unlike the one he had had as a child at Christmas when he had woken and found presents under the tree. He liked the thought that the world didn't stand still while he slept. If he had thought about it deeply, he would have realised that it made him feel a little less lonely in the world, but Roland never allowed himself deep trains of thought; the headlines were just about all he could bear and then he switched off.

It was about midday that he noticed a man at the gate. Roland watched him a little while from a gap in the curtains. He thought it must be one of those vendors who appeared so frequently these days. If they weren't selling things – everything from fruit and vegetables to second hand books – they were selling services: have your pool cleaned or your gutters cleared or your car seats reupholstered. All for an extortionate fee, of course. Roland waited. He heard the gate rattle and the man call out. 'Hello. Is there anyone home? Hello?' Still, Roland waited. The man took two steps back from the gate and appeared to be in retreat when Roland made his big mistake, he reached out and pulled the curtain closed. He knew the man had seen him, but he still refused to acknowledge him. The next thing he saw was him grip the gate tightly, haul himself onto the top, waver a little and then fall over the other side, one foot remaining caught in the mesh.

The comedy of the moment was lost on Roland whose stomach lurched as he started in a quick spasm of fear. He knew he should have had the gate replaced a long time ago. It was far too low and unintimidating. The doors were all locked; Roland always kept them locked – and bolted – but that probably wouldn't stop someone coming in if they wanted to.

But burglars didn't wait until they saw someone was home before they broke in, did they? Nor did they knock. Perhaps they did if they wanted an easy way in. Knock on the door and then knock you on the head. Roland felt himself looking madly round. The heaviest and most obvious thing to pick up was a large vase that had belonged to his mother and which stood on the floor near the fireplace in the sitting room. But that was an expensive item and certainly not worth using if it didn't work. Roland wasn't quite sure he would be able to hit someone on the head with it. He wasn't the most physically strong of men and imagined he would be easily overpowered. Better something long and sharp like a knife, he thought, and dashed to the kitchen. It was then that he heard a knock on the kitchen door and a voice called out: 'Hello? Hello? It is the police. I need to ask you some questions.' Roland lifted the curtain of the little window near the back door and peeped out. He jumped when he saw someone looking back at him. The person smiled and repeated their request. Roland relaxed and then called out:

'Show me your police ID.' The man fumbled in his trouser pockets and produced what looked like an ID; Roland had no idea what a Zimbabwean police ID should look like. He imagined something like a sheriff's badge and was slightly disappointed it was nothing like that.

'What do you want?' he called out, trying to make a visual evaluation of his caller through the small square of window. He looked like a policeman. Was it to do with the murder? He felt his body tense suddenly and a wave of panic rose in his chest. He wasn't prepared. What would he say?

'I'd like to ask you some questions, please,' said the policeman. His voice was soft. 'It won't take long – just a few minutes.'

Roland took a deep breath, counted to five and turned the latch on the Yale lock, undid the chain and slipped back the two bolts that held the door locked. Slowly, he opened the door and stood back to let the policeman in.

'Thank you,' he said with a nod of his head. 'My name is Chief Inspector Edmund Dube.' He held out his hand, which Roland looked rather dubiously at before giving it a limp shake. Almost immediately he wanted to wash his hand, but refrained from doing so as he knew it might have caused offence. He had a sudden flash of his mother holding him up to the sink as a little boy and frantically washing his hands with a large bar of soap. 'Dirty boy! Dirty boy! Playing with those dirty people! You'll get sick. You hear me? You'll die.' Instead he slipped his hand into his cardigan pocket and made a mental note to wash it as soon as the policeman had gone.

'Mr Sherbourne. Roland Sherbourne.' He wished he hadn't mentioned his first name. It was too friendly. He hoped the policeman didn't call him Roland. Or Mr Roland. He hated that.

Roland led the way awkwardly to the lounge. He made sure to offer the policeman a chair he hardly used and secure his own favourite before the officer had a chance to sit in it. In the clear winter light of the lounge, Roland studied the policeman's face. It was one of quiet, perhaps even sadness, when he wasn't trying to be the jolly policeman and put Roland at his ease. Roland saw him take in the room: the antiquated furnishings, the old photos in silver frames and the piano in the corner. He started as the inspector got up and went over to it.

'Do you play?' the policeman asked, running his hand softly over the polished wood of the lid.

Roland felt mildly irritated. Wasn't this man a police officer? Wasn't he here to ask him questions? 'No,' he answered, with an impatient shake of his head. A faint look of surprise registered on the other man's face and he added, 'It was my mother's. She played.'

'Ah. And she is now?'

'Dead. She died a few years ago.'

The policeman straightened. 'I'm sorry to hear that she has passed on.'

Roland hated the expression 'passed on'. He disliked it as much as 'passed over'. One was dead and that was all there was to it. Nobody passed on anywhere else, to heaven or to hell or to some magical realm. Dead was dead.

The policeman continued to survey the room. One of the pictures on the wall caught his eye and he went over to look at it.

'It's my father's war medal,' explained Roland, exasperated.

'Impressive. What did he get it for?'

'His ship was torpedoed. He rescued three men from drowning. On the third rescue, his own leg got trapped under some heavy machinery. He managed to get free in time, but his leg was badly damaged and had to be amputated.'

'A brave man indeed.'

'Perhaps you could ask me your questions?' said Roland, making a point of looking at his watch.

'Ah yes, you have somewhere to go?'

Roland didn't, but he raised his eyebrows and tilted his head ever so slightly to suggest acquiescence. He didn't like lying and thought the wordless answer might exculpate him from the crime of doing so.

'Do you know about the murder next door?'

'Murder?' Roland's voice came out high-pitched and strained. He coughed loudly and cleared his throat. 'No. I heard there had been a death. I... well, I saw the police there and I asked the maid what had happened. She said the madam had died.' He gave a short laugh and found Edmund looking questioningly at him. 'These people,' he said by way of explanation. 'Death is all the same to them, isn't it? Sickness, murder, accident. It's all the same.'

'By "these people" you mean...?'

Roland looked slightly embarrassed. 'I mean, you know, maids, gardeners.' His fingers played nervously with the large buttons of his cardigan. The man thought he was a racist, he was certain.

The policeman continued. 'You say the maid told you. Perhaps I could speak to her when I have finished with you?'

'I don't mean my maid. I don't have a maid,' said Roland hurriedly. 'Hers. Theirs. You know, the maid next door.'

'When did you see her?'

'When the police were there.'

'Where was she?'

He noticed a slight flicker on the policeman's face.

'I don't understand why you are asking me these questions.'

Edmund gestured to the window. 'You've got quite a high wall there, Mr Sherbourne. I don't see any gaps in it and I don't imagine you would shout over it looking for information. I was just wondering how you managed to get her attention.'

'She was outside the gate.'

'Outside the gate. I see. What was she doing?'

'What do I think she was doing? Why are you asking me?'

'Was she here the whole afternoon yesterday?'

'Yesterday? Well, no, not if Mrs Pullman was murdered. No, I assume not.'

'You *assume* not?'

86

Roland looked at his shoes.

'Were you here all day yesterday?' continued Edmund.

'No,' answered Roland, his eyes now on the pattern on the carpet. 'In fact, I was out all day yesterday.'

'Pity,' said the officer, getting up and walking over to the window. 'You have a good view of next door from here. You might have seen something.'

Roland couldn't help feeling the officer's eyes gently boring that little bit deeper.

'Where were you?'

Roland was taken aback. He hadn't expected any further questioning. His first response was that it was rather rude to be asked anything else.

'Well, I can't remember off-hand,' he said irritably.

'You can't remember?' The police officer's voice was still quiet, but a faint tone of what – incredulity? – had entered it. 'It was yesterday.'

'Shopping... yes, quite a lot of shopping. And I stopped somewhere for coffee. And, of course, I went to the library... Well, I can't remember everything. All my days are exactly alike. One just rolls into another.'

'You mean you go out every day?'

'No, no, I mean... my shopping days. Once a week, sometimes twice, I go shopping.'

'Where do you go?'

'Look, this is ridiculous! I thought you were here to ask questions about that dead woman next door. Not what I do during the day! For goodness sake, this is a waste of both our time!'

'Not quite,' said Edmund, not raising his voice in return. 'I'd like you to answer my question, Mr Sherbourne. How did you spend yesterday?'

'Shopping. I told you.'

'And you were back at what time?'

'Four o'clock. No, no, no. I mean five. Five o'clock.'

The police officer looked sideways at him as though he wanted to challenge him but refrained.

'You knew her?'

Roland didn't answer at once; when he did his voice was scratchy and coarse. He cleared his throat. 'Mrs Pullman?' he asked with a feigned sense of casualness. 'Yes. Well, she was my neighbour.' He shrugged his shoulders as though that explained everything.

'People don't always know their neighbours,' answered the policeman, his quiet voice making Roland feel instinctively uneasy. 'She was a friend?'

'Well, no, I... look, what is this all about? What do you want to ask me? Really? What is it? Did I see something? Did I murder her? What? It's more likely to be the gardener. He did something... something she didn't like. Perhaps he... scratched the car or... or he broke something valuable. I don't know. Perhaps he planted a geranium in the wrong place and it was the final straw and she went mad and fired him.' Immediately, he regretted his outburst. He took a deep breath and let out a sigh of exasperation. 'Why are you here? Why are you asking all these questions? '

'Really, you think it may be the gardener?'

'I... of course... I don't know if it was him... it's just, well, the most obvious explanation.' spluttered Roland.

Edmund turned slowly from the window and stared hard at Roland, who flinched slightly and looked away.

'Something just doesn't fit the bill, Mr Sherbourne. We haven't found the gardener yet, that's true, but nor is he missing.' Edmund decided not to tell him that the gardener had left the Pullmans' employment a week before. 'But in the meantime I'm looking for someone else. Someone with a grudge; someone who is clever, who sat and planned a murder meticulously. This is not a crime of passion, Mr Sherbourne. This is something far, far more complicated than that.'

Chapter Eight

Edmund uttered the last words to Roland with a definite sense that he was playing a role. He felt like a detective on television and that, had he been in a film, the camera would have zoomed right up to his face at that moment, perhaps with a crescendo of background music before the credits began to roll.

As it was, he was staring across Roland's sitting room at a rather anxious looking man who appeared to be still in his dressing gown at midday. If only he could sustain the role: walk with hands behind his back, his head a little in the air and a knowing look on his face. If only he could always sound assertive, 'in the know', authoritative. It worked with some people; people whom he felt more confident than. With others, like Mr Pullman, he fell to bits, feeling small and awkward, as though the very words he spoke had little hands that reached up and held onto his throat, refusing to come out.

He faltered now as he tried to maintain a sense of mystery.

'Um... so Mr Sherbourne, I'd... er... appreciate it if you could call me on this number if you happen to think of anything important.' Edmund held out a piece of paper on which he'd written his phone number. He noticed the look of disdain on Roland's face as he took it gingerly between finger and thumb.

'Chief Inspector Edmund Dube,' said Roland, reading the piece of paper. He gave a nod and just as gingerly placed the piece of paper on the table behind him.

Edmund walked to the door of the living room and turned. 'I'll see myself out. Thank you, Mr Sherbourne.' He gave a slight bow and turned to go, thinking his words carried a certain sense of aplomb, but Roland was at his side in a second and pushed past him in a sudden fluster.

'No, no. I'll show you out,' he insisted, rather breathlessly and Edmund noticed how he dashed ahead and closed the door that led down the passageway. He tried to do it surreptitiously, but his movements were awkward and clumsy and the door banged shut.

'Such a wind today!' exclaimed Roland in a contrived tone of surprise.

'Yes,' replied Edmund, his voice non-committal as he made a mental note of Roland's actions. He heard Roland lock the door behind him as he went down the three steps from the kitchen door to the path. He stopped suddenly, realising that he had forgotten to ask Roland to open the gate. He looked back at the closed door and decided against knocking again. Instead, he attempted to climb the gate with a little more panache and managed to jump down on the other side with a certain spring. He was happy that progress had been made in at least one area.

Something wasn't quite right there; he had found the man's attempts to distance himself from the scene of the crime almost laughable. He had been amateurish in his efforts, almost as though he was playing a character in a film who had to deliberately appear suspicious only because he wasn't, whilst the real criminal would be a little old lady who made tea and appeared kind and homely and suitably vague. He had a sharp, angular body and his movements were jolting and staccato-like. He seemed ill at ease within his own space, but Edmund imagined him to be like that all the time and not just because he was talking to a police officer.

Why did he act in such a guilty fashion? Yet Edmund hadn't gone to the house to interview him as a possible suspect. The fact of the matter was that Edmund was determined to carry out a thorough investigation. He was tired of the police having a reputation of being a waste of time; he was tired of being laughed at. He had seen Nigel Pullman's face the day before: the sneer and look of contempt and he wanted to prove him wrong. He was going to carry out a proper full-scale investigation and get to the bottom of this mystery.

Back at the police station, chaos ensued. Two policemen were leading a handcuffed man off the back of a police truck whilst a woman stood and screamed at them.

'How dare you just come on to my property and arrest this man without due reason? she demanded, her lips pursed together in indignant rage. 'What's the problem? Has he said something about the government? I suppose he was wearing an MDC T-shirt and so you thought you'd send a truckload of heavies round to give him a hard time? What has this country come to?'

'Can I help you?' Edmund asked, approaching her with hesitation for she looked rather volatile.

'Yes, you can help me,' she snapped, turning on him. 'Are you the person in charge here? My gardener has just been arrested for a crime he most certainly didn't commit.'

'Please come this way,' began Edmund, when a figure standing in the doorway to the charge office spoke over him.

'Mrs Ncube, please come inside.' Both Edmund and the woman turned their heads in his direction. It was Detective Inspector Khumalo; he was watching the proceedings with an unsmiling ruthlessness. Even the aggrieved employer halted in her tirade, looked surprised at being summoned and then followed orders.

Edmund looked after them, dug his hands in his pockets and then followed behind. The door to Khumalo's office closed just as Edmund reached it. He stopped, his hand on the handle, turned to go and then turned back, gave the door a light knock and opened it before there was any chance for anyone to refuse him entry. Khumalo was at his desk, his hands clasped in front of him. The woman was perched uneasily on a rickety chair. 'Questioning!' she scoffed. 'I know what you guys do! Hmm? I know.' She jabbed her finger in her chest as she spoke. 'Anyway, what has he done? What's the problem?' She said the word 'problem' in a voice heavy with sarcasm.

'Stabbed someone,' Khumalo replied simply and watched as her face changed.

'And... are they dead?'

Khumalo nodded.

'He's a good gardener... ' she began as though that were reason enough for him not to be guilty of such a crime. 'Who? When?'

'A woman in Suburbs. Yesterday.' He ran his finger slowly under his chin as he awaited her response.

'Oh! I know who you are talking about. Marcia Pullman. I heard she had been murdered.'

Khumalo was silent.

'I used to belong to her book club. But this is nonsense. Malakai was at my house all day yesterday.'

'As I said, Mrs Ncube, this is just routine questioning.'

'Then why is he handcuffed? Is that usual? I don't think so? Hasn't he got a right to have a lawyer present?

Khumalo's face was unmoving. 'We will keep you informed of all progress. Thank you. That will be all.' Without looking up at Edmund, he added: 'Please see Mrs Ncube out.'

'I'm going to get legal advice on this. You do know that, don't you? You haven't heard the last of this, mark my words.'

Khumalo looked briefly up at Edmund then and gave a slight nod.

'Please, come this way, Mrs Ncube,' began Edmund.

Mrs Ncube looked uncertainly between the two policemen and then stood up, shaking her head in despair.

'Definitely won't be the last you hear of this,' she went out muttering.

'Please, Mrs Ncube, this way,' said Edmund, showing her down the corridor to his office and closing the door behind him. She looked around at the piles of files and papers and the lone typewriter on his desk.

'There's no order,' she said, throwing her hands up in the air. 'No order at all. No wonder good men go to jail.'

'That's what I'm trying to do. I'm trying to establish some order,' said Edmund, opening a file to show her and flicking through pages of typed charge sheets. 'There's a lot to do.' He felt like a child pleading with its teacher for some respite over incomplete homework.

'I need to talk to you.'

Her eyes narrowed suspiciously. 'Go on.'

'About your gardener, Mrs Ncube. How to help him.'

She glanced at the closed door and seemed to hold her handbag closer to her body. 'Now listen, let me make this very clear from the beginning. I am not paying anyone any money.' She stared hard at him, her mouth drawn into a grimace.

'Oh, no, no, no,' he began, holding up his hand in protest. 'That is not what I am suggesting. Please, Mrs Ncube, would you take a seat.' He motioned to the chair in front of the desk. She didn't move. 'Please.' She hesitated and then stepped forward and sat on the chair, still gripping her bag tightly.

'Are you a hundred per cent sure that Malakai was at your house yesterday afternoon?'

'Absolutely. One hundred per cent.'

'What time does he finish?'

'Five o'clock.'

'You work?'

'Yes, I do work – from home. I would have known if he'd gone out.'

'You knew Mrs Pullman?'

'Yes. When I heard that she'd got rid of Malakai, I took him on at once. I'd seen what he'd done in Marcia's garden – he's a wonderful gardener! It's *very* difficult to find a good gardener these days.'

'Had he worked for her long, do you know?'

'A couple of years, I think. She paid him well – in fact, she was *very* generous in what she gave him, I can tell you that. He's had to settle for less with me.'

'She looked after her domestic workers well?'

'Oh, yes. But she made sure they worked for it. The maid, Dorcas, is there all hours of the night and day.'

'Did he mention any trouble with the Pullmans, Mrs Pullman in particular? An argument? Any accusations made?'

Mrs Ncube shook her head. 'He had been fired over some mishap with the car, but I don't think he felt particularly aggrieved, especially as he found another job so soon.'

Edmund jotted down a few notes. 'Even though you were offering a lower wage?'

'Yes.'

'I see,' he said, staring at the open notebook.

'Do you? Does that mean Malakai can go now?'

Edmund looked uneasy. 'I'll see what I can do, Mrs Ncube. I will try.'

She rolled her eyes. 'I don't get it. Who's in charge of this case? Why are you asking me questions when the last guy wouldn't give me the time of day?'

'Like I said, Mrs Ncube, I'll see what I can do. I'll do my best.'

The look of suspicion settled on her face again. 'You're all as crooked as each other,' she said, standing up. 'Just a bunch of crooks.'

Edmund stood as well. In his haste, his chair fell backwards. His whole state was one of apologetic confusion as he tried to right the chair and not turn his back on Mrs Ncube.

'You are not from here, Mrs Ncube? Your accent... '

'I lived in Britain for ten years.' She gave Edmund a long, hard stare. 'I won't put up with this police brutality. I tell you, I won't.'

In the front office, they met Malakai sitting handcuffed on a bench, a policeman either side of him. He stared at the floor, sulky and silent, while his employer spoke quietly but firmly to him, reiterating the need to 'just tell the truth' and reassuring him that he'd be back soon. In a louder voice, with each word carefully accentuated, she said: 'And any problems, you just let me know, Okay? Okay, Malakai? Anybody lays a *finger* on you, you let me know.' She looked sideways at Edmund as she said this and pursed her lips defiantly.

Edmund went back inside his office and compiled a list of interview questions. He would like to have typed them out, but there wasn't enough time. He'd better get the interview over and done with so the real criminal could be found.

Edmund found the charge office empty.

'Where has the suspect been taken?' he asked the officer behind the desk who was filling in a form.

'They have taken him to be interviewed,' was the curt reply.

Edmund sighed and took a deep breath. 'Who is *they*? Your use of a non-specific pronoun is incorrect in this instance.'

The officer glared at him over the counter. 'Khumalo took him for questioning.'

'Khumalo? When?'

A shrug was the only reply and the officer carried on filling in his form.

Burning with indignation, Edmund made his way down the corridor to the interview room. It was locked. He knocked, but no one answered. He knocked again, but still no one answered.

'The General is looking for you,' said an officer passing him without stopping.

'Sir!' Edmund called after him. 'The General is looking for you, sir!'

The man continued to walk away and Edmund turned back to the closed door. He was about to knock again, but decided against it.

Dispirited, Edmund wandered down the corridor towards the Senior Assistant Commissioner's office deep in thought. It wasn't the gardener, this Malakai man. It just obviously wasn't him. Edmund had worked in the police force long enough to know the look and the actions of a guilty man. If they had found him drunk or hiding in a relative's house somewhere, that would have been different, but to pick him up at a suburban house where he was tending the garden seemed wrong. Suburbs and Burnside were far apart: even if

Malakai had possessed an extremely fast car, it was unlikely that he could have popped down to Suburbs to break into a house in such a short time that he wouldn't be missed in the garden in Burnside.

Yet why the conspiracy? If it was just police laziness then why the closed doors and the silence? Why was Khumalo involved when it was Edmund's case? Baffled, Edmund stopped before he got to the Chief's door. He didn't feel like talking to him at the moment. Instead, he returned to his office and sat for a few minutes with his head in his hands. It stung, this lack of confidence in him, this sheer absence of faith in his ability to do anything well. He picked up the book next to his elbow, *Being in Control: A Practical Guide to Self-Confidence,* and stared at it crestfallen. He flung it to the corner of his desk and sat back, his arms folded across his chest.

He glanced at a sheet of paper next to him. It contained details about Craig Martin: age, address, telephone number. Despite Dorcas's claims of the night before, no one had been sent to find Craig Martin. Edmund thought for a bit, pressing his lips together and leaning back in his chair. Murder wasn't usually this difficult to work out, he thought as he tapped his pen on the desk. It usually involved someone hitting someone else on the head and then trying, unsuccessfully, to hide the body. He stood up resolutely and made his way to the door. He would go and see Craig Martin himself. He was scared of something, that much was obvious, but it was doubtful he was a killer. He must know something, though, and that knowledge had filled him with the fear of either being thought the murderer or giving someone else away. Hardened criminal? Unlikely. They didn't run off down driveways at the first sign of being recognised. No, they were the ones who tried to talk their way out of things, often with a smile and a laugh and other forms of trickery.

Edmund arrived at the address half an hour later. He had to get public transport again and the driver had been reluctant to stop just anywhere to let his passengers off.

Edmund thought he made rather an elaborate show of *not* breaking the rules: driving at a reasonable speed, not shooting through the traffic lights or letting passengers alight on street corners. Just because Edmund was who he was: most police officers were known to the tshova drivers. As long as he didn't open his mouth; that was the requisite for being taken seriously. If he just sat and looked silently, there was something slightly imposing about Edmund. When he spoke, however, it all fell apart and he could feel them turning away, laughing; uninterested.

Chapter Nine

Edmund surveyed Craig's house with mild interest. He lived in a small semi-detached double storey in Bradfield. The driveway ran alongside an oblong of brown garden, which was bordered by flowerbeds empty of any sort of horticultural life. Instead, upside down empty beer bottles had been pushed into the ground at various random intervals. There was a small verandah to the house on which sat a single chair, the kind one might find in a doctor's waiting room. It looked neither comfortable nor particularly well kept, for the seat cover was torn and the foam cushion was visibly thin in places, a dirty yellow. An empty whisky bottle lay toppled on the floor next to a crumpled cigarette packet and an over spilling ashtray. On the far wall was a dartboard, hanging slightly askew, with three darts in the bull's eye.

Was this the house of a potential murderer? Edmund contemplated the scene for half a minute and then knocked on the door. No one answered and, as he walked round the house, surveying it from different angles, he saw that all the curtains were drawn. He was about to turn away when he had a sudden feeling that there was someone in the house. He knocked again and then he called out:

'Mr Martin? Mr Martin? I think you are there. Please can you open the door?' There was no response so he tried again. 'Mr Martin, it is me. Chief Inspector Dube from CID. You gave me a lift the other day – in your Renault 4. A fine car – do you remember? I just need to talk to you about... well, about a few things... please.'

There was still nothing. Edmund took a deep breath, was about to say something, stopped and then shrugged and said it anyway. 'I can help you. Otherwise you are in a lot of trouble, Mr Martin. You help me, I help you?'

He didn't mean this last sentence to be a question. He didn't want to sound begging or uncertain and he wondered if he should say that bit again with more force. However, to his surprise, he heard the sound of the door being unlocked and pulled slowly open. A troubled face appeared, the eyes looking furtively around.

'It's okay, Mr Martin. I'm here by myself. Look, I don't even have a car! If I were to arrest you, I'd have to ask for a lift!' Edmund laughed good-naturedly and shrugged his shoulders. 'I just want to ask you a few questions. May I come in?'

A long time ago, when Edmund was growing up under the tutelage of Mr MacDougal, he had been taught not only the value but the power of good manners. People, he was told, would respond to him in a more positive manner and it was likely he would get what he wanted. It was a lesson that had proven true for Edmund many a time, especially when dealing with members of the public, who for some reason always expected the police to be the most unhelpful and ignorant of creatures.

Edmund was allowed into an alcove that might otherwise have served as a small dining room, but here contained a table that was piled high with files and papers and topped with another overflowing ashtray. There was one chair, which was offered to him; Craig sat on a wooden stool with a green rayon covered cushion with a silky fringe and drummed the fingers of his right hand in a hard, agitated manner on the table. He looked old and lined and coughed periodically, a deep, throaty smoker's cough. He wore an old pair of shorts and a red and white striped golf shirt, and looked as though he had been hiding in a dark cellar for the past few days.

'A drinker,' thought Edmund. He knew the signs and it accounted for the prematurely aged look he had. Heavy smoker, nervous. Far too nervous and lacking in resolve to have committed a premeditated crime. He got angry quickly, he had seen that at the police station. He was an angry person, yes, he could see that, too. There was no joy in the house – he remembered the beer bottles in the garden and could imagine Craig pushing them into the hard, unrelenting ground with great vehemence. Perhaps he *could* drive a knife into someone whilst they slept. Perhaps... if he hated them enough.

Before Edmund could speak, Craig began: 'I didn't do it. You have no proof. Absolutely none and I won't be hounded like this. It's... it's... unconstitutional. That's what it is. You guys can search this whole place if you like. You won't find anything because I didn't do it.' He lit a cigarette and Edmund watched how his hands shook a little as he held the match to the cigarette end, half-closing his eyes as he did so.

'Calm down, Mr Martin,' said Edmund, speaking softly. 'I have a few questions, that's all. You ran away – why?'

'Because that nut case of a woman was running after me, shouting that I was the one who had done it.'

'If you didn't, why the need to panic?'

Craig blew out a stream of blue smoke and looked away.

'Mr Martin, the maid's name is Dorcas Hlabangana. She said you were at Mrs Pullman's recruitment agency yesterday morning. Is that right?'

'Ah, jeez!' sighed Craig with a shake of his head. 'I'm not going to get out of this one easily, am I?'

'Just tell the truth, Mr Martin.'

'Sure thing! The truth will set me free, yee-hah! Praise the Lord!'

Edmund waited.

Craig scratched his head and turned to face Edmund. 'This is going to sound weird and you probably won't believe me.'

Edmund shrugged and leaned back in the chair as much as he could, for it was a hard, upright one, which dug into his back.

'I... I belonged to a group... a dating group. You know what I mean?' He looked slightly embarrassed.

Edmund nodded. 'I think so.'

'We met every month, sometimes twice a month. There is

a lady who organises everything. Sometimes it's a party, sometimes we met at a bar. She has a friend who owns a lodge; we used to go there often.'

Edmund nodded again, watching Craig's eyes as they looked away from him. His voice seemed to falter somewhat as the story progressed.

'I stopped going. I wasn't getting anywhere. There were some nice people, but... well, no jackpot. You know what I mean?'

Edmund nodded slowly.

'Well, anyway, sometimes, if this lady knew someone she really thought I'd like, she would arrange a date so I didn't have to go through the whole going to the party stroke bar stroke lodge rigmarole. She – Shantelle – rang me up a couple of days ago.'

'Shantelle?'

'She's the woman who arranges the... the...'

'Appointments?' suggested Edmund.

'Yes, well... appointments!' He threw back his head and gave a loud chuckle, which soon descended into a hacking cough. Edmund watched as he tried to take another puff of his cigarette as though that would help calm him, but all it did was start another round of coughing. Craig's hands alternated in a windmill of covering his mouth and waving smoke out of his face.

'Sorry,' he eventually managed to wheeze. 'It's that word – *appointments*. Seems like whichever way you try to mention blind dates in respectable terms, it always manages to sound incredibly dodgy.' He coughed again. 'A sort of mixture of the erotic and a visit to the dentist!'

Edmund smiled.

'I suppose you're married?' asked Craig, rather suddenly stopping coughing.

A little surprised at the forwardness of the question, Edmund hesitated a moment before answering, 'Yes.'

Craig made an expression that suggested he knew that the answer was inevitable. 'Religious, too, I expect.'

Again, Edmund was rather taken aback. He smiled awkwardly and tried to change the subject. 'You were telling me about Shantelle?'

'Hm? Yes. I was, wasn't I?' Craig stubbed his cigarette out in the ashtray, pushing a mountain of ash over onto the table as he did so. '*Shantelle.* Well, she called me and asked me if I wanted to go out with this aid worker of some sort. You know what it's like in this place. Everyone wants to get out.'

Edmund raised his eyebrows in a question.

'Zimbabwean man meets foreign aid worker. Fall in love. Move to Nice Democratic Country with water and electricity and Human Rights. You know what I mean?'

Edmund wasn't sure that he did, but he nodded anyway.

'She thought I'd be interested. Why wouldn't I? Sad old Craig Martin who hasn't had a date in months. I'd jump at the chance, wouldn't I? Not just a date, a chance to get out of here.' He swept his arms out in front of him. 'Yep, poor little old me.'

Edmund watched Craig light another cigarette. He was beginning to find the smoke claustrophobic.

'You met her, this aid worker?'

Craig tilted his head back and nodded, his mouth full of smoke. He blew it out in a thin blue plume.

'Disaster. As usual. She seemed to want to quiz me on being white. What did white people think of this and what did they think of that? Who cares, that's what I'd like to know?'

Edmund wasn't sure he was quite following the train of Craig's thoughts. He was wondering how his failed date with a foreign aid worker had anything to do with the death of Marcia Pullman.

'It's a funny thing, you know, being white,' continued Craig. 'Well, a white Zimbabwean. We're so nearly extinct we've become an object of anthropological interest. Where did we come from? Have we the ability to survive? To change? We're a bit like the dinosaurs. The world's waiting to see what we're going to evolve into.' He paused. 'Crocodiles, probably. White crocodiles.' He seemed to think he had said something very funny and proceeded to laugh in a bitter, halting fashion.

Edmund still struggled to follow Craig's pattern of thought. The man had obviously had some bad experience, but he still wasn't sure where Marcia Pullman entered the picture.

'How does Mrs Pullman come into this?' he interjected, trying to lead the conversation back in the direction of the investigation.

'Mrs Pullman? Oh, her. *Marcia.*'

Craig stopped and momentarily looked rather lost. 'Well, she was the owner of this crap agency that employed Shantelle, who set me up with a ridiculous aid worker in the hope that I might find luuve.'

'I don't understand,' continued Edmund. 'What do you mean?'

'Mrs Pullman,' Craig spoke slowly, tapping out each syllable on the table with a tobacco stained finger, 'runs the agency where Shantelle works. Top Notch Professionals or something equally stupid. They're hardly professional. They're maids that's all. Nothing professional about them.'

'So the lady who organises the *appointments* works at the agency?'

'Yes, it's not a full time job, the... you know... the dating bit. She wants to go full time one day, but until then I suppose it's just a hobby.'

'Do you pay?'

Craig squirmed in his chair. 'There's a joining fee, for want of a better word, and... well... a charge if you do actually go out with someone.'

'Did Mrs Pullman know what Shantelle was doing?'

Craig shrugged. 'Doubt it. Joining the group was by invitation only and once I had done so, Shantelle contacted me by Whatsapp. I was told specifically not to come to the office.'

'How did you get to threaten Mrs Pullman's life?'

'I'm getting to that,' said Craig, wagging his cigarette held hand at Edmund. 'And by the way, I didn't actually *threaten her life*. I got the hell in. The date was a disaster. *Com-plete* disaster. And I suppose I blamed *her*. Shantelle, I'm talking about. I had one mega babalas. You know – hangover?'

Edmund nodded.

'Sorry,' apologised Craig. 'You *are* religious, aren't you? You have that look. I suppose you go to one of these evangelical churches. No drink, no drugs, no sex before marriage. Now the good old Catholics, they've got it right. Alcohol is the answer to everything. They even brew their own. The monks, I mean. I wouldn't mind if you were a Catholic.' He paused. 'You're not, are you?'

Edmund shook his head. 'Mr Martin, please. If a dangerous person is at large, I – we – need to find that person. I need to know what happened between you and Mrs Pullman.'

Craig nodded and once again crushed his cigarette butt into the pile of ash, once again sending a wave over onto the table.

'I went into the office. I – I was angry. I suppose I shouted – well, okay, I did shout at Shantelle. I did feel bad about it afterwards. I went back later and took roses–'

'Mrs Pullman was – where?' interrupted Edmund.

'She must have been in a back room.'

'And?'

'And Shantelle asked me to leave and so I did. But I came back. I had this... sudden surge of anger.' Craig stopped, realising he may be getting himself into deep water. 'I was angry, all right. I was angry with Shantelle and her aid worker and her stupid bloody idea. Then there was this big bossy woman in this... this... funny pair of shoes. She was a type – you know? Like a schoolteacher or a matron. Big and bossy ordering me to keep quiet and get out and I couldn't take it. I couldn't take it!' He was shouting now, his face red and angry. 'I hated her. At that moment she stood for everything I hate. She wasn't just a woman who ran a pathetic pseudo upmarket employment agency, she was the kind of woman I have despised all my life. The kind who believes they have power over you and can tell you what to do and think and feel. The kind that works in schools and libraries and... and at the British Embassy.'

'The British Embassy?'

'Yes, and other places that decide the destinies of mere minions.'

'And what exactly did you do then?' persisted Edmund, foreseeing that he was going to get waylaid by more vitriol if he didn't.

Here Craig paused and looked embarrassed again. 'I might have threatened her.'

'Might have?'

'Okay, so I did. I did this really stupid thing that I regretted as soon I had done it. I – I put my hand to my head as though it were a gun and I – well, I fired. Imaginary, you know.' Craig waved his hands around his head again, seemingly reluctant to re-enact his actions.

'I see,' said Edmund, trying to lean back in the chair again. 'This was just a threat – a gesture, even?'

'Yes, you know. Bad movie stuff. If there'd been an audience, they'd probably have laughed. American sitcom canned laughter.' Craig gave Edmund a sideways glance as if he suspected he probably didn't understand the reference, but Edmund nodded his head and looked back down at his notebook.

'But you didn't actually say you would kill her?'

'No.'

'This was what time?'

'Sheez, I don't know.'

'Ten, ten thirty?'

'Hell, I'm not up then. Not with a babalas. More like eleven thirty.'

'Where do you work, Mr Martin?' asked Edmund, looking about the room.

Craig cleared his throat. 'I work for myself. Bit of this and

that. Well, actually, not a hell of a lot of either this or that these days. I mend things, I suppose. Here, here's my card.'
He put his hand in his pocket and drew out a rather battered wallet. From it, he took a small grey dog-eared business card.

'Craig Martin,' read Edmund, 'Your Fix It Man. No job too big or too small.'

'It should read: some jobs far too big, but nothing is too small for a twenty dollar call out charge.'

Edmund whistled. 'Twenty dollars! That's just for getting there?'

'That's the plan,' said Craig with a cynical smirk. 'But then there are old ladies who can't pay and poor people who can't pay and even some fairly well off people who *won't* pay and what am I supposed to do?' He ran his fingers through his long greasy hair and gave Edmund an unexpectedly friendly smile. 'I would offer you some tea, officer, but I'm broke. You won't be able to squeeze a teabag out of me, I'm afraid. Squeeze a teabag. Get it?' He laughed and reached for his cigarettes, which was just about all that Edmund could bear. He got to his feet hurriedly.

'Let's just make this clear, Mr Martin. You ran yesterday because the maid at Mrs Pullman's house recognised you and you had made a threatening gesture to Mrs Pullman earlier that day?'

'That's right. Amazing coincidence, isn't it? Small world, Bulawayo.'

'No other reason?'

'No other reason. Stupid, I know. I knew it as I ran away, but I could hardly stop.'

'Why didn't you stay in the car? Why come in and wander around the garden?'

'Just some morbid fascination really. I had no idea how long I was going to wait for you and I didn't think it was going to be five minutes so I thought I'd have a look round the garden. I didn't think anyone would see me.'

'Not the best idea, Mr Martin, at a murder scene. You could have inadvertently destroyed evidence.'

'Sorry,' Craig smiled apologetically. He lit a cigarette.

'Thank you for your time, Mr Martin,' said Edmund as Craig's face disappeared behind a cloud of smoke. 'I'll be off now.'

'Just one thing. How did she die? You see, I don't even know that.'

'It's not clear,' Edmund hesitated. He did not wish to say that Mrs Pullman was already dead when she was stabbed. 'She was attacked. With a knife.'

Craig's forehead wrinkled into a question.

'I'm afraid I cannot discuss the case in more detail until all the forensic tests are back.'

'I see,' said Craig, although he obviously didn't. 'I'm not going to be hounded, am I? I'm not a wanted man or anything like that?'

'No. Leave it with me. But I may need to ask you some more questions, Mr Martin. Don't go anywhere.'

Craig spluttered into laughter. 'Don't go anywhere? Oh all right – I'll cancel my trip to Bermuda!'

'Good morning. I will see myself out, thank you.'

'No, no, please, let my butler do it! Jeeves!' called Craig with another hacking laugh. 'Please show this gentleman to the door.'

Edmund managed a half smile and made for the door. Once again, the winter air was quite a relief.

Chapter Ten

1979

'Always remember, a sharp pencil is the tool of a sharp mind.'

Mr MacDougal sat at the table, sharpening each of Edmund's pencils; he tested the points on the palm of his hand.

'There you go. All sorted for tomorrow, eh, Edmund?'

Edmund nodded his head. He perched on a chair opposite Mr MacDougal, clutching his new satchel he had been bought just that morning. It looked and smelt brand new and he was loathe to put it down in case he dirtied it.

They had spent the morning at the shop that sold uniforms. The Indian man behind the counter had looked sharply at him when Mr MacDougal had asked for the uniform for Sir Herbert Stanley Primary.

'Sir Herbert Stanley Primary,' Mr MacDougal had repeated, used to having to say things twice because of his accent. 'This lucky boy is starting next week.' He had rocked back on his heels and sucked his cheeks in and for a moment looked like Edmund imagined he would when arresting someone: cool and calm and in control. Then his face changed as he looked down at Edmund and smiled.

'You'll be out of these in no time at all, I bet,' he said as he held a grey pair of trousers up against Edmund. 'Breathe in.'

Edmund took a deep breath and held it.

'How long can you do that for? Two years, d'you think?'

Still Edmund held his breath, his eyes wide. Mr MacDougal laughed.

'It's all right, laddie. Breathe! These are well big enough for you.'

To the man behind the counter he said: 'We'll take these and we'll need a shirt, too, and some socks.'

'Blazer?' said the man, eyeing Mr MacDougal with increased suspicion.

Mr MacDougal thought for a second and then nodded. 'Yes, we'll take a blazer, too.'

The man disappeared into a storeroom at the back of the shop and Edmund felt his stomach lurch with excitement as they waited for him to return. He watched as the brand new blazer was taken from underneath its plastic covering and removed from the hanger. He was afraid to touch it, never mind put it on. When he did, he felt the soft silky inside hug his shoulders. Mr MacDougal bent over and did up the three brass buttons. He turned the collar down neatly and gave it a superfluous brush with his hand.

'Perfect,' he said at last. 'Clever boy. What about a tie?'

As he walked down the road to join the main one, Edmund found himself thinking about Craig's question. 'I suppose you're religious, aren't you?'

He hadn't answered the question, partly because he didn't want to be drawn into sharing any personal information, partly because he didn't know how to answer it.

His mother was a devout churchgoer, always had been. So had the MacDougals. It was church every Sunday: neat Presbyterian services with vases of purple and yellow flowers on the altar and tea and biscuits afterwards. The MacDougals took his mother and him along, but his mother insisted they sit at the back, although Mr MacDougal said they were all equal before God. But even after Independence, his mother insisted that their place was on the very last pew and there they sat, often by themselves, sideline participants, watching and learning the right way to worship.

His mother, Edmund always thought, became something of a snob in this regard. She was rather scornful of those who didn't don their Sunday best and go off to Church, Bible in hand once a week. She was proud he knew what the Litany was and that he could recite the Lord's Prayer at the age of four. Most of all, she loved to sing. 'All Things Bright and

Beautiful', 'Bread of Heaven' and 'To Be a Pilgrim'. She sang as she worked, as she cleaned and polished and cooked and it wasn't just that she was singing or praising, she was saying: 'Look at me, I'm Presbyterian. I believe in God, in our dear Lord Jesus. I'm going to heaven.'

Later, when the MacDougals had gone and she worked for another family, the Thornes, who weren't religious, Edmund's mother had carried on for a number of years to tread the known path to Church once a week where she continued to sing the songs, albeit without quite as much gusto. By this time, at least a quarter of the churchgoers were also black and so she finally condescended to move three rows up from the back.

In recent years, however, she had faltered in her religious duty. She missed the occasional service and then she attended the occasional service. Failing health was partly to account for this, but even when Edmund offered to pay for a taxi to take her, she just pulled a face and shrugged.

'I don't need a church to believe in God,' she said and would spend Sunday afternoon stretched out on her bed with her Bible.

'You don't believe any more, do you?' she challenged Edmund one afternoon when he had visited and she asked him to read through the Psalms with her. She was lying down, which seemed to be more and more her habitual position these days and her Bible was spread out before her.

He paused before he shook his head and said softly, 'No.' He had expected her to be more vocal in her response and admonish him for his loss. Either that or pray for forgiveness, but she didn't say anything in response. When she did finally speak it was just to acknowledge his words.

'I thought so,' she said, quietly. 'Will you read still? Psalm 23. "The Lord is my Shepherd".'

'The Lord is my shepherd, I shall not want,' began Edmund and he read the whole psalm, quietly and clearly, but feeling no emotion at all.

Edmund sat opposite Janet at the kitchen table. Her hands were wrapped around a mug of coffee, which she stared at without focusing. The kitchen was cold; it seemed to emanate from the floor, which was a concrete one, but looking around, Edmund also saw a hole in one of the window panes, patched with a piece of cardboard and masking tape. The kitchen itself was quite bare. Faded curtains hung at the window and the paint had come off the kitchen cupboards in places. When Janet opened the fridge to get out the milk for the coffee, he noticed it was practically empty.

When Edmund had arrived that afternoon, he was ushered into the sitting room by a slightly nervous and over-zealous maid, eager to please. He had sat there while awaiting Janet, who was apparently still getting ready although it was already two thirty. From the window, he looked out onto the brown square of garden.

The house was old, probably late '20s, with a small garden that was neatly laid out and criss-crossed with stone paths, but empty of any plants or grass. A plant in a pot and an African Violet in an old ice cream container on the verandah were the only signs of life.

There was a bench in the corner of the garden that was, at this time of day, flooded with sunlight. On it sat an old lady, Janet's mother, he supposed. She leant forward on a stick and stared off into an ornamental fountain that no longer worked. She had on a bright pink jersey, which contrasted with her neatly brushed bob of soft white waves. The collar of a white shirt was folded over the V of her jersey and a patterned kerchief tied round her neck. She seemed ready for something, prepared. A stark contrast, Edmund thought, to her daughter who now sat before him, looking down.

Janet was wearing a long grey cardigan that, despite being mohair, looked rather old and worn. Edmund studied Janet's face. She wasn't someone who was ageing well: her skin was rough, particularly on her cheeks where broken lines bloomed in two round pinches of pink; her eyes were puffy and rather droopy – an old person's eyes, thought Edmund, who looked briefly down at his notes and saw that she was 61.

Edmund took a sip of his coffee and cleared his throat.

'Do you work, Mrs, er, Peters?'

'Peters, that's right. Yes, yes, I do. At Twice Loved. It's a shop at Ascot, a charity shop.'

Edmund cocked his head slightly. He hadn't heard of it.

'People donate things and we sell them. All the proceeds go to help elderly people in Bulawayo.'

'Ah, I see. And you should be there now?'

'I only work part time. It isn't open on Mondays so I work Tuesday to Saturday. I do the morning shift, but today I... I couldn't. I couldn't... I just couldn't go in this morning. They understand. They've told me to take a couple of days off.'

'Yes, a good idea,' nodded Edmund, making notes. 'Mr Peters – where does he work?'

Janet's head flicked up sharply. She said, rather defiantly, 'There isn't a Mr Peters. Hasn't been for a long time. It's just my mother and I. I have a son, too, in the UK.'

Edmund jotted down 'Elderly mother. Son in UK. Income? Charity shop – Twice Loved. Check.'

'If I could just clarify the events of yesterday afternoon,' he began again. He looked down at his notes. 'It was your day off. You were at Mrs Pullman's house to do a stocktake of the books,' he prompted her.

'Yes,' said Janet with that faraway look in her eye. 'I went early to help her.'

'This was usual, was it?'

'The stocktake? Oh no. Not every month. We did a yearly one; it was supposed to have been done in May, but I hadn't got round to it. She... Marcia... she, well, she had been on at me for a while. Books had been going missing.'

'Missing?'

'Yes. Louise Eastman, I think it was, asked to borrow that new Follett and Mary had been the last one to borrow it and said she'd given it back in March, but no one had seen it since. And then Lydia Ncube was leaving and asked for her books back – you can do that, you know, if you want – although many people just donate them. Anyway, Lydia wanted her books back and three out of five were missing.'

'And they were?'

Janet stopped, surprised. 'I'm not quite sure off hand. I think they were all Nora Roberts... does it matter? It's not important, surely?'

Edmund shrugged and jotted down the name.

'Why did Mrs Ncube leave the book club? Do you know?'

Janet thought for a moment and then shook her head. 'I can't remember. She's a Zimbabwean, but she lived in the UK for a long time. Twenty years, I think. She wanted to come back home and, when we started using the US dollar in 2009, it looked like things were on the up. She moved back with her husband, but I feel we disappointed her.'

'In what way?'

'We're boring. We have small town lives. Small town dreams.'

Edmund couldn't help but hear the bitterness in her voice.

'When did Mrs Pullman ask you to do the stocktake?'

Janet thought. 'Tuesday last week.'

'She phoned you?'

'Yes, we didn't mix socially except for book club.'

'She was ill on Friday. Did you know that?'

Janet shook her head. 'No. But it doesn't surprise me.'

'Why is that?'

'She wasn't the healthiest of people. Got out of breath easily and the bottom of her legs were puffy. Didn't drink enough water if you ask me.'

'You went to the house early to do the stocktake?'

Janet nodded.

'At four o'clock. Book club was at six?'

Janet nodded again.

'And the stocktake would last approximately how long?'

'An hour, an hour and a half maximum. Marcia was a whizz

at these things. She'd have them all laid out in alphabetical order and it was just a case of ticking them off. We might do a couple of repairs, although most of the ladies are very good at looking after the books. We also set aside any that no one has shown much interest in and we ask the owners if they'd like them back. If not, we donate them to charity.'

'So, if you began at four, finished at five, what would you do then? What else was there to get ready?'

'I wouldn't get anything else ready. That was Dorcas's job. She laid the table with all the glasses, plates and soup bowls. Marcia did the food. I would just be there. Just there, you know. In case I was needed for anything, I suppose.' She shrugged and pursed her lips as though she had just thought of it.

Edmund watched her intently. Her brows furrowed as though she were struggling with a maths problem or trying hard to remember something.

'Tell me about Marcia.'

Janet took a small sip of her coffee and Edmund noticed how like a little bird she was, hunched over her mug. A bird who has fallen out of its nest and injured its wing and stares up at the nest far, far above it somewhere, miles out of reach.

'She ran the book club. She was the one who started it, about five years ago. I've been a member for about three and a half years.'

'It's always held at her house?'

'Oh, no. We take it in turns. Or at least, we're supposed to.' She looked apologetic. 'Marcia always did such a good job, you see. She made lovely things to eat and she had such a lovely house. I – well, I could never produce what she did. We live on such a limited income, my mother and I.'

'We live in a harsh economic climate,' said Edmund, ostensibly to make her feel better, as if she might find comfort in the thought of a communal suffering, but instead he thought he sounded like a ZBC reporter. The words were cliché now in Zimbabwe.

'Yes, yes of course we do,' said Janet. 'Of course everyone

is struggling. Even the ladies with fairly good jobs. And husbands. We're all struggling.' She took another sip of coffee. 'Some of the ladies team up together when it is their turn. Share the costs you know. That's what Brenda and I did. We had it at her house, of course. I – well, I wouldn't have it here. We haven't enough glasses for a start.' She gave a short laugh and then looked sadly back at her coffee. 'Actually, Chief Inspector, we aren't all struggling. Some people in this country make a lot of money. Sometimes they make it out of other people. Do you believe you can make money out of doing a decent day's work here? By being a teacher or a bank clerk or running a shop? I don't believe it. I think anyone who is rich is crooked.'

Edmund nodded his head in tacit agreement.

'I understand Mrs Pullman ran a domestic employment agency, is that correct?'

'Yes. I believe it is somewhere in town. Can't remember what it's called now.'

'Top Notch Domestic Agency.'

She raised her eyes in acknowledgement. 'That's right. It used to be a secretarial employment agency. You may remember it as The Professionals?'

Edmund shook his head. 'Have you any idea why she decided to change the secretarial agency into a domestic agency?'

'Jobs became scarce. You know how it is here. People get jobs because they know someone who knows someone. They don't go through agencies; they go straight to the job. Top Notch! What a joke!'

'Mrs Pullman had a flair for the imaginative?'

'Oh, I don't think there was anything imaginative about it at all, Chief Inspector. She just knew how to make money. Let me tell you something, Chief Inspector, Marcia wasn't interested in placing your average domestic workers or tea boys. There's no money to be made. These were highly trained carers of the elderly – night nurses, companions. Top Notch stuff indeed. '

'There is a call for this sort of work in Bulawayo?' Edmund was doubtful.

Janet hesitated and then went on. 'One thing you might have noticed about the white population of Bulawayo is that we tend to be rather elderly. The young people leave as soon as they can. A couple might stay on but not many. We grow older – and frailer – on our own. Family might come and visit once in a while, but not often. So the question remains: who is going to look after us when we can't look after ourselves?'

'I see.'

'Marcia realised one important fact a long time ago. There's no money to be made out of the white population. It's not that we're too small, it's that we don't spend money. We're watchful, not relaxed, I suppose. After the whole farm invasion scenario, we don't put money into staying. Into maintenance, yes, but not into anything new. You won't see us buying suites of furniture for instance, but you'll see black people doing it – even when they can't afford it.'

Edmund considered Janet's words.

'What I'm saying is, if you want to make money in Zimbabwe, don't aim your product at the white population. Many people have done this and failed.' She made it sound as though she were describing an expedition up Everest. '*Unless,* unless, of course, you are aiming it at the old Rhodies living abroad: those who don't want grandma to come and live with them in Perth or Toronto or Edinburgh; those who feel she is better off where she is with a nice little home and a neat little garden and a household of servants to look after her.'

Edmund could almost taste the bitterness in her voice. No money, a failed marriage perhaps, lonely.

'Isn't it expensive?' he asked.

'Expensive? Do you know how much care costs in the UK? People sell their houses to pay for it. Believe me, it's much cheaper here – and Marcia knew it.'

Although Edmund listened carefully to what Janet was saying, he wasn't sure he picked it all up. Beneath her words lay an innuendo he couldn't get at. He would have to think about what she'd said. For the moment he gave up and tried to pick up his original line of thought. 'The agency is fairly successful would you say?'

'Oh yes. I am sure it is. Marcia never invested in failure.' Although Janet had drunk half of her cup of coffee, she stirred it with a spoon and then added a teaspoon of sugar and stirred it again. 'Not her only source of income though, Chief Inspector. Her husband, you know, has a safari business.'

'For black people?' Edmund couldn't help asking, with a smile on his face.

Janet smiled back. 'No, for people who *don't live* in Zimbabwe!' she laughed. Edmund felt a change between them, as though something settled and she now felt more at ease with him.

'Do you know if Mrs Pullman's working hours were flexible? She could take the afternoon off to prepare for book club?'

'I don't think Marcia Pullman actually ever *worked*, Chief Inspector. She *ran* things. Things and people. Including her husband, I might add. You know his safari business belongs to her, don't you? It's not her husband's.'

'Isn't it?' said Edmund, his ears pricking up. 'You mean he just runs it?'

'Yes. She used to joke about it – how her husband worked for her. She was definitely the source of the money and she was one wily businesswoman, Chief Inspector. No one had the upper hand with her.'

'You didn't like her?' He had to ask. It needed to be brought into the open.

Janet looked away for a couple of seconds and then looked back. 'Hard to say, Chief Inspector,' she said, rather cryptically. 'She gave orders and I obeyed. Let's put it like that.'

'But you are shocked at her death?' asked Edmund, his head on one side.

'Of course I am shocked at her death!' exclaimed Janet, banging her mug down on the table top with such force that some of the coffee spilled out. 'I was the one who found her with that, that thing sticking out of her!'

'I'm sorry,' apologised Edmund. 'I need to know what she was *like*, Mrs Peters. I need to know why someone would want to kill her.'

'But wasn't it some person off the street looking for something to steal?'

Edmund watched Janet's face carefully as she spoke. She was flustered. He could understand why, but there was something else in her demeanour that bothered him and he couldn't quite put his finger on it.

'Do you *really* think someone just wandered in off the street on the off chance of stealing a few items or is some homicidal maniac wishing to cause harm?' persisted Edmund. 'A locked house, an unlocked gate, a letter opener through the heart, but no sign of a struggle. A few things moved, a couple of drawers pulled out, but nothing stolen?'

'No, not at all,' she agreed, nodding sadly.

'Why did you tell Dorcas to tell the police that the gardener was missing?'

'I didn't. They asked if there was a gardener. She said no, he'd been gone for a week.'

'I see. It was interpreted a little differently at the police station. You are not protecting someone, are you, Mrs Peters?' Edmund felt rather grand when he said the words. It spurred him to continue: 'Mr Pullman, perhaps – or Dorcas?'

'Mr *Pullman? Dorcas?* Absolutely not. I don't even know them. I'm just the book club secretary. They are nothing to do with me!'

'Thank you, Mrs Peters, I see,' said Edmund, watching the woman's lips tremble as she struggled to regain control of herself. That was point eight in *Being in Control: A Practical Guide to Self Confidence*. Agreeing with someone who was arguing with you cut them off. They automatically backed down. Edmund was pleased to see point eight working with Janet.

'If you know of any reason that either of those people would wish to harm Mrs Pullman, I do need to know.' His voice was quiet after her outburst. 'Because it is not the gardener, or ex-gardener, and I don't believe it was someone who walked off the street. Somebody disliked her enough to drive a knife into her. That somebody knew her.'

Janet's eyes were suddenly wide with a look of fear. 'Surely not...' she began and then stopped.

'So you see, I am looking for reasons why someone might want her dead.'

It was a few seconds before Janet answered. 'That I'm not sure of. She could be bossy. A bit domineering, but if you did what she wanted, there were few problems.'

'What if you didn't do what she wanted?'

Janet looked slightly surprised. 'I wouldn't know,' she answered with a slight smile. 'It didn't happen to me.'

'One more thing,' said Edmund, aware that Janet would not stand much more questioning. She was pale and drawn and her eyes drooped as though they were pulled down with weights. 'Do you happen to know who Mrs Pullman met for lunch yesterday?'

Janet looked surprised. 'No. I haven't a clue.'

'Somebody known by the initials S.P.?'

'S.P.? Really?'

'Do you know who I mean?'

'Sandy? No... she's Buchanan. Sipho? Susan?'

'It doesn't have to be a woman,' smiled Edmund.

'No, no, of course not. Steven?'

'We could be here all day guessing, Mrs Peters. If you do think of someone (he wanted to say *who actually exists*) please let me know.'

'I will, Chief Inspector. Most certainly.' Janet seemed to brighten a little, probably guessing the interview was at an end.

'Thank you, Mrs Peters,' said Edmund, closing his notebook with a thoughtful look. 'Thank you for your time.'

1979

Edmund ran to his mother, who was waiting at the gate. His satchel knocked against his back as he ran; he could feel his reading book inside going up and down.

'I've got words,' he breathed excitedly. 'To learn.' He looked up at her. She looked serious, her brow slightly furrowed as though she was trying to work something out.

'You must learn them,' she said very stiffly. 'No messing around when you get home.'

Messing around was far from Edmund's mind.

'Dick, Jane, Spot, Sally, Mother, Father,' Edmund recited on the walk home. 'Dick and Jane are brother and sister – and Sally's their little sister. They have a dog called Spot. And a red car. Father drives the red car to work.'

Edmund's mother listened but did not say anything except when she stopped him to tie up his shoelace or told him not to walk too close to the edge of the pavement.

When they got home, he took his book out of his bag. He had a little notebook in which were written five words for him to learn.

'See,' he said, holding it up to her face. 'See my words.'

His mother pushed the book out of her face. He waited for the slap, wondering what he had done wrong. Instead, she gave him a mug of tea and two thick slices of white bread and margarine. At two o'clock, she went back to work.

The next day when his mother fetched him, she was in a hurry.

'Walk fast,' she said. 'We need to get home as quickly as possible.'

Edmund ran beside her, trying desperately to keep up with her long strides. She clicked her tongue with irritation whenever he stumbled. Once home, he was told to wash his hands and tuck his shirt in. Then he was led up to the main house.

'Come in, Verna. Edmund.' Mrs MacDougal stood at the

back door in a light blue floral dress. She had a double row of pearls round her neck, which she now touched with her hand as she stood by to let them in.

Edmund's eyes were wide as he was led into the house. He was taken down a passageway and into another room in which Mr MacDougal sat at a large table. He appeared to be just finishing his lunch and looked up as they entered.

'Ah, Verna. Good, good,' he said as he put his knife and fork together. He dabbed his mouth lightly with a napkin and pushed his chair back to stand up. 'Edmund, my boy, how are you lad? How's school?'

'I am fine, thank you,' replied Edmund, convinced that there must be something that he had done wrong. What was so terrible that his mother had decided to call in extra forces?

'Don't look so worried, pet,' soothed Mrs MacDougal. 'We're only here to help.'

Edmund looked searchingly at his mother and then at Mr MacDougal.

'We've decided, Edmund, to give you a bit of help with your homework. Now I will start with maths because I have to get back to work after lunch. Mrs MacDougal will help you with your English. All right?' He smiled favourably at Edmund. Then he burst out laughing. 'It's all right, laddie, you're not in trouble. We're only here to help, aren't we, Edna?'

Mrs MacDougal smiled. 'Ooh aye. It's been such a long time since there was a child in the house. It'll be lovely.'

'Right, ruler, pencil, rubber, sharpener. Let's get started.'

It was just the beginning. Mr MacDougal would teach Edmund maths after lunch every day while Edmund sat straight-backed at the dining room table, his pencil case placed neatly at the side of his exercise book, a present on his birthday from the MacDougals. In it, there were two Staedtler HB pencils, sharpened and eager to be used; a long white rubber with a small blue end for rubbing out ink; and a fifteen centimetre wooden ruler, newly varnished.

He delighted in the clock ticking gently, filling the room with a kind of peace. It was marking time, of course, but instead of indicating how much had passed, it gave Edmund time, as though it were a present. There seemed, between each swing of the pendulum, to be a great swathe of eternity. There was no rush, no bustle; all was quiet.

There was nothing he looked forward to more than the time he spent doing his work with the MacDougals. Mr MacDougal, his glasses half way down his nose, wrote sums in pencil on a piece of lined paper. All the working out was done on another piece of lined paper, everything laid out neatly in rows. He didn't jot things down randomly as Edmund had since seen other people do, some writing diagonally across the paper in scruffy hardly readable handwriting.

'It's all about order, Edmund,' he would say, looking up and pushing his glasses back up his nose. 'It's all about order. If only the world were a little more ordered, it would be a much happier place.'

Chapter Eleven

The next stop was Pullman's Bespoke Safaris. Rather surprisingly, it was situated on a busy street in the middle of town, flanked on one side by a bank and on the other by a shoe shop. Edmund stood outside and hesitated to go in at first. Even the lettering on the sign seemed to admonish him and for no other reason than being him. It was hard and black and the letters of the motto were long and thin and curling, the type he associated with menus at expensive restaurants and orders of service at weddings. They reached out like tendrils, with all they suggested of money and the power and decadence of money, then they arched back on themselves, cold and aloof and uninterested.

The door was closed and guarded by a security gate. A notice on the door informed Edmund that he must ring the buzzer to enter. He did so, expecting that someone would come and let him in, but they didn't. He rang the buzzer again and waited a full two minutes before trying a third time. Then he stepped to the side and tried to look through the tinted glass of the window. The next thing he knew, the door was flung open and an irate woman with short brown hair glared at him.

'How many more times are you going to ring the buzzer, hey?'

'I'm sorry,' began Edmund, 'I was waiting-'

'Waiting? Waiting for what? Look, you press this' – she pressed the buzzer – 'and when you hear a click that means the door's open and you can come in.'

'I'm sorry...' repeated Edmund, feeling very small and foolish.

Her eyes ran over his ID and narrowed slightly in the corners.

'Come in,' she said, turning back into the office. Edmund

followed her. She sat down behind a large, heavy looking desk and picked up a pair of glasses that lay on her computer keyboard.

'How can I help you?' She assumed the detached efficiency of the office worker, but before she did so, her eyes caught those of a young woman working at another desk and they shared a look, a look that said 'why me?'

'I'm investigating the death of Mrs Pullman,' began Edmund, watching her face carefully. Immediately, she assumed an expression of doe-eyed sadness.

'Very sad. We're all devastated.' There was a beep and she turned to look at her computer screen. Then she moved her mouse around with a few gentle clicks. 'Sally-Anne, it looks like that booking for the 21st has just come through.' She continued to look at the screen for a minute or so before turning back to Edmund. 'Mr Pullman's in his office. He's with someone at the moment. Would you like to wait?'

'Perhaps I can ask you a few questions first if you don't mind.'

'Me?' She was surprised. Once more there was a look exchanged with the younger woman.

'Yes. Your name is?'

'Um, it's well, it's Linda. Linda Palmer.'

'Could you tell me about yesterday? Who was here in the office, anybody who wasn't?'

She pulled a face that suggested he had asked her to recall the events of a random date ten years before.

'Um, well, I'm not quite sure what you mean.' Edmund noticed she had picked up a pencil and held it horizontally between the fingers of both hands, bending it upwards as though she were about to snap it.

'How many people work here?'

'Three of us. Mr Pullman, Sally-Anne and I.'

'What time do you start in the morning?'

'Mr Pullman comes in early at about seven. Sally-Anne and I are in at eight.' She looked across to Sally-Anne as though looking for agreement. The younger woman nodded.

'And you leave at five?'

'Sally-Anne works a half day so she finishes at one. I finish at four and, again, Mr Pullman stays on until five.'

'A workaholic.' The words were a statement, but Linda interpreted them as a question.

'Oh, yes, definitely. He works very hard indeed.'

'He was here the whole of yesterday?'

'Absolutely.' There was an emphatic nodding of the head. 'All day.'

'And you would know if he was in his office or not?' Edmund looked across to the closed door behind which Mr Pullman apparently sat.

Her face darkened. 'Yes, of course. What are you implying?'

'Nothing. Nothing at all. I just need the facts, Miss Palmer.'

'Mrs. It's Mrs Palmer.'

'I'm sorry. Mrs Palmer. What does Mr Pullman actually do?'

Linda rolled her eyes in obvious indignation. Before she could reply, Edmund interrupted. 'What I mean is, what's his role in the company?'

'He's the managing director.'

'Which means?'

Her expression was one of shocked amazement. 'Well, he's in charge. He oversees the running of the business.'

'You misunderstand me,' said Edmund, surprised that he managed to talk so calmly. 'If I'm a tourist and I want to go on one of your safaris, I come in here and I – speak to whom?'

'Me. I arrange everything.'

'And your colleague in the corner?'

'She keeps the books.'

'So you arrange my trip and I pay and she handles the payment.'

A nod of the head. 'Yes.'

'Who will take me on the trip?'

'We have a driver.'

'A driver?'

'Yes, business isn't too busy these days. If we need to bring in another driver, we have a couple of guys who work for us on a part time basis.'

'But Mr Pullman doesn't take the tour?'

'Oh, no. No.'

Edmund thought of Mr Pullman in his safari gear and wondered why he sat in an office all day.'

'So he...?'

'I told you, he oversees the running of the business. There's marketing and talking to clients...'

'I thought you spoke to clients?'

'Yes, but he manages our US clients as well.' She gave him a look that suggested this was far out of the realm of Edmund's imagination.

'Did Mr Pullman leave the office at all yesterday? Did he go out for lunch? Did he go home for lunch?'

She shook her head a little too quickly. 'No, he was here all day.'

'Or at least until you left?'

She shifted in her seat. 'Yes.'

'You don't go out for lunch at all?'

'Sometimes. Not yesterday.'

'Do you close for lunch?'

'Yes. The office is locked.'

Edmund held her gaze until she looked away.

'I read my book,' she said, reddening. 'It's good to have time out.'

'What are you reading?'

She rolled her eyes, opened a drawer next to her with sudden vehemence, took out a book and slapped it down on the table in front of him.

'Nora Roberts,' noted Edmund.

'Yes, I have about four more here,' she growled, reaching into the drawer and flinging more books onto the desk. 'See? They keep me busy. *Very* busy at lunch time.'

'I am sure they do,' said Edmund, standing up and pushing his chair back. 'Do you belong to Mrs Pullman's book club?'

'No.'

Edmund turned back the cover of the top book.

Her eyes flicked between the book and Edmund's face. 'I borrowed them from a friend.'

'I see. Thank you for your time.'

'Don't you want to speak to Mr Pullman?'

'No thank you. I spoke to him last night.'

She exchanged a look of confusion with Sally-Anne who shrugged her shoulders and looked uncertainly at Edmund.

'It surprises me that you're not closed today,' said Edmund, walking to the door.

'Mr Pullman wants everything to go on as usual,' said Linda, standing up as well and pushing the button to open the door.

'He wants everything to go on as usual,' repeated Edmund, looking around the office and taking in as much as possible. The eyes of both women were on him. 'Like nothing happened.' As he spoke, the door opened and a slightly red-faced and out of breath Pullman entered, ushering in a policeman, a tall, intimidating man. Khumalo.

'What the-?' began Pullman as soon as he laid his eyes on Edmund. He shook his head slowly, his mouth open and his tongue pushed up against his teeth and turned to Khumalo.

'What's this guy doing here? I thought he was off the case, hey? What's the story?'

Khumalo looked Edmund straight in the eye. He was chewing gum and even doing that he managed to impart a sinister air. He jerked his head towards the door. Very unwillingly, Edmund followed him outside.

Khumalo didn't say anything at first. Edmund stood waiting, feeling a mixture of apprehension and annoyance.

'This is my case, understand?'

Edmund stared him in the eye for a few moments. 'We need to follow protocol. You *know* we need to follow protocol.'

Khumalo raised his hand immediately. 'This is not your case, Dube. You understand? I don't want you to have anything more to do with it. Go back to the office. Go back to your typing or filing or whatever it is you do, but stay away from this case.'

He stepped forward and placed a hand on each of Edmund's shoulders. Edmund could feel their grip tighten.

'I can make things very difficult for you, Eddie. Very difficult indeed. You like your job in Bulawayo, don't you? And we like you, we like you here. We'd miss you if you weren't here.'

'If I weren't here?' Edmund could feel Khumalo's fingers dig deeper. 'What do you mean?'

'I mean just what I say.' Khumalo's face was an inscrutable blank, his voice cold. He let go of Edmund's shoulders and patted his cheeks, just that touch too boisterously to be termed friendly.

Edmund stood still as Khumalo walked away. He was tense with expectation and yet, too, a tingle of excitement shivered through him. What were they so afraid he would find? Why was he off the case? He leaned back, digging his hands deep in his pockets, watching as Khumalo disappeared inside the office and the door closed behind him with a click. Then he made his way slowly down the road.

1979

'Hey! Teaboy! Where's my lunch?'

Edmund looked up at the figure blocking his way. Jasper Meyer stood in front of him, his thumbs looped through his satchel straps, legs widespread. His pudgy eyes fixed Edmund in a steely gaze while his mouth settled into a thin line of hate.

'I'm looking for my satchel. I want to go home.' Edmund glanced along the empty row of satchel hooks outside the classroom and then back at Meyer. The fat boy smiled: not a friendly, benevolent smile, but a small, spiteful, derisive one.

'That yours?' He motioned behind him with a jerk of his head. 'If it is, you're in trouble, making a mess like that.'

Edmund looked beyond Meyer into the playground. A satchel lay in the mud, its contents strewn about: lunch box, cool drink bottle, reading book and pencil case. The book fluttered open in a weak wave to him and then closed again.

'My bag,' began Edmund, starting towards it and falling headlong onto the cold concrete of the corridor. Meyer's foot was at fault.

'Oh dear, did you trip?' the large boy sneered. 'Here, let me give you a hand up.'

Down on the ground, Edmund lay catching his breath for the fall had knocked the wind out of him. Naively, he reached for Meyer's hand and felt himself being jerked up with force. Meyer's face was so close to his he could feel his sweet, sticky breath on his cheek. Fingers gripped Edmund's arm tightly, twisting his wrist into a spasm of pain. The back of his throat ached with tears, but Edmund refused to cry.

'You don't get it, do you, Teaboy?' Edmund tried to look at Meyer's face, but only one pudgy eye could be glimpsed. Edmund fleetingly thought Meyer was going to kiss him – or bite him. He stood stock still, trying to overcome a strong desire to urinate.

'We don't want you here.' The voice was a harsh whisper through clenched teeth. There was a pause and then the face retreated. 'Get it now, Teaboy?' growled Meyer, standing back. Edmund didn't reply.

'I said, get it now, Teaboy?' Meyer yanked Edmund's arm behind his back and held it there. 'Get it?'

'Yes,' Edmund wheezed, with a sharp intake of breath.

Meyer shoved him against the wall; a satchel hook dug in his back. 'And don't you forget it! Go home. Tell Mama and Baba you want to go to the school for piccanins in the compound. Yebo?' He stared Edmund straight in the eye and then stepped back.

Edmund eased his arm back and forth. Tears welled in his eyes, but still he refused to cry.

'Cheer up, Teaboy,' said Meyer, slapping Edmund's cheeks. 'You'll be better off when you're back where you belong.' He smirked then ambled off to get his bicycle, stopping on the way to kick Edmund's satchel further along the ground.

Edmund waited until he had gone, then tore across the playground and picked up his belongings. The bottle and lunch box could be washed and so could the pencil case, but the book could not be salvaged. Edmund turned the pages, horrified. What would Mrs Fourie say? What would his mother say? Mr MacDougal?

Mud stuck to the pages. Dick and Jane's happy pink faces were covered in an ugly brown smear and Father's smart city suit was sullied beyond repair. Edmund tried to wipe the pages, but only succeeded in creating a sepia tinged world. Mother's skirt, Spot the dog, their shiny red car: all were covered in a dark, dirty stain.

Edmund walked home slowly, engulfed in a cloud of despondency like none other he had felt in his seven years of life. His future, which had lain open to him at the beginning of term, a clean white crisp page, was now blotched, smudged, spoilt.

The initial excitement over the buying of uniforms and stationery had dissolved like salt in water, leaving only an indefinable bitter taste. For there had been other incidents, too. Some were minor, like being prodded in the ribs with a sharp pencil; others were not quite as negligible.

Only that day, Mrs Fourie had asked Martin Bateman to hand out the English books, but when he got to the end of the pile, Edmund still didn't have his.

'Where is your book?' boomed Mrs Fourie, bearing down upon him, tapping the desk with a long wooden ruler.'

'I don't know, Mrs Fourie,' began Edmund. 'I handed it in.'

'Are you suggesting that *I* lost it?'

A titter of laughter rose from the class.

'Quiet!' Mrs Fourie banged the ruler hard on Edmund's desk, making him jump, while she glared at the rest of the boys. She turned back to him.

'Where – is – your – book, Edmund?' She spoke slowly, pronouncing every word deliberately.

Edmund squirmed. 'I don't know.'

'I don't know,' she mimicked in a child-like voice. A second, smaller burst of laughter was even more short-lived than the first; Mrs Fourie quelled it with one look of fury.

'Edmund, find your English book or stay for detention,' she barked. 'Work on a piece of paper for now. You can copy it in later.'

'He can't speak English, so how can he write it?' said a voice from somewhere in the class and a wave of laughter followed in its wake.

'Quiet!' Mrs Fourie barked, her eyes scouring the classroom for the source of the remark. The class fell quiet again. She turned back to Edmund.

'Find your book,' she ordered, 'and bring it to me.'

Before she dismissed the class, Mrs Fourie handed him a note for the school secretary, giving him permission to phone his mother to say he had to stay for detention. He didn't know what was worse: the nasty suspicion in Mrs Fourie's voice or the humiliation of having to wait in the front office whilst a message was delivered to Mrs MacDougal.

'She'll pass the message on to your mother,' said the secretary, replacing the receiver with a certain smack of her lips that suggested he was in a lot of trouble. 'You'll have to walk home by yourself after detention.'

'Thank you,' said Edmund, his heart sinking further. By the time he would get back, Mr MacDougal would have gone back to work. There would be no maths lesson that afternoon. Edmund walked slowly out of the office and down the steps. The classroom block loomed in front of him, solitary and foreboding. He took a deep breath and tried to console himself. If he could finish quickly, surely Mrs Fourie would let him go. He could run home. It wasn't that far, was it?

Then Edmund found his book in his desk. He wasn't sure

how it had got there, but he was hoping he could now go home. Mrs Fourie pursed her lips and shook her head when he told her, expecting to find his work unmarked, but it wasn't.

'Oh. That's funny,' was all she said.

'I promise I handed it in.'

Mrs Fourie continued to scan his work, as though looking for a sign of further fraudulence.

'*Somebody's* marked it,' she said, turning towards him with raised eyebrows.

'I think,' Edmund hesitated. 'I think somebody took it and hid it,' he began.

'Nonsense,' she snapped, waving him away. 'You must take responsibility for your own actions, Edmund. You lost it.'

Realising the hand of fate was against him, Edmund slunk away. Then he discovered his satchel was missing.

Edmund's mother turned the pages of his reading book slowly, shaking her head in disbelief. Eventually, she put her hands over her mouth and looked upwards to heaven, or at least he supposed it was heaven, from whence she drew her comfort in times of trouble. The silence was intimidating, as was the wait for it to burst suddenly and a hand strike him rudely on the cheek or a tirade of threats to be unleashed, unbending in their ferocity. He didn't know which was worse, the pain of the slap or the sting of the words, which continued to beat their little fists in his head long after the smarting on his cheek had subsided.

Neither ensued. This crime was ultimately the worst he had ever committed, residing beyond mere anger and punishment. If it already needed God's intervention, Edmund knew he was doomed. His mother didn't even look at him; she clasped the book to her bosom as though it were a tiny baby, and rocked back and forth in anguish.

Edmund bowed his head in shame. What now would the MacDougals say?

The office of Top Notch Recruitment Agency was closed. A notice stuck on the door announced that 'Due to a tragedy, this office will be closed until July 14th'– the following week. Edmund didn't think it was a good idea to mention a tragedy in connection with an employment agency; some people might read something deeper into it: maid poisons employer; cook beats woman to death with rolling pin. Gardener murders madam. He tried the door but it was locked. He would have to get a contact number for this Shantelle lady from Mr Pullman. 'S,' he suddenly thought. 'What was her surname?'

'It is closed until next week.'

Edmund turned to find a man standing and looking at him from the doorway of the next-door office. He looked like he could have been a janitor, dressed as he was in blue overalls and a peaked tartan cap. A bunch of keys jangled from a belt loop and he had that air of superiority peculiar to people who believe their jobs are far more important than they really are.

'Salibonani,' said Edmund. 'Do you know where the lady is who runs this office?'

'Look,' said the man, walking over, jangling as he did so. 'Due to a tra-ge-dy, this office, that is *this* one' – he poked the door with his finger – 'this office will be closed until July 14th. That is *next* week. The 14th.' He made a wave movement with his left arm to suggest 'next week'.

'Yes, I can read,' Edmund answered with a sigh. He wondered how many times he would be told that the office was closed. 'I want to know where the lady is. The one who works here.'

'She is not here.'

'Do you know where she is? Do you have a phone number? Are you the caretaker?'

'Yes, I am the one who looks after this whole building.' He swept his arm out to show the immenseness of his realm. 'But I don't have a phone number.'

'It is very urgent that I contact this lady. I have to ask her questions.'

The man looked suspiciously at Edmund and then looked back at the notice.

'She will be in next week,' he said eventually. 'Come on the 14th.'

Edmund walked slowly down the stairs, each step heavy with despondency. Top Notch was situated within a block of flats that had been converted into offices and doctors' surgeries. It was in a quiet part of town with large shady trees in the car park and a security guard lounging on the steps.

A car drew up as Edmund emerged from the stairwell. It was red and looked fast and jaunty, like all red cars do. The tinted windows made it impossible for Edmund to see the driver, but he didn't have to wait as a woman got out immediately the car stopped. She seemed in a hurry, harassed even, for her movements were quick and uneasy and she appeared flustered about something. Edmund approached her.

'Shantelle?' he hazarded. She spun round, her eyes wide and alert, but not frightened, 'Chief Inspector Edmund Dube, CID.' Edmund loved saying that. He felt grand and important; the trick was keeping up the façade of confidence.

'Yes? What can I do for you?' In a split second, her face snapped into that of the efficient office worker. What was she hiding, Edmund wondered, as she brushed a loose strand of hair out of her eyes? Attractive? Yes, in a red car way. She liked to look good: lipstick and make up and tight fitting clothes. But really attractive, deep down inside attractive? No, although Edmund was sure there were plenty of men who would disagree with him. She was wearing a silky white tracksuit and a pair of white and silver takkies with a heel. Edmund had always found these a rather strange invention as he associated takkies with sport and fitness, not fashion.

'I need to speak to you about the death of Mrs Pullman.'

'Yes, it's very, very tragic what happened. But I was under the impression she had died naturally? Didn't she?'

'I assume you are going to your office? Can we talk in there, please?'

'Oh?' A slight scowl passed over her face, replaced by an over-zealousness to do exactly as he wanted.

'Of course. Come this way, please.' She picked up her bag, locked her car with a beep from something in her hand and made for the stairway. Edmund noticed she made sure she didn't walk with him, but in front. She opened the door to the agency and went quickly inside to a little box on the wall behind a desk. It was beeping in that way that Edmund always found slightly menacing, as though a bomb were about to explode. She punched in some numbers and the box fell silent. Edmund looked around the office. It was rather blandly decorated; there were pictures of the innocuous type: 3D prisms of different sizes on backgrounds of bright primary colours and fake flowers in vases. Edmund was surprised: it wasn't Marcia.

Behind the desk was a large grey filing cabinet on top of which was a flower pot with something with long thin green fronds growing in it. To the left of the cabinet was a closed door. The desk had a calendar and a photo of a little boy on a toy motorbike. There was a small waiting area, which consisted of a sofa, a low coffee table and a few magazines and a water dispenser. Shantelle settled herself into the large black office chair on wheels behind the desk. Edmund sat in front of the desk on a rather less comfortable and much smaller chair.

'How did you hear about Mrs Pullman?'

'Oh, er, her husband phoned me last night.'

'He told you she had died of natural causes?'

He watched her face carefully as she answered. 'Yes.'

'Did he tell you Mrs Pullman had also been stabbed?'

Shantelle paused, as though considering her answer.

'Yes,' she said, slowly. 'He did mention it.'

'He mentioned it.' He waited for her to say something else but she didn't elaborate. 'He told you to shut the office for a week?'

'Yes. But look, I would have done anyway. I mean, you know, as a sign of respect.'

She gave a gentle nod of her head and looked straight at him.

Edmund cleared his throat. 'I need to know about yesterday. There was an incident here, I believe.'

Momentarily stumped, Shantelle shook her head slowly.

'A Mr Martin threatened Mrs Pullman?'

'Oh *that*. It wasn't really anything–' She stopped. 'Who told you about it?'

'Dorcas Hlabangana.'

'Dorcas. I see.' Edmund's words were like a small stone landing in a still, smooth expanse of water, sending shivers of meaning across her face. 'Dorcas? Of course. Yes, she was in the kitchen. So you mean you think...? Craig? Noooo.'

'Could you tell me please, in your own words, what happened?'

At first she hesitated and then she pulled herself closer to the table and leant towards him, her hands clasped together on the table. Edmund noticed her false red nails. He always associated them with hard, fast women, but perhaps that was his mother's doing for she abhorred all signs of vanity.

'You think it has something to do with her death?'

'Perhaps.'

'Do you think he stabbed her? Oh my God! Craig!' She put her hand over her mouth in what Edmund found a slightly affected way. He couldn't imagine that much tugged upon the strings of Shantelle's heart. 'He's the one who stabbed her. Oh my God! It's Craig, isn't it? Oh my God!'

Although Edmund had lost his belief in God, he still recoiled to hear His name taken in vain. Edmund had often ruminated on the fact that it is what you learn as a child that stays most tenaciously with you as an adult. It was the waste of words, too, that Edmund detested.

'If you have to repeat yourself, you're making a hash of it, laddie, always remember that,' Mr MacDougal used to say. 'Economy is everything in life.'

'Please just tell me what happened.'

Shantelle settled herself in her chair as though she were at a drinks party and about to tell a funny story. 'So then this guy, right, he comes in and he's mad. He's really, really mad and his face is like this (ugly grimace) and he's spitting and raging.' Edmund could see the red fingernails flashing through the air, shredding it as she spoke.

After she had recounted the events of the day before, Edmund asked: 'What I don't understand is why?'

'Why?'

'Why was he so angry? You say he did some work in the office. Was he not paid for it? Did he do a bad job?'

'If he's psycho, does he need a reason to be angry?'

'You called him Craig, not Mr Martin or even the repair man. I think you know him more than you may suggest?'

He could see he had her cornered. She ran her tongue lightly over her lips.

'I have a little' – she searched for the right word – 'side interest. I like to, you know, bring people together.'

'A dating agency?'

'Hmm, not quite an agency, although I'm hoping one day, you know, to go out on my own. At the moment, let's just say I like to play Cupid.'

She watched Edmund's face carefully. He nodded.

'I have some clients. We meet up for drinks and a bit of a party every couple of weeks. You know what I mean?'

'I think I do.'

'Craig is one of my clients. I always thought he was a nice guy. I mean, nothing to look at really. It's the hair, it's too *eighties*.' The red fingernails hovered around her head like some sort of manic butterfly. 'He doesn't look good, you know. Not in good health. He needs to go to the gym, lose some weight, have a haircut.'

Edmund shifted in his seat. He wasn't sure he had either the time or the inclination to hear how Craig Martin could improve his success with women. 'What happened?'

'He gave up coming to the socials. You know these white guys; they just want white chicks. They won't try something different. They won't go for blacks, not even a mixed race woman. Not that any self-respecting black woman would go for him.' She rolled her eyes to emphasise the ludicrousness of the idea. 'Well, that's his priority, but it does cut things down a bit.'

'Prerogative,' interrupted Edmund before he could stop himself.

'What?'

'Pardon,' he corrected her. 'It's not his priority. It's his prerogative.'

'I don't know what pre-whatever means. I'm talking about his *priority*. It's his *priority* to choose who he wants to go out with.'

Edmund looked at her without comment. She sat back in her chair, letting her arms drop to her sides as though to suggest the futility of the situation.

'So, sometimes, when I did get a white girl come along, which is very occasionally, I arranged a private date with Craig.' She shook her head again. 'Even they struggled to find him attractive. Man, that hair... He was very lucky, you know. *Very lucky*.'

'Had he been on a date recently?'

'As I was saying,' she looked darkly over at Edmund as though he was going to interrupt her again, 'he was very lucky because I got him this date with an NGO lady. Now, those do not come up very often, I can tell you, and this one was very difficult.'

'Difficult? Why?'

'I had gone to this NGO place to advertise the agency. Mrs Pullman had this idea that they would pay big money for maids. Do you know how much they get paid? Well, it's *big* money, I tell you. I was to inform them that we could also arrange gardeners and provide extra maids for parties. But with this chick she got it wrong. Turns out she's all into human rights and equality and all that stuff, right? She thinks it's horrendous that maids are paid so little.'

She shook her head and whistled. 'Man, she was nuts all right.'

'So you set her up with Craig?'

'Well, he's not exactly sane, is he? What happened was that I could see she was new to the country. A bit *naïve*, if you know what I mean. When we first met, before she'd had a cadenza about equal pay and whatever else she was on about, we'd exchanged cards. Business cards, you know what I mean?'

Edmund nodded. 'Of course.'

'I phoned her. I asked her if she'd like to meet some Zimbabweans. Get to know the culture, you know? And, to cut a long story short, she agreed *eventually* and I set her up with Craig.'

'I see.'

'So first he's all shy, he says he doesn't have time, he's busy. I mean, *come on*, is this guy for real, I'm thinking? Then he agrees, like I'm pushing him into something. I mean this woman works for an NGO!' She rubbed her thumb and middle finger together. It was a vulgar gesture, Edmund thought and he could understand some of Craig's exasperation.

'So they went out?' he prompted her again.

'Yah. I don't know where they went or what happened.' She suddenly looked totally uninterested in Craig and his rich date. 'But he comes in the next day and he's shouting' – the nails flashed again – 'and he's saying he hates me and he hates my effing dating group and how he's sick and tired of people like me who are out to get money.' She rolled her eyes and pointed at herself as if to suggest that that couldn't possibly be true of her of all people.

'Anything else?'

'He never wants to see me again. He was going to report me. I'm disgusting. He hopes the place burns down. Something about corruption in Zimbabwe and there's no respect for human rights and blah, blah, blah, blah, blah.'

'And then?'

'I was just like *so* upset. I couldn't handle it. I rushed into the back room.' She gestured behind her.

'And then?'

'I've told you. Mrs Pullman came out. She asked him to leave or she would call the police. Then he went out.'

'And that was it?'

'No. He came back. About five seconds later and started all over again. Then he made a threat and left again.'

'What kind of a threat?'

'He pointed his fingers to his head as though he had a gun. It was creepy. He looked at her, you know, with so much *hate*. There was *so much* hate in his eyes. It just shows, you never know what people are really like. Even a very nice guy can be a killer.'

'Do you think he is capable of murder?'

'Craig? Well, he must be! He made a threat and the next minute Mrs Pullman is dead. Hey yey yey!'

'Except that Mrs Pullman was already dead.'

Shantelle dismissed this statement as irrelevant. 'He had to make sure, didn't he? He had to make sure.'

'Why didn't he kill you? You arranged the date. Why Mrs Pullman?'

She shrugged as though the answer were of little importance. '*I don't know.* Who knows with these psychos what goes on upstairs?'

'Have you had this sort of trouble before?'

Shantelle widened her eyes and shook her head vehemently. 'No, not like this. Sometimes, *very* occasionally, someone is unhappy with their date.'

'Really? Why's that?'

'Most of the time it's nothing serious. Just sometimes there are those people who think they are *guaranteed* to find love, but, you know, love just isn't like that.' She appeared to want to brush the whole thing off.

Edmund resisted commenting on her matchmaking skills and pushed on with the questioning.

'Did he know her?'

'Not that I know of.'

'Had he met her when he worked here?'

'No.'

'You said he hated her. It's difficult to hate someone you don't know.'

Shantelle clicked her tongue irritably. 'He hated *everybody* at that moment.'

'And afterwards, when he had left, did Mrs Pullman say anything that suggested she knew him?'

Shantelle thought. 'No.' She shook her head. 'She just said he was a disgusting piece of humanity.'

'Those were her words exactly?'

Shantelle nodded her head. 'And white trash. That's what she also called him.'

'When he left, did he say anything at all?'

'Something like "I'll be back soon" or "I'm coming back".'

'What about "I'll be back"?'

'Oh yes, that's it. "I'll be back." That's what he said.'

Edmund doubted Shantelle had the imagination to exaggerate. 'What did you do when he had gone?'

'Mrs Pullman told Dorcas to make some tea. She told me to go for a walk, but I didn't. In case he was outside somewhere. He might have *killed* me or something.'

'It must have put you in a difficult position. I take it Mrs Pullman didn't know about your 'second job'?'

'Absolutely not. I tell all my clients never to come to the office. We operate by Whatsapp.'

'She must have asked who he was and why he was there.'

Shantelle thought for a moment and then shook her head. 'No, she didn't. If she had, I would have said he was the guy who did some work in the office a while ago and he had a bit of a thing for me. Couldn't take no for an answer' – Shantelle flicked her hair back – 'she just said he was white trash, that's all.'

'Did he come back at all?'

'No, but he left some roses outside the door. I threw them away at once.'

'You don't believe he was genuine?'

'Oh, I don't know. I thought maybe he was one of those psycho guys, you know? One minute all nicey-nicey, next minute carving you up with a knife.'

Edmund took back what he had assumed about Shantelle's

lack of imagination. No doubt her opinion of Craig the previous afternoon was informed by hindsight rather than any genuine knowledge about his mental well-being at the time.

'You didn't think of calling the police?'

Shantelle gave him a look that said she felt sorry for him. 'What you guys going to do, huh? Sorry, but most of the time you are useless. Not you,' she added as though to soften the blow. 'The other guys, you know? Very useless people.'

'What time did Mrs Pullman go home?'

'About twelve fifteen.'

'Was that usual? Did she only work in the mornings?'

'Mrs Pullman didn't exactly work here,' said Shantelle, a slight smirk on her face. 'She came in sometimes to check how things were going.'

'Was that a regular thing? Every Monday?'

'No. Whenever she had the time.'

Whenever she had the time. But did she? Book club usually took up most of her day, apparently, yet here she was checking in at the office and meeting someone for lunch as well as giving the maid the afternoon off.

'Do you know if she was going to meet anyone for lunch?'

'No.'

'There wasn't someone she met on a regular basis at all?'

'I work for her, but I am not her secretary, Inspector. I don't know what she does beyond these four walls.' The nails flashed again as she held up her hands in supposed ignorance.

'Was there anyone else in the office? Anyone else who witnessed Mr Martin's outburst?'

'No. No one else.'

'What about Dorcas? Did she hear what was going on as well?'

'Yes.'

'Did she often work at the office?'

Shantelle was hesitant, guarded. 'Ah, yes. Sometimes.'

'She cleaned I take it?'

'Yes... yes. When our cleaner is away.'

'What time did she leave?'

The question appeared to stump Shantelle who made a show of thinking hard about it, eyes tightly closed, face tilted slightly upwards as though she were trying to mentally add up a long string of figures.

'Maybe half twelve.'

'Do you stop for lunch at all?'

'No. Lunchtime is our busiest time generally. It's when most people come in and register.'

'You don't get hungry?'

'I make tea whenever I want. I don't eat much. I make my shakes – my energy shakes – and that's enough for me.'

'What time do you finish work?'

'Three o'clock.'

Edmund looked at his watch. It was a quarter to four. 'So I am lucky to have found you here today, especially as you closed the office.'

'Mr Pullman told me to. I'm just doing some' – the hands whirled frantically as the nails slashed a word out of the air – 'paperwork. It seemed a good day to catch up with it.'

Edmund raised his eyebrows.

'Hey! Look here, why are you asking all these questions? Why are you asking about me? I haven't done anything wrong.'

'Facts,' said Edmund, 'are very important.'

Shantelle looked blankly at him. He could see she was about to launch another attack so he asked quickly, 'Let's get back to Dorcas. Have you ever heard of any problem between her and Mrs Pullman?'

She took a deep breath before answering. 'No, no, not at all.' Shantelle's voice had become strange, slightly thin and raspy. Edmund noticed how she kept looking away, how the red fingernails had settled uneasily on the desktop.

'What about you? How did you get on with Mrs Pullman?'

'Me? I... oh... very well. Very well indeed. She was very kind and very generous.'

'Too many verys,' thought Edmund. Once again, Marcia Pullman was kind and generous to those who worked for her. Yet nobody seemed to like her and nobody seemed to miss her.

'Did you mention the incident in the office to Mr Pullman?'

'No... no... I didn't.'

'You didn't consider it important? You said you were afraid he was a madman.'

Shantelle pulled her shoulders upwards in a shrug and gave him a coquettish smile.

'Don't know,' she admitted in a baby voice.

Edmund snapped his notebook shut and stood up to leave. Shantelle, he couldn't help noticing, looked relieved. Edmund handed her his phone number.

'Please give me a call if there is anything else you remember Miss...?'

'*Mrs* Johnson.'

'Mrs Johnson.' He nodded, put his notebook in his pocket and went out of the door.

Edmund walked slowly to the end of the block. He wasn't happy. He thought back over the conversation. He remembered Shantelle's darting eyes that moved constantly to and from her cell phone, the way her fingernails clicked nervously on the desk. She was definitely on edge and he wondered why.

Chapter Twelve

1979

Mr MacDougal said it was a splendid name: Edmund.

'Are you going to climb mountains like Edmund Hillary?' he'd say. Or 'You'll have a lot of mountains to climb in your life, laddie, but you'll do it, I know. You've got the look. He's got the look, eh, Edna?'

Auntie Edna would smile and pat him on the back and say, 'That he has, Jack, that he has.'

After his maths, when Mr MacDougal had gone back to work, Edmund did some reading with Mrs MacDougal, sitting next to her on the big, wide sofa. She had a smell that was soft, powdery and sometimes almost sweet, and he loved it the most when she put her plump red hand on his knee and laughed about something, leaning her greying head closer to him, the sweetness engulfing him. Then he was on top of the mountain. When he had read, she read to him, poetry mainly. Scott and Burns and Shelley. He struggled at first to recite it, although he loved the sound of the words, the way they seemed to drop off her tongue as though he could catch them and keep them and hold onto their musical beauty.

'It's a gift,' Mrs MacDougal would say. 'Poetry is a beautiful gift to keep your whole life long.'

She was right, of course, for many years later he could still recite many of the poems.

> *O my Luve's like a red, red rose,*
> *That's newly sprung in June:*
> *O my Luve's like the melodie*
> *That's sweetly played in tune.*

For a long time he had felt like Edmund Hillary. It was as though he was constantly at the top of a mountain, rejoicing. Not just celebrating his own victory, but having someone celebrate *him*, showering him with affection. There was always a biscuit and tea on a tray and then he could go and play in the garden if he wanted to, but he didn't. He sat and read his book or went over his maths.

There was nobody, nobody in the whole wide world happier than Edmund. He was happy with a happiness that enveloped him, that engulfed him. Happiness and love.

It was that feeling, that warm loved feeling that he occasionally woke with some thirty five years later. He had a strong sensation of having been elsewhere, a wonderful place, and he would open his eyes cautiously, feeling disappointment creep slowly through his body. He'd try to cling to the dream by closing his eyes and hoping to fall back asleep, but it never worked. He would lie a while, adjusting to reality, acknowledging the bed and the room in which he lay; the life he occupied. He'd feel the dream slipping slowly away, like a mystical lover disappearing as the dawn lightened and hardened into day, and later he might not even remember he had had it. Eventually, he gave in to the inevitability of getting up and ready for work.

Was he not loved, he asked himself on numerous occasions? He'd look over at his wife sleeping next to him: her relaxed form always looked so peaceful and free from worry. She had pretty, soft features, the kind that make a woman look younger than she is and the type of mouth that seemed to be always smiling. It was her mouth that he had originally found her most attractive feature because it was different; other girls perfected sulky pouts in order to appear mysterious and becoming, but she had this beautiful warm, wet mouth, the lips just slightly heart-shaped, that brimmed and quivered with expectation.

Lately – or had it been for quite a while now? – she had begun to irritate him. He'd come home from work and there she'd be talking over the fence to the neighbour, laughing away.

'How was your day?' she'd call as he walked up the short path from the road to the house. It was a phrase he'd come to hate; it was empty, it was banal, it belonged to TV scripts, not his life. Did she know so little about him and about what he did that she could turn to him so lightly and ask such a question? Increasingly, Edmund felt Mary was like a doll, a beautiful doll with a set face. He wanted to shake her sometimes, violently even, but what he feared, perhaps even more than hurting her, was receiving that smile in return.

Then at other times he pulled himself short and was ashamed of his behaviour. It was his turn for the questions: isn't this what he wanted – a wife who stayed at home, a respectable job in town? Wasn't he father home from the office? Father in his pinstriped suit, brief case in hand? What should his answer be? 'Fine, thank you, my dear. No problems on the trains today, but London was awfully busy.'

Today, Edmund had woken again surrounded by the remnants of his beautiful dream. Once again, he tried desperately to cling to it and keep it and, once again, felt it slip away. He opened his eyes and glanced at his alarm clock. He had five minutes before he needed to get up and, as time is always precious early in the morning, he felt he needed to make use of it wisely. It was his time, his alone. He reached into the drawer next to his bed and rummaged under some papers until he found what he was looking for, a photo. It was black and white with a thin white border to it. The picture was of a small boy in school uniform standing in front of a car with a house in the background. The boy was smiling, a soft, shy smile as though all the joy inside of him threatened to rise up and burst his heart. The car was a Renault 4. It was blue, he remembered, an unusual egg shell blue. Edmund ran his finger lightly over it and sighed. Next to him, Mary stirred and he quickly put the photo away. Long ago, he had told her about them, about the MacDougals, and he had shown her the picture. It was in the early days of their courtship when he had been keen to show her every nook and cranny of his life, or just about. She had laughed and cooed and called him cute and he, in turn, had smiled happily in the warmth of her interest. But they were rare gems that he shared with her and even then he had a certain reluctance to tell her everything about himself. Now, many years later, his reluctance had hardened into a refusal. She would show kindness in a silly, affectionate sort of way that he detested. The mouth, the slippery smile – he couldn't bear anyone, least of all his wife, to smile at his pain.

'Day Two,' thought Edmund as he sat up in bed and switched the alarm clock off a second before it rang. He wound the clock – it was one of those old-fashioned ones – and put it back on his bedside table, aligning it with the lamp and the edge of his Lesley Charteris novel. Mary woke and snuggled up against him. She reached up and ran a hand through the hair on his chest.

'Five more minutes,' she said with a provocative smile. 'I'll make it worth your while.'

Edmund took a deep breath and got out of bed.

'There's a murder enquiry on. I must get to work early.' He pulled on his trousers and took down his shirt from where it hung, neatly ironed, on a hook at the back of the cupboard door.

Mary pulled a face. 'Edmund – always so enthusiastic.'

Edmund buttoned up his shirt and then leaned over and kissed his wife.

'See you later,' he said. 'I will get something to eat on the way to work. You go back to sleep.'

A keen wind whipped against Edmund as he walked down the road. It was early still and, being winter, the sun was still struggling to rise; everything was infused with a thin grey light. Pieces of litter accosted him along the way: an old coke can rattled into the ditch next to him, a plastic bag blew into his face, a piece of cardboard lying in the road rose up as he passed, buoyed forward by the wind.

What struck Edmund most about his walk to the bus stop these days was the silence. Nobody stopped, few people talked. Their heads were bent as though they were afraid of being beaten if they looked up. They huddled into coats and jackets and then onto buses and taxis. The empty silence was the worst, an invisible oppression bearing down on everyone. Edmund thought uneasily about the way things used to be: the hustle and bustle of people going to work, the sense of purpose, the hope.

If he closed his eyes so they were only open the tiniest bit, and concentrated on the cold and the wind, he imagined he was in Scotland, or at least what he imagined Scotland to be. He was walking over bracken-covered hills, whistling while he collected heather. It was cold. It was about to snow. Suddenly, Edmund heard a frantic beeping of a horn and a minibus cut across his path and stopped. Several people got out, but several more ran to catch it. Despite being the person nearest the bus, Edmund was the last on.

The bus was full. Edmund felt people look away as he got on. He was quite used to it. Sometimes, they thought he had got on the bus to cause trouble; perhaps fine the driver for speeding or overloading the bus, or having no indicators or brake lights. Generally, most of the drivers in his area knew him and knew he was harmless. Innocuous. Edmund hated that word. It suggested weakness and powerlessness, an inability to be taken seriously.

A couple of stops into town, Edmund found himself squeezed against the window. A very large woman in a long shiny green skirt and matching top with huge sleeves that stood out like two spiky blossoms sat next to him, smelling strongly of something more like air freshener than perfume. Edmund moved to open the window, but it was jammed shut. He closed his eyes and thanked God he wasn't claustrophobic.

Next to the woman, and completely dwarfed by her, were two tiny school children in navy blue uniforms. They carried plastic bags in which they kept their pencils and a plastic bottle of water. 'No food,' thought Edmund despondently.

No money for food. The little girls looked up at him over the large woman's bust. Their faces were gentle and innocent, their eyes absent of the use and abuse of the world. There was a time when people were proud of going to school and of being able to give their children an education. Edmund remembered those days; the buzz of excitement before school started, buying pens and pencils, the smell of new exercise books, the small square plastic box in which he kept his lunch. He remembered how his mother washed his uniform every second night while he lay naked under the blanket; how she woke early to iron it and how she treasured the picture Mr MacDougal had given her of Edmund in his school uniform.

It was perhaps due to his earlier wander down memory lane that Edmund decided to visit Janet's place of work first that morning. Ascot shopping centre was somewhere that once held a certain fascination for him as a child. He remembered it when there was a cinema and an antique shop and when the supermarket there had a milk bar where one could order milkshakes and ice creams. Not that he ever had one of these great delicacies. Mrs MacDougal would take him and his mother there on the last Saturday of every month, when his mother was paid, and they would buy mealie meal and ration meat and a large bag of kapenta to last them the month. At the end of every school holiday, his mother bought him two pencils and five exercise books to keep him going through the term. They would load everything into the tiny boot of the Renault 4 and go home, feeling replete and happy.

'Thanks be to God,' his mother would say as she packed everything away into the small cupboard in the khaya. 'Thank you, God, that we can afford these few things.' She would raise her eyes to the roof as though God were crouching up there in the bare rafters.

'Why doesn't he give us more, Mama?' Edmund had once asked and she had smacked him sharply on the side of his head.

'You!' she exclaimed in horror. 'What are you saying? The Lord has given us this and you want more? Shame. Shame on you.'

But later, when they lay asleep together on the large mattress on the floor of the tiny bedroom, his mother had stroked his head where she had hit him and said softly, 'We must be grateful, Edmund. Mr and Mrs MacDougal are very kind to us. We are lucky to work for white people like them because they treat us properly. If you work well for them, they will look after you, Edmund. Remember that.'

'They had,' thought Edmund as he got off the bus and walked in the direction of the shops. For a while, at least. They paid for his school fees and they paid his subscription to the Public Library. They helped him with his homework and read to him in the afternoons. He had felt loved and treasured. One of the family, that was the expression. In his mother's family he was known as the white boy and, although it was a name that set him apart from others, he never denied it. He kept quiet and stared solemnly back at those who bandied it at him. Inwardly, he loved it. He knew it was meant as a slur, as an attempt to rein him in and bring him back down to earth, but he luxuriated in the thought. He didn't give the game away though. That thought was his and his alone and he wasn't going to be so stupid as to spoil it all by becoming smug and full of himself. He kept it and buried it deep within himself.

Edmund surveyed what he still referred to as the 'new' Ascot. Gone were the antique shop and the cinema. He remembered the thrill of looking at the posters of new releases and what was 'coming soon', the way the posters were edged with tinsel and how plush the carpet looked from where he peered in through the glass door. Sometimes he had watched the moviegoers buying their cartons of popcorn and plastic cups of Coke and Fanta before disappearing through the purple curtains into the land beyond.

It was all gone now; it had all disappeared. As a young police officer, he had been involved in raiding some of the more dubious movie houses in the centre of town. In the act of chasing prostitutes and drug dealers out of the back rows of these sordid institutions, he had glanced round to see what he had been missing all his life and had felt slightly cheated to see only a wide screen and rows of seats. In his mind's eye, there was always something more, some magical element, that existed behind the purple curtains and he refused to let reality tell him otherwise.

Twice Loved was easily found; a small shop full of second hand clothes and pieces of chipped crockery. There was that smell, the one always associated with second hand shops: musty and slightly damp and old, the smell of years pressed together and stored away. Edmund's eyes passed quickly over the rows of clothes and shoes. There were a few books, nothing of interest, things like *How to Play Contract Bridge* and *Wonderful Cape Town*. There were bits of cutlery, one or two nice looking silver spoons and a brass candelabra and a couple of pictures, mainly of the sea crashing over rocks and one of a vase of flowers next to an open window.

The manager was a Mrs Reilly, a rather formidable woman in her early 60s, Edmund guessed. Her hair was set in waves of light orangey-brown with streaks of grey at the top, making her look like a raccoon. Her eyebrows were pencilled on in dark brown and her eyelids were thick with light blue eye shadow. Edmund felt more than slightly overwhelmed. He was once more back in the classroom at school, feeling Mrs Fourie behind him, breathing down his neck, waiting, just waiting for that great hand to come crashing down on his book and the exclamation, 'Punctuation, Edmund! Punctuation is the foundation of all understanding!'

'I heard about Marcia's death yesterday,' she said, at first rather interested as to why Edmund was asking her questions. 'A friend of mine was due to go to book club at Marcia's on Monday evening and then of course she got the call from Janet that it was *cancelled* and *why*.' Mrs Reilly had a habit of bending her head forward every time she emphasised a word. 'Kidney failure, I hear.'

'Could I ask you a few questions about Mrs Janet Peters?' asked Edmund, feeling his throat closing up again. Mrs Reilly was quite a daunting presence, but he must try to be in control. *Being in Control: A Practical Guide to Self Confidence.* Step 5: *Assume a position of authority.*

'Janet?' she said, eyeing him suspiciously. 'Why, what has she done?'

She had ushered him in to a small back room that was crammed full of black bin liners bulging with more second-hand clothes. Then she had squeezed herself into a tiny chair behind a desk and motioned for him to sit on an even smaller chair opposite her. Edmund felt the indignity of his school days return with even greater force.

'Please understand, Mrs Reilly, I am not accusing Mrs Peters of anything. This is just a routine investigation.'

Mrs Reilly's smile didn't waver, but her eyes narrowed.

'Has something been stolen?'

'Why do you ask?'

'Why else are you asking questions?'

'How long has Mrs Peters worked here?'

'She's not a thief. I don't believe she would have stolen something.'

'I'm not saying she has, believe me. What is her job exactly?'

'Janet has worked here for about a year now. We've never had any problems with her. She takes the odd day off – but she always phones and lets us know. So, no problems there. It's very quiet at the moment. I told her she could take a couple of days off.' Mrs Reilly folded her hands in front of her on the desk and gave Edmund a tight-lipped smile as though to suggest the questioning was over.

'This is a charity shop, yes?'

'Yes, that's correct.'

'The money goes to help the elderly?'

Mrs Reilly's eyes narrowed again. 'Yes, correct again.'

'May I ask how? I mean, do you give the money to an organisation or do you handle the money yourselves?'

A definite shadow came across the lady's face. Her voice was hard as she said, 'We give it to an organisation, Friends of the Elderly. All their money comes from fundraising. Not a cent from the government. Without them, many elderly people would have died.'

'That is good,' said Edmund, feeling the force of the woman's animosity. 'It is good that something is being done.'

'Yes, no thanks to our corrupt government.' Her mouth was thin and flat as she spoke.

'Does Mrs Peters get paid for working here?' asked Edmund, trying to plough ahead with the questions.

'I don't see that that is any business of yours, Inspector,' said Mrs Reilly, an ironic smile now curling her lips upward.

'Not mine, personally,' he agreed, 'but it is police business so there are some questions I really need to ask.'

'Well, if you must know, all the people who work here receive a small wage. Very small. Basically, it covers their transport to and from home.'

'So the type of person you have working here is not doing it for the money, obviously,' said Edmund trying to lean back in the chair but not succeeding for there were three dresses slung over the back. A coat hanger dug into him.

'Yes, you could say that. All of our staff are female and they are supported by husbands.'

'Except Mrs Peters.'

Mrs Reilly seemed to register something for the first time.

'She lives with her old mother, you know. She might be one of these old dears on a good wicket with a British pension. I think Janet has a son or daughter as well in the UK. It's possible they send money.'

'Do you know where she worked before this?'

Mrs Reilly pulled a face and tapped her fingers on the desktop. 'Dentist's surgery, I think it was. Receptionist, that sort of thing.'

'The shop is closed on Mondays, is that right?'

'Quite right. We're open Saturdays, so we close on

Mondays. Nobody's got any money on a Monday anyway.' She gave a little laugh without opening her mouth.

'Well, thank you for your time, Mrs Reilly,' said Edmund, standing up awkwardly.

'Not at all, Inspector. As I said, Janet is... well, Janet. Nothing else to say, really. Good woman, lacks confidence sometimes. Not always good at adding up. I've had to go through her calculations more than once.' She gave a brief laugh and Edmund once again had the feeling of being back in class.

'Did you know Mrs Pullman at all?'

'Marcia? Yes, sort of. She came in here sometimes looking for things.'

'She came in here?' Edmund was surprised a person like Marcia would set foot in Twice Loved.

She nodded. 'Looking for things, you know.'

'What sort of things?'

'Antiques. She had an eye for them, if you know what I mean. You and I, we could look at that pot for instance' – she pointed to a deep blue China pot on her table – 'and we'd say nice pot. My African Violet would look good in that. I'll give you five dollars for it. Now Marcia would look at it and see a ninth century Chinese vase worth twenty thousand dollars. She'd still offer five dollars for it – but that's what made her quite well off.'

'She collected antiques? And she made a lot of money?'

'Look, I don't know, officer, how true these things are,' said Mrs Reilly, shrugging her shoulders. 'One hears these things on the grapevine, but, as my late husband used to say, there's no smoke without fire.'

'What did you hear?'

Mrs Reilly leaned closer. 'Well, I think it was Janet herself who told me about it. She had gone to book club one evening and Marcia had boasted to everyone how she'd found a picture in here which she bought for ten dollars and it turned out it was worth ten thousand.'

'Really? What did she do with it?'

'Sold it. Took it to Christie's in Joburg and they sold it for her.' She paused, running her tongue along her teeth. 'We didn't get a penny though. Janet thought she might have made a donation of some sort, if not to us at least to the elderly lady to whom it had belonged. Five hundred dollars. One hundred, even, but there was nothing.

'Was Mrs Peters upset? Was she angry about it?'

'Janet? Angry? I don't think Janet could get angry, officer. No, she was disappointed, let's say, but angry? No.'

'Did it ever happen again?'

'Not that I know of, but occasionally Marcia came in here and had a good look around.'

'Did Mrs Peters ever mention *anything* concerning Mrs Pullman?'

Mrs Reilly thought for a moment and then shook her head. 'Not that I remember.'

Edmund closed his notebook and put it in his pocket. 'Do you mind if I have a look round?' he asked and saw Mrs Reilly's lips pinch slightly.

'No, no, go ahead but remember if you break it, you buy it!'

Edmund looked along the shelves of odd bits of crockery and ornaments and then along the line of battered paperbacks. Then he turned his attention to a small display case with various bits of jewellery arranged inside. He was just about to turn away when his eyes caught something. It was a small knife with a very sharp tip like that of a spear and a beautiful smooth black handle. Without thinking, he opened the cupboard and picked it up. He held it up to the light to see better.

'That'll be five dollars,' said a voice beside him. Edmund jumped as Mrs Reilly suddenly appeared at his side and shut the door of the cabinet firmly, her bust billowing out like the sail of a ship. 'Everything needs to be paid for. Our elderly people depend on the money we get from selling things. We get no help from our dear government at all.'

Unprepared for her sudden descent on to him, Edmund

felt himself shrink considerably. He should have been angry, but he felt humiliated. He was a small, small boy looking up at Mrs Fourie and feeling the eyes of the class on him as she pointed and prodded him.

'This young man, *this African boy,* has stolen two dollars from my bag. Two dollars! This is what happens when we let *anyone* into our schools. God alone knows what the future holds.'

Edmund put his hand in his pocket and brought out a five dollar note.

'I'll buy it then,' he said and saw the anger on Mrs Fourie's face wobble uncertainly.

'Mary will see to you,' she said, motioning to a lady at the till. She turned away ostensibly to neaten a rail of clothes. 'That's if you want it. Good day.'

1979

Mr MacDougal was sitting on the end of the bed in the spare room, turning down the tops of the long woollen socks he had on and smoothing them carefully.

'Sometimes, laddie, you have to take matters into your own hands, d'you know what I mean?'

Edmund didn't. He squatted on the floor looking up at Mr MacDougal, watching carefully his every move. Mr MacDougal was getting ready to attend the annual Burns' night celebrations held by the Caledonian Society. He kept his kilt, along with the heavy winter coats that he and Mrs MacDougal had arrived with many years before, in the small cupboard.

'There was a fella I knew back in Kinlocheil; Roddy Buchanan was his name. Liked to throw his weight around. He was a big boy, very tall and *big*. Solid. Well, one day Roddy took things a step too far and picked on a wee lad half his size, little Johnny Craig. Scared the hell out of him. Fellow wet his breeks he was so afraid. I hate that, you know, laddie. I hate bullying.'

Edmund nodded, waiting patiently to hear the end of the story. Mr MacDougal stood up and looked at himself in the full-length mirror on the wall. He moved his kilt very slightly to the left and shrugged his shoulders so that his shirt sat a little more comfortably on him.

'Well, Roddy was not the brightest star in the galaxy. Bullies often aren't. It so happened that one day Roddy needed help with his homework and what did he do? Aye, you've guessed it. He waited for Johnny after school and demanded that he do it for him. He thought it would all be plain sailing, right? Johnny was scared of him and he would do the work and Roddy would be sitting high and dry as a result.'

Edmund nodded.

'Well, it wasn't to happen. You see, what he did not understand is that in demanding Johnny help him, he was giving the little boy the upper hand. You know what that is, Edmund? It means that Johnny was in the driving seat. Oh aye, Johnny did his homework all right for him, but he did it all wrong, didn't he? Made a right hash of it, he did.'

'What happened?' asked Edmund, his eyes wide at the thought of Roddy Buchanan's reaction.

'Oh, he was beaten. Six of the best by the Latin master, Old Jeffries.'

'And?'

'And a new respect was born. You see, violence need not be countered with violence. Use your head. Know your own strengths. Know what I mean?' He opened a drawer next to his bed and took out a little knife. 'Know what this is?'

Edmund shook his head.

'It's a sgian-dubh. A Scottish knife.' He held it up so that it glinted in the light, spat on it and then shone it with a handkerchief.' 'Going back many years in Scotland, it was considered polite to declare your weapons before entering someone's house. But I say, be prepared. You never know who's going to stab you in the back.' He slipped the knife into the top of his sock so that the shiny silver handle stuck out. He patted it fondly. 'Everyone has a weapon, Edmund. You need to find out what yours is and use it. Use it wisely, 'cause likely as not, you haven't got another one. You understand me, Edmund?'

Edmund nodded slowly. 'I understand. I understand.'

Chapter Thirteen

Nigel Pullman swung his legs off the side of the spare bed and sat up. His body felt heavy and his senses dull.

'Not good,' he thought. He could hear Dorcas in the kitchen and knew that she'd been preparing his breakfast. Sausages, bacon and eggs on toast. Life really did carry on, didn't it? The first night he had spent away with a friend. The body, the police, all that frenzied investigation. He could never have slept in the house that night. But the second night he was back. This was not out of any desire to be near Marcia or even out of concern for the safety of the house. Rather, it was a need to be surrounded by familiar things and follow a routine. Anyway, he was never good at staying with other people.

Nigel Pullman was born to be master of all he surveyed and didn't take well to being a guest, unless it was at a safari lodge for which he was paying big money and therefore didn't need to feel grateful. He hated being looked after or pitied and so he had returned home, much to the consternation of Dorcas who did not appreciate the order to be back at work so soon.

The rest of the week opened up before Nigel as a tunnel might do to a train about to enter it. It would be dark. There were things to do: a funeral to arrange and personal matters to sort out. He wondered how much Lindy at the office might be able to do. Nigel wasn't one for paperwork and making plans. Marcia had always seen to that side of things – and done it so well. Nigel had already decided on a cremation so if Lindy could put out a notice about the memorial service and organise the wine and snacks for the reception afterwards, that would be a load off his plate. He didn't mind paying, for money was not an object and it was very useful sometimes to be able to throw it about a bit.

Dorcas appeared to be hovering uncertainly in the kitchen. She put his food on the table and made a great deal of arranging the salt and pepper shakers and smoothing down the tablecloth. He watched her out of the corner of his eye. Surely she wasn't going to ask for a pay rise.

He ate in silence. Dorcas hovered still. Still watching her carefully, Nigel Pullman put the last piece of toast and scrambled egg in his mouth, wiped his mouth with a napkin and sat back. He pushed his plate towards her.

'We need a new gardener,' she said, standing back and twisting her hands in front of her. He waited. Was that it? Before he could respond, she turned and went back into the scullery. He heard the sound of water filling the sink. A new gardener. Did she think it was all going to carry on as usual? Did she assume he was going to stay here? He didn't know himself. A raise of his eyebrows was all the recognition he had given her that he had heard her words.

Before he left for work, Nigel Pullman put on his cap and picked up his cooler bag. In it was his lunch and his blood pressure pills. He thought he should say something to Dorcas – give her some instructions or something. Her back was turned towards him as he entered the scullery area where she was washing up.

'Dorcas,' he growled.

'Yes, baas.'

'Just clean the house same like madam told you. Nothing's changed, hey.'

Dorcas kept her eyes averted, slightly wary of her employer, but she nodded her head. Nigel liked the domestics to be frightened of him. 'Just tell them, you break anything I'll give you one of these,' he would boast to his friends, showing them the flat of his hand. 'Never let them have the upper hand because otherwise you're done for.'

'Everything is the same. Nothing has changed. You understand me, Dorcas?'

Her eyes darted from the plate in her hand to the sink.

'You mean...?'

'You know what I mean. We just do things slowly and quietly and get on with our lives. No problems. No need to speak to anyone. We don't want gossip, do we?'

'No baas,' said Dorcas, dropping the plate into the sink with a clunk.

He turned to go, but suddenly she said: 'What about the police? Are they coming back?'

'I've sorted things with them. But if that one who was here the first night comes back, you don't speak to him. You understand? He's bloody penga. Arsehole!' snapped Nigel. 'Phone me if he comes here, hey Dorcas? Don't let anyone in without my permission. You hear me?'

Dorcas nodded.

He turned and walked out through the kitchen.

Janet Peters woke up slowly. She had a distinct feeling she had overslept and, looking at her alarm clock, she had. Her eyes were heavy and sticky with sleep. Sleeping tablets, she thought ruefully as she pushed her feet into her slippers and stood up. She was stiff and her hip ached. I hate winter, she thought. Well, my bones hate it.

In the kitchen, she found Loveness wiping down the kitchen counter. The baby on her back peered round and eyed Janet blankly. Light streamed in through the window, a brutal reminder to Janet she had missed half the day. Janet hated waking up late but she seemed to do it more and more these days, even before Marcia's death. It was the sleeping tablets. They only seemed to kick in at three o'clock in the morning and then they hit her like a steam train, pushing her into a dark oblivion until nine in the morning. When she worked at the shop it was a struggle to wake up, especially in the dark winter mornings, but luckily she only had to be in for half past eight.

'Morning, Loveness,' said Janet, tying her dressing gown belt around her and switching the kettle on.

'Tea is in the lounge,' said Loveness with a big smile on her face. 'Madam has already made it.'

To Loveness, Janet was Mrs Peters; madam was her mother. Janet raised her eyebrows in surprise and clicked the kettle off. She was taken aback to find her mother in the little used sitting room. Tea was on a tray on a small coffee table and the curtains were wide open so the light flooded in. As Janet entered the room, her mother replaced a photo she was looking at on the dresser.

'Good morning, Janet,' she said brightly. As Janet bent over to kiss her, her mother grasped her by the shoulders and looked searchingly at her. 'How are you, dear? Did you sleep well?'

'No, not too well.' Janet straightened up and looked out of the window. 'Too much going on up here.' She tapped her head.

'Look, I've been thinking. Why don't you go off into town today? Without me. Have a nice day out.'

'A nice day out in Bulawayo? Is that possible?'

'Come on. First of all, you need to because we didn't get anything done on Monday. Secondly, then you could go and have a nice cup of coffee. You can't stay indoors all day, it's not good for you.'

All through Janet's childhood, her parents had subscribed to the idea that fresh air cured all ills. Whatever the ailment, a good walk outside would do you the world of good. It was something that bookish Janet had struggled with somewhat, especially as a teenager when she had just wanted to lie in that extra five minutes on a Saturday morning or read her book stretched out across her bed on a lazy afternoon.

'When I was in Kan,' her father would tell her occasionally, speaking of his time in a Japanese prisoner of war camp, 'I used to walk the length of the fence about seven times a day. It wasn't long, but I worked out it gave me a decent bit of exercise.'

'Weren't you out every day cutting down the jungle and hardly fed anything?' she had once asked. 'I wouldn't have felt like a walk if I had to do all that.'

'It's one thing someone forcing you to do something, it's

another choosing to do it,' was his reply and she had bitten her tongue and not made any reference to the fact that he might be forcing her to go for a walk. Her father was far from a jailer.

'Why don't you come with?' said Janet to her mother as she poured out some tea. 'This is all very ceremonious, isn't it? Having tea in the sitting room?'

'Your father and I used to do this every morning, if you remember.'

Janet thought. She wondered if her mother was right about that. Wasn't that only weekends? Then again, people seemed to have had so much more time forty years ago that perhaps it was quite likely that her parents started each day with this tea-drinking ritual.

'No, I am not going to come with,' said her mother, replying to the first question. 'I think you should go by yourself.'

'Mum, I don't mind. I really don't. Who am I going to talk to if you're not with me?' Janet smiled.

'You don't need to talk to anyone at all. It's probably better not to. Take a book, find a table in the corner and have five minutes to yourself.'

'Oh, Mum,' said Janet, putting down her teacup and coming over to her mother's side. 'Why do you always think you are a burden? You're not. You're really not.'

'Who said anything about me being a burden?' Her mother feigned a shocked look. 'Anyway, I'm your mother and you should listen to me. Mother knows best.'

They sat in silence for a couple of minutes and it struck Janet how light and cheerful her mother seemed. She could feel it herself. It was like a heavy coat had been thrown off. The sunlight filling the room gave the morning a sense of expectation: something was going to happen. For the first time in a long while she experienced an almost girlish excitement, a pull towards the day as though she must get up immediately and rush off and get dressed. She felt a shiver of anticipation and immediately chided herself.

'I wonder when the funeral will be?' she asked, getting up from her mother's side and returning to her chair. At once the room seemed to darken.

'Whenever they're ready, I suppose,' said her mother, taking a sip of tea and smacking her lips. 'Nice cup of tea. We must get that brand again.'

Janet didn't answer. Her mother seemed, perhaps unintentionally, callous. Yet it was hard to feel much sympathy for Marcia. It was just the shock really, Janet thought. The body... she stopped. There was something she had to do.

'All right, I'll go to town,' she said, standing up with sudden energy. 'Don't say I never take your advice.'

Chapter Fourteen

Janet reversed her car out of the short driveway with a certain burst of freedom. It reminded her of the time, many years ago now, when she passed her driving test. Her mother had taken her and brought her home and, when they got back, her father was waiting at the gate, sucking on his pipe. He had changed out of his work clothes for he was in a string vest and a pair of khaki shorts, which always embarrassed Janet when her friends came round. He was a doctor; she felt he should dress like one all the time, not like an inmate of a Russian gulag.

It wasn't just that. His body had never fully recovered from the time he had spent in the prisoner of war camp. His rib cage was visible under his skin: he had never relearnt the art of eating on his release in 1945; not that he was a picky eater: he couldn't bear to have wasted any food, but his portions were never large. He ate purely to fuel his body and never took food for granted. It was for that reason they hardly ever ate at restaurants; the servings were overwhelming and made him unhappy for days afterwards.

She had wanted to go for a drive. Somewhere. Anywhere. Her mother hadn't been too keen on the idea. After all, Janet had only *just* got her licence, but her father had waved her mother's concerns away with a wave of his pipe-holding hand. She had driven around the block and then up Twelfth, right down Borrow Street and right again down Selbourne Avenue. She had wanted to go somewhere, anywhere, just get on the road and head on out. She was eighteen. It was 1973. February and it hadn't rained for two weeks. The sun shone, the sky was blue. She had wanted to roll back the sunroof and drive along with a scarf round her head like Grace Kelly, except there wasn't a sunroof and she didn't have a scarf. Still, she had been excited. Young and excited.

Janet paused before reversing out onto the road. She glanced tentatively at herself in the rear view mirror and winced. She looked old: her face was lined and her skin, although soft, was broken by little red lines that hared off all over the place. It looked painful, although it wasn't, and Janet wished she could afford some makeup to hide the red marks.

She took a lipstick out of her handbag and applied a thin layer of red, rubbed her lips together, had another look at herself in the mirror, ran her hand through her hair to try and give its some 'oomph', rather than fuzz, and then turned back to the urgencies of the moment.

Nigel Pullman would be likely to be out. What about Dorcas? Janet wondered what her plans would be for the future. She recalled the time Dorcas had asked her for a job. She had been surprised, of course, for she knew Marcia paid her well and she got more than adequate accommodation. She remembered thinking Dorcas looked scared: she twisted her hands and looked over Janet's shoulder as she spoke as though there were someone there.

Janet couldn't afford Dorcas, couldn't even begin to compete with what she was used to and she had insisted that Dorcas stay with Marcia. Since then, Janet had found the young woman cold towards her. Sometimes the coldness bordered on insolence or a complete lack of interest in anything Janet said to her.

At the last book club meeting at Marcia's house, Janet had complimented Dorcas on how lovely the house was looking. She had expected Dorcas to be pleased, to smile and at least say thank you, but her face was blank and expressionless as she shrugged and turned away.

One road down from the Pullmans' was a nursery school with a high durawall. Janet parked her car – a blue Datsun Pulsar – here. There were two other cars outside so she wouldn't draw attention to herself by leaving the car here. She quickly walked back up the road and turned right. The Pullmans' house seemed to loom larger than ever in the clear winter light. She hadn't quite realised before how big the plot was. In comparison to the other houses on the street, it took up the equivalent of two stands. Janet wondered briefly who lived next door to them on the right hand side. The house was obviously lived in, but she had never seen anyone either go in or come out.

Janet couldn't help noticing how beautiful the garden was. It was the kind of garden she longed for: green and lush and full of all sorts of flowers. At one time, quite a few years ago now, she and her mother had thought of sinking a borehole in their garden. They had lived moderately well then on her parents' pensions. Every month, Janet would change a hundred pounds of it into Zimbabwe dollars and she and her mother would pay their bills and do a little shopping. They weren't big spenders. A treat was a carton of cream or a triangle of blue cheese and sometimes they bought a fillet of beef. With the introduction of the American dollar, it had all gone downhill. Prices had shot up; retailers continued to work a degree of inflation into their prices and general greed had ensued.

They had started to sell things: paperbacks and clothes, the not so treasured things at first and it had been a great way to get rid of a lot of rubbish. Then it was a couple of pictures, those that weren't too old and faded. Then a table, a bookcase and a set of tiny porcelain figures that Janet had known throughout her childhood.

The money received was a pittance. A week's groceries, sometimes not even that. The figurines paid for a large water bill, the result of a broken pipe underground in the garden. She had longed for the security of childhood: for her more than capable father who had loved her completely and protected her from all the evils of the world, the evils he himself had experienced so well. He had been so organised, leaving a clearly written will and making sure that she and her mother were well provided for by the investments he had made. But all the shares and securities, all his carefully laid plans had come to nothing, for no one, absolutely no one twenty-five years ago, could have predicted what was going to happen: inflation then hyper-inflation, then the introduction of the American dollar and the excessively high prices. The loss: how years of investments lost all value overnight. Her mother had cashed in her life insurance policy and bought a tray of eggs; Janet had sat stiffly in the chair as her investment advisor had told her the shares her father had bought years ago in a Zimbabwean mining company were now worth nothing; the company itself had filed for bankruptcy.

Janet had been gripped by fear each night when she went to bed. The dark shadow of poverty raised its ugly head as she lay and planned and plotted. Schemes, business ideas, loan proposals. But they were no more than that and really Janet couldn't blame anyone but herself. When she sat and looked at herself in the mirror every morning, at her dull skin and her lifeless eyes and the lines that seemed to multiply overnight, she didn't think that she would offer herself a loan either. But then one day, quite out of the blue, she had stumbled across a brilliant plan.

Janet rang the buzzer. At once she was taken aback by the familiarity of the action. She half expected to hear Marcia shouting for Malakai to open the gate.

'Dorcas. Good morning.' Janet didn't know why she had greeted the young woman in such a hearty way, and nor did Dorcas for she stared at Janet with wide eyes as though she had been caught doing something she shouldn't have been. On seeing Janet, her face relaxed into its usual blank stare.

'Good morning, madam,' she said in her low, monotone voice. Janet noticed she had dark rings around her eyes and her cheeks were sunken.

'Is anyone here... anyone else besides yourself, I mean? Police... or anyone like that?'

Dorcas shook her head. 'No, it is just me.'

'Good. I'm just returning some books, Dorcas. Some books that belonged to the madam.' Janet tapped her sling bag that rested on her hip and wished she could sound a little more natural and not as though she were talking to someone hard of hearing or a bit simple. She would never have made a good detective, she thought.

Dorcas put out her hands to take the books and Janet hesitated.

'I'll bring them in,' she said. 'I know where they go.'

Janet wondered if it were just her imagination or did Dorcas move so as to block Janet's way in.

'Mister Pullman says I must not let anyone in without his permission.

'But it's me, Dorcas. Just me. Mr Pullman knows me. He means other people. Strange people.'

Dorcas eyed Janet with deep suspicion and then stood aside uncertainly and Janet, smiling rather too brightly at first and then with a nervous hesitation, entered the house with clumsy, halting footsteps.

'Thank you. Won't be two seconds,' she called and walked a little faster, hoping that Dorcas would not follow her. She went into the large lounge and looked around blindly.

'It must be here. It must be here,' she kept saying to herself. Carefully, she closed the lounge door to the passageway, making sure that she did not make a sound as she did so and then she stole over to an old-fashioned writing desk in the corner. It was locked. Her heart sank. She pulled the drawer underneath the desktop and was surprised that it opened. Inside it were a couple of pads of flowery notepaper, a packet of airmail envelopes and various birthday and Christmas cards. Janet felt around the bottom of the drawer, but there was no key.

Next, she looked up on the mantelpiece. Her heart leapt when she saw a tortoiseshell jewellery box. She looked inside, but it was empty. She looked in all the vases and on the shelves. Aware of time moving by, she looked wildly round the room. Every time her eyes came back to the locked bureau. How did they do it in films with only a hairclip or a piece of wire?

She heard footsteps coming towards the room – the

floorboards creaked in these old houses – and quickly took the books out of her bag and put them in the box of book club books which was under a table. She turned to see Dorcas in the doorway, staring at her.

'Ah, Dorcas, just rearranging a couple of these books which aren't in the right order.'

The fact that none of the books in the box were in any order whatsoever was irrelevant, thought Janet, who didn't think Dorcas would have any idea as to how these things worked.

'Great,' she said, standing up. 'That's all sorted out at least.' Turning to Dorcas, she said brightly, 'That little writing table in the corner, I suppose it's locked, isn't it?'

Dorcas walked over and tried the lid. 'Yes,' she replied.

'Just wondering, just wondering, that's all,' Janet mumbled, contemplating whether she could get away with not giving an explanation at all. 'About the paperwork for book club. Not a problem. I'll phone Mr Pullman and ask him. Unless... you don't happen to know where the key is, do you?'

Dorcas looked at her blankly before shaking her head, making Janet feel mildly exasperated. What was wrong with the girl? Was she suffering from grief? Hardly, she had never seemed happy with Marcia. Maybe that was just the way she was, just her: one of those people who was never happy. And yet Janet couldn't help thinking there was some invisible burden on the woman's shoulders, something holding her down.

Janet made her way despondently back to her car. She had set off with a certain excitement and feeling of daring, but it had come to nothing. They must be in the house she thought. They must be. She got in the driver's seat and pulled her scarf loose from around her neck. She looked at herself again in the rear view mirror and was surprised to see a pinkness in her cheeks. She couldn't help but smile, but then looked away guiltily and started the car.

Later that morning, Edmund was back at Janet Peters' house.

'She is out,' said Loveness, duster in hand, leaning against the door jamb as though she didn't want him to come in.

'Do you know when she will be back? It is important that I speak with her.'

'She will be back just now,' she said shaking her duster emphatically. 'J-u-s-t now. Now now.' She obviously wanted to put him off, but also wanted to protect Janet in case, by being out, she had broken some law.

'I'll wait, thank you,' said Edmund. 'No transport.'

She took a deep breath and admitted defeat, let her hand slide to her side and opened the door so that he could go in. She showed him into the sitting room and, after giving a side table a quick dust over, made for the door.

'Your daughter is not with you today?' he asked, attempting a little light conversation.

'Daughter! Hah! You see my grey hair and you ask me about my baby daughter!'

'Your granddaughter is not with you today?' Edmund attempted the question again.

'She is in the kitchen. She is too small to be left alone.'

'Too young. You are lucky to have such understanding employers.'

'Yes.' She glared at Edmund, as though the situation were somehow his fault. 'Only women know how difficult it is to have a baby and a job.'

'Mrs Peters – was she here all day on Monday?'

Loveness's eyes narrowed. 'Why are you asking me questions? If you want to know, you must ask Mrs Peters.'

'I am asking you,' said Edmund noting her defensive manner.'

'She is here ev-ery day, ev-ery day with her mother.' Loveness wagged her finger at him. 'Not one day does she leave her by herself.'

'Except to go to work.'

The finger stopped in mid-air as Loveness conceded she may have exaggerated, but the acknowledgement was temporary and, if anything, gave her added momentum.

'There is *always* someone here. *Always*. Madam Peters does not go anywhere. To see friends, or to meet someone or to travel to Harare. No! South Africa, no! Botswana, no!'

'But she did go to book club alone?'

'I am here on those nights,' Loveness declared with a shrug of self-assurance as her hand fell by her side. 'People are struggling. We are all struggling. Why don't you leave people alone?'

'I'm a policeman investigating a death.' Edmund paused. 'In mysterious circumstances.' He hoped his words sounded suitably weighty. 'I can't always leave people alone.'

Loveness clicked her tongue with vehemence. 'Mrs Peters is a good woman.'

'Good. I assume she was here all day?'

She sucked her cheeks in and gave a little nod, as though afraid to give assent to something that may get Janet into trouble later on.

'The other madam, she is here?' asked Edmund, looking out of the window.

'The other one is sick. She is in a wheelchair.'

'Please tell her I am here. It is polite for her to know who is in the house.'

The maid raised her eyebrows, glanced about the room as if to make sure all was in order – or was she counting the ornaments? – and then left, closing the door behind her.

Edmund looked about him at the room. Janet Peters was by no means well off. Her whole life was frayed around the edges. Frayed or faded or stretched out of shape. She didn't seem to like Marcia Pullman, but was she glad she was dead? Edmund pulled his lips in and gave a little shake of his head – he was talking to himself again – but there was something unusual about her set up: two women living in a house in Suburbs, employing a maid, still needed an income. They still needed to pay bills and buy food and drive their small car.

'Go with how you feel in your heart,' he remembered Mr MacDougal saying, his hand over his left breast. 'It's your heart that knows, laddie.'

He had thought a lot of the MacDougals recently and was rather enjoying this trip into the past, however painful it was at times. Everything seemed to remind him of them, even this lounge, thought Edmund, looking around. It was a sparsely decorated room, in a way that had once been tasteful, but which was now considered old-fashioned. The furniture was old and heavy, the solid, square type from the 50s covered in a rose pink, rather worn chintz. Despite it all looking a little threadbare, there was something warm and unintimidating about it. Edmund felt a sudden urge to sit in an armchair and read the newspaper.

A long oak sideboard stood between two large windows that opened out onto the garden. It was covered in photographs. Edmund's eye was drawn to a black and white one of a man's profile. He was wearing an army officer's hat and the collar of his uniform was just visible. There was a wedding photo of the same man, this time in a light grey suit, with a woman in a white knee length dress. It was not a wedding dress, but it was smart and stylish and she wore a coat over it, buttoned at the waist. The woman held a small bunch of flowers as they stood on the steps to some sort of building, not a church. A registry office, Edmund guessed.

Another photo was of a young girl. It was a studio picture, the kind one used to go and sit for. It was almost a rite of passage at one time. A card his mother had called it. *We must get your card done.* He had vague memories of a hot afternoon, of being forced into his one and only suit, a little short in the legs, but nobody would see his ankles in the photo. His mother had ordered a taxi, a rare occurrence, which she hadn't even done when her brother Silas was on his deathbed and had called for her or when Tete Ruvimbo had had her baby and asked her to get the next train up to Harare, but she had insisted in case he got his clothes dirty.

He remembered seeing photos the other boys brought to school. Photos of holidays to Durban and fishing trips to the Zambezi. Barefooted white boys kneeling next to the impala they had shot or eating ice creams on the beach. The closest he got to such carefree exuberance was the photo of him next to the MacDougals' car. He was happy, grinning widely; it was a true moment of joy in his life, a far cry from the cardboard smile at the photographic studio.

On that occasion, he had been sullen, irritated with his mother. He had despised her for her excitement and her pride, her naivety in believing the photo was the culmination of something: success or happiness or education; a sign he was on the right road. Then how he had despised himself for all his ugly thoughts. He was her only child, her pride and joy; who was he to deny her happiness? Edmund felt a pang and wished he didn't feel himself superior to her in intelligence; wished he still believed in her as he had done as a young child.

He recalled how proud he had been of her as he sat at the MacDougals' dining table doing his homework when she would come into the dining room with a tray of highly polished cutlery and put it away in the drawer of the dresser ever so quietly in case the noise disturbed him. She would smile – the smile of a proud mother – and every time Mr MacDougal told her how clever he was, she would squeal with delight and clap her hands and thank God.

'A penny for your thoughts, officer,' said a voice and Edmund turned to see the elderly woman whom he had seen sitting in the garden the day before. She was in a wheelchair that she manoeuvred into the room and turned it so that she faced Edmund. 'Brr, it's cold in here. We hardly ever use this room.'

Edmund started. 'Good morning. Yes, it is cold, isn't it?' He smiled. 'Is this you?' He pointed at the wedding photo. Immediately he felt embarrassed, as though he had overstepped an invisible mark. 'I'm sorry, I was just looking at the photographs. They are interesting.' He stepped back and put his hands behind his back as though to demonstrate that he wasn't touching anything he shouldn't be. He waited for the comment, for the 'well, that's none of your business' or for the suspicious look that suggested he were casing the joint so that he could come back in the dead of night and rob them blind.

'Yes, that's my husband, Edward, and me on our wedding day in 1952.'

Despite her age, he could still trace elements of beauty in her face. She had high cheek bones and sharp blue eyes and that lovely soft pink skin that elderly white women have; women of a certain era who hadn't spent years basking in the sun. Women who have worn hats and gloves and for whom sun tanning was rather common.

'No wedding dress?'

No wedding dress? He bit his tongue, which seemed to have a life of its own this morning. This time she did look surprised and one eyebrow arched upwards as though Edmund had been rude or as though he were suggesting something wasn't quite au fait about the event.

'The war was over – except in my husband's mind. He could not abide any form of waste and frills and foppery were considered waste. It was a good suit though. Irish linen.'

Edmund smiled, a conciliatory smile. She was sharp about the edges and he had no wish to annoy her. They were difficult, this generation of white people. They had a respect for the law, a great respect often – the police was their first port of call in an emergency – and they were polite – very polite – called you 'Chief Inspector' and spoke kindly. But there was something else at the same time. There was no ease. The younger whites – the ones who had no faith in the police whatsoever – they were different. They didn't belong to a generation forbidden to speak to black people. They were more open, more relaxed, less on their guard.

'Your husband – he has passed away?' ventured Edmund, hoping his question wasn't too forward. Her eyes flickered downwards for half a second and her face softened.

'About twenty five years ago.'

'A long time to be on your own,' said Edmund, softly. Automatically, his hand stretched out towards the photo frame. He stopped and let it fall beside him. Her eyes, he noticed, narrowed and he realised he had struck a chord.

'You wanted to see my daughter, Chief Inspector? She's out at the moment. Shopping.'

'She's not back at work?'

'Tomorrow. They gave her a couple of days off at the shop.'

'I thought she might be resting at home and I could ask her some more questions.'

'We usually do our shopping on a Monday. We only go into town once a week and pay our bills. We'll top up with electricity and then we do a little shopping. All the new fruit and vegetables come in on a Monday at about eleven o'clock so we make sure we are at the supermarket by then. Then we change our books at the library and occasionally we may have a cup of coffee at the café next door. One has to be so careful these days, Chief Inspector, so frugal. We're usually home by one.'

Edmund, who had grown up on British detective novels, had an innate admiration for the British sense of time: people who could pinpoint exactly where they were at exactly what time. 'I left the room at seven minutes to six, officer.' or 'The murder couldn't possibly have happened before ten o'clock as, at approximately three minutes after the hour, I saw Mr Johnson in his garden.'

Routine, he often said to Mary when he came home and saw her talking to her neighbour over the low wall that separated the properties, is the backbone of our day. He hated the lack of structure in her day: the slapdash attitude to meal times, the way she lay in bed for an extra twenty minutes in the morning, how she wasted time talking and braiding friends' hair. Mary's life was governed by the movement of the sun across the sky, not by the measured tick of the clock.

'You didn't go shopping on Monday, Mrs...?'

'Whitstable. No. I wasn't feeling well at all – pain. I had a hip replacement last year. It wouldn't heal properly and it has been endless trouble ever since. That's what has put me in here. My... ' She motioned to the wheelchair.

'I'm sorry.'

'Why? It's not your fault.' She sighed and shrugged. 'I've had a good life, Inspector. If I had the choice, I wouldn't end it like this, but one does not always have a choice. There are things we have control over and things we have absolutely no control over and you just have to trust the process of life on those occasions.'

'You believe in fate?'

She thought for a second. 'A flexible fate,' she decided. 'It's all about this.' She tapped her head. 'Thoughts determine one's fate as much as character. The tragedy of life is that most people look to some outside influence instead of inside themselves.'

Edmund looked away. He had a feeling he was being pulled into a conversation he didn't want to enter into. Fate, God, the meaning of life: conjecture and supposition, but not much besides. He had had enough of that growing up and having to listen to his mother ramble on about the Holy Spirit. He delicately tried to turn the conversation to book club.

'Did Janet go shopping?

'No. I had had a bad night's sleep. I told Janet I'd be all right, but she insisted on staying with me.'

'Until she went to book club?'

'Yes. It was me who insisted then. I told her she *must* go. I didn't want her getting into trouble with Marcia.'

Edmund nodded, but let the comment go. 'Who looks after you when your daughter isn't here?'

'I don't need looking after!' She waved the suggestion away with her hand. 'Watching, sometimes, in case I fall, but not looking after! When I'm in this, I'm all right.' She tapped the arm of the wheelchair. 'Loveness is always here if Janet isn't and that's not often besides when she's at work. She bought me a cell phone as well. I haven't a clue how to use it, but it makes Janet feel better. When Janet has book club, Loveness works the morning and then has the afternoon off and comes back in the evening. It works for all of us. I rather think she enjoys watching the television.'

Edmund's gaze now shifted to a small bookcase next to the dresser. He ran his eyes along the titles swiftly.

'You like crime,' he smiled, looking up at her. Her eyebrow raised slightly again in surprise. Edmund had experienced this sort of reaction before from people who didn't imagine he would recognise titles and authors. Policemen weren't supposed to be well-read.

The Bookcase Glance, as Edmund referred to it, was an introduction to all sorts of things. What someone read could often suggest opinion, and opinion, character and motivation.

'Yes,' she said. 'I do like a good murder.' There was a hint of a smile on her face as she added: 'A fictional one, of course.'

'In books everything is solved,' said Edmund, hooking out a novel with his forefinger. He opened it to the first page. 'Number 310. Lesley.' He read and then shrugged.

'Book club,' she said. 'Janet gets them for me. Lesley is the person who owns the book.'

'I see. You don't want to go there yourself?'

She shook her head and indicated the wheelchair.

'You could still go,' insisted Edmund.

'No, no.' She turned the wheelchair and approached the window. 'It's Janet's night off. Her evening out away from me. Why should she wheel me around there as well?'

From behind, Edmund saw an old lady with white hair. Her shoulders were slightly hunched over.

'Besides,' she added, looking some way out into the garden, 'I couldn't stand her, you know, I really couldn't stand her.'

'Mrs Pullman?'

'Yes, Marcia.' She turned the wheelchair round to face Edmund. 'She was a real *bitch*, Chief Inspector. A right bloody bitch. And I tell you what, I'm glad she's dead. I'm really very glad.'

Chapter Fifteen

Edmund wasn't quite sure if he was shocked by Mrs Whitstable's outburst or not. Because she was elderly and in a wheelchair, perhaps there was an assumption she should be meek and passive, living with her fragility with a kind of "Little Nell" smiling acceptance, but it was more likely to be the other way round. Those who are most bitter are those who have been most disappointed, and disappointment springs from hope and expectation.

Edmund knew all about disappointment, although he had never thought of himself as a bitter person. In fact, he had an unusual capacity to buoy himself along, mindful always of his dream, which he kept constantly before him, a dream of one day running a competent police force and fighting crime effectively. It wasn't bitterness, but sadness he faced; a raw lonely sadness which ate away initially, but which he had come to live with.

'Why did you dislike her so much?' His voice was soft. The clock ticked with a calm gentleness, dissipating the vindictiveness of her words.

'She was greedy. Nothing was ever enough. She had so much money and yet she wanted more. She took, she never gave.'

'From what I have seen, she looked after her domestic workers very well.'

She gave a scornful laugh in response. 'Marcia never did anything unless it served a purpose. Yes, she had lovely servants' quarters by all accounts. She wasn't one for overcrowded hovels with blackened walls and children playing in the dirt. Oh no, Marcia couldn't put up with some ghetto at the back. Everything was for show, even the people who worked for her. They had show homes as a bonus, but tell me – were they happy? No. Not at all.'

'How do you know?'

She pointed her finger and said with something of the air of a schoolmistress, 'What's her name, the maid there? She's asked Janet for a job more than once. How could Janet give her a better salary? The wonderful salary, the accommodation – it was all a trap, Chief Inspector. An exquisite Venus flytrap; beautiful and exotic and enticing, but once the poor creature is there – SNAP! There is no leaving. She kept people with money. In this country at this time what do people want more than anything, more than happiness? Money.'

'Why did she want so much to keep her workers? Jobs are so hard to come by, she could easily have changed them every month.'

'Ah, but a woman like Marcia Pullman does not do so, Chief Inspector. She spends a lot of time training her staff into doing things just the way she wants. I have no doubt that her maid is probably quite a capable young woman. Good brain, but no opportunities, like so many young girls. In another place, in another life, she could've had a good job in a shop or done clerical work, or perhaps even gone to university. Things being what they are, however, she is a maid.' Mrs Whitstable smacked her lips together and gave Edmund a look to say that she knew what she was talking about.

'What about the gardener?'

'Oh, he'll be the same. Taught how to prune and plant and take a cutting. How to clean the pool and shown where to go if sent on errands. Oh yes, one doesn't have to do too much if one's servants are in order.'

'And yet he cleans the car with Vim,' mused Edmund, a little smile on his face.

'Oh dear. Really, he did that?'

'Yes. Someone cleans the car for two and half years with car shampoo and water and then one day they clean it with Vim.'

Mrs Whitstable smiled. 'Well, there's no accounting for human nature, is there? We had a young girl who worked for us many years ago now. Violet, her name was. I had a beautiful red dress that I often wore if my husband and I were going out for the evening. It wasn't washable, but I didn't take it to the dry cleaner's every time I wore it, I rubbed out any spots and checked it for marks and put it back in the cupboard. I showed Violet how to do this and she did it for at least three years with no problems at all. Then one evening, I went to take it out of the cupboard and – there it was, hanging there as it always did – with white spots on it.'

'White spots?'

'Bleach. Well, that was it, of course. The dress had to be thrown away.'

'What happened to Violet? Did you fire her?'

'No. I was angry and threatened all sorts of things, but in the end I had to accept there was nothing I could do.' She gave a wry laugh. 'She left soon afterwards of her own accord. Sometimes I think she wanted to get fired.' She shrugged.

A silence sprang up between them. The tick of the clock seemed to fill the air. Edmund stared at the timepiece and wondered if he should go and then come back. He was surprised to find Mrs Whitstable looking at him. Her sharp blue eyes seemed to be doing some kind of analysis of him.

'You have an intelligent face, Chief Inspector. I think you are a very clever man.'

'Thank you,' replied Edmund, rather surprised and awkward. He was momentarily reminded of Auntie Nonnie, his mother's sister, pulling at his cheeks when he was about twelve. 'Soo handsome, huh. Beautiful boy.'

'You don't believe me, do you?'

Edmund smiled a self-deprecating half smile.

'Believe me. When you've lived as long as I have you learn to separate the wheat from the chaff. In your life, you will meet a lot of people who will try to make themselves appear clever or handsome or good. You will learn to see who is real.'

Edmund had an odd feeling then, as though Mrs Whitstable wasn't really a person, but a being, a messenger.

He looked across at her frail frame, her hands with the fat blue-black veins rising out and pitted with liver spots and freckles, and the idea disappeared into nothing.

'I went to Sir Herbert Stanley Primary School,' he said, without really knowing why he said it. In his embarrassment he wanted to find a reason for his intelligence, as though it wasn't his, like he didn't deserve it. 'I was very fortunate to have been sent there by my mother's employers.'

Her wry smile broadened. 'You're very lucky. But intelligence has little to do with education. I know a lot of educated people who aren't very clever at all.' She wheeled her chair round to the door. 'You must excuse me, Chief Inspector, I get so tired these days. I need a little nap. It was so nice talking to you. I don't know what time Janet will be home, but I'll tell her you called. Does she have your telephone number?'

'Yes, yes, she does,' said Edmund. 'And I have hers. I'll arrange a proper meeting with her. Good morning, Mrs Whitstable.'

1979

'Do you want to play?'

Edmund looked up from his book. It was Rupert Hargreaves. He was swinging along the monkey bars in the playground and now let go and dropped to the ground. Surprised, Edmund looked around. There was no one else nearby. Rupert heaved himself back on the bars; Edmund went back to his book. Every now and then he looked at Rupert over the top of the page. Eventually he put the book down, slipping it into his satchel. He stood by the side of the jungle gym, watching Rupert swing across. When he got to the other side, Edmund hauled himself up and reached out for the first rung. His elbow joints pulled as he made his way across the bars; right hand, left hand, right hand, left hand. His legs swung beneath him, the momentum pushing him along. When he got to the end, Rupert was waiting for him.

'Can you do this?' he asked and swung his feet up between the bars, hooking his knees over them and dropping his head down so that he hung upside down. Then he folded his arms across his chest. Edmund followed suit. Rupert nodded his approval, suspended as he was like a bat in a cave.

'Clap your hands.'

Edmund clapped his hands.

'Touch the ground.'

Edmund reached tentatively towards the ground. 'I can't touch it. My arms aren't long enough.'

'Touch your head.'

Edmund touched his head.

Rupert was rather red in the face now. He pulled himself up and dropped to the ground. So did Edmund.

'My mom's here,' Rupert said, picking up his satchel from under the tree. 'I'll see you tomorrow.'

Edmund watched him go. 'See you tomorrow,' he called, hardly raising his voice. 'Goodbye.'

After leaving Mrs Whitstable, Edmund felt restless and decided to walk down to the Pullmans' house and have another look around. He wanted to talk to Dorcas again and, when he found the gate closed but unlocked, he assumed she was there.

Although in the same suburb, and in fact separated by only two streets, Janet's and Marcia's houses couldn't be more different. Janet's was suspended in time – the dry rose garden with the broken sundial and that musty smell that was present even out of doors; paths that no longer led anywhere, the door knocker mended with putty. Janet's old was a poor old, the old of worn carpets, paperbacks with broken spines and chipped porcelain jugs. Marcia's old was different. She had antiques: a walnut writing table, crystal wine glasses and Persian rugs. A wide verandah swept down to a soft blanket of emerald green grass. A path led to an ornamental fish pond full of carp and goldfish, and various other paths led off across the immaculate lawn. The flowerbeds overflowed with lavender, roses, nasturtiums, dianthus, daisies and snapdragons, while a creeper of early jasmine hung full of scent along the fence.

When no one answered the buzzer, Edmund pushed the gate. It slid open easily. He walked up the drive to the back door. It was locked, as was the front door. He decided to have a wander around the premises. At the back, a wall cut off the servants' quarters from the rest of the garden and another lower wall to the left of this marked out a vibrant herb and vegetable garden. Edmund peered into it over a black iron gate: fat, ripe runner beans hung, heavy and green, tied to wooden stakes; great flowers of broccoli and cauliflower pushed their heads through soft black soil; peas clambered up a wooden frame on the back wall. All this life, thought Edmund, all this life carrying on.

Edmund peered round the wall into the servants' quarters; the building consisted of two separate living quarters, both of which were shut up. The outside doors were painted bright blue and large pots of lavender were placed on either side of both doorsteps. A large black bin was placed round the side of the building. Everything was very neat. Spick and span was the saying, thought Edmund, briefly remembering Mrs MacDougal using it in her broad Scottish accent. Not bad for servants' quarters. Some people don't know how good they have it – or was it an exquisite Venus flytrap as Mrs Whitstable had suggested?

Edmund thought of the expression on Dorcas's face that first evening, of the dull, blank look in her eyes. Was she bored – or scared? Edmund stood still a moment, his chin raised a little as he thought. Was she hiding something – about herself or someone else – or was she merely a young woman who didn't really like her job, but did it out of necessity, waiting for the day when she could leave? He thought of the small red moons of nail polish left on her nails. There was something about Dorcas that was all wrong. He thought again of Mrs Whitstable's words. *In another place, in another life.* Was it that she could have a better job and be someone else? Young girls didn't want to be maids anymore; they wanted cell phones and wigs and high heel shoes. But jobs were hard to come by and at least this one provided good accommodation, which was rare.

Edmund thought of the room at the MacDougals' that he had shared with his mother, who had kept them neat and spotlessly clean although they were dark and shabby: the ceiling board sagged dangerously in the middle after a particularly heavy rainy season and there was no indoor tap, only a sink outside in which his mother washed all their clothes and the cutlery and crockery. She boiled water for his bath on the fire and poured it into a big metal tub. He remembered dancing round in agony on more than one occasion because the water was far too hot.

The gardener, Nyathi, lived in the room next door to them. He was old and missing many of his teeth and those left stuck out at various angles, brown and yellow, like falling tombstones in a deserted graveyard. He was a nasty, cantankerous old man who could sometimes be heard laughing to himself, the sinister whoop of the hyena who hunts at night. Once when Edmund was having a bath outside in the tin tub, Nyathi had come round the corner and, instead of walking on, had stopped and looked closely at him, running his tongue over his protruding teeth and then sucking his lips in with a slippery slurping sound. Edmund had drawn his knees up to his chest and crossed his arms which made the old man cackle with an unsettling delight and then walk on to his room.

The reason the khaya was usually screened off was because no one wanted to see – or know – what was going on behind it. The one occupied by Dorcas was different – pots of lavender, curtains hung properly at the windows, a brightly painted door: all a far cry from the usual: the family crouched in the dirt or huddled around the cooking pot on a small fire in the yard; pokey windows with rags of curtains looped up at erratic intervals. He knocked on the door, but no one answered. He pushed the door, but it was locked and the curtains at the window were drawn.

He walked back the way he had come, stopping again to look at the vegetables, and noticed a few weeds pushing their way surreptitiously through the earth. A couple of the butternuts were browning and the beans were more than ripe, yet no one had picked them. Edmund turned and looked back towards the khaya. Something was wrong about the whole picture. Something wasn't joining up, not meeting. Marcia Pullman was a woman whom no one seemed to like, yet she was so generous to her maid. Where was the maid now? The husband was still living in the house, although he was away all day. Edmund knew he was the sort of man who was unlikely to make his own bed. He probably liked a full breakfast in the morning and a neat house. So where was she?

He walked round the side of the house to the kitchen. He saw a floor cloth hanging out to dry on the kitchen pipes and leant over to feel it. It was damp. He pursed his lips. The maid who never seems to be at work, he thought.

He walked round the front of the house and was just about to try the front door again in a re-enactment of Janet's steps when he thought he noticed a movement in the garden. He walked round the side of the house treading quietly and saw a figure kneeling on the verandah, looking into the lounge window. From the back, it looked like a man, but when the figure stood up and turned, he saw it was a woman with dark hair in a short sleek bob.

She jumped when she saw him and looked surprised and rather embarrassed.

'Good morning,' she greeted him, eyeing him with some hesitation. 'I'm sorry, I'm' – she turned back towards the house and gestured vainly – 'looking for someone. I tried the front door,' she added by way of explanation.

'You are looking for Mr Pullman?' asked Edmund. 'He's at work still.'

'No, Mrs Pullman. Marcia. I believe she lives here.'

'Can I ask why you have come to see Mrs Pullman?' asked Edmund, approaching her slowly. By the olive hue of her skin, he reckoned she was of mixed race. She was certainly very striking.

'She has an appointment with me at twelve,' she answered, a look of slight perturbation crossing her face. 'Sorry, is there something wrong? Where's Marcia?'

'You obviously haven't heard,' began Edmund. He hated this sort of thing, delivering bad news. 'I am afraid she has died.'

'Died?' She took a deep intake of breath, her hand clasping her chest. 'What – how? I don't understand. She had an appointment.'

She wasn't indignant, but surprised, as though death were no excuse for Marcia to miss an appointment.

It was Edmund's turn to ask questions. 'You knew the deceased?' It was such an awful term to use that he regretted his words as soon as he said them. Deceased? What was he talking about? That was office jargon. He was like one of the officers who sat and took calls and filled in incident reports that were then filed for eternity in a growing stack of paperwork on a back shelf somewhere.

'Well, no. Not really,' she admitted. 'I'm not related or anything like that. I'm... well... I'm here to give her a treatment.'

'A treatment?'

'Yes, I'm' – she hunted in her bag and brought out a card, which she handed to Edmund – 'a therapist.' She said the last word a little loudly as though it needed enunciation. Or was she embarrassed, Edmund wondered? It was almost like a rubbish collector might announce himself as a garbage technician, with a self-conscious emphasis that in itself was a giveaway.

Edmund looked at the card. Sandra Smith. Life coach and therapist. Auras cleansed. Positive thinking coach. Colour therapist. Pet therapist.

'Pet therapist,' read Edmund slowly. 'You're a vet?'

'No, no,' she gave a short, embarrassed laugh. 'I sort out any problems you might have with your pet.'

'Problems?'

'Yes, you know, if your dog has a stronger personality than you and won't listen then I can, well, sort it out.'

'I see,' said Edmund, not sure that he did really. 'Mrs Pullman had a problem with her dog?'

'No, no. Not at all. She wanted some advice – I think. I can't say.'

'Do you mind if I ask you some questions, Mrs Smith?'

'Miss – Ms – Smith,' she corrected him. 'No, ask away.'

'Ms Smith. You see, Mrs Pullman was stabbed,' said Edmund, simply, watching her gasp again in horror.

'That's terrible. Absolutely terrible.' She shook her head, her forehead furrowed into a frown of concern.

'She was already dead,' Edmund added, 'but she was stabbed nonetheless.'

'Oh?' Sandra looked at him, uncertain how to proceed.

'Was she upset about something? Was that why she called you in?'

'I don't know,' said, Sandra. 'I really don't know. She phoned me and made an appointment. That's all I know.'

'And you usually go to someone's house? They don't come to you?'

'Not always. Some people want to be in the privacy of their own homes. Some people like being in a totally different place.'

'This was her first appointment?'

'Yes.'

'And she didn't say what it was for?

She hesitated a moment, seemed about to say something and then didn't.

'I really don't know.' She looked Edmund straight in the eye, but he did not believe her.

'Can I ask you why you were looking in through the door?'

'I wanted to see if she was home.'

'You were not content with the fact that no one came to the gate when you buzzed?'

'I – well, no. No, I suppose not. She told me that the gate doesn't work and to just come in. It wouldn't be locked. I knocked on the door, but no one answered. I thought – that maybe she hadn't heard me. Or that perhaps she was asleep.'

Edmund didn't say anything. He was about to ask her more about her job when his phone rang. The earpiece was damaged so that he had to put on loudspeaker to hear anything at all. He felt self-conscious as the voice on the other end boomed through.

'Inspector Dube?' Edmund was so used to people giving him the wrong title that he didn't bother to correct them anymore.

It was Craig Martin. 'Yes, Mr Martin.'

'There's something I've been thinking about. About Monday. I don't really want to discuss it on the phone. Would you be able to come round to my house?'

Aware that the conversation could be heard, Edmund walked down the verandah steps and onto the grass. 'Yes, give me about forty-five minutes to an hour. I'll be there.' He hoped the information was worth it as he would now have to catch two minibuses across town and two back.

'Ms Smith,' said Edmund, slipping his cell phone back into his pocket. 'I may need to ask you some more questions.'

She looked slightly alarmed and then shrugged her shoulders. 'If I can help in any way, I will, sir,' she said, sounding exactly like a schoolgirl in front of the headmaster. In fact, there was something very schoolgirlish about her, Edmund thought. The petite frame, the bobbed hair and rather childlike way of folding her arms across her chest as though she were carrying a load of school books. 'You have my card.'

They walked down the drive together to the front gate. Edmund saw her car parked outside. She wasn't being very discreet if she had ulterior motives.

'Which way are you going?' she asked as she unlocked her door. 'Perhaps I can give you a lift.'

'Bradfield. Opposite the Trade Fair grounds.'

'Sure. Jump in.'

Edmund got in the passenger seat and put on his seat belt. He felt suddenly the joy of having your own transport and imagined it was him driving. The Saint in his Hirondel beating it down Twelfth Avenue while all stood by and watched. Edmund smiled faintly. He would never have made a private eye he was sure.

Chapter Sixteen

Craig didn't know why he had asked Edmund if he was religious or not. He assumed all black people were. Even African dictators and leaders of genocides seemed to hold onto their faith. In fact, it seemed to buoy them up at times and give their senseless actions a hint of a meaning. Or at least that's how Craig felt.

Edmund wasn't a dictator, yet there was something about the policeman's calm, quiet ways that unnerved Craig. The big, hearty guffawing type of policeman one could joke around with, perhaps share anecdotal evidence about the problems with women or the cost of a bottle of scotch – there was none of that feeling with Edmund. With him, one had the sense one was talking to a – what was it? A priest? No, priests were often smug and distant; at least Catholics were in his experience. A lawyer? A judge? A teacher? Edmund seemed to belong in his own category. Not of his time. That was the phrase that occurred to Craig as he stood at his kitchen sink, washing a mountain of ash down the plughole, a phrase that fitted the quiet policeman in his long coat very well. It was as though he had stepped out of the pages of a novel. Craig couldn't imagine where he lived or what he did in his time off. Edmund wasn't the sort of person one imagined in a pair of shorts or watching a football match on TV, beer in hand, shouting at the screen.

Craig felt a vague sense of disquiet, as though he had shown his true feelings to someone he knew very little about. Perhaps it had all gone over his head. Perhaps he wasn't going to come back with copies of *The Watchtower* or some other form of salvation, or even just pray privately for Craig or light a candle in church. Maybe he was just a normal guy who enjoyed kicking a ball around and liked the ladies. Yet somehow, Craig didn't think so.

Craig had noticed the lack of a reply to his comment about religion. It probably meant Edmund was part of some weird apostolic cult, or maybe he was a Jehovah's Witness. He always found them rather cagey about their choice of religion, as though you weren't to utter its name. He remembered a man he had once given a lift to. He was white and Craig was always wary of giving white people lifts. Why didn't they have a car? If they didn't have one, it was often either because they were elderly and couldn't afford to run a car on their pensions, or down and out.

The elderly he didn't mind. He admired their spunk, the way they took to walking everywhere as though it were a Boy Scout expedition. He had even given a lift to an elderly woman who had a packed lunch with her because she hoped to find somewhere cool and quiet to stop and have a bite to eat. But other white people were more suspect. Drink was usually the reason they had nothing. You could smell it when they got in the car, a mixture of stale body odour and alcohol, and you could smell it long after they had got out.

Craig detested this sort; they unnerved him, perhaps because they made him realise the only thing that stood between him and them was a 1975 Renault 4. He had become very circumspect as to whom he gave a lift. This man, the one who turned out to be a Jehovah's Witness, looked quite clean and respectable. He had on a white shirt and a tie and there was nothing in his demeanour that was lacking or begging. He was just a man looking for a lift. But once inside the car he began to talk in riddles. He was going for an interview because he had been fired from his last job and Craig had raised his eyebrows in alarm. Was he a drinker after all? But then it turned out that he had been fired because he refused to wear a Santa hat over the Christmas period.

'I don't believe in Christmas,' he had said to Craig, their eyes meeting in the rear view mirror. The man was sitting in the back on account of Craig's shopping – two bottles of whisky, a carton of cigarettes, a packet of polony and a cabbage (it was reduced to clear) – taking up the passenger seat. 'The world is still waiting for the birth of the Messiah.' That had been it; that was all he said. After he had dropped him off, Craig had wondered why the man had been so secretive about his beliefs. What was the problem? Perhaps he feared being dumped on the side of the road. In some way, Craig recognised the man's reticence as a sly invitation to join him, a bit like having some sexual rendezvous in a lay-by on the side of the road. Nothing said, but everything meant. Rather like joining the Masons, he thought. Secret handshake, knowing glances, certain telling words used in otherwise innocuous greetings.

Craig was a Catholic, however, and that in itself was like being a Mason. You could never leave. Even if you renounced it, decried it, threw your willing self onto the sacrificial bed of Anglicanism or paganism or even atheism, there was always some small, but very significant part of you that remained the property of the Catholic Church. Craig sometimes imagined the Vatican City must have a huge room, among all its other huge rooms, that was a record room of all the souls who had absconded in some way or other. A bit like lost library books, they still belonged to the Church and, as such, should be taken back. Sometimes they were, like books found forty years after the borrower had taken them out because stamped all over them in huge capital letters was IF FOUND, PLEASE RETURN.

He had had, a long time ago now, a girlfriend who became Born Again. It had been one of the singularly most devastating moments in Craig's life, the day she had come to him and said she had something wonderful to tell him. They had been together about three or four months and were still at the early stage of getting to know each other. Craig was young then, about twenty-two, and he had a long way to go before he grew bitter and cynical. He didn't even smoke, and, although his hair was still à la mullet, at least it was in fashion then.

It had flashed across his mind that she was going to tell him she loved him; that she wanted to be with him always and, although the thought was an overwhelming one, a large part of him had rejoiced in the sensation that he had found his soulmate. The joy was short-lived as she told him how she had found Jesus and that she wanted to share the love of God with him. The news had knocked him sideways. God was something you thought seriously about when you were old and just about knocking on heaven's door. It wasn't relevant when you were young; at least not before forty. He had looked at her, at her beautiful clear skin and her soft brown hair and thought that dying was so far away; it was incomprehensible. For that's what God was for, wasn't it?

He had listened to her speak about how religion was to be lived, how it must be a part of their lives, how she wanted to live and live and feel the bountiful love of Jesus. With much trepidation, he had gone along with it for a while, although his answers to her questions as to whether he 'felt it' were always rather non-committal. He wasn't quite sure what he was supposed to feel – an overwhelming love? A light shining in his face? A sensation of walking on air? These were things he felt when he looked at her, not a bearded man in robes who seemed to stand between him and any kind of happiness he had ever had.

He went along to the Church, too, for a bit. They were greeted at the door by overly-enthusiastic boys with acne and their jeans pulled up just that little bit too high. She saw them as warm and friendly, he as strange and predatory. He suspected their quick, sharp movements and their all-too-friendly hugs and slaps on the back. Inside, were more of the same, both male and female. A group stood at the front, clustered around microphones. A young man with longish hair and a droopy moustache played the guitar and a thin, wispy woman in extremely tight jeans and T-shirt that showed her midriff swooned over a keyboard. Always a keyboard, Craig often thought, never a piano.

They sang and closed their eyes in ecstasy and all but made love to the microphones they gripped in one hand while the other stretched up to the ceiling and beyond.

'Yes, Jesus, yes,' they cried as the music played on and on, verse after verse, the chorus repeated ad nauseam.

'What a friend we have Jesus. What a friend. Yes, sirree,' a man at the pulpit had once declaimed. 'He's my friend; he's my buddy. He's not some person way up there.' He gesticulated towards the iron roof of the church, if it could be called this as it was an old warehouse. 'He's here. He's here.'

Craig had looked around briefly for a man in robes and sandals, but everyone was in jeans and T-shirts. The same man had talked about a 'guy' called Paul who had been a non-believer and how, when he had been converted, he had to tell all his buddies about it.

'Now imagine you're at a braai with a few oans and you're having fun, maybe having a couple of beers and this dude appears. "Hey," he says, "Have you heard of the Son of God? You haven't? Well, have I got something to share with you."'

This is perhaps when Craig shifted the most uneasily in his chair (not pew). As a Catholic, he had always imagined God to be serious; a solemn man who sat before the huge open book of life in white flowing robes and wrote slowly and deliberately with a stiff white quill, recording each misdemeanour, action and good deed with methodical accuracy. Craig couldn't quite imagine either Him or Jesus as one of the 'oans'. It was hard enough imagining God smiling, never mind cracking open a Castle and knocking it back.

He loved the formality of the Catholic Church, even if he didn't believe anything they said. The silence, the incense, the swish of robes, the feeling of something greater than oneself looking down from the heavens, not across from you in a pair of jeans and a tie-dye T-shirt.

At forty-two, Craig couldn't deny that he was drawn towards it all, the comfort and security religion offered. It was why he never made fun of believers. He understood that need and only wished he hadn't lost the belief. It would be great to live with the assurance of something to watch over you and guide you; something to pray to; to believe with all certainty in an afterlife, a place of peace. A new life.

Always he felt the loss of that faith. It was like the loss of a childhood belief in fairies or Father Christmas. What was the difference in those beliefs – God and Father Christmas – except that at a certain age someone told you the truth about the latter and let you go on with the former? What would life be like as an adult if you still believed in a great fat bearded man who came down the chimney once a year? You'd be mad. Yet a God who was never seen, never had been seen, lived on and on – and on.

Sometimes, at Christmas maybe, although he had spent at least eight of the past ten Christmases alone and sad and often drunk, he caught whiffs, glimpses of that old belief. Just briefly, for seconds maybe, and it almost hurt, that pull to the past, to something that can never be resurrected. Then the brief blanket of security, that child-like conviction that no harm could ever come to him, was whipped away and he was left standing, shivering in the cold knowledge of his aloneness, of his vulnerability, his mortality.

He lay in bed that evening, thinking of the events of the past couple of days. He had given up trying to finish a novel he had been ploughing through for the past month or so. It involved a crime and a private investigator called Manning and various beautiful women with names like Giselle and Luciette, who either lay next to the swimming pool in scanty bikinis drinking martinis, or performed Kung Fu stunts in catsuits while looking wickedly appealing. Trash. Craig had long ago worked out who the criminal was. It didn't take long to work his way round ridiculously obvious red herrings and characters that were far too suspicious to be *it*. He looked at the lettering of the author's name – D.P. Radley – in bold black font on the cover. Who was he when he wasn't writing novels? Was he some great swashbuckling type who wrote books with one hand and held a cigar in the other? A man who lived on an enormous ranch in America somewhere with moose heads hanging on the wall and large boisterous dogs at his feet? Some ruddy-faced ex-policeman who wanted to share his experiences with the world? Or was he some lonely no one? A small man, hunched over slightly, strands of hair brushed from one side of his balding head to the other. Someone everyone overlooked. Someone who projected his sorry one-roomed life into the character of Manning, a brave, confident womanising detective who drove fast cars and drank whisky late at night in bars full of sexy women?

Craig found himself wondering about the drawbacks of being an author. Did you ever run out of plots or ideas? Did you ever worry that you had become boring and predictable? He looked at the cover of the book. It had a cigarette burn right where the breasts of the bikini clad Luciette should be, a wide gaping brown hole through which the words of the first page showed. It had belonged to Craig's dad who had given his books to his son when he moved into a nursing home in Harare.

'Here, I can't take any of these,' he had said, shoving a box into Craig's arms. 'There's not room to swing a cat.'

Craig hadn't wanted them at first and had left them in the car intending to drop them off at the SPCA shop whenever he was passing. Except he didn't seem to pass it. On one long, boring Sunday, he rediscovered the box and had idly picked up the first book to hand and started to read a few pages.

The sun was high in the sky by the time Manning awoke. He lit a cigarette and lay back against the pillow. A figure moved next to him. It was the beautiful Ronette from the Tropicana Club on 48th Street. Her soft, ivory skin complemented his tough, tanned skin. He was a man of the outdoors. A man of adventure.

Craig was drawn to the simplicity of the words, the quick moving plot and a world that was intrinsically uncomplicated and easy to navigate. Every book was the same: the indomitable Manning, his way with women, his quick thinking mind, his lack of a need to be with anyone on a full-time basis. He didn't get lonely or down or even very philosophical. He was always himself.

Craig looked at the picture of Manning with his silky brown moustache, in his open shirt and the jeans with the large buckle, standing feet akimbo and pointing his gun towards the reader. He'd be old now if he were real. He might even be dead. What happened to old investigators? Did they marry the last blonde they encountered and settle down in some safe, quiet life in a cabin in the mountains – or maybe by the sea, taking long walks across the beach every day and writing their memoirs? Or did they die in single rooms in old age homes?

Craig found himself thinking of Shantelle and whom she would have put Manning in touch with had he joined the agency. He wondered how Manning would have fared with Coralee and Jade, whether he too would have gone home and got drunk?

'Women,' thought Craig, 'are the bane of a man's life. Beautiful women...' He found himself falling asleep. Images swam in front of him. There was Edmund sitting across from him at the table and Marcia Pullman's house and Jade's scornful smile. The office, Shantelle and roses. Suddenly, his eyes opened and he sat up a little. Dorcas, that's who he was remembering. He turned onto his side and closed his eyes again. He must phone Edmund the next day and tell him about Dorcas.

Chapter Seventeen

Craig Martin greeted Edmund at the door like an old friend.

'Inspector! *Chief* Inspector, even. Please, this way.' He made a sweeping gesture with his arm.

Edmund entered rather gingerly. The gloom of the small hallway hit him immediately, smelling as it did of stale cigarette smoke and something overly sweet, which was somewhere between air freshener or deodorant and the smell of cheap confectionary. However, he was pleasantly surprised to find Craig had attempted a clean-up of his dining area, even if everything had just been piled on one end of the table. He had also opened the windows and a light breeze blew in, lifting the thin faded curtains.

Craig had been in the middle of making tea and he returned to this task with cheerful gusto, fishing the teabag out of the milky mess and squeezing it so hard against the side of the mug that it tore.

'Tea, Chief Inspector?'

Edmund hesitated. 'Just a glass of water, please.' Immediately, he wished he hadn't asked for anything as he saw Craig pick up a dirty glass by the sink, give it a rinse under the tap and then stick a rather dubiously grey dish rag in and swirl it around. He placed the glass, full of water, in front of Edmund. The outside of the glass was still wet and trickles of water formed a little puddle around the bottom.

'How's it all going?' asked Craig. There was something jaunty about him, thought Edmund, like a little light had been switched on in his eyes. He had shaved, although he had missed a bit just below his left jaw bone, and his hair was washed and he had on a navy blue sweater that helped subdue the redness of his cheeks.

'All right,' answered Edmund, rather warily. He was not about to discuss a police investigation with anyone, never mind a suspect. Edmund hadn't quite crossed Craig off the list of potential suspects, although he held him in the 'unlikely' category.

'I've been giving this case a lot of thought,' said Craig, knocking a cigarette out of its packet and waving it around, unlit, as he talked. 'It's a tricky one, but I think it's just got to be the husband.'

Edmund's heart sank. Was this why Craig had phoned him? To go over details of the case and speculate as to who was 'It' as though they were playing a game or were characters in a film?

'Why do you say that?' he asked.

'Always is, isn't it? Isn't there some kind of statistic about this sort of thing? Ninety percent of people who are murdered are murdered by their spouse? I'm sure I've read that somewhere. Easy to engineer when you think of it. Go home at lunch time, kill your wife and then say you were at work all day.'

'He has an alibi,' Edmund said and immediately regretted giving away information.

'Alibi!' scoffed Craig. 'Where were you on the night of the eighteenth at seven o'clock? Who remembers what they were doing at any specific time?'

Edmund nodded his head slowly. 'Yes, sometimes that is the case, but not all of the time.' He could see Craig waiting for him to say more, but he didn't.

Craig sat back and lit his cigarette. Foreseeing another relatively long conversation in which he would be drowned in second hand smoke, Edmund decided to move the discussion on.

'You had something to say to me, Mr Martin?'

Craig nodded, wagging his finger at Edmund while he blew a perfect plume of blue smoke above his head.

'The maid. Now she, I would say, is the next on the list after Mr Husband. She's at home all day and she knows where the knives are kept. Madam goes to lie down and wapaa. Good night, Mrs Pullman.'

Edmund didn't know where he would start to disprove such a theory. Hesitant to discuss any more details of the case, he chose his words carefully.

'We are looking at a variety of options at the moment.'

'A variety of options,' spluttered Craig. 'It sounds like you're choosing what colour you want your house painted.'

Edmund felt embarrassed. He concentrated on wiping trickles of water off the glass while Craig went on to laugh by himself. Eventually, he stopped.

'What I wanted to tell you,' Craig said, stubbing out the cigarette 'is about the maid.'

Edmund hoped the information wouldn't be long in coming.

'I remember her.' Craig nodded his heading a knowing way. 'You might even say I know her.'

Edmund waited patiently.

'But not from the office.' Craig pushed his tongue into his cheek and said with a meaningful raise of his eyebrows: 'From Ivory Lodge.'

Edmund cocked his head in a question. 'Ivory Lodge?'

'Ivory Lodge, Malachite Hills Lodge, Eve's Executive Accommodation and Exquisite Dining Lodge.' He sat back in his chair as though he had delivered some very profound news and was waiting for it to sink in.

Edmund was none the clearer.

'The dating agency,' cried Craig. 'Find love in the comfort of your friends.'

'What?'

'That's her mission statement. Weird, hey?'

'What would Dorcas be doing there?'

'Looking good. Little black dress, heels, a bit of make up.'

'But what would she be doing?'

Craig made a stupid face and rolled his eyes. 'I'll leave you to work that one out. I remember her passing snacks round on one occasion and arriving with a couple of girls on another occasion.'

Edmund tapped the tips of his fingers against his lips while he thought about this.

'Are you sure?' He thought uncertainly of Craig's irrational temperament and his predilection for alcohol.

'I'm very sure. It's the short hair, you see. The wigless head. It stood out. I was just going to sleep last night when it just came to me, just like that.'

'Just came to you? In a dream?'

'No, I remembered. You know what it's like. You're relaxed and just drifting off and sometimes your mind throws these things at you. It's like match replay – and because you see things in slow motion, you suddenly see these little details that you overlooked the first time. Worth looking into, wouldn't you say?''

Edmund was still sceptical, but it was worth noting anyhow. He took a little sip of the water as a sign he was thankful for the information.

'You could have phoned me,' he said.

'I did. I would have phoned you sooner, but my battery was dead and the electricity was off. That's why I only got to phone you at lunchtime.'

'I mean, you could have told me this information on the phone.'

'I could have – but I prefer to talk face to face. You might want to ask me questions. It could take time. Phone calls are short – and expensive – and you have to think quickly.'

Edmund glanced quizzically at Craig. He wondered if he wasn't quite enjoying this now. It was a bit of excitement in a dull life, something to interrupt his loneliness and give him something to think of besides himself.

At that point, there was a knock on the front door. Craig sat up with a start and looked beseechingly at Edmund.

'It's not your guys, is it?'

'Not that I know of,' Edmund replied, thinking it rather sad that Craig lived such a lonely life that the only possible callers would be the police.

'You go,' Craig ordered Edmund, nodding his head in the direction of the front door.

'How's that going to help?' asked Edmund, wondering

what a visitor would think when the door opened to a police officer.

'Please. Just do it,' whispered Craig in what Edmund thought was an exaggeratedly hoarse whisper.

He walked through the small hallway and was about to open the door when he stopped. He replaced the chain that Craig had left off that morning and then opened the door.

It was Sandra Smith.

'Hello,' she said, peering at him under the chain. 'Edmund?'

He was at that moment quite swept away by her beauty. He hadn't noticed it at first when he had met her on the Pullmans' verandah. He had been too busy asking questions and getting details, but here and now, her face close to the door, he saw her in a totally different light. Her face was soft and elfin-like. The sharpness of her hair cut accentuated these features and made her eyes appear very wide. Beautiful eyes, he thought. Such beautiful eyes.

'Edmund?' she said again uncertainly. 'Your phone. You forgot it in my car.'

Edmund fumbled clumsily with the door. 'Thank you,' he said, opening it wide, 'for bringing it back.'

Sandra peered into the hallway, looking behind him at a shadowy figure watching from the entrance to the kitchen.

Edmund checked his phone for any messages or missed calls and then slipped it in his pocket. 'It's all right, Mr Martin. This is Sandra Smith. She gave me a lift to your house and I forgot my phone in her car. She is just returning it.'

'Oh,' said Craig, coming out of the shadows. 'Would you like to come in?'

Edmund was surprised that a man who had minutes ago been unwilling to open the door himself should now welcome a complete stranger into his house.

'No, thank you,' she smiled. 'I'm on my way into town. Just thought I'd see if Edmund were still here.'

Edmund. She used his name. It seemed to roll smoothly off her tongue as though she smiled when she said it.

'You're going back into town?' asked Edmund. 'Could I possibly get another lift?'

'Yes, of course.' She smiled again.

'I just need to make a couple of phone calls. Could you... do you... mind waiting? I won't be long.'

Did that smile falter slightly? Edmund wasn't sure.

'Of course. Go ahead. I'll... er... wait.' She looked around uncertainly.

'Could I get you a glass of water?' asked Craig who had now moved fully into the hallway. 'Or tea?'

'Water,' she replied. 'Thank you. I don't drink tea.'

Edmund squeezed his eyes in sympathy for what was to come and went outside into the garden.

Chapter Eighteen

'So, you're a *ther-a-pist*?' said Craig slowly, stirring his second mug of tea without much attention to the amount that was slopping over the sides and onto the counter.

'Yes, I help heal people.'

'Right,' said Craig, his lips firmly pressed together in a look of utter seriousness. 'Yes, well, a good job to have I would have thought. Everyone needs to be healed. Heal the world, make it a better place.'

She smiled a polite smile and he snorted and then looked away.

'Here's my card,' she said and handed him a small white card with a yin and yang sign in the top left hand corner and a flower in the bottom right hand one. Craig read it sceptically.

'A life coach,' muttered Craig. 'I've never met one of those before. Is it anything like a tennis coach?'

'Not quite, although there may be some similarities. I help people make the right decisions in life.'

'Can't imagine most people like being told how to live their lives. I certainly wouldn't.'

'It's not about *telling* people anything. I show you the way. We discuss options.'

Inwardly, Craig cringed. Discuss options? He hated phrases like that. Empty, meaningless words. As though life gave you options and it was simply a matter of pressing a button and – hey presto! – you got what you wanted.

'I suppose it helps to know what your options are in the first place,' said Craig, returning the card to her. 'Pet therapist, too? Dogs have options as well? Should I chase the cat? Should I not chase the cat?'

'We all have options. We just don't see them as such. We put up barriers. We say no.'

Craig thought this would be a good time to take a sip of his tea. It saved the necessity of talking.

'We have to return to our original selves.'

Oh dear, thought Craig. Any minute now she's going to start talking about the inner child. He had once been on a date (also disastrous) with a vegetarian called Rhoda. It was a long time ago now, just after the Born Again Christian. Craig couldn't even remember what she looked like, but he did remember her talking about karma and past lives and how one had to get in touch with the Inner Child (the capital letters were hers), who was not the immature you who still liked to lick dry jelly powder out of your hand or take the stairs two at a time, but your real self who knew what you really wanted.

'Think of a baby,' Sandra said. 'They know what they want.'

Bingo.

'They're totally self-centred, I would have thought.' Craig contemplated lighting a cigarette, but then thought better of it and took another sip of his tea.

'There's a difference. Babies are not afraid of asking for what they want. They do what they want, too. When they're upset, they cry; when they're happy, they laugh. They haven't learnt to hide or disguise their feelings like we have.'

Too much like a magazine, Craig thought. One of those he read at the dentist's – *Women & Home* or *Fair Lady*. 10 Things We Can learn From Babies.

'Surely it's a bit more complicated than that,' he said, the scepticism clear in his voice. 'What I want and what a baby wants are two different things, aren't they?'

'Yes... and no. What *you* want may not be quite as straightforward as the baby, but why should the asking for it be any more difficult?'

'Babies don't ask. They demand.'

'So should you.'

'It's not polite.' Craig laughed, a slight sneer turning up his nose.

'No, not from other people. From life, the universe.'

'Is that with a capital letter, Universe?' He imagined it was. Visions of Rhoda the Vegetarian raised their ugly head. Sandra seemed to sense his hesitation.

'What I mean is, if you want something, believe it's yours and that you have the right to it.'

'The right?' Visions of Jade the Expat replaced the Vegetarian. It was now a Human Right to demand what you wanted from life?

'Believe you are entitled to it. So often we want something, but somewhere in our consciousness is this idea that we don't really deserve it. When we don't get it, we accept it because we feel it was right that we didn't get it.'

Entitlement. Consciousness. The Vegetarian was back. 'I'm not sure I agree with you.'

'Aren't you?' she interjected. 'Why are we always so surprised when something good comes our way? Why isn't a positive outcome expected? Why aren't we as surprised when things *don't* come our way? All our lives through – parents, teachers, religion – tell us to be grateful, tell us to accept what we are given and not to ask for more. We don't deserve it. We aren't worthy. We come to believe it as an actual fact.'

Craig shrugged. Sometimes it was all too much to think about. He didn't like conversations like this; conversations that took you down steeply winding roads with an ever more feeble light. Whatever you said, there was some BUT which popped up like a signpost at a crossroad and pointed you in a different direction. Sometimes you felt you had been this way before; sometimes you found yourself agreeing with something you had earlier contradicted. It always ended in 'See. See what I mean? I'm right, aren't I?' except you weren't saying the words and you weren't even sure what you were supposed to see.

'You need to connect to your inner self,' said Sandra, tapping her chest with a closed fist. Craig groaned somewhat audibly and avoided looking her in the eye.

Inner self. The cliché of clichés. Some of the emptiest words in the English language. He picked up an old receipt for beer and cigarettes that was lying on the table and began to fold it in half.

'God is within,' continued Sandra, unperturbed. Craig managed to groan inwardly this time. 'It's the difference between a candle and electricity.'

Craig raised his head in a question.

'Candles blow out. They burn away. They don't last.'

'And electricity does?' He didn't think electricity was a good analogy to use when wanting to describe something constant and reliable in Zimbabwe.

She gave a small laugh. 'You know what I mean, don't you? In an ideal world.'

Craig leant forward and was just about to say something when he stopped. He remembered Verimark Girl then and he held back.

'All these things,' he said, quietly. 'All this talk of consciousness and inner selves. It's fine if you're sitting in London or San Francisco and all you want to do is clear some karma. But here, in this place, I don't know, it all looks pretty, well, irrelevant. We *haven't got* electricity and we *have got* candles, what does it all mean?'

She didn't answer. A smile played on her lips and he couldn't help feeling slightly irritated. Did she think she had some superior knowledge, or perhaps she had heard this argument so many times, she saw through it? He looked at her, at the soft expanse of her chest through the V of her T-shirt, her smooth neck and her face devoid of all makeup. She was beautiful in a simple way, in a way that the world needed to be reminded was true beauty: freckles were ultimately more attractive than great gashes of pink blush and clear skin more eye-catching than eyes outlined with black or blue and lizard skin eyelids.

'Tell me,' he said, 'before you got into all this inner self stuff, did you like country and western?'

She burst into laughter, leaning forward as her eyes creased and then rocking backwards in her chair. 'Country and western, what? What on earth gave you that idea?'

He looked embarrassed. His attempt to sting her with words had backfired so he shrugged instead. 'You look the type. All that sentimentality.'

'No, no I didn't – I don't – listen to country and western.'

'I suppose it's all dolphin songs and waves crashing on the beach?' He was intent on hurting her.

'Sometimes.' She was still laughing and it irritated him.

Then she stopped laughing and an awkward silence spread between them. Craig continued to fold the little piece of paper into smaller and smaller squares.

'Would you like to try some meditation?' Her voice was soft, but serious. He caught a momentary look of shyness on her face as though she feared his refusal. 'Not now though – another day?'

He turned back to his paper folding and didn't answer.

About a minute passed before she pushed her chair back and slung her handbag over her shoulder.

'Well, I must be off,' she said in what could only be called a breezy tone. 'I wonder if Edmund is ready to go. I have yoga at five.'

'Can't interest you in a beer then?' he joked.

She smiled and shook her head. ''Fraid not.'

He got up and walked her to the door. Edmund was coming up the drive to meet her, phone in hand.

'Thank you,' she said before she walked down the steps. 'It was great chatting.'

He was reminded of his mother then, how she stood behind him on the rare occasions when she remembered to collect him from an afternoon of playing with friends. 'Say thank you,' she would hiss between clenched teeth. 'Say thank you for having me.' She may have been a drunk, but she was a drunk with manners.

Craig managed a crooked smile. 'I'm not the type, you know. Yoga and all that. Meditation. It's just not me.'

She nodded and looked away and then looked back, straight in the eyes this time.

'The first response to change is resistance.' She smiled and waved and got in her car and was gone.

Later that evening, Craig sat on his ridiculously small verandah with its iron bars and its high wall and its limited view of his neighbours' back garden. He liked to sit here in the evening. It was the lightest place in the house when the electricity was off and the warmest in the winter. He liked to watch the neighbours. They were the kind of people who lived their lives according to some clockwork mechanism. They maintained a small, neat garden with a row of daisy bushes along a short drive and a cluster of pawpaw trees in the back garden with a whirly washing line and a clay tub full of parsley and basil.

Every day they left home at the same time and every day they returned at the same time. The car was parked in a lock-up garage; it never lingered carelessly in the drive or waited impatiently at the gate. They had probably had the same car for years; it was a blue Ford Escort. Craig doubted they went very far in it. It was looked after and washed and polished and put away. They didn't live extravagantly; he imagined they were the type to spend cautiously. They probably splashed out on a limited bouquet on DSTV, something that afforded them a movie channel and one of sport and one of the news. They watched the same programmes every week and never flicked, never wondered what else there was. The kind of people, thought Craig, whom you could find anywhere in the world: Australia, America, England, France. They weathered Zimbabwe because they never changed. They had set their expectations at a certain level and never wanted to live beyond it. In that way they were never disappointed. Craig marvelled sometimes at the simplicity of life. It was then that he believed maxims as banal as 'Simplify your life'. It was then that they meant something.

Craig opened a bottle of beer and lit a cigarette. He had

meant to make a meal that evening, the first proper meal in a long time, but now he felt a sudden sadness and emptiness descend. The advent of Sandra had, he had to admit, given him something to think about. He had imagined, hadn't he, that he might ask her round for a drink sometime, although she probably didn't drink alcohol.

He might even have offered her a meal. He'd have loved to have asked her in some nonchalant manner, as though he had people to supper all the time. He'd have loved to have flung open the fridge and rummaged around amongst the basil pesto and the fresh (home-grown) romaine lettuce, the tahini and the crème fraiche and conjured up something suitably healthy and good for the Inner Self. Instead, he thought of the packet of Vienna sausages he had bought a couple of days earlier and a frozen single serving of Cape Malay curry from the Indian takeaway. He took another sip of his beer.

Next door, the neighbours arrived home. Mr Neighbour (Craig had never asked his name) stopped the car in front of the garage and Mrs Neighbour got out. He then drove the car into the garage while she unlocked the front door. He locked up the garage and went down the drive to close the gate, which he also locked. Craig imagined that she put the kettle on and put two biscuits on a plate. Mr Neighbour entered the house and closed the door behind him. In exactly ten minutes, Craig knew he would appear again in a pair of shorts and a T-shirt and water the daisies with a big bucket.

It was better not to be aware of your existence, wasn't it? It was when you became mindful of the routine, when you could see yourself standing in the garden with a bucket of water, that's when it all fell apart. It was when you looked over your neighbours' wall and became conscious that you were looking, when you were aware of the packet of viennas in the fridge, when you felt your loneliness like an ache, when you were alert to the utter sham of your life and the failure of dreams; that's when it all collapsed and the precarious house of cards you had built around yourself began to fall.

Craig felt himself slipping deeper into thought. It was a kind of religion, wasn't it, all this inner self stuff? The once distant God who existed way beyond the clouds and could only be called upon in Latin, who barely deigned to grant wishes and answer prayers unless accompanied by the pillaging of cities or the wearing of a hair shirt, had been distilled into something much smaller and much closer to home. God had descended the golden stairs from heaven and made his way to ground level. He had got a job in a band and wore T-shirts and open sandals and wanted to share a beer and be your buddy. Then, not content with being lead guitarist, he had made himself smaller, very small indeed, and had managed to be swallowed whole by those who looked for religion as some sought pills. Now he was called the 'inner self', someone you could talk to and question; someone who, when connected to, gave you what you wanted just because *you thought you were entitled to it*. A great power was in evidence. You could control the world at your fingertips if you could but *believe* you could. If you were *connected*. If you had a more consistent power supply than ZESA. If your candle didn't waver in the wind of self-doubt. Imagine – a world of little gods, each entitled to what they believed was theirs, and nothing, except themselves, to hold them back?

Craig finished the beer and rested his head in his hands. He didn't want to drink. He really didn't want to drink. He wanted to pretend he had just locked up his car and he was watering the daisies and he would come into the house and drink a cup of tea and eat a ginger biscuit. The family would sit down to a home-cooked meal after which he'd help the children with their homework and then read them a bedtime story. Warm little bodies lying next to his, a hand against his cheek; loving him; needing him; wanting him.

At that point the electricity went off for the second time that day and Craig sunk heavily into the gloom. He made his way to the kitchen, lifted down a bottle and poured himself a large whisky. Then he went upstairs to bed.

Chapter Nineteen

Edmund had spent the last twenty minutes making phone calls and waiting for answers. Answers that didn't come. How far his world was from the world of novels and films where policemen had information at their fingertips. Previous cases, previous charges and suspects' profiles could all be produced by punching a few words into a computer – or even looking in a simple filing cabinet. But here, in Bulawayo, things were very much slower.

'Dorcas Hlabangana. Hla-ban-ga-na. Dorcas. Dor-cas. D O R C A S.' So it went on as he tried to find out information about Dorcas's past. He had his doubts about Craig Martin's claims as to the fact that Dorcas was not in the office when he threatened Shantelle. Perhaps he was just trying to undermine Dorcas and cast a shadow over her insistence that she recognised him. However, if she hadn't been there, how did she know that it was him who had threatened Marcia?

When, after fifteen minutes, nobody called, Edmund phoned back. The phone just rang and rang. He tried a second time and somebody answered.

'Where is Mpofu?' Edmund asked.

'Mpofu is not here.'

'Not there? Why?'

'Why? It is lunchtime.'

'Lunchtime? I've just spoken to him. Who else is on duty?'

'I don't know. They've gone for lunch.' The voice was cold and dismissive.

'This is Chief Inspector Edmund Dube. Do you understand? You are disobeying a senior police officer.'

There was a pause and then a long, thin noise seemed to reach to him out of the phone. It wasn't insolent, it wasn't derisive, it was a threat, suggestive of a lion ready to spring or a snake ready to strike. And then the dry rasp of laughter.

Edmund almost dropped the phone as the noise rushed through him.

He found Sandra looking at him with great curiosity.

'Could you – may you – drop me back on the corner of Clark Road?'

'You going back?' she said, curiously, as they got in the car. 'How long do the police take to investigate a crime scene?'

'I have some more questions to ask.'

'Mr Pullman?'

'No, the maid.'

'Oh,' said Sandra, her eyes intent on the road. Edmund glanced across and wished for the second time that day that he had not said anything to anyone about the case.

'Routine questions,' he added in the vain hope that the words neutralised any possible suggestion of suspicion.

'You just need to be sure,' she said, patting her chest. 'Here.'

Edmund didn't say anything. Police work involved more than being sure in your heart. A conviction needed something called evidence.

'You lack confidence, don't you?'

Edmund looked uneasily at her and then out of the window.

'You need to connect to your core. Your still small voice of calm. Stop. Listen. All the answers are within you.'

Edmund managed an unsure smile. This was unusual territory for him. He was used to God and asking Jesus for help – and even the occasional Saint – but this was something else. She was telling him to listen to *himself*, not a higher authority.

A part of him felt like he would like to ask her more. What did she mean? How could he put her words into action? But they were already at the Pullmans' and the opportunity was lost.

'Thank you,' he said to Sandra as he struggled to get out of her car. He seemed to be fumbling and dropping things.

He felt embarrassed that he had thought her attractive, as though she knew his feelings like she seemed to know all the others.

She smiled. 'I hope it all goes well. Think positively.'

He nodded and managed a half-smile and then shut the door.

'Goodbye. I may need to ask you a few more questions though. I have your card. I might – ring you?' The words stumbled out. He was at once too jaunty and melodramatic. Perhaps he sounded insincere, creepy even.

She waved and he lifted his hand uncertainly in response as the car drove away.

The Pullmans' house was deserted still, and the gate was still unlocked. The floor cloth on the pipe outside had dried. The early afternoon sun was bright and the garden was alive with a frantic vibrancy, yet in the shadows it was cool and dark. Even the butterflies shied away from the edges and corners of the garden, dancing manically around the flowers in the sun, as though they too were afraid of what might befall them if they wandered off. Edmund glanced at his phone. No messages. No missed calls. He doubted there would be any information received today regarding Dorcas.

He went out of the gate and turned onto the road. Then he stopped, went back a few steps and climbed over the gate of the house next door. He was now becoming quite good at this and managed it without falling over the other side. Mr Sherbourne still had some questions to answer and, while Edmund was here, he may as well ask them.

The house was quiet and shut. Roland was not the sort who left the back door open all day, or at all. Edmund imagined all the doors were locked and bolted. The windows of the lounge were open a couple of inches, however, suggesting someone was home, so Edmund thought he would knock on the front door. The house being slightly elevated meant that he could pass beneath the windows without being seen. As he did so, he could hear voices – a woman's voice and a man's. He couldn't quite make out the words for the woman was talking fast. The man's words were far more intermittent and monosyllabic.

Edmund stood very still, trying hard to listen, to catch something of the conversation. The man's voice came nearer and Edmund realised he was standing at the window. He pressed himself as close to the wall as possible.

'I doubt they will investigate any further. Please, let's not worry about it.'

The woman's voice was high-pitched and insistent.

'You are white. It's okay for you. They will leave you alone.'

'Look, they're pretty useless at the best of times. Just carry on for now. Just let Pullman think life is carrying on as normal. Let it go for a couple of months before you do anything. Come, I want to show you something.' The voice moved away from the window and Edmund assumed he crossed the room. There was a silence and he realised they had left the room.

He contemplated what to do. Should he proceed to the front door and probably scare the hell out of them, a police officer arriving when they were talking about the proficiency, or rather lack of it, in the police force? Or should he try and leave the premises without being seen and return at a later date?

Edmund took a deep breath and moved noiselessly back down the drive. Then, changing his mind, he approached the garage, which lay to the right of the house. The garage door was shut so he went round the side where there was a narrow strip of ground between the garage and the garden wall. There were two windows on this side, surprisingly dirty ones considering Roland's penchant for cleanliness.

Dusty cobwebs and lack of light made looking through the window difficult and it took a few seconds before Edmund could discern the objects inside.

There was a car, a large one, under a dustsheet. The shape suggested it wasn't a modern one, and where the sheet ended he could see the half moons of wheels and old-fashioned hubcaps. There was no other car, no motor bike, no bicycle.

There was a workbench, but it was clear of any tools. An old number plate was propped against the window on the house-side of the garage, but otherwise the room was empty of any immediacy, any sense of interaction with the outside world.

He heard a noise and peered round the corner of the garage wall. He drew back as a figure passed. It was a woman, a woman in a maid's uniform, carrying a large bag with GAME in pink letters on the side. She walked with a sense of purpose, her flat black shoes tripping precisely down the drive. When she got to the gate, she took a key out of her purse and unlocked the padlock on the chain. Edmund stared. The woman was unmistakably Dorcas Hlabangana, the late Marcia Pullman's maid.

1979

'Psst! Hey, do you think it was your dad' – Jasper Meyer brought his hand down hard on Edmund's shoulder – 'who killed *your* dad?' His left hand landed firmly on Rupert's shoulder. 'Do you think?'

Jasper had descended on Edmund and Rupert as if from nowhere. They were sitting in a secluded corner of the playground playing noughts and crosses in the sand.

Rupert went red. He shrugged Jasper's hand off. 'Go away. Leave us alone.'

'Aar, what's wrong? I'm just *asking*.'

Rupert didn't say anything. He continued to draw crosses in the sand with his finger.

'I mean, I was just wondering, you know. Didn't your dad have his head blown off? Or was it his legs?'

Edmund watched his friend's face darken to a deep crimson and his eyes fill with tears. Suddenly, Rupert launched himself at Jasper, knocking him to the ground. Grabbing him by the neck, he hit his head on the ground again and again.

'Leave us alone. *Leave us alone!* Do you hear me?'

Jasper's mouth filled with spittle; his lips were drawn

back in a tight grimace that made his podgy face seem momentarily thinner. With a hard shove, he pushed Rupert off him and stood up, dusting off his clothes.

'You think you can fight me, hey? You think *you* can fight *me*? You and your pathetic little sidekick here.'

The bell rang for the end of break.

Jasper pulled himself straight so that he towered over Rupert.

'You watch your step, arsehole. You and Teaboy, you understand? Or someone's going to go BOOM just like Daddy did.'

Rupert wavered. His chin wobbled and he looked away. Boys were passing them, some looking, some not even noticing.

'Line up! Line up!' The monitors were shouting. 'Hey, Meyer! Hargreaves! Dube! Into line!'

Chapter Twenty

'I'd like to talk to you, Mr Sherbourne. Please open up.' Edmund leant closer to the door as he spoke the words. His voice was calm, but surprisingly strong. He felt fired up. It wasn't just Dorcas; it was the car. It was obvious it was never used. It was an old car, one of those kept by a collector who might take it for a short spin on warm, Sunday afternoons. It was not an everyday car.

Edmund watched the mottled panes of glass change colour as Roland approached from inside.

'Yes?' he called. A hesitant, irritated voice. 'Who is it?'

'Chief Inspector Dube.' He paused and then added, 'CID.'

There was a silence. Not even the panes of glass showed any movement. Edmund was just about to call out again when he heard the sound of the door being unlocked.

Roland opened the door and stood back, his figure crouched over as though he expected Edmund to throw rotten tomatoes at him. His hair was slightly dishevelled, but otherwise he was quite smartly dressed in a pair of khaki chinos and a white cotton shirt. Roland wasn't the sort of man Edmund imagined wearing a pair of shorts and a cap. He didn't seem to relax into what he was wearing, as though it was some sort of uniform that must be worn properly, but without much enjoyment. In fact, enjoyment and Roland Sherbourne did not seem to go together at all. Edmund looked at his sharp, pinched face and his pale, thin lips and thought: here is a man who does not forgive. But is he capable of driving a knife through someone's heart? Edmund wasn't sure.

'May I come in?' asked Edmund, moving up a step towards the front door. 'I need to ask you a few more questions.'

A funny sort of spluttering noise erupted from Roland.

'What?' he exclaimed. 'What on earth about? Why do you keep bothering me? This is harassment!'

A slight exaggeration, thought Edmund. Was the bluster hiding something?

'It won't take long. I really do need your help with the investigation, Mr Sherbourne.' *Being in Control: A Practical Guide to Self Confidence.* Step 4: Make other people feel important. They will respond to you better. Edmund had used this tactic at ZIMRA before and found it quite useful. Minor officials with far too much power who didn't even look up from their newspapers in acknowledgement of your presence, suddenly became rather useful when you made them feel like a fount of knowledge.

Roland seemed about to say something, appeared to think better of it and blew hard through his mouth.

'All right,' he said as though the words were stuck in his throat. 'But I don't have a lot of time.'

Edmund suspected he was lying, but he played along anyway.

'You are going out?'

Roland nodded non-committedly. Not a good liar, thought Edmund.

Edmund followed Roland into the sitting room. He was quick to look around. As Roland hadn't been expecting him, he would not have had much time to put away any evidence of Dorcas being there. Edmund noticed two empty glasses on a tray on the table and two plates with crumbs on them. He was aware of Roland watching him and aware that he had seen what Edmund had. He was more nervous and fidgety than usual.

'I'm a busy man,' he began. 'If you'd called five minutes ago, you would have found me in the middle of a piano lesson.'

'Really?' said Edmund, without conviction. 'You teach or you were being taught?'

'I teach,' answered Roland, his voice edged with impatience.

'The last time I was here, you said you don't play.'

Roland reddened. 'I'm sorry,' he stammered. 'I lied. I don't like people to know.'

'Yet they know you give lessons?'

'I like to keep it quiet. Under the radar.'

Edmund thought it was a strange way to make money.

'And now you are going out to give a lesson?'

'Yes, yes that's right.'

'In your car?'

Edmund was certain he saw Roland hesitate. 'Of course.'

'Which is a what?'

'What do you mean which is a what?'

'I mean what kind of car do you have, Mr Sherbourne?'

'It's a... well, it's none of your business, is it? If you've come here to ask me questions about Marcia Pullman's death then ask me them and be gone.'

'I asked you what sort of car you drove, Mr Sherbourne.' Edmund was resolute.

'This is ridiculous,' insisted Roland. 'Absolutely ridiculous. What's your number, your police number? I'll report you to your superior.'

Edmund gave a small laugh and rocked back on his heels. He felt his confidence soar. 'What for? Asking you what sort of car you have? It's hardly a crime.' He thought of the Police Commissioner stuffing his face with Meat Supremo pizza and chips. He imagined him talking to Roland Sherbourne, bits of pizza flying out of his mouth as his great jaws sunk into it. 'You must put it into writing. Triplicate copies.' Edmund reckoned Roland would be severely disappointed with this response.

'It's a Mazda 323,' said Roland, quickly, perhaps also realising the futility of his threat.

'And it's parked outside?'

'In the garage.'

'Under the dust sheet?'

'What! – have you been snooping around?' he cried, his face red with a mixture of indignation and embarrassment.

'I'm a police officer. It's my job,' said Edmund, simply, not raising his voice.

'I don't care who you are, I–' began Roland, but Edmund cut him off, suspecting they were going to go round and round in circles with Roland making various unreasonable and unrealistic threats.

'Mr Sherbourne, as I have said before, this is a police investigation and, as such, I need to make enquiries. I came here the other day to ask you some questions about the day of Mrs Pullman's death. Had you seen anything? Had anything seemed suspicious? I don't think those are unreasonable questions, but you lied to me then as you lie to me now.'

The earlier confidence he had felt began to blossom in him as though he had been injected with something. It was a combination of knowing he was in the right and knowing Roland knew he was in the right. He had a strange sense of growing taller and wider, like he was filling the room. He took a step towards Roland, who took two steps backwards.

'I put it to you, Mr Sherbourne, that you were here the day in question. Perhaps you saw something – someone – but for reasons known only to yourself you want to protect that person. You fear they were involved and you don't want to get them into trouble. It's natural, Mr Sherbourne, to want to protect those we love.' *Being in Control: A Practical Guide to Self Confidence.* Step 3: Make people feel comfortable with you. Show a shared sense of feeling for and response to the world.

'Not at all,' insisted Roland, a white spot appearing on either side of his mouth. 'There is no one I wish to protect.' Edmund watched him open and close his left hand.

'But that person may not be guilty,' said Edmund, walking towards the window and looking out. From here, he had a clear view of next door's drive, garage and the back door. 'Maybe there is some perfectly innocent explanation for that person being where they were and maybe this matter can be sorted out.'

'What do you mean, sorted out?' Roland's voice was thick and rasping. 'Are you... are you looking for a bribe? Because I can tell you–'

Edmund turned, startled. This wasn't the response he had predicted.

'No, no, of course not,' he insisted, but his voice sounded thin and artificial. 'That's not what I meant. I meant... well, I meant that if you tell me the truth, it can be forgotten about.'

'*Sorted out. Forgotten about.* I know what you mean. Give me fifty dollars and we can call it quits. No one will look any further. Oh, I know your type, *Chief Inspector* Dube. You're all the same, aren't you? Not one good egg among the whole lot of you! That's why you're here every two minutes, asking all these questions and pretending you're Inspector Clouseau with that ridiculous long coat of yours. This is what we've come to is it? Do you know my father used to be a police officer? Many years ago now and thank God he is dead. He was a good man. A man who believed in justice and peace and the Law. The Law! What does it mean to you – to anyone anymore?'

'Mr Sherbourne,' insisted Edmund, feeling extremely embarrassed and insulted. 'Let me make it clear that I am not here to ask for a bribe. I am here to solve a crime. I don't want money, I want information.'

'Why?' continued Roland, the white patches now two puffs of cotton wool on his face. 'She was an awful woman. She was a liar and a cheat and a bully and I'm–'

'Glad she's dead?' finished Edmund. Roland stared at him for a few seconds and then looked away. His hand opened and closed, opened and closed.

'Strong words for someone you didn't know. Yet you're not the only person to say that – or suggest it, so what I see here is a number of people who are glad to see Marcia Pullman dead and I ask myself do they hate her enough to have stabbed her?'

'I heard she died naturally. Kidney failure wasn't it?'

'She was stabbed as well. Somebody hated her so much, they couldn't bear the fact that she died peacefully in her sleep. They wanted everyone to know how much she was hated. *Hated.*'

Roland was quiet and still, except for a certain heaving of his shoulders and the noise of someone trying to regain their breath after a long run. At this point, Edmund would usually feel sympathy for the person being questioned and suggest a break, but today Edmund had no sympathy whatsoever. He felt driven, not out of any need to vindicate Marcia, but because he would not be made a fool of. He was going to solve this case at whatever cost.

'What do you think?' persisted Edmund. 'Was it the husband or the gardener or the woman from the office – or the maid?' He watched Roland's face carefully to see how he reacted to those last words, but Roland was blowing his nose in a large blue handkerchief.

'It certainly wasn't someone who came in from the road and decided to stab her. Some stranger or weirdo.'

'Why not?' asked Roland. 'It happens all the time.'

Edmund gave a short laugh. 'In books, yes, and films. Not in Bulawayo. If something had been stolen, maybe, and if she had been found in the kitchen with a machete in her head, perhaps.'

'Stranger things have happened,' said Roland without much conviction.

'Do you know what I think, Mr Sherbourne? I think that someone, like you, hated Marcia Pullman. They hated her with a passion and they wanted her dead. So they plotted and they planned. They knew there was no gardener and they made sure the maid was out for the day. They knew, too, Mrs Pullman's routine and what happened on the day of book club. Who was expected and at what time.'

Roland shrugged, but his eyes were yellow with fear.

'It could have been you, Mr Sherbourne. Watching from this window' – Edmund pointed out of the window towards the Pullmans' house – 'noting the comings and goings in the house. What time the husband left, when she was alone in the house, all those sorts of details. Most people are, of course, creatures of habit.'

The colour rose in Roland's cheeks again. He drew his head

back like a cobra about to spit. Edmund wouldn't allow him his opportunity to talk. He held up his hand and carried on.

'Then, of course, it could have been someone else. The maid, for instance. Mrs Pullman is difficult, she is nasty. She keeps Dorcas working all hours and doesn't pay her well. One day, Dorcas just snaps and...'

'Rubbish!' declared Roland. 'Dorcas is well paid. She wouldn't need to do such a thing.' He stopped, realising he had said too much.

'Oh, you know Dorcas?' Edmund acted surprised, but his voice held a slight trace of something more patronising.

Roland shifted uneasily. 'Vaguely. As one does.'

'Enough to know how much she earns?'

'Look, that's just a surmise. I see her sometimes – from my window. She always looks well dressed.'

'Happy? Does she look happy?'

'Happy? How the hell do I know? What a ridiculous question!'

'Is it? If you notice someone's clothes, I would have thought you'd notice their face. The eyes, you know are the window to the soul.'

'Eyes are the window to the soul.' Roland spat the words back at Edmund. 'Who are you? You're not a policeman. You're some sort of con artist, aren't you?'

'I'm Chief Inspector Edmund Dube, CID,' said Edmund, his voice growing in a confidence that surprised him. 'And I'd like to know exactly what your relationship with Miss Dorcas Hlabangana is.'

Chapter Twenty-one

Dorcas walked quickly up the drive of 274 Clark Road. She felt a pang of guilt for she hadn't locked the gate, expecting only to be out for a short while. The house was quiet with an eerie sort of silence. She didn't like it. Ghosts. Isipoko. Whatever you wanted to call it, the fact of the matter was that the place was creepy. She didn't like to be alone in the house anymore. Everything had changed, yet everything carried on as usual. She was up early to make Mr Pullman his full English breakfast before he left for work. When he left, she rushed through her jobs: washed up the breakfast things and gave the floor a quick sweep. Fed the cat. Dashed into the bedroom where Mr Pullman slept to make up the bed and clean the room. Then she threw his clothes in the washing machine, quickly scrubbed the bathroom and hurried out into the garden.

She was astounded that Mr Pullman carried on living in the house. Didn't he have relatives he could go and stay with? Perhaps after the funeral and once the furore over the circumstances of his wife's death had died down, he would think of moving. It was all very well him saying that life just carried on as usual, but she didn't want it to. She was hoping to have been given notice. Three months' wages would be very nice. Perhaps she could go to Botswana and buy goods to sell in Bulawayo, like her cousin Veronica did.

It was her suggestion that she do some watering since there wasn't a gardener. She suggested it for three reasons: one, that it got her out of the house and gave her a legitimate reason to be outside in the sun; two, because she hoped Mr Pullman would employ a gardener so she wouldn't be on her own too much longer even though that would negate point one. Thirdly, she hoped that mentioning a gardener might prompt him into some thought about the house.

'We need a new gardener,' she managed to utter in his presence, while he sat with his mouth full of scrambled egg.

There was no response at first. He carried on shovelling food into his mouth, his little pig-like eyes apparently on a spot just in front of him. Dorcas went back to the scullery and ran the water for the washing up.

She felt his presence like a dark shadow, a heaviness that pervaded the house. For a big man, he was surprisingly silent and sometimes she would turn and find him there, standing, staring. She made sure she did everything correctly. She packed his lunch bag and set it out on the table with his car keys and she made sure his clothes were properly ironed and put away. It was essentially a simple job, yet it exhausted her. As though she were waiting for something – a hard smack on the side of her head or a punch to the stomach. Waiting.

She didn't mind the mornings too much. She opened all the curtains in the house, even the ones that Mrs Pullman had told her to keep closed at certain times of the day when the sun came in directly and could spoil the furniture. The sunshine cast warm puddles of light along the corridor to Mrs Pullman's bedroom and there was something so alive, so immediate about the tiny specks of dust that danced in the illuminated air that gave Dorcas a strange reassurance. She didn't dare go right along the passageway to the bedroom. It was a mess, she knew, after the police had been in and muddled everything. Mrs Pullman would not have been pleased. Dorcas could just imagine her, hands on hips, ushering them all outside – 'Out, out, out, out!' – and giving them strict instructions to take their shoes off before they even thought of entering someone's bedroom.

Outside in the garden, while she stood watering, Dorcas loved to hear the birds chatting busily in the jacarandas and watch the bees disappearing into flowers. Everything alive, everything unconscious of tragedy or loss. Wasn't that the best way to be? For a long time now she had envied animals and insects, even plants and flowers, their absence of knowledge. To not know sadness, to not carry that ever-increasing burden of responsibility, was nirvana in itself.

Dorcas had a memory, a very faint memory of sitting next to the fire with her grandmother. She was young, perhaps four or five, and her grandmother had told her stories of animals. *The Lion and the Hare. How the Elephant got his Trunk.* Stories in which everything was resolved in the end. The lion was sent away with his tail between his legs, defeated by the cunning of the hare who was clever and quick-witted and so saved his own life by talking and bargaining.

There had been an incident in the village, a rape, but Dorcas did not know this until many years later. Her grandmother had taken her away while the elders talked. She had sat with her in the warm darkness of the hut and told her story upon story. As she talked, her voice changed. Sometimes she was the lion, sometimes the elephant or the rhinoceros. Sometimes, she was a dove or an ant. She gesticulated wildly, pointing here and there and clicking her tongue and pounding her feet on the floor. All the time, the elders sat outside discussing the fate of the unfortunate girl and the perpetrator of the crime.

'Some things are not for children to hear,' Dorcas heard her grandmother tell Dorcas's mother. 'Be careful what you say. Children understand much more than you think.'

Six months later, Gogo died. Dorcas remembered how she had crept into the hut when the darkness of night had descended and no one was looking. She had bent over her grandmother's body, which was wrapped in blankets. Her face was unexpectedly peaceful, but she was afraid to hold her hand, although she wanted to. She wanted to lean over and say, 'Gogo? Gogo, wake up.' She didn't because she knew it wouldn't happen and, rather than have her fears confirmed, she held onto her words to avoid disappointment.

Dorcas viewed the time before her grandmother's death as her insect life, the time when she played, oblivious to any danger, when days were filled with glorious adventure without any sense of harm. The day began at sunrise and ended in the gathering darkness when she curled up next to the old lady and fell gently asleep. Everything lived forever, everything stayed the same. Her insect days: the days before Fear.

While she watered the Pullmans' garden, Dorcas looked at the large, bright bushes of lavender and daisies and the glorious pink geraniums that spilled out of the pots on the verandah and she thought how temporary human life was, how the rest, the flowers and the trees and the bees and sunbirds, all went on, whatever happened indoors.

It seemed to Dorcas then that her life was taking a new direction. There had been many times in the last few months when she had felt that this was it. This was all life was going to give her. She had felt trapped and afraid. She had been easily led down a path littered with all sorts of distractions and she had been so busy looking at them that she failed to notice that at the end of the path, coming nearer and nearer was a single cell, a room with no windows and a tightly locked door. It was into this she had been led and left. What would happen now? Would the walls fall away and the sky fall in?

It's what they had discussed this afternoon. They had to be quiet and keep a low profile. It would all blow over. Give it a couple of weeks, that's what he said – but she wasn't so sure. It was that policeman. He was asking questions, investigating. He had seen madam's diary. He would find out. He was far too clever, too knowledgeable somehow. He with his clean-shaven open face with those eyes that seemed to see into you somehow.

The kind of policeman she was used to was watchful, but for other reasons. Their eyes followed you with a watchful greed. How could they get what they wanted, be it money or goods – or sex? But the truth, the truth was rarely something a police officer looked very hard for unless it benefitted them in some way. She had too much experience of their kind to make her trust any of them, ever.

Roland was adamant everything would be okay. She made lunch for them and they watched a DVD. It was her favourite – *The Wizard of Oz*. Usually, it would absorb her completely. She had watched it so many times, she came to imagine herself as Judy Garland. She wished her own house, her little khaya, would be picked up by a tornado and deposited in a magical world. She imagined herself singing and dancing as she skipped down the yellow brick road, her two plaits flapping against her back as she ran along. *We're off to see the Wizard, the wonderful Wizard of Oz!* Today, she had been distracted and irritable and hardly followed what was happening. Roland could sense her unease but he could do little to placate her. It's not that he was not sympathetic, but he found it difficult to reach beyond himself. The arm around her shoulder was tentative and awkward; his glum face said it all as his hand slipped from her and he sunk back into the chair.

When she left, a feeling of heaviness lay between them. She didn't want to go back next door, but she didn't want to stay either. It would be quiet at home. Silent. He never asked her to stay though and she wondered if he ever considered her life beyond the confines of his house. Sure, she had told him about the job, but what else did he know? She had existed before all this; she had had another life, but she had folded it up with all her other secrets she wished to forget and had got on with this life, giving it everything she could.

It had been exciting at first, working in such a beautiful house. She had been afraid of dropping things and was always careful when she washed the dishes that nothing was chipped or broken. It was a boring job in many ways; her friends at the market did not envy her. Their conversation was always full of life and colour as they spoke of the characters who frequented their stalls and the competition between vendors to sell the most or have the most popular stand. Dorcas's life was lonely, but she was content. In particular, she loved routine: polishing the same steps day after day, dusting the shelves, dipping dirty plates into hot soapy water and watching them emerge with a silky clean whiteness; stacking them to dry on the rack and letting her eye run along them. She enjoyed being alone, comforted by the sound of the clock ticking and the cat rubbing against her ankles when he wanted to be fed.

At the end of every day when she looked into the kitchen to check that it was clean and tidy, she felt a surge of pleasure; everything was in its place, everything was content. Even the cupboards and the table and the vase of flowers were happy, beaming at her with an innate joy. Another day lay before her ready to be unfurled and lived and she wallowed in its latent monotony.

And then one day, something else had entered the picture, a shadow in which lurked the figure of Mrs Pullman. Dorcas remembered how she had been mopping the floor and humming a very low tune when suddenly she had become aware that she was not alone. She had jumped when she saw Mrs Pullman watching her from the doorway to the passage and her humming had stopped immediately.

'Mrs Pullman... madam...' she had faltered.

But Mrs Pullman had turned away and disappeared before she had even finished uttering the words. Was that it, thought Dorcas sadly, was that when it had started?

Dorcas disliked late afternoon; she always had. It was the time when visitors arrived. There were drinks and snacks, dinner parties. There were bridge evenings and there was book club – and she was there until late, her legs aching, washing up and putting things away. Mrs Pullman hated any washing up to be left at the sink. She thought briefly then of the two plates and two glasses found next to the sink on the day Mrs Pullman died. As she walked up the drive and round to the khaya, she wondered if she should have told that policeman about the phone call.

She approached the khaya and stopped just before she got there, key in hand. She was reminded of how she first felt when she saw it two years earlier. She had been completely lovestruck, completely bowled over. It was neat and clean and even included a proper bed with linen and something called a duvet; a cupboard and a two plate stove and there was a flush toilet and shower with hot water. Curtains! She had never had curtains before. She remembered how she had lain on the bed and spread out her arms and felt a great thrill of success shudder through her. She had made it. After everything: her short-lived marriage, the death of little Farai, the grief. Her life was going to change forever. A good salary and a place to live. What could be better?

There's no such thing as a free lunch. Isn't that what he had said to her that day she had told him? Certainly not in Zimbabwe, anyway.

She would have to hurry now into the house and close all the curtains. Mr Pullman was eating out that night so she didn't even bother to set the table. She was late. If she closed all the curtains by four, she wouldn't be in there when the darkness started to come down, for in the late afternoon a shadow crossed the garden and house which fell into a deserted quiet.

'Quick,' she thought to herself, looking at her watch. 'Time to move.'

Chapter Twenty-two

Roland felt quite sick. His head seemed to be full of some strange buzzing noise and he wondered if he weren't about to have a heart attack.

'Oh, God,' he thought wildly, 'this is it. This is how my life will end.'

The world whirled around him in a halting staccato way, a bit like a DVD that has got stuck. He put out his hand and steadied himself on the back of an armchair and leaned against the wall. The flowers on the curtains seemed larger and brighter than usual as they loomed close to his face.

'Mr Sherbourne? Mr Sherbourne, are you all right?' A voice came from far away and he was aware of someone else in the room. The someone came closer and became a long dark coat. The policeman – he was still here. The nightmare was not over.

Roland felt himself being led round the front of the chair and made to sit down. He collapsed into it and felt an instinctive urge to curl up in a ball and rock himself to sleep. A glass of water was put into his hands and someone clasped his fingers round it and held it up to his mouth.

'Mr Sherbourne, are you all right?' The voice was slightly louder and firmer than before. Roland took a deep breath and looked around him. He looked down at the glass and then up at the policeman.

'Here now,' he began, feeling a flush of irritation again. 'What's the meaning of this, going into my cupboards, in my kitchen and–'

'Getting you a glass of water? It's not a crime, Mr Sherbourne. I'm trying to help.'

'Help?' spluttered Roland, but all further argument died. He felt too weak to argue. If he could just muster enough strength to get this man out of his house once and for all.

He seemed to zone out again as the next time he became aware of the policemen's presence, he was holding a DVD cover out in front of him.

'Is this yours, Mr Sherbourne?'

Roland looked at it, pulled a face and looked away.

'Mr Sherbourne, I've asked you a question. Is this your DVD?'

'What if it is?' snapped Roland and immediately regretted the amount of energy it took out of him. '*The Wizard of Oz*. It's hardly pornography, is it?'

'Hardly,' agreed the policeman and again Roland had that strange feeling that he wasn't really a policeman at all. He wouldn't be surprised if he disappeared and was never seen again, like a being from another dimension. Roland wasn't the sort who believed in either angels or demons or anything supernatural. His hard-core atheism was an anathema to the imagination, but he still couldn't quite help feeling that he was in a strange dream. Was this Edmund Dube who he said he was?

'You watched it this afternoon, didn't you? You watched it with Dorcas Hlabangana in your bedroom.'

'I...' began Roland, feeling a wave of heat rise in him again. He stopped. He was exhausted. Dorcas, Marcia Pullman, this investigation, a strange man in his sitting room who had obviously not only been in his kitchen, but into his bedroom as well. He was losing control; all he had left was gradually spinning away from him.

'Yes,' he admitted wearily. 'Yes, I watched that DVD this morning with Dorcas Hlabangana in my bedroom. What are you going to do about it, arrest me?'

'I could,' replied the Chief Inspector simply. Roland's face fell in surprise. 'You lied to a police officer. You told me you didn't know Miss Hlabangana, but it's obvious you are in some sort of relationship.'

Roland choked and spilt water from the glass as he struggled to straighten himself in his chair.

'Please tell me the truth.' The policeman's voice was

harder now, although he did not raise it. 'I want to know where exactly you were on the day of Mrs Pullman's death. I want to know where Miss Hlabangana was.'

Roland was on the edge of the seat now. He was aware of himself making funny little spluttering noises, rather like those horrible toys that squealed in a high-pitched wheezing fashion when you stood on them.

'She wasn't with me. I... I don't know where she was. We don't normally – not during the day – only on Sundays. I mean–'

'You mean it's only since Mrs Pullman's death that you have been able to meet during the day?'

Roland nodded meekly. He was cornered, he knew. He felt like an errant child, the boy caught picking his nose and made to stand in front of the class and admit it. The figure of the policeman loomed over him. His coat seemed to billow out so that he looked like some sort of black Dracula who, hands clenched like he was used to perching on a branch somewhere, dominated the room and all in it.

'Are you protecting her?'

'Not at all. She's the maid, for goodness sake. Not some hardened criminal.'

'Everyone has the potential for murder, Mr Sherbourne.'

Roland didn't know what to say. If truth be told, he didn't know where Dorcas was that day. He believed her when she said she had been given the afternoon off and only returned at four. He had given her money to buy new clothes the Saturday before that fateful day, and Dorcas had told him she had spent the afternoon in town, looking for a suitable outfit.

'Did Marcia Pullman know of your involvement with her maid?' The Chief Inspector's words hit Roland like a steam train. It was the first open acknowledgement of his relationship with Dorcas and he shied away from it in acute embarrassment.

'No. No, she didn't.' Roland's voice was hoarse and low. He sounded like a man on a life support machine.

'Are you sure? Women have a way of knowing these things, you know? They see things that pass us men by: shared looks, eyes that rest that quarter of a second longer on another's face than they should, hands that touch accidentally.'

'Well, how could Marcia have seen any of that? I didn't go there.'

'But Dorcas came here. Mrs Pullman might have seen her.'

'I didn't know the woman. I had nothing to do with her.'

'Really?'

'Yes, really.'

'Yet you called her Marcia and not Mrs Pullman.'

'So?' spluttered Roland. 'Does it matter what I called her?'

'Perhaps not,' assented the policeman. He was silent for a moment while he paced the room, hands behind his back. Roland wondered if he did this for effect, but suspected he didn't. 'You have been involved with Miss Hlabangana for how long?'

'It's not what you think...'

The policeman raised his eyebrows and Roland wished he had never uttered such a cliché. That's what everyone said when they were caught red-handed.

'It really isn't,' he insisted. 'We don't... we aren't... it's not a *relationship*.'

He hated the policeman's stare; it unnerved him completely.

'I see. You just watch movies together. *The Wizard of Oz*.' He turned the DVD over in his hands, as though inspecting it for fingerprints.

'Yes,' said Roland, weakly. 'It's her favourite.' He smiled a very rare, sad smile. 'Judy Garland, that's who she wants to be, you know? A little white girl in Kansas with a dog called Toto. We used to joke that she – Marcia, Mrs Pullman, whatever you want to call her – was the Wicked Witch of the West and one day she would get so angry that she would disappear – pouf! – in a cloud of smoke.'

'Mr Sherbourne, tell me please why you disliked Marcia Pullman so much. I suggested earlier than she mistreated

Dorcas, but she didn't did she? I've seen the accommodation she was given. It's pristine. Do you know how many maids would love to have what Dorcas had?'

Roland put his head back, squeezed his eyes shut and let out a deep breath. 'There is a price to pay for everything, Chief Inspector. That is the way of the world.' Roland looked sad and defeated. 'Well, she had to be there all the time, sometimes until quite late at night. They were always entertaining. Parties, dinners. Lots of people passing through. Hunters, I gather. They come here for the season. They paid huge amounts of money and dinner with Marcia was often thrown in as a freebie. Lots of imported wine, whisky, good food. That ape of a husband of hers would tell them some hunting stories from his repertoire to get them in the mood and then off they'd go to have their very own African experience.'

'All this you got from Dorcas.'

Roland sighed wearily. 'She's no fool that girl. She shouldn't be a maid really.'

Edmund turned to the window and looked out at the house quiet and lonely next door.

'Do you ever leave this house?' The question hit Roland hard. He felt like a character in a movie who has taken a few punches and struggles up from the floor only to find a boot in his face.

He shook his head. 'Rarely. I don't like the outside world, Chief Inspector.'

'Shopping?'

He shrugged. 'Dorcas does it for me... and I have an arrangement with a small supermarket. The owner's known me for years. He delivers once a week.'

'You don't work?'

'No. I was left some money by my parents. I... play the market. Stocks and shares.' He looked over at the policeman who seemed to be eyeing him suspiciously. 'Not here. I have some money outside the country. It's not a fortune, but it's enough. My needs, as you can imagine, Chief Inspector, are not great.'

The policeman nodded and seemed to be contemplating whether to ask another question. Eventually he said: 'Mrs Pullman met someone for lunch on the day that she died with the initials S.P. Do you happen to know who this might be?'

Roland shrugged as though Edmund had just asked him who the first prime minister of Lithuania was.

'I thought you might have seen someone. Perhaps a person who has been before?'

Roland shook his head, but his eyes wouldn't meet Edmund's.

'Is there anything else you want to tell me?'

Another shake of the head.

'Do not think of going anywhere, Mr Sherbourne. This matter is still under investigation and I will need to speak to you again.'

Roland's mouth opened and then closed. He looked away, tired and scared. He had an awful feeling the world was about to rush into his reclusive kingdom and haul him out.

Chapter Twenty-three

That night Edmund had the dream. It was a long, long time since he had had it last. He was alone. He was young, a small boy looking for his mother. He had walked home from school as he usually did, and lifted the latch on the gate. It squeaked open, as it always did, and he walked up the drive, as he always did. There was a silence; the silence of Sunday morning when even the birds are quiet and the house is absent of the sound of sweeping or washing or voices calling to each other from different rooms; the hurried voices of the week; orders, plans, lists; voices that get into cars and leave the house while a gate swings shut with the fluid assurance of midweek attention to detail.

But it is not Sunday. It is Wednesday. He drops his school satchel outside the screen door of the kitchen. He peers through the green mesh; the kitchen is empty.

'Mama. Mama?' he calls, gently. His mother has told him many times not to shout.

He opens the door and steps inside. He will get into trouble, he knows. You cannot just walk into a house like this, but something pulls him, drags him through. Room after room is empty. Empty of everything. Tables, chairs, beds, the dresser, the radio, the tea set on the silver tray. Everything is gone.

'Mama!' he calls, louder now, more intense, more desperate. 'Ma-ma!'

The wind blows through bare windows and a piece of newspaper skitters across the floor. Squares of sunlight glare at him, the trees outside loom closer. He runs from room to room. The rooms never end; they fold out like a line of dominoes falling one after the other. Each one is empty, silent, full of a strange kind of yellow light that is at once airy and claustrophobic.

'Mr MacDougal. Mrs MacDougal. Where are you?' He stands still and calls. The words come back at him, *you, you, you*. He shouts, he screams. But there is nothing, nothing, nothing.

Edmund had woken that morning with a strange sense of longing. He had glanced at the photo of the Renault 4 again, but this time, instead of putting it back in his drawer, he had slid it into his little notebook and put it in his pocket.

The newspapers were a day late in reporting the death of Marcia Pullman. One paper bore the headline: 'Woman Dies in Frenzied Attack' and another 'Mysterious Death in Suburbs House'. Both stories were rather scanty on the truth. Mrs Pullman had been murdered in her bed with a kitchen knife ran the first story. There was blood all over the walls and there was evidence to suggest a violent and prolonged struggle. The domestic worker, Miss Dorcas Hlabangana, had found the woman dead when she wondered why she hadn't seen her for a while. Someone may have come in through the window.

The second story suggested the gardener's hand in events. He had damaged Mrs Pullman's car and she had taken the money out of his wages. He was so angry he came back to confront her but he found her dead. In his anger, he stabbed her four to five times.

The Senior Assistant Commissioner, Constantine Magwali, otherwise known as The General, was reading the newspaper when Edmund entered just before lunchtime. He placed it on the desk in front of him with a sigh.

'Yes, Dube.' He stared up at the younger man with obvious irritation. 'Sit down,' he ordered, motioning to the chair with a nod of his head.

An interminable silence reigned, in which The General drained his teacup with a very long and noisy slurp and then sighed a great many times. He was a large man with glasses and greying hair; his bulbous features made him look like an oversized bullfrog behind the desk. He took great pride in sharing his first name with Constantine the Great of Rome, a man who, as he often told the force, not only converted to Christianity at a time when it may have cost him his life, but was also a great strategist and military general. Eventually, he folded the newspaper and placed it in front of Edmund. The headline glared up at him.

'The truth, Dube, is, like the saying says, in the eye of the beholder.'

Edmund didn't think it was worth trying to answer. He adopted an inquiring look instead.

'You know what I mean, hah? You know what I mean.' Edmund was about to hazard an interpretation when he realised his superior was not waiting for an answer. 'Everybody's truth is different, Dube.' He stabbed his short fat fingers into the newspaper. 'Yes, everybody's truth is different.' He settled back into his chair as though he had said something quite profound, but Edmund was still at a loss at understanding.

Edmund leaned forward to say something, but his boss carried on. 'What we need is one truth. One truth, Dube. You understand?'

'I'm not sure I do.'

'What I am saying, Dube, is that we need to come together, to agree. You understand me, huh? You understand?'

'Yes, but–'

'I have the pathologist's report,' he carried on, opening a drawer and removing a plastic file. He placed it on the desk near his elbow, making no attempt to show it to Edmund. 'It appears Mrs Pullman died of kidney failure. She had been suffering for a while. Her doctor has confirmed these details.'

'What about the stabbing?'

'She did not die from the stab wound. She was already dead.'

'Yes, but why was she stabbed if she was already dead?'

The General was silent for a moment. The older man stared hard at Edmund, his mouth working as though he were chewing on something. Edmund couldn't see his eyes, only his own reflection in the Senior Assistant Commissioner's glasses.

'I have given you more information than you are entitled to hear. Now, you must be satisfied that this is not a murder investigation, but a case of breaking and entry.'

'But, sir–' began Edmund.

'Enough. I want you to leave this case alone. Do not get involved. You hear me? I've put Khumalo in charge. The gardener is in custody as we speak. Malakai Ndimande.'

'He's not involved.'

There was a wry smile and something of a snort. 'You have *evidence*? You have evidence he's not involved?'

'Do you have evidence he is?'

The fist banged on the table so loudly and so unexpectedly that Edmund visibly jumped.

'You think you know everything, don't you? You think you know as much as me?'

'I am sorry, sir. It's just that I have an idea. I've been thinking a lot about the case. I do not think the ex-gardener had anything to do with it. If I could just explain to you why–'

'You are doubting me?' The head's lip quivered with anger as he pushed his glasses back up his nose.

'No... I mean...'

They sat in silence for a minute. Edmund tried to summon the courage to put his argument across, but he could feel the General's anger simmering as he fiddled with the top of his pen.

'May I be excused, please, sir?' Edmund longed to be out of the office and out of sight.

There was silence.

Edmund tried again. 'Please, sir–'

'Rumour tells me you let someone go. A Mr...' he looked down at his notes – 'Mr Martin Craig?'

'Craig Martin. Yes, but–'

'But nothing. You think because he has a white skin he cannot do anything wrong?'

243

'No, no, it's not that it–'

'He ran away from a crime scene and you let him go?' He threw up his hands in despair.

'I *didn't* let him go. He ran away. I gave instructions for him to be picked up at his house.'

The General spluttered into laughter. His long, yellow teeth seemed to spring forward like that of a hyena. 'I see, I see. *You gave* instructions. You sent two police officers away from the scene of a crime when you had no authority to do that.' His face suddenly became very serious. The yellow teeth disappeared and the flap of skin under his chin grew taut. He looked intently at Edmund. 'My friend, you are getting yourself into very deep water. You understand? You understand what I am saying? You have no idea the trouble this could get you into.'

Edmund felt a tingle of fear run down his spine. He wished he could stand up, call him an idiot and disappear out of the door and into his faithful Hirondel. He sat still, refusing to nod his head.

At that moment there was a knock on the door and a young woman by the name of Catherine entered with a brown paper packet smelling strongly of grease and vinegar.

'Ah, my lunch?' said the General looking up. 'What is it, a burger?'

'A chicken burger and chips, sir,' she said, placing it on the side of his desk.

'Chicken? I said beef, hey? Beef. Why did you bring me chicken?'

'There was no beef,' she replied placidly, placing a pile of paper napkins next to the bag and lining up a plastic knife and fork as though she were laying the table in the restaurant of a grand hotel.

'Did you get extra salt?'

'Yes, sir.' She placed four packets of salt next to the knife and fork.

'They never give enough salt,' he said to Edmund as though it were the worst thing in the world. He reached into

244

the bag and brought out four long greasy chips and stuffed them in his mouth. He shook his head. 'Give me the salt.' He licked his fingers and scattered a sachet of salt across his chips. Edmund felt his argument dissipating in front of the arrival of food.

'You can go,' said the Chief, with a flick of his hand as though dismissing an errant child who has been formally reprimanded. 'Just remember what I said.'

Edmund's heart sank as he realised any protest would be in vain. 'Yes, sir,' he said, standing up. 'Good afternoon, sir.'

'How's that paperwork coming on by the way, Dube?'

Edmund was just approaching the door, his hand on the handle.

'Fine. Fine, thank you, sir.'

'Good, good. That's what I like to hear. Progress is good.'

Once outside the office, he kept his head down and disappeared into his office telling the front desk that he was busy finishing the traffic incident reports and was not to be disturbed. He tried to inject a confident, serious tone into his voice, but couldn't help see the way that Bhebhe sucked in his lips, trying not to laugh. They knew of course, everyone did, that he had been taken off the case. But this time Edmund felt he had an ace up his sleeve. He'd show them who was boss when he had everything worked out. Once alone, he worked on compiling his notes on the case and carefully typed them up. It was usually an activity that gave him quiet satisfaction, but today he felt on edge. It was a mixture of excitement and unease and, at about nine o'clock, he made sure his desk was tidy and set off to catch a kombi.

'Tea, Inspector?' Mrs Whitstable leant forward in her wheelchair and turned the teacups over onto the saucers.

'Yes, please,' said Edmund. 'Milk, no sugar, thank you.'

He had arrived at the house on the pretext of seeing Janet Peters whom he knew was at work. He'd offered to come back later, but Mrs Whitstable had asked him in instead, as he had hoped she would.

'There was a time when everyone had sugar in their tea. Now it's tantamount to asking for a cigarette.'

Edmund took the teacup from her outstretched hand.

'We used to smoke, too. All of us. We all smoked and drank gin,' she laughed. He watched her face soften as she did so and caught a glimpse of a younger woman. 'Even when pregnant. But everything is a sin nowadays, isn't it?' Edmund looked up at her as he took a sip of tea. It was surprisingly hot and made him wonder if he didn't usually drink his lukewarm.

'Nice teacups,' he said, admiring the dark pattern of red roses and little green leaves.

'Thank you. They were a wedding present. From my husband to me.'

Edmund became uncomfortably aware of holding something quite precious. She seemed to read his thoughts for she said: 'Don't worry. I know you won't drop it. I used to take it out for special visitors only. Nowadays, well, we don't get many visitors, special or not.'

'Thank you. I'm honoured.' *Thank you, I'm honoured?* Where did those words come from? Edmund had begun to feel strange. Not unwell, just as though he was having some sort of out of body experience. He had never been to England, but he felt he was there now. The carpet was old and threadbare, the walls needed a paint and the pictures in the room were dated and faded. Yet they all combined, with the grandfather clock, the tea service and the crystal decanters to give him a picture of something *real*. Marcia's house, for all its finery, wasn't *real*. It was only made to look so.

'I used to do a lot of entertaining when I was younger. There was always somebody around for tea or dinner. Of course, between my husband and I, we used to belong to many different groups and societies. Edward was a Lion for many years and I belonged to the Women's Institute. I used to give talks on the wild plants and herbs out in the bush. I was very interested, you see, in traditional medicine. I also loved amateur dramatics and I started a reading circle, too.'

'A reading circle? Like book club?'

'Book club!' she spat. 'I don't know what that's all about, Chief Inspector, but it's not about books.'

'Oh?' Edmund's ears pricked up.

'It's all about showing off. What you can provide in the way of drinks and snacks. What your house looks like. How many people you can accommodate. It was never like that in my day. We were genuinely interested in books. We did things simply, but properly.'

Edmund nodded in agreement and looked round the shabby room. He saw a house that had once welcomed visitors with tea in teacups and cake to be eaten with small delicate silver forks.

'I got so angry the other night when Marcia phoned Janet to organise the stocktake.'

'Why's that?'

'Well, everything with Marcia was orders – orders to do this and that. She never asked and, of course, Janet never protested.'

'I can see why that made you angry.'

'Oh, that's not what made me angry exactly. I'm used to it, although that doesn't make it sit any better with me. What made me really angry was her comment about the mushrooms.'

'Which was?'

'She asked Janet if she knew anywhere she could get mushrooms. A couple of the shops had sold out. She wanted them for some canapés she was making for her bridge club people and, before Janet could even answer, she said "Well, you're the wrong person to ask, aren't you? You and your Marie biscuits, you wouldn't know what a canapé was if it landed on your head."'

'How did Janet take it?'

'She was very upset, but she suggested Marcia phone another member of the book club who had made stuffed mushrooms the meeting before.'

'When was this?'

247

'Last Monday? Tuesday? I can't remember exactly, but I know it was at the beginning of the week. You and your Marie biscuits! I am infuriated by comments like that from complete Philistines. My husband was a doctor. When he was alive, we were comfortably off. Not rich, but we didn't need to be. We didn't worry over money. Not like we do now.'

'This is your house?'

'Yes, it is. We've lived here since 1958. We were in the bush for nearly five years. My husband was a doctor in Shangani. Then in '58 we moved into Bulawayo.' She smiled a tight, closed mouth smile. 'A long time ago now.' There was a pause while she seemed to be thinking. Suddenly she brightened. 'Janet moved back here after her divorce. It was supposed to be a temporary measure but that was about seventeen years ago.'

'Was that to look after you?'

'Me? Oh, I see. Absolutely not. She was hard up with a small child. I've only been in this' – she tapped the arm of the wheelchair with the flat of her hand – 'for about nine months.'

'It annoys you?'

'The cost annoys me. The operation and the subsequent treatment took what little savings we had and my grandson had to send money too.'

'I'm sorry.'

'To answer your question, yes, being in a wheelchair does annoy me. I've always been very active. People of my generation were, Chief Inspector. Far more than they are today. I was at one time a very keen amateur lepidopterist. You know what that is?'

Edmund shook his head.

'A butterfly collector. It was more than a hobby; I was quite serious at one time. Here, let me show you.'

She wheeled herself over to the oak sideboard and opened the left-hand cupboard.

'In there, if you wouldn't mind getting it for me, is the last bit of my collection.'

Edmund reached in and carefully lifted out a wooden tray

with a glass lid. It was thick with dust that she brushed off with her hand. She blew gently on the lid and then held it up for Edmund to see.

'My favourites. *Danaus chrysippus*. Beautiful, aren't they?'

Edmund nodded, looking closely at the row of butterflies, their brown and orange wings fixed forever in flight.

'Do you know that there are pictures of the *Danaus chrysippus* on the walls of ancient Egyptian tombs?'

Edmund shook his head.

'Butterflies are the souls of the dead waiting to pass through purgatory.' She spoke in a broad Irish accent.

Edmund turned to look at her.

'It's an Irish saying. Mind you, the Irish weren't alone in thinking that. The Romans believed a soul left the body through the mouth and it is often depicted in their art as a butterfly. The Greeks believed a new human soul was born each time an adult butterfly emerged from its cocoon.'

Edmund nodded and replaced the tray of butterflies in the cupboard, gently shutting the door.

'The Japanese believe something similar. One butterfly is a good omen, usually signifying that the soul of a loved one is visiting. Large numbers of butterflies, on the other hand, are not such a positive sign; they portend disaster.'

Standing up, Edmund's attention was drawn to two paintings on the wall. One showed a group of men and women at a feast. The men were wrapped in swaddling cloaks that fell about their torsos, revealing bodies rippling with muscles. The women who weren't naked served the rest of the company great clusters of grapes while exposing their breasts to all and sundry; those who were naked, stretched themselves luxuriously across the table in attitudes of lassitude and torpor. Cupids flew overhead whilst from the heavens another barely clad male figure reached down, offering the banqueters a golden goblet.

'What are they doing?' he asked.

'Drinking ambrosia, the nectar of the gods. It confers immortality or longevity on whoever consumes it.'

'I can see why it might have been popular.'

'Well, all may seek it, but it was only the gods who were allowed to drink it. The consumption of ambrosia is the demarcation of the division between humans and the gods.'

'Could the gods stop the humans from drinking it?'

'Oh, they had their ways. Through fear, mostly.'

The other picture was of a cluster of small mushrooms growing close to the roots of a large tree. A naked baby, lying on a pile of white cloth, reached its hands upwards as a thunderstorm raged. A great bolt of lightning cut across the sky.

'Filii Deorum,' Edmund read.

'The Sons of the Gods. Both the Ancient Egyptians and the Ancient Greeks believed there was a link between mushrooms and gods. Wild mushrooms were 'the sons of the gods' who had been sent to earth by lightning. They grew after thunderstorms and didn't have seeds like other plants did.'

'Who's the baby?'

'That's Dionysus. He's often referred to as the god of wine and fertility, but I prefer to think of him as the god of mystic illumination. His father, Zeus, was in love with his mother, a human called Semele. They became lovers, although she never saw him or even knew which god he was. Hera, who was both Zeus's wife and sister, found out about the relationship and convinced Semele to get Zeus to reveal himself to her in his true form. When he next visited her, she made him promise to agree to do whatever she asked him, which he did because he loved her so much. Obviously, he could not break his promise even when he found out what her request was. By revealing himself to her, he killed her with one of his thunderbolts and she burnt to death.'

Edmund's eyes opened wide in surprise. 'What happened?'

'Zeus managed to rescue their unborn child and sewed him into his hip so that he could be reborn at a later stage. Continuing to be eaten up by a jealous rage, Hera followed the boy, even arranging for him to be torn apart by the Titans – but that's another story.'

'Did you paint these?' he asked, looking back at the pictures.

'Only the second one. I painted it for my husband as a twenty-fifth wedding anniversary present.'

'It's good,' he said with a nod of his head.

'Well, all based on sketches I did. Even the baby is Janet as a baby. I could walk for hours as a young woman. Sometimes, I'd go out for two or three days in the bush, sketching and collecting specimens. Not just butterflies, plants too. There are cures for everything to be found in nature. In fact, some of the most poisonous plants are also medicinal; it just depends on how much is administered.'

'You are interested in herbal medicine? In my culture, we would call you a n'anga.'

'I don't do the funny stuff – you know solving marital problems and putting a curse on your neighbour and all that sort of thing.' She smiled. It was a cliché to say it, Edmund knew, but her eyes really did seem to twinkle. She leaned closer to him and tapped her right temple. 'I know how it's done though. The power of suggestion works wonders.' She wheeled herself nearer the table.

Edmund nodded his head slowly, but remained sceptical.

'I see you don't believe me, Chief Inspector. It works the same way as religion does. If you've done something wrong, you expect to be punished, not necessarily by the law, but by the law of God or the universe or whatever you want to call it. The Law of Retribution. What goes around, comes around. So the cheating husband is not surprised when he starts to feel various aches and pains or when he starts bleeding from his nose. He goes along with it because, somewhere deep inside of him, he knows he is being punished and he knows he deserves it. He becomes more and more ill and eventually he dies.'

Edmund thought hard about her words, but still wasn't convinced. He sat down again and picked up his teacup and saucer.

'Are the aches and pains real or imagined?'

'Oh, they're real enough. A bit of this or that in your food every day. It's the response that's so important. For many, perhaps even the vast majority, there is an understanding that a moral law has been broken and there will be a price to pay.'

'Some people don't have a conscience.'

'Hmm, Marcia Pullman. Those people, I'm afraid, are the hardest to deal with. Their idea of justice is everything working their way.'

'Did you ever meet Mrs Pullman?'

'No. I didn't want to. From what I gather, she was an awful woman, Chief Inspector. The nouveau riche is what we used to call them. Her money and her antiques and her fine wines. But who was she really, that's what I want to know? I guess, like a lot of white people here, she was nobody; a big fish in a small pond. We used to see it a lot in the 50s, you know, during the big immigration drive. People who came here with nothing, absolutely dirt poor, and suddenly they were someone: house, servants and car. They made money, but money can't buy class. Manners maketh man but Marcia certainly didn't have any.'

Manners maketh man. The words floated across to Edmund and he sat up with a little start. She noticed.

'You've heard the expression, Chief Inspector? It means–'

'I know what it means,' interrupted Edmund and then felt a little embarrassed for doing so. 'Excuse me, I was just remembering someone else who used to say that quite a lot.'

'A teacher? They're usually the type to come out with such maxims.'

'No... and yes. The man my mother used to work for. A long time ago now. He used to teach me in the afternoons.'

She didn't say anything; she took a sip of her tea and smiled blankly as though she had just missed part of the conversation.

'It's strange,' he continued, 'I've thought about them on and off for years, but since I started investigating this case, I seem to have continual reminders of them.'

There was no response again. Edmund wondered if she wasn't deaf. Her eyes were on him though. Surely she could see his lips moving. There was an awkward silence in which Edmund drank his tea as delicately as possible. It made him break out in a sweat and the cup wobbled precariously in his grasp.

'Such as?' she said suddenly and he looked up rather surprised.

'Oh... er... well such as a Renault 4 and... well... Ascot shopping centre.'

Her brow furrowed. 'Ascot?'

'We used to go there, you see. Mrs MacDougal would take my mother and me there at the end of every month. In her Renault 4. We'd go shopping. It was such a treat. I hadn't been there for such a long time and then I went there last week. It's funny how, even when a place changes, it still has the capacity to remind you of a time gone.' He smiled sadly and met her eyes with a shrug.

'And what happened to these people, the MacDougals?' She spoke in a Scottish accent.

Edmund took a deep breath and, in letting it out, felt himself collapse back into the chair slightly. He felt suddenly quite tired.

'I'm not sure. They left the country quite suddenly. Just before Independence.'

'For Scotland?'

'I don't know.' It was true, he didn't, but if the truth be told, nor did he think they had just moved. Initially, he thought they must have been kidnapped and were being held to ransom somewhere in Bulawayo. Then he thought they must have been Western spies, outlaws of the government, perhaps held in a top security jail somewhere. It broke his heart to think of Mrs MacDougal having to eat prison food. In some daydreams, he entertained the idea of Mr MacDougal managing to break out of prison by using his strong logical brain and mathematical ability. He imagined him sizing up the length of the jail bars with his little wooden ruler, making numerous calculations and then planning his great escape.

It had all been so sudden. He remembered coming back from school and finding his mother in tears. She had cried and sung sad hymns about Jericho and that was always a sign that someone had died. Except that no one had died this time. 'One day I came back from school and they had gone. They never said goodbye and we never saw them again.'

There was a pause. Edmund heard the clock ticking softly. 'You missed them?'

Another pause. 'Very much,' he said at last. 'Yes, I missed them very much. They taught me a lot. Maths and English. Poetry.' As he spoke, he had a very clear picture of his mathematical set. Mr MacDougal would place his ruler under the words that Edmund read. It was so neat and precise. Edmund had never met anyone else with a wooden ruler. 'I'd like to find them again though.'

Edmund became aware that he had entered some sort of reverie and sat up hurriedly. 'Tell me, Mrs Whitstable, how does your daughter manage financially?'

If he wasn't mistaken, he saw her mouth harden slightly and her eyes narrow.

'I suppose you get away with asking that sort of question by being a policeman. Well, things have been very hard for us both in the last few years. Janet used to work for a dentist, she was a receptionist, but then he left the country and Janet was out of work for a while. The way this country has gone, Chief Inspector.'

Edmund nodded. 'But one still needs to survive.'

'Yes, of course. Well, she got a job at Twice Loved and very lucky she was to get that.'

'But I understand that is a charity shop and she doesn't get paid?'

The mouth definitely hardened this time and she gently thumped the arms of the wheelchair with her hands. She moved it across the room with surprising speed. From a large and rather ugly writing desk she took a small notebook.

'I get an army pension from my husband. It's not very much, about a couple of hundred pounds a month, which is paid into my bank account here. I also get a very small pension of my own which is similarly paid out. It used to do us really well before we changed to the US dollar lark. Three hundred pounds was a lot of money to live on a few years ago. Janet didn't have to work. Then it all changed and she found it hard to get back into the job market. People asked questions, they inferred things, things that weren't true. We had to sell a few things at first. I had some good silver I had hardly ever used and some china. It tided us over for a while.'

'Mrs Peters has a son, I gather?'

'Yes. Jamie. He's in England. He sends money occasionally, mainly for big repairs. The geyser went last year and the year before that the car needed a new exhaust. He's a good boy, but he has his own life.'

Edmund wished his mother would say something similar. He could never do enough to help her.

'I'm sorry to ask you such personal questions. You probably don't think they are relevant to the investigation.'

'Not at all. Not many people are just murdered because they happen to be around at a particular place at a particular time. Every moment in our lives counts towards the next and even the moments in our neighbours' lives can count towards ours. We are all connected, aren't we? A butterfly flapping its wings in Brazil causes a tornado in Bulawayo.'

He looked at her, not understanding her reference.

'The chaos theory. Every action has a knock-on effect. Something seemingly irrelevant to you can have a profound effect on your life. If only we knew the full extent of our actions.'

'Technically, I'm not looking for a murderer,' said Edmund. 'Mrs Pullman was dead before she was stabbed. It appears she died of kidney failure.'

Mrs Whitstable nodded. 'I see. That's strange. Almost a bit disappointing.'

'Maybe not disappointing...'

'You don't believe it, do you?'

Edmund didn't reply.

'You think there's more to it, don't you?'

'Perhaps. I'm not sure.'

'I take it the will has been read?'

'Everything goes to the husband,' replied Edmund, thinking of Mr Pullman's angry outburst when he had asked him a few days earlier.

'Well, there you are!' She clasped her hands in glee. 'Case closed, I'd say.'

'You think he did it?'

'Nine times out of ten, it's the spouse. Didn't you know that? The person the police look at first is the spouse and it usually is them.'

Edmund wasn't quite sure of these rather sweeping statistics but didn't say so.

'Your crime stories wouldn't be very exciting if that were the case.'

'Oh, stories!' She swept the word away with a wave of her hand. 'This is real life.'

'All right. Why then? Why stab his wife?'

'That's a cover. She died of something else. Perhaps he poisoned her?'

Edmund shook his head. 'No. She had been suffering with kidney problems for a long time. Her family doctor has confirmed the information. The contents of her stomach revealed nothing remarkable. It doesn't appear that there was anything to hide.'

'Hmm,' muttered Mrs Whitstable. 'It's certainly a puzzle. I still think it's him though.'

'But *why*?'

'Why? A woman. It's generally a woman – or money. Or both.' Edmund watched her face brighten with delight at her simple solving of the puzzle. It was beginning to dawn on him that Mrs Whitstable's mystery solving skills were quite basic.

'Why does he have to kill her to have her money. She'd

already given him enough to start a safari business. She'd do that again, surely?'

'Would she? Perhaps his business had run into problems, ones she wouldn't have any sympathy with. Perhaps his woman wanted more and more. Maybe she wanted him to leave dear old Marcia, but a divorce would leave him penniless, death wouldn't.'

'Then why do it in such a way? If, as so many people think, no investigation is going to be carried out, why stab her? Why not poison her slowly or make it look like the gardener did it? Why not *pay* the gardener to do it?'

She was momentarily stumped but then waved her finger in the air knowingly. 'Conceit.'

'Conceit?'

'Yes, every murderer is conceited. If you have to prepare and plan down to every last detail and make sure that every eventuality is prepared for, then you have to be quite clever. Some part of you must want the police, the detective, the press, the public, *everyone* to know what you did and how you did it and how clever you are.'

'You wouldn't be very clever if you got caught.'

'But think how wonderful it must be to have everyone running around after you, how you must watch them trying to decipher clues and work out motives. It doesn't really matter if you get caught.'

'I'm not sure Nigel Pullman is that type.' Despite his bulldog personality, Edmund guessed Pullman was a man of simple thoughts.

'People will surprise you,' she said. 'When you get to my age, you are no longer able to be shocked. It's amusing sometimes to watch how people try to keep what they feel is shocking news from me. All I think is hurry up and be done with it. I'm eighty-three years old. What haven't I seen?'

Edmund smiled. He could imagine Mrs Whitstable was a force to be reckoned with. He wandered over to the sideboard and looked closely at the photo of a young woman. It was a close up of the head with the hair curled back from the forehead in soft waves. He recognised the large, intelligent eyes and the sharp nose, rather like a horse's.

'This is you?' His voice held a note of admiration.

'It may surprise you to know I wasn't always old, Chief Inspector,' Mrs Whitstable said, coming up behind him in the wheelchair. 'That was me in England, just before we came out here in '53. I hadn't long been married. My life was ahead of me then: all those years just waiting to be lived.'

Edmund cocked his head towards her. He couldn't tell if she were sad or grateful.

'Why did you leave England?' he asked. 'Why come here?'

'It was a different place then,' she smiled. 'A land of opportunity and adventure. Nowadays it seems it has become a land of opportunism and misadventure.' She looked at him and then away out of the window. 'I hope you don't mind me saying that, Chief Inspector. I don't want you to think I am some old colonial who can't let go of the past. I am sure you won't believe me if I say it was a very different world back then and our ideas were very, very different. I didn't come here to colonise anyone. It was going to be fun, *adventure*. But anyway, a lot of wrong has been done and here we are, many years down the line, paying the price.'

Edmund shot her a quizzical look. 'You think you are paying a price for the past?'

'We all do, Chief Inspector. And so will you, too, or your children, for the wrongs done today. The collective debt of a nation, that's what I call it. Collective karma. I believe in karma, Chief Inspector. Do you know what it is?'

'Hmm, not really,' he admitted, glancing briefly at the clock on the wall and aware that he ought to leave.'

'Basically, what goes around comes around.'

'You reap what you sow?'

'Yes, yes exactly. Except that you could reap it in another life.'

'Another life?'

'We live many times. Each time, our soul learns something new, sometimes through the mistakes made in a past life.'

Edmund nodded slowly.

'You're sceptical, I can see. Everyone is at first. My husband lost his faith in Christianity due to his experiences during the war, but he became interested in Eastern beliefs; it was he who told me about karma and I came to believe too. It's what makes revenge meaningless.'

'Revenge?'

'My husband was interned in a Japanese prisoner of war camp from 1942 to 1945. It was an awful time. I cannot even begin to imagine what it was like: people dying around you from typhoid and malaria and just plain exhaustion; fighting over a quarter cup of rice, being punished by being made to stay out in the sun, finding maggots in your food – and eating them – no, I cannot begin to imagine what it was like. He had a friend, Jack Sprall, everyone called him Jack Sprat, who survived with him, but he was so eaten up with grief and anger and a terrible need for retribution that he returned to Japan years after the War in the hope of finding his former captors.'

'And did he?'

'No. He searched for months. One day he was found dead in a hotel room. Slit his wrists.'

There was a silence. A light wind blew the curtain gently outwards.

'You have the windows open,' Edmund said, glad for the chance to change the subject. 'It's cold.'

'Old habits die hard,' she said. 'My husband had them open all the time. He couldn't bear to feel shut in. That's why we moved here – sunshine and space.'

There was another pause. Edmund had the sudden sensation that a lot of time had passed. Somebody would probably be looking for him – he had switched his phone off before coming in as he had not wanted to be disturbed. It was as though he had fallen into a slumber and must now awake.

'The point I was trying to make, Chief Inspector, is that searching isn't always a good thing. If something is going to come our way, it will do so of its own accord. Don't get lost in the search.'

'You mean...?'

'Your friends, the MacDougals. Sometimes it's best not to look too hard.'

Edmund was silent for a moment. Was it disappointment he felt? Had some tiny part of him thought she would help him find them?

'We all pay in the end for what we have done in our lives.'

'Do we?'

She smiled as though he should know.

'What did Marcia pay for?'

'She was nasty, really nasty.'

'Nasty enough to be murdered?'

She shrugged and seemed to have become very small and shrunken again. 'Everyone is called one day to settle their karmic account. Each of us will face our day of reckoning. This time it was Marcia's turn.'

Chapter Twenty-four

At half past six that evening, Edmund was still at the police station. For the past couple of months, he had found himself staying longer and longer at work. Ostensibly, it was to avoid the rush hour crush in overfull commuter omnibuses and it gave him the opportunity to catch up on paperwork. If he was honest with himself, it was also because he felt there was little to rush home for.

Mary would be chatting as usual to neighbours and friends and she seemed reluctant to come in and start making the evening meal. He saw a look on her face sometimes that was resonant of a feeling he had had as a child, when he was having fun at Rupert's house, jumping boisterously onto the mattress in the bedroom from the window sill and Rupert's elder sister had walked in and warned them both to calm down or they'd be in *big trouble*.

The police station was a different place at night. It grew considerably more interesting the later it became. There were drunkards to contend with and the nightly round up of prostitutes who were brought in on the back of a truck. The officer in charge would stand and laugh as they struggled to jump off in their high heels and minute skirts, but even then there was a feeling of bonhomie as the women laughed and clucked their tongues at the charge officer as he tried to look up their skirts. Some of them entered the cells with an exaggeratedly suggestive gait and called to the young officers through the bars to bring them water and something to eat as though they were ordering food in an expensive restaurant.

Edmund missed his time working nights. Since he had been promoted, he only worked daytime hours. He loved the feeling of being awake while the world was asleep. He loved the colourful nocturnal characters who came alive in all their splendour in the dark of night and disappeared, like vampirish unearthly creatures with the dawn. There was a camaraderie in the station itself that wasn't there during the day. Those on night duty were more willing to share food and stories and volunteer to make tea. It was as though there were an acknowledgement somewhere that it was a special time that existed outside the bounds of normal hours and therefore normal behaviour.

It was easy to enter the records room without being noticed. The door was never locked and no one worked in it at night. There was no reason Edmund shouldn't enter it; he was a Chief Inspector after all. Yet he couldn't help feeling that he was doing something he shouldn't be. He had a feeling of being watched, even when eyes weren't on him and everyone else at the station seemed to be getting on with their jobs, oblivious to his presence. It was as though all his movements were being recorded by some invisible presence, a something that hung in the air and permeated the tiniest nook and cranny of the police station. Something vengeful.

Edmund closed the door of the records office carefully behind him and glanced around; the place was a mess. Every shelf, every filing cabinet, every desktop and every chair was covered in files. Piles of papers, folders and dossiers stacked untidily on the floor leaned precariously towards each other like miniature towers of Pisa, ready to topple at any moment. He was in the records room every day, filing traffic offence charges. It was he who had tried to bring some order to it by sorting the files into year order, even if every visit meant almost starting again as it seemed impossible for anyone else to grasp the idea and advantages of an ordered and effective system.

Edmund sighed. Perhaps she was right: Mrs Whitstable that was. Was it worth chasing the past, trying to track it down and shake the truth out of it? Or was it best left alone, folded away carefully, layer upon layer pressed firmly down before the drawer is locked and the key hidden?

The older records were the easiest to find, stored as they were in steel grey 1950s filing cabinets, each drawer fronted by a typed name card denoting the alphabetical placing of the contents inside. Still, it was not uncommon to find an empty drawer, or one missing a bottom or one that couldn't open properly as it had come off its runner. Edmund even found one that contained only an empty coke bottle, a newspaper from two years ago and a half eaten packet of lemon cream biscuits.

'Mc' and 'Mac' were listed together. MacDougal, Archibald Balfour. Edmund pulled out the file. He cleared a chair to sit on and took a long deep breath and breathed out.

On opening the file, the first thing he saw was Mr MacDougal's photograph. He was younger than Edmund remembered him: he had more hair and his face was smooth and wrinkle free, young, looking to the future.

Edmund scanned over the details: date and place of birth, schooling, qualifications, height, weight. His eyes darted over the papers. Rank promotions, applications for leave, a letter confirming his position as Chief Inspector CID, Bulawayo Division, another praising his efforts to improve police performance. There was nothing, nothing to suggest his retirement or otherwise: no reason for his sudden disappearance.

Edmund went back to the details at the beginning of the file. He was aware he was reading too fast and not taking everything in. He started again. And that's when he saw the note, right at the bottom of the form listing personal details. October 19th, 1979 – suspended from duty pending further investigations. Edmund almost dropped the file. He turned sharply and glanced towards the door. It was ever so slightly open and he was so sure he had closed it firmly. He slipped the file under his coat, put the coat over his arm and made his way out of the records office, his heart beating faster than usual. He walked quickly past the front desk and down the steps of the police station into the darkness of the winter night. The street was quiet. At the end of the road, he stopped and looked back at the police station illuminated in a pool of light. There was no one there, no one at all, and yet he couldn't help feeling someone was following him. He hugged his coat closer and crossed the road.

Ndhlovu was easy to find. Most nights he could be found at the end of the counter in the bar of The Flame Lily Hotel, a small establishment in the middle of town. It had once been popular with middle class salesmen who liked its proximity to Bulawayo's business district in the daytime and its restaurants and bars in the evening. Now that business was on the decline and most eating places of any repute had moved into the more salubrious suburbs, it was slightly down at heel and in need of a makeover. However, although the smell of stale beer was a little too strong, the carpets worn and the framed prints of flame lilies had faded into a uniform yellow, it still maintained a small dedicated clientele. Ndhlovu was surprised when Edmund sat himself beside him, but happily accepted his offer of a drink.

'You're not having one?' He took a long drag of his cigarette and blew the smoke out of his nostrils.

Edmund shook his head. 'I'll get to the point right away.' He was nervous, his words jerky and unwieldy in his mouth as they tumbled out one after another.

'Chief Inspector Archibald MacDougal. You remember him?'

There was the slightest of nods as Ndhlovu stubbed out his cigarette.

'What – what happened to him?'

Ndhlovu laughed. 'That was a long time ago. You are talking to a madala now. This' – he tapped his forehead – 'does not work so well any more.'

Edmund shook his head. 'If anyone can remember, you can. What's the saying, elephants never forget?'

Ndhlovu pursed his lips as though to suggest he didn't have much faith in the saying.

'Please, help me,' insisted Edmund.

Ndhlovu appeared to think long and hard.

'Edmund, why is it that you wanted to be a police officer? Tell me that.'

'I wanted to put everything right in the world. I wanted to do good. Isn't that every police officer's dream?'

Ndhlovu laughed; his lips drew back and his yellow teeth protruded. 'No, Edmund,' he said. 'It's not.'

He carried on laughing, even when he began coughing. He waved Edmund away with his hand.

'What do you know about Mr MacDougal? What happened?' Edmund persisted.

Ndhlovu sat shaking his head. 'The past is best left in the past. What has gone has gone.'

'What do you mean? What happened? I need to know. Why the mystery?'

Ndhlovu took a small sip of his beer and stared hard at the glass.

'You ask too many questions. Leave Pullman alone. It's not your case, Edmund. Leave it to the people who can do their job properly.'

'Pullman? I'm not asking you about Pullman!'

Ndhlovu stared hard at him. 'Mrs Pullman died of natural causes.'

'Mrs Pullman...?' Edmund's mind was abuzz with confusion. He knew he must pick his words carefully.

'The PM showed quite clearly that she was dead before she was stabbed. It is no longer a murder investigation. She died of kidney failure after suffering from kidney problems for a long time.'

'As confirmed by her doctor.'

'As confirmed by her doctor–'

'Who wasn't called to the scene.'

Ndhlovu stopped, his mouth set in a thin, hard line.

'Yet you were.'

'Do I need to remind you I am a government medical officer?'

'As well as Chief Pathologist.'

'As well as Chief Pathologist, yes.'

'Mrs Pullman's death–' Edmund began.

'Is none of your business.' Ndhlovu turned and faced

Edmund. His face was dark, his lips pinched. 'You're not a well man, Edmund. We've all tried to help, tried to put up with it. But now, well, it's getting dangerous, Edmund. We can't keep playing children's games just to make you happy. I had to cover you the other night until Khumalo arrived. If Pullman knew...'

Edmund stood very straight next to the bar counter, not either believing or understanding what Ndhlovu was saying. Children's games? Not well?

He opened his mouth to ask another question, but Ndhlovu was getting ready to light another cigarette. As he struck the match, his eyes narrowed and he looked sharply at Edmund through the thin curl of smoke.

'Thank you for the drink,' he said, looking directly into Edmund's eyes. 'Stay away, Edmund. If you know what's good for you, stay away.'

Edmund had the dream again that night, except this time it was different. He was small, he had to reach for the door handle. The door swung open easily.

'Mama!' he called. 'Mama!'

The rooms were empty. The white walls stretched up beyond him. He couldn't see where they ended, couldn't see the ceiling. They just went on and on, swaying, swaying, about to cave in, about to cover and crush him.

And then he could hear crying. Someone was weeping. A woman.

'Mrs MacDougal?'

Another room empty. Shadows from the trees outside fell in through the open window.

'Mrs MacDougal? It's all right. I've found him. I've found him. He's here. Here in my pocket.' Edmund took the photo out of his pocket. Mr MacDougal – so young. Not a mark on him. He'd live for years yet.

He could smell her before he saw her. That soft, powdery smell of rose talc. Coty, wasn't it? She sat in the corner, her large face red with crying. She mopped at her eyes with a white handkerchief. He tugged at her dress, he pulled her arm. He wanted her to see. *I've found him*. But she wouldn't listen. She was consumed with tears, with grief.

'Edmund, *how could you?'*

A white flower fell at his feet. A white rose. It shook wings from its petals and fluttered upwards. There was someone behind him. He had shut the door. He knew he had. Who was it, who was following him? His heart was pounding. His mouth was dry, his throat tight with the pain of fear.

A girl. The girl on fire. A girl doing cartwheels across the room, oblivious to the flames that consumed her. She was laughing, laughing as she turned.

She's going to die, thought Edmund. He wanted to shout, he wanted to tell her, but when he did the words came out all wrong.

'I'm going to die!' he screamed. 'I'm going to die!' She laughed, a deep belly laugh, on and on, her mouth red and smiling. Mary's mouth.

I'm going to die!

Edmund jolted awake. It was dark and cold, but he was sweating. He leant over to turn his bedside light on. The switch clicked futilely. The power was off. He felt about carefully until his hand located the glass of water next to his bed. He drank it all at once and then lay back against the pillow and tried to calm himself. The dream had changed. What did she mean? *How could you?* He tried to remember that day, but everything was a blank. Yet there was something there, something he couldn't quite grasp. A feeling, a memory. If only he could remember what had happened. As his eyes became used to the darkness, he began to make out various shapes and objects. He began to feel more assured, less afraid as he did so. He felt a sense of relief. It was just a dream, just a nightmare. It wasn't real.

He picked up his clock and peered at the time. It was eight minutes to four. That meant it was eight minutes to three in Scotland. He wondered what they were doing, whether they were even alive, whether they ever thought of him and his mother and what had become of them.

His mind drifted and he thought of Marcia Pullman and who could have stabbed her. A slight panic arose in him. It didn't seem to matter to many people. How could it be that someone could be so universally disliked and yet no one had challenged her? Other people would have been shunned, ignored, left out of book club and bridge evenings. Yet she was like a planet around which many moons orbited. She was rich, she was greedy, she was nasty and yet everyone wanted to come along to her parties.

At times like this, Edmund despaired of human nature. Or was it as widespread as that? Was it just in Africa – just in Zimbabwe, even – where a culture of greed and mediocrity was not just encouraged, it was positively envied? People revered idiots as long as those idiots were rich beyond the dreams of the average person. Plunder was applauded, the blatant abuse of funds went unquestioned. It was less to do with fear, thought Edmund, than a misguided sense that those in a certain position should be allowed to wield absolute power.

People didn't want to see government ministers in second-hand cars, doing their shopping in a supermarket and talking humbly to those who voted them in. Instead, people liked to see their taxes well spent, to know that the money that could have mended roads or built a hospital, paid for a weekend in Paris, a night at the Ritz. There is a delight in opulence, even if it never spreads its golden fingers over your cold, grey existence or deigns to speak to you in words other than orders to move out of the way or get me this or that. If we cannot have it, somebody else shall and we must buoy that person up at all costs.

Mary stirred. It was as though she had read his thoughts and was waking him up to tease him. She always made fun when she felt he was 'being serious'. She turned over and snuggled down underneath the blanket. Edmund sighed. He thought of Craig Martin, sleeping alone every night, and how he probably envied Edmund his wife – the company, the comfort, the togetherness – and Janet Peters, also alone and yet was she lonely? Edmund couldn't imagine that she longed for male company. He thought she was beyond that and probably preferred to be on her own.

Mrs Whitstable – he felt her loss more than he felt Janet's. Hers was the loss of somebody dearly loved, a soul mate, a true love. How many people got to that stage anymore? How many seemed to give up along the way? He thought of his mother and how she had kept the existence of his father secret for many years.

Edmund looked at his clock again. It was half past four. He swung his legs out of bed and into the cold morning air.

'What are you doing?' It was Mary; she peered at Edmund through half closed eyes.

'I'm going to work,' he said, putting on his shirt and buttoning it up.

'It's early. Are you mad?'

'No. I just can't sleep. You go back to sleep. I've got quite a lot of work to do. See you later.'

He was about to leave the room when he hesitated momentarily and returned to Mary's side. Leaning over her, he gave her a quick light kiss and then turned hurriedly and walked out of the door.

1979

Edmund thought he was dead. A liberation hero, a man who died so that others may live in peace. He had never known his father so he could hardly miss him, but sometimes when he saw families walking down the road together or fathers dropping their sons at school, he felt the loneliness of the mother and son twosome he inhabited and wondered what it would be like to have a father. It was that same loneliness that brought Rupert and him together in their strange, strained friendship, and the same one that drew him to the soft comfort of the MacDougals.

One night, Edmund had woken to the sound of an argument. He could hear his mother's voice and that of a man and he had peeped through the curtain that separated the mattress from what his mother very ostentatiously called the sitting room, which was an old green sofa that the MacDougals had sold to her the previous year when they were replacing their lounge suite. She couldn't afford the whole suite so the two armchairs were sold to Nyathi, the gardener.

'You are *my wife*,' he heard the man's voice insist. There was a hint of menace in the tone, a sense of appropriation that attempted to smother his mother's protest.

'And where have *you* been for the past five years, my husband, hah? You tell me that. Where have *you* been?'

The voices continued for some time. There were insults, threats of recriminations, argued points. Then suddenly, the voices had stopped and Edmund heard a door close and he hurried back onto the mattress.

In the darkness, he heard his mother crying softly next to him. He did an unusual thing then, strange for him who kept his emotions locked so securely away. He put his arm around her and patted her shoulder. He was shocked then at her reaction for her gentle sobs became heaving, relentless tears. The sadness she had kept hidden in her heart for so long was let free at last.

Chapter Twenty-five

By seven o'clock, Edmund was outside the National Archives building. He was early but he wanted to be there when it opened. It was cold; the air was fresh with an icy bite. It would warm up later, but in the hollows of doorways and the shadows of buildings, a dark shiver lurked. The early morning sun was not enough to warm oneself in and Edmund found himself rocking forward on the balls of his feet and rubbing his arms, trying to get warm. He had got to the police station early that morning only to find the records room padlocked. The officer on duty had looked shiftily at him when he asked for the key and then said that it had been locked for the sake of security.

'But I am your senior officer. I have every right to the records room. Give me the key.' But the man just shook his head and said he didn't have it. Edmund sat in his office fuming silently. He was on to something; he *must* be on to something. Why the closed doors and the averted eyes? Why the turned backs and the barely veiled warnings?

They could keep him away from police records, but he doubted they could keep him away from the national archives. However, he did not sign the register of visitors in his own name, using instead the unremarkable pseudonym of S. Nyoni. He was the only visitor there the whole morning. A woman, who seemed far too young to have the responsibility of preserving the city's past bestowed on her, found the relevant newspapers he was looking for and placed them on a desk in the reading room.

'No photocopying without permission,' she smiled at him, a piece of chewing gum protruding through her teeth. 'And no photographs.'

Edmund nodded and watched her clip-clop out of the room and back to the reception. He turned to the tome in front of him. *October 1979.*

1979

Edmund was full of excitement. His mother was going away for two days. She said she was going to visit Tete Ruvimbo who lived in Salisbury, but Edmund knew better. He had been playing outside the kitchen door when he heard his mother talking to Mrs MacDougal. His mother had been acting strangely lately: she was happy for once, as though she had made up her mind to do something that had been bothering her.

After his father's nocturnal visit, a letter had arrived. Edmund's mother rarely received post and when it did arrive it was usually of morbid or demanding content: someone, usually a vague second or third cousin, had died. Money was needed for the funeral. Money was needed for transport into town to get the death certificate. Money was needed to feed and clothe the remaining children. There was no end to the reasons money was needed.

Mrs MacDougal had given him the letter to give to his mother. It was in a khaki envelope and the name and address were written in a small, sloping secretive handwriting, as though each letter were trying to hide behind the one before.

His mother had looked at it questioningly, a look of slight perturbation in her eyes. The letter was on cheap newsprint, a sheet torn out of a school exercise book. Edmund watched her reading it, how her eyes and lips moved slowly over the words, which she mouthed silently to herself.

He didn't ask her what it said. He supposed that soon enough he would hear who had died and what troubles the family were having burying the body. She had folded the letter carefully back into the envelope and slipped it inside her uniform. She was unusually subdued that afternoon as she put the knives and forks back in the dresser drawer. Edmund watched her from the table where he sat doing his maths homework. Mrs MacDougal looked up from her place on the sofa where she sat threading a needle.

'Verna,' she said, her voice soft and kind. 'I have an idea. We'll speak later.'

His mother obviously knew what she referred to as she nodded her head respectfully and left the room.

He didn't hear all of their conversation, only bits of it. He had finished his homework and sat on the rock outside the kitchen door, watching a lone ant make its way up the smooth surface, marvelling at its ability to know and stick to its path.

'You will need to go to Salisbury.' Mrs MacDougal's voice floated out to him. 'It will be quicker.'

'But Edmund...' Edmund's ears pricked up at the sound of his name.

'Edmund will be all right. Don't you worry. We can take the lad to school. He'll be no problem whatsoever.'

Edmund waited anxiously to be told the news himself, but it was a full two days before his mother, just as they were eating their breakfast porridge, said: 'Edmund. I'm going away. To see Tete Ruvimbo. You remember her?'

Edmund thought and then shook his head.

'Yes, you do,' said his mother, a note of irritation in her voice. 'You do remember her. I am going to see her. In Salisbury. I will be gone for two days.'

Edmund pretended to let the news sink in.

'Who will look after me?'

'The MacDougals.' She watched his face closely as though not sure of the plan herself. 'They will take you to school and look after you.'

Suddenly she threw herself onto the floor in prayer position. 'Thank you Lord! Thank you, Lord!' she cried, looking up at the ceiling. When she had stopped rocking back and forth, Edmund noticed that her eyes were wet with tears.

'Will I stay in their house?' ventured Edmund.

'Ah, you!' cried his mother, turning on him vehemently.

'You can sleep on the floor. You understand? You say thank you to Mr and Mrs MacDougal. You praise God we have such good people to work for.' She stood next to him and twisted his ear until he cried out in pain. 'Don't mess it up. Do you understand me? Don't mess things up.'

Edmund had waved his mother away early the next morning. Mrs MacDougal stood at the gate in her powder blue dressing gown, the belt pulled tightly round her waist and her grey hair tied back into a bun. They had stood and watched his mother walk down the road, her little suitcase in her hand and her red doek tied round her head. Then Mrs MacDougal had taken him by the hand and said:

'What about a wee bit o' breakfast, my boy. You like oats?'

Edmund shrugged his shoulders. He had only ever had mealie meal porridge. 'I don't know.'

'You've never tried them? Oh well, we definitely have to have some then, hadn't we?'

"Chief Inspector Archibald Balfour MacDougal has been reported missing along with his wife, Elizabeth MacDougal. The couple was last seen on Thursday afternoon by their gardener, Mr Simeon Nyathi, at their home in Suburbs. Mr Nyathi said he had been surprised when they paid him early but was told they were going away. MacDougal, who was described by his colleagues as an exemplary police officer who had excelled in his role, had recently been suspended from duty pending further investigation. He was the senior investigating officer in the case in which a local businessman was wrongly accused of running a house of ill repute said to be a favourite of Rhodesian soldiers. The officer investigating the couple's disappearance said that they were doing everything possible to locate their whereabouts."

Edmund walked quickly through the streets of Bulawayo. It gave him time to think. He felt he was close to something, as though he could see a shape moving behind a curtain, but he couldn't quite catch it yet. The words sent him reeling, even now, walking down a street in the clear light of day, they fluttered like butterflies in front of his eyes and try as he may, he couldn't catch hold of them, couldn't snatch them out of the air and pin them down. Edmund stopped for a moment. He needed some time to think so he turned and looked in the window of a shoe shop. The world turned slowly in front of him as a memory surfaced. He was standing on the top of a flight of steps looking down. He remembered the driveway, the shadows cast by the tall trees along the fence. What was it now, that feeling? Boredom? No, but he had been waiting a long time. Why was he waiting? Who was he waiting for? The feeling dissolved, as did the picture. Edmund was once again in the centre of town.

Edmund looked at the reflection of the busy street. People were walking purposefully along the pavement; even in these times of economic constraint, so many people seemed to have somewhere to go; they had a sense of purpose. Hawkers haggled on the pavements, selling windscreen wipers and phone chargers, packets of oranges and avocados. Shops advertised special offers and discounts or announced the latest arrivals with double exclamation marks.

Behind the smiles and the chirpy greetings, behind the jaunty swing of attaché cases and the bustle of people moving to and fro, darting into offices or glancing in shop windows, was a thin thread of desperation, pulled so taut it could not be seen, but which lent all these movements, so everyday, so commonplace anywhere else, an uneasy edge of desperation. The smiles were brief, the greetings strained; the movement of people just that little bit too quick as though everyone was late for an appointment, but in reality they were going nowhere: the brief cases were empty, as were their pockets and stomachs and futures.

Something changed then about the picture that Edmund looked at, like a kaleidoscope moving round. He saw a hardness in some faces, and shifty glances in others. He saw money slipped into pockets and fat greedy smiles as hands were shaken and greetings exchanged.

Edmund thought of the Pullmans, of the permanently full cupboard, fridge and freezer. He thought of Mr Pullman and his boorish face as he sat behind his well-stocked bar and drank double (imported) whisky. He thought of Mrs Pullman and her bridge parties and book club meetings and her hospitality, which was at once generous and alienating and made the recipient of it feel they were bound to her and her desires. Somewhere in that house with all its beautiful furniture and cut glass crystal and fine bone china was the answer.

Edmund made his way quickly towards the police station. He had to find more information. He had to find all the details. By the time he got near the station, Edmund was hot. His coat felt heavy and he stopped on the corner of the street to take it off. Looking up he was surprised to see Nigel Pullman leaving the police station. He walked quickly, his great bulbous eyes focused on a spot in front of him; he didn't see Edmund standing transfixed at the end of the road.

What could he have been at the station for? A part of him thought Nigel Pullman might have gone in to find out how the investigation was going. Perhaps he wasn't involved in his wife's death and he genuinely wanted to find out what had happened to her. Edmund watched him climb into his khaki Land Cruiser and reverse into the street.

Once inside the station, Edmund had an overwhelming feeling of trepidation. The entrance hall, usually teeming with people, was peculiarly quiet. The duty officer was bent over the counter, reading through a number of charge sheets and a lackadaisical cleaner was sweeping a damp mop across the floor without much enthusiasm. Somewhere, a long way off, a door banged. Even the noise of the traffic from the street seemed to retreat.

The feeling followed him into his office where he stared at his desk for a minute or so, convinced that something had been moved on it. He went through a mental checklist of what should be there, even down to his pen-holder and mug.

He opened the drawers and peered in. The top drawer was locked; he took out the key and opened it. All was in order. Except–

'Bhebhe!' There was no answer. 'Bhebhe!' Edmund called more loudly. There was a scraping of a chair and the duty officer came in, a little too slowly for Edmund's liking. It irritated him.

'Bhebhe, there was a file here. Where is it?'

Bhebhe rolled his lips into an 'I don't know' gesture.

'There was a file here on a man named MacDougal. An old file. Bhebhe, stand up straight please. Remember who you are speaking to.'

Bhebhe languidly pulled his limbs together and stood away from the doorway, which appeared to be holding him up. He saluted, as though pretending to be serious. Edmund kept his eyes on the man's face, convinced he could see the officer smothering a grin.

'Listen, there was a file here on a MacDougal. It's very, very important. It was in my drawer here, which was locked, and now it has disappeared.'

Bhebhe made a great show of coming round to Edmund's side of the desk and looking quizzically at the lock of the drawer.

'But it looks like it is okay,' he said, turning the key back and forth. 'It has not been broken.'

'I didn't say it had been broken. I said the file is missing.'

'Oh.' Bhebhe stood back with his hands behind his back and didn't say another word.

'Get out!' ordered Edmund in a sudden fit of fury. 'And get me the file on Marcia Pullman.'

'Pullman?'

'Yes. Marcia Pullman. You know who I am talking about.'

Bhebhe stood shuffling his feet and looking down at his hands.

'What? What is it?' demanded Edmund.

'I can't... You are not allowed access to those files.'

'Who said? *Who said?*'

'Khumalo.'

Edmund pushed past him and strode out of the room and up the corridor to Khumalo's office. Khumalo was seated at his desk giving instructions to a policewoman who appeared unusually good-looking for the job. She smiled at Khumalo with a pretty pout of her lips that reminded Edmund all too much of Mary.

'The MacDougal file, please,' Edmund demanded, stretching his upturned hand across Khumalo's desk, his anger giving him a sudden surge of confidence. 'And I want access to the records room.'

Khumalo was remarkably calm in response; calm, thought Edmund afterwards, with the reassurance that he was in control and there was nothing Edmund could do about it.

'I don't know what file you are referring to. MacDougal? I've never heard of it. As for your access to the records room, you don't need it. *As I have already informed you,* I am managing the Pullman case. I don't need you interfering and causing me any more headaches than you already have.' He turned to carry on giving instructions to the good-looking policewoman, talking quietly and nodding sagely like a doctor considering a medical case.

Edmund felt the world move slowly round him. His chest was tight, as was his throat. He wanted to shout, but he was unsure. There was something about Khumalo, something about the stillness of the man that he found intimidating. There were times, too, in Edmund's life when he felt a strong sense of what he must do, an inner voice, perhaps, which piped from the depths of his self and spoke words of pure wisdom. He heard it now. Be quiet, it said.

He took a deep breath and considered ignoring the inner voice, although it had always proved to be correct. 'I'd like permission to see the file of Marcia Pullman.'

'We have made an arrest already. The suspect is in the cells.' Khumalo's eyes did not meet his. He began writing something on a pad of paper.

The room spun again. Edmund struggled with the inner

voice. 'Who?' The word sounded strained and unnatural, as though he were being strangled.

'Malakai Ndimande. He has been charged today with unlawful entry and violation of a corpse.'

'Charged? Malakai?' Edmund felt a wave of indignant rage sweep through him. 'This is why Pullman was here?'

Khumalo took a deep breath and leant back in his chair, which Edmund couldn't help but notice was a proper office chair on wheels; his own was a wooden one. 'New evidence has come to light which is enough to have the suspect charged.'

'New evidence?'

'Yes.'

'Are you going to tell me what this new evidence is?'

Khumalo remained quiet.

'Please,' attempted Edmund, biting his lip.

'Okay. If you will stay out of this case once and for all.'

Edmund held Khumalo's gaze.

'Edmund? Once and for all?'

Edmund looked away. He nodded once.

'Some valuable ornaments belonging to Mrs Pullman were found in Malakai's khaya. The man is a thief.'

Edmund froze. Surely not, he thought. Surely it wasn't Malakai after all?

'Did Mr Pullman confirm they belonged to his wife?'

'Yes, he confirmed he had seen them in her possession.'

'Which khaya?' he asked. 'At his new place of work or the old one.'

'The new one.'

'Are you saying he stabbed Mrs Pullman and then stole the ornaments?'

Khumalo shrugged. 'She was already dead.'

'And what were these things that he stole?'

Khumalo reached into his top drawer and brought out a bag from which he took two small elephants. One was green, the other covered in a medley of jewels. He laid them before Edmund as though to suggest the case was now closed. 'Happy now?'

'He took these?' said Edmund, 'Just these? Nothing else?'

'*Just these?* These are very valuable. Who knows what else he took? He could've sold things on.'

'Did you find any money?'

Khumalo shrugged. 'No. Didn't need to.'

'Do you not think these are unlikely objects for someone to steal? Why not take the dead woman's cell phone or the DVD player or her jewellery? Something easier to sell on.'

Khumalo leaned back in his chair with his arms folded and surveyed Edmund with a look of sheer contempt. 'Malakai Ndimande has been arrested and will be charged with unlawful entry and violating the corpse of Mrs Marcia Pullman. Do you understand?'

'Is Mr Pullman happy with this?'

Khumalo sighed. 'Everyone is happy except you.'

Edmund was silent for a moment. There was a lot he wanted to say and questions he wanted to ask, but the inner voice was screaming now and stamping its feet. Edmund took a long look at Khumalo and then turned and left the room.

He walked out into the sunshine of the late July day. The silence had gone now. There was noise. Loud noise: cars and trucks and hooters and people talking and shouting, cell phones ringing. A baby cried. Yet it was all far, far away. He needed to walk out of the chaos and find somewhere quiet. Down Leopold Takawira he walked at a stiff pace, down towards the park and the museum. It was a road well-travelled by him; the route he used to take home every day. It was like that day so long ago now, when he had wandered home, alone as he always was, but heavy, too, with the events of the day hanging over him.

'This is what happens when we let anyone into our schools.'

'This boy.'

'This thief.'

And then the next day, he had returned home to find the MacDougals gone.

Chapter Twenty-six

Sandra Smith sat at her kitchen table, looking rather blankly at the envelope in front of her. It was early – five thirty in the morning – and she was still in her dressing gown. Her breakfast comprised a cup of green tea and a slice of crisp bread with sesame seed spread – homemade, of course – but she was interested in neither at this particular moment in time.

The envelope was old, but it had been kept well, so there was little damage to it. In fact, it was only the writing on the front that gave it away as being old. The envelope was addressed to her, just her first name: Sandra. The handwriting was old-fashioned cursive, the sort of flowery, loopy type that was sometimes difficult to read, but which looked quite pretty on the page. She could imagine the pen moving along the lines, stringing words out behind it like the tail on the end of a kite. Despite the loops and twirls, it was neat and each word rested carefully on imaginary lines. There was not a spelling mistake or a punctuation error. It was perfect. The perfect letter.

The ink on the envelope was faded. Besides her name, which was in the middle, there was a brief instruction at the bottom of the envelope, which read: To be opened on your twenty-first birthday. Sandra had read the letter many times since then. She remembered her initial surprise when her mother, or at least the woman whom she called her mother, had handed it to her.

She had been excited; it was her birthday after all, and she was young still, young enough to yearn to get older and look forward to the day with a sense of expectation. There was to be a party and a tent had been hired and her cousin Marcus was going to bring his records and all her friends had been invited. There was even a theme – 1950s Hollywood. She had wanted the Roaring 20s, but Marcus had pulled a face. How on earth would he find the right music? 1950s Hollywood was okay because there was Elvis and Dean Martin and rock n' roll, at which Sandra had grimaced and said she didn't like rock n' roll. She wanted Greta Garbo glamour not Bill Haley rocking around the clock. Marcus had rolled his eyes and asked her if she knew where they lived. This was Bulawayo, not New York.

She just wants something special, she had heard her mother say to Marcus later on. You know what she's like. She just wants everything to be perfect.

Perfection, thought Sandra, staring at her name on the envelope, following the curls and loops and wavy lines, the long line of the back of the 'S' and how it swooped down and outwards and flicked up again behind. It had haunted everything she had done: her eating disorder, her alcoholic binges, her short-lived marriage and even now, where she was at this moment, sitting in this chair having breakfast. The need for healthy food and drink, her profession putting the emotional needs of others to right, the distancing of herself from relationships. All this was underpinned by a need for perfection.

Sandra had long ago delved into the depths of herself. She knew what made her the way she was, what she liked and disliked. She knew how food affected her, how the need for and then the complete hatred of it controlled her. She knew what sort of people had different effects on her and so she had learned to pick and choose her life. It wasn't easy; every day there were situations that threatened to draw her in and people who threatened the autonomy of her space. It's why she worked for herself and lived only with her son and chose whom to take on as a client and whom to politely refuse.

The envelope. She remembered making a tiny tear in the top of the flap and then taking her father's long, thin letter opener and tearing it open, careful to do it in one swift movement so there were no jagged pieces. She was aware of her mother watching her, aware of a certain fidgetiness in her manner, the way she smoothed down the hair at the side of head like she did when she was worried. 'I'll give you some time to yourself,' she had said and left.

The letter was a page long. It was on thick notepaper, folded into thirds. Dear Sandra, she read. Dear Sandra... There are moments in one's life that are thresholds, although they appear to be just like any other moments in the aeons since the world began. There is no heavy door to push open, no bell to ring, no thought to make before stepping over it.

But the sensation afterwards is so tumultuous, so shocking that one feels oneself slipping, sliding, falling about foolishly in all directions as though the ground itself is moving, has disappeared even and you are falling... falling into oblivion.

So she had felt as she had taken the letter and wandered out into the garden. The men had finished putting up the tent and were arranging the chairs. Her mother was giving instructions and laying tablecloths at the same time. Sandra had looked hard at her, how beautiful she was, how in control. She was the person who had answered every question, the pillar they all leaned against. She was always there, always had been: picking Sandra up from school, sitting next to her on her bed when she was ill, watching sports' matches and school plays, wrapping birthday presents, sitting up late into the night to make sure she came home safely.

Sandra watched the tablecloth billow out as it was flung across the table and it was as though everything it represented – home and childhood and the long years that link one to another – in the moment of becoming tangible, became nothing. She saw her life as someone else might see it and herself as an object within that life. Her mother saw her then and their eyes met. She stood immobile for a few seconds, the tablecloth limp in her hands. At that precise moment, Sandra knew that what she had read was true and a door shut heavily behind her.

It was a beautiful afternoon in August. She had always loved August, loved spring. From inside, she heard Marcus playing Madonna. 'Well, she does look *a little* like Marilyn

Monroe and *she's* glamorous,' he had argued, but now, just at this minute, she couldn't hear anything except a buzz, like the sound her father's radio made when he was searching the short wave bands for the BBC World Service.

In the kitchen she had found a tin full of fairy cakes, with swirls of green-black icing covered in edible glitter and tiny stars. 'Three dozen Hollywood star cupcakes coming through!' her best friend's mother had announced early that morning as she strode into the kitchen, her arms full with two cake tins. Now Sandra picked one out and took a bite. It was sweet; over-sweet, the kind of sweetness that children love and adults baulk at. She felt like a child then, a very small child, and she took a cake and sat in a corner of her father's study, shoving the cake in her mouth with both hands and crying, sobbing, 'Please God, don't let it be true.'

That was a long time ago now. Seventeen years. Her father had since died and her mother had moved to a retirement complex near Durban. Sandra had lived there herself for a while after the breakup of her marriage, but instead of finding her way, as her mother had hoped, she felt lost amongst people with money and beautiful homes and the time to sift through malls of fashionable shops. They had provided her with an income, that much could not be denied, for they all worried about their pets and their past lives and how they could improve their karma without upsetting their bank balances too much.

Then one day she had decided to come home. To Bulawayo, a crumbling edifice in the desert of Matabeleland.

> *Round the decay*
> *Of that colossal wreck, boundless and bare*
> *The lone and level sands stretch far away.*

Her father had been a great lover of poetry and, although she didn't quite follow in his footsteps, snippets remained. These words had struck her with extra force when she arrived back with her small suitcase and her son.

Barnaby was seven, small for his age with very dark hair and eyes. An introvert, he longed for the company of other children and the stereotypical trappings of a normal home: two parents, siblings, a dog, a cat, a bicycle and three meals a day. Sometimes Sandra felt a pang of guilt when she served lentil burgers instead of some great big juicy steak for supper or when she put carrot sticks and hummus in his lunch box for school, and made him drink water instead of juice and lemongrass tea instead of coffee and fizzy drinks.

But he was healthy, wasn't he, and if you're healthy, you're happy, isn't that right? One day he would be old enough to appreciate all she had done for him. One day, he would look back fondly on all the arguments they had had over eating raw broccoli and he would thank her because she wouldn't have insisted unless she loved him, would she?

Sandra took a sip of her green tea and thought hard. Marcia wasn't supposed to die. That wasn't part of the plan. She would have to get the information another way – but how? She thought of Edmund; she thought of Craig. In another room, she heard her son stir. It was six o'clock. In another hour he would be at school and she would have plenty of time to plan her next move.

Chapter Twenty-seven

1980

It was hot in his costume. Craig shifted uneasily on the stage and longed to sit down. It wasn't easy being the front end of the donkey. It was difficult to see through the round holes that were the eyes; in fact, it was impossible to look out of both at the same time. He closed one eye and stared out at the audience: all the mums and dads and brothers and sisters sitting in rows in the school hall.

A ridiculously small fan beat somewhere in the heights of the ceiling, thumping the air with great enthusiasm but not much output. Ladies fanned themselves with folded programmes and men mopped their faces with handkerchiefs – but not his mum and dad; they weren't there.

Craig had looked for them as soon as his part was over and he had a chance to stand still and focus outside the hole. He glanced along the lines of parents, all smiling kindly, laughing at the right times, waving secretly to their children on stage. All except his parents.

They said they would be there. Only yesterday afternoon his mother had helped sew up his donkey costume where the stitching was unravelling. She was all right in the afternoons; not bleary-eyed and vague as she was in the mornings and not sad like she was in the evenings. The afternoons were his time. After homework, they would play cards or she would read him a story. At four o'clock they had tea, which Wilson brought in on a tray. Two Willsgrove brown cups and saucers and a Kango teapot. A small, white crocheted cover protected the sugar bowl from flies. It was edged with tiny white beads that tinkled when touched. Sometimes Craig sat with it on his head. Trying to make her laugh, trying hard not to let her cry.

After tea, they went out into the garden, he running, she hanging back in the shadows as much as possible. Afraid of the glare, of the affront of the sun, even now when it began to wane. He pointed out flowers, new blooms, butterflies, ants, dragonflies, blades of grass, grains of sand; anything to keep her focused, keep her in the moment. His hand looked for hers as they walked back inside. He wanted to lead her away, to keep her in the sunshine, to drag the day out just that little bit longer. He knew it was over when they reentered the house. His father would come home and Wilson would set the table: just for the three of them. Only three of them now Callie was gone.

Dinner was difficult, awkward, clumsy. His father asking him what he did at school. Nodding, but not listening. The scrape of his knife on the plate, his eyes watching to see if he'd be told off, the disappointment when he wasn't. His mother's hands on her knife and fork and then the way she pushed her plate away and shook her head. The look on his father's face.

'Not hungry, love?'

'Not tonight.'

She would stand up then and take her plate to the kitchen. He would hear the click of Wilson's tongue, could imagine the expression on his face. There was nothing more to say then, no small talk. His father would finish his food, never varying his pace and never looking up until the end.

'Good boy,' he'd say then. 'Finished your homework?'

'Yes.'

'Good. Go and have a bath and then I'll come and say goodnight to you.'

Lying in the bath, his head half submerged in the water, he'd hear the clink of bottles, the soft pleading of his father's voice. Tears. She was gone then, gone for the night, into her own little world that no one could share. Was she happy? He never knew. For all her movements, the lolling of her head, the staggering down the passageway, the thick slurring of her words; all were edged with pain.

The hall door opened suddenly and a figure stumbled in. She had on her best dress, the one he liked most. It was a buttercup yellow with tiny pink flowers. It was her smart dress, her happy dress. She walked as though her shoes were too big for her, stopping and leaning on someone's shoulder for support. Behind her, walking quickly trying to catch her up, was the school secretary. Her mouth was white, pinched with anger.

'Mrs Martin,' she whispered. 'Mrs Martin. Please come with me.'

'I want my son,' his mother said, stumbling, falling into the row on the other side of the aisle. People looked, people frowned.

'Mrs Martin, the headmaster has asked you to stay away. You're in no fit state...'

'I'm here to see my son.' Her voice got louder, angrier. 'Please, let me see my son.' She shook off the secretary's clutch and carried on walking towards the stage. Craig bowed his head in shame. Mary turned and sniggered with Joseph. Craig was red; he was hot. He was burning up. Lines of sweat wiggled their way down his cheeks. He longed for somewhere cool, somewhere soft and cool. The shadows in the garden, the dark of his bedroom, the silence of midnight.

Suddenly there was even more of a commotion as two men from the audience caught hold of his mother's arms and pulled her away from the stage.

'I *want to see my son*! I want to see *my son*!' she screamed as she was dragged from the hall. She was stumbling, falling backwards, her hands clawing the air. She fell with a hard thud, her legs askew, her dress pulled up to her thighs. The children on the stage laughed behind their hands, the parents gasped and shook their heads.

'Please, please! Craig! I'm here Craig! Let me go! Please let me go.' Her pleas descended into tears as she rocked back and forth, oblivious of her dress and her visible underwear, oblivious of the world which peered in and watched her pain rise and fall with each racking sob. Someone helped her to her feet, someone put an arm round her. They knew, everyone did, about Callie. They led her out gently and closed the door firmly behind her. An astonished twitter ran through the audience as they settled back into their places.

The deputy headmaster whispered something to the music teacher who nodded and immediately flung herself into the opening chords of *Once in Royal David's City*. She motioned to everybody to stand and, bewildered as they were, for the song was not due for two scenes yet, they sang with gusto as though by doing so they were driving out the demon who had so rudely interrupted the show.

Afterwards, once more a small boy and free of the donkey costume, Craig stood outside the hall and waited to be picked up. He saw the glances in his direction, the smothered smiles, the looks of concern, the hurried whispers – 'Which one's Craig?' 'Poor boy.' 'What to do with a mother like that.' 'Remember the child who died...'

It was the secretary who fetched him and took him to the headmaster's office.

'Your mother has been taken to see a doctor,' he said. 'She will be all right. Your father will stay with her tonight.'

Craig nodded, his hands behind his back. 'Is she in hospital?'

'Yes, yes. A nice hospital. She will be all right. She'll be looked after.'

'Yes... sir. Thank you, sir.' Craig's voice was a whisper, barely audible.

'You can stay here tonight – in the sick bay. Matron will look in on you.'

Craig nodded again, thinking of his pyjamas, his bedroom, his Incredible Hulk poster.

'Craig, your mother...' the headmaster hesitated as though he wanted to say something and then changed his mind, 'is going to be all right.' He smiled, the kind of smile that says, 'Good, get on with it. Chin up. You'll survive.'

'Well done on your performance tonight,' he said, just as

Craig was about to leave. 'Not an easy part to play, but you did it very well. The audience had a good laugh. It's always good, always good to make people laugh.'

Craig had never been much good at keeping in touch with either friends or relatives. With the exception of his dad, whom he phoned every Sunday evening, he hardly called anyone. He had joined Facebook about two years previously, but rarely ever checked his account. He didn't own his own computer and whenever the faint need or desire to look up old friends actually did occur, which wasn't often, it usually coincided with the consumption of a couple of bottles of whisky, after which he was in no state to drive to an internet café.

He had, like most people who subscribe to such networking sites, initially been quite interested in finding out what had happened to so and so and so and so and all the other so and sos who had come and gone in his life. It was interesting to see where they all lived; not many friends were left in Zimbabwe. There was one in a happy clappy church in Harare and another one who sold tyres in Kwekwe, but otherwise they all appeared to live in places such as Adelaide, Southampton, Edinburgh, Auckland, Port Elizabeth or Washington DC. They posted pictures of Sunday brunches next to cool, clear lakes or children tumbling on velvet green grass while smiling women in straw hats looked on with maternal pride.

There were holiday snaps of exotic destinations and snow-filled Christmases. There were pictures of exciting cities like New York and Shanghai. All these people that Craig had known, had grown up with, who had also begun life in Zimbabwe, had somehow managed to take flight and had soared to wonderful heights. They had wives or girlfriends (perhaps even mistresses) who wore bikinis and sunglasses and brightly coloured sarongs and who lay on the beach drinking multi-coloured cocktails. They had children who posed in sweet little dresses or school uniforms or looked cute in oversized sunglasses. They had all these things: they had a life.

Gradually, Craig had become more and more disillusioned with Facebook. He couldn't help despising the artificial cheeriness and the constant need to tell everyone how happy or loved or saved – there were plenty of religious nuts out there – you were. One friend, whom he hadn't seen since 1984, regularly sent him inspirational messages. 'Yesterday has gone, Tomorrow is a promise and Today is a gift' was one of them. All very well when you are lying on the beach drinking daiquiris with a half-naked woman next to you, Craig had thought sarcastically.

He had been consumed by a need to find out who was as miserable and as lonely as he was and so he had spent a number of anguished hours going through the profile of every person he could remember he had ever met. He had even woken in the middle of the night and looked on the website using his phone. He wanted to find someone who wasn't smiling or laughing or clutching a baby or with his arms round some beautiful woman.

There were a couple of profiles that belonged to the shadowlands of Facebook pictures: those in which quotes were used instead of photographs. One friend had rather enigmatically used an empty armchair as his picture. Craig had initially been drawn to this and had messaged him in the hope that he had found a kindred soul in cyberspace. However, he was disappointed to find Brian Whittaker as happy as the rest of them, working in London as a graphic designer and 'earning far more money than I deserve'. He had offered to show Craig around the London Docklands where he lived and worked the next time Craig should be in London. Craig had written back and said that would be great and he would let him know when he was *in town* next, which wouldn't be this year as this year was all Cape Town, Bangkok and New York, with a trek through Patagonia thrown in for good measure. But if Brian should ever find himself back in Zim, Craig would love to show him round some of Harare's Docklands, beautiful as they were. Of course, that's if he ever got time off from earning more money than he deserved. Craig never heard back from Brian.

That had really ended Craig's sojourn in social networking reunions. He decided that if he didn't keep in touch with old schoolmates, it was because there was a reason. He would choose whom he wanted to see and whom he didn't. As a result, he didn't see anyone. The people who usually phoned Craig were those wondering how much it would cost to fix a roof or do some painting and even those calls had waned somewhat recently. Someone, an elderly lady in fact, had once told him that he should get his act together more.

'You do a good job,' she had said, 'but you don't *look* like you do a good job. You know what I mean?'

Craig had nodded and agreed, but somehow couldn't quite pull himself out of the hole in which he seemed to be falling faster and faster. Another company had started up doing exactly what he did. Bill and Ben the Fixit Men, it was called. Bill and Ben, Craig doubted it was their real names, drove a dark green Morris Minor van with big fat wheels and a shiny silver exhaust. They wore matching green overalls and flat caps, which made them look like extras out of *Annie* and as if at any moment they would burst into song, slap their thighs and do cartwheels across the bonnet of the car. They had business cards made and left at every convenient place across town, they put up notices and they had their children, cute little people in matching green overalls, give out leaflets outside a large supermarket. It was a cunning trick, Craig had thought ruefully when he had seen how people cooed over the two children, patting their heads and pulling their cheeks. He wondered if a little Craig would work at all, imagining a much smaller version of himself in frayed jeans and a red tartan shirt, hair hanging greasily down his neck, smoking fifty a day. Probably not.

The Fixit Men charged twice what Craig did, but people were prepared to pay for the duo. Somehow or other the souped-up Morris Minor inspired a confidence that Craig's

Renault 4 didn't and the matching green overalls did something for Bill and Ben that Craig's attire failed to do for him. The result was a general slump in business for Craig and a boom for the Fixit Men. Instead of fighting back though, Craig had lain low. In fact, he had lain so low, he couldn't get up any more. He had one, perhaps two, phone calls every couple of days and sometimes those were just enquiries: 'I'm just wondering how much it would cost to install a new geyser? Really? The Fixit Men charge twice that.' And yet the Fixit Men got the business and Craig didn't.

No, Craig did not receive many calls and he certainly didn't make many. Funds were running low, the rent was due and the car hadn't much more than a quarter tank of petrol in it. His once a week phone call to his father had even been reduced to giving the superintendent in charge of the home a message: 'Please tell my dad I called.' It was therefore something of a novelty to Craig that he found himself dialling Sandra's number. He had memorised it from the card she had given him the previous day. Despite all the alcohol Craig consumed, he still had an extremely good memory for figures and could often recall phone numbers and bank account numbers from years before.

'Hello, Sandra Smith speaking.'

'Sandra! Er... hi... this is Craig. Craig Martin from yesterday?

'Oh, yes. Hello, Craig. What can I do for you?'

'I was... er... wondering if I could come for a massage. Say around three?'

There was a silence.

'Hello?'

'Yes, I am still here. The fact is I don't do massages.'

'Oh, don't you? That's a pity.' Craig gritted his teeth and kicked himself. He wished his memory worked as well for facts as for figures.

'I can give you the number of someone who does do them. Just hold on a minute.'

Great, thought Craig, absolutely wonderfully great.

Sandra came back to the phone and read out a number that Craig pretended to write down.

'Colour therapy!' he said suddenly, remembering one of the things that Sandra offered. 'What about that? Can we do some of that this afternoon?'

The voice was hesitant. 'Yes, sure. It's forty dollars an hour.'

Craig gulped. A fine sweat broke out on his forehead. 'Forty? Okay.' His voice was high and raspy. He sounded as though he were being strangled.

She gave him her address and he rang off. He did a quick calculation and reckoned he would have saved himself thirty-four dollars had he been brave enough to ask her out for a cup of coffee instead, especially as she probably didn't drink coffee and would have had a glass of water. He had a quick look in his wallet, which yielded the total sum of seven dollars in disgustingly old one dollar notes and five rand. He had another ten in his drawer upstairs and a lady in Northend owed him ten for some plumbing he had done for her a while back. Twenty-seven dollars. He wondered if he could have a half an hour session instead. Then he would still have seven dollars left.

Craig sighed despondently. He picked up his phone and redialled Sandra's number.

'Hello, me again.'

'Hello.'

'I'm sorry. I won't be able to make it today.'

'All right. Tomorrow?'

'Actually, I won't be able to make it any day.'

'Oh.'

'The fact of the matter is that I just wanted to see you again. I enjoyed our talk.'

There was a pause.

'Hello?'

'Yes, I'm here.'

'You wouldn't want to go out for coffee, would you – or a glass of water? I mean... you can have whatever you want except that you probably won't want half the things on the menu. Sugar and caffeine and all that.'

'All right,' she said, as though agreeing to eat something questionable in appearance. 'Except that it won't be until later. Is four o'clock too late?'

She named a café as Craig felt the world spin. Four o'clock! Four o'clock! Four o'clock! He heard a whirr and a buzz and a little cuckoo shot out of a clock and did a jig and shouted four o'clock in an insanely doolally manner.

'No, no, not at all. I'll meet you there, shall I? Or I could pick you up.'

'No, no. No need. I'll meet you there.'

Craig rang off and caught himself smiling in the mirror. He ran his hands over his face and thought he probably needed a shave. He scraped his hair into a ponytail and for the first time in a long time considered cutting it. 'Nah,' he thought, letting it go. A wash would do just as well.

Sandra put her phone down and sat for a few moments in silence. She was glad she had accepted Craig's offer. She hadn't been sure at first, the call about wanting colour therapy had made her suspicious, which is why she had doubled the price. The last thing she wanted was to be alone with a man who had other intentions.

The thing was that she really did want to speak to Craig, pick his brains a little and find out what he knew about Marcia, which probably would have been a lot more difficult had she been required to talk about what colours he should wear and how to cleanse his aura. Sandra knew the café they were to meet at closed at five so she would not be subjected to too long a time with Craig. She took a deep breath. Marcia's death had presented an unexpected hiccup and Sandra didn't deal very well with things not going to plan. She rolled out her yoga mat in the living room and assumed the lotus position. Positive thoughts, she told herself. I will find it, I will find it, I will find it.

Chapter Twenty-eight

'Why are you here? Really. You don't want to sit having tea with an old woman.'

Edmund moved uncomfortably in his seat. It was as though he had been caught out: like a little boy who loves to visit an elderly relative just because she is generous with sweets. He felt embarrassed, but he couldn't explain it, the feeling that he had when he was in the house: the lovely sense of quiet, of time falling softly within it like swollen raindrops dropping from a leaf; the welcoming feel of the old carpet and the worn chairs.

It took him back, back, back and he was that little boy again, looking up from the MacDougals' dining room table. He remembered its walnut brown warmth stretching away from him and how when he swung his legs, there was a great sense of joy and freedom; all this space between him and the carpet. He wanted then to never grow up, to never have legs long enough to touch the floor. But when he did touch it, when he stood or walked, the feel of the carpet under his bare feet was one of protection. He spread his toes and dug them in and felt he could stretch and stretch and grow and grow, but never fill the room, never be too much for it. There would always be space, more and more of it; he would never outgrow the house.

When the MacDougals left, his mother found work almost immediately with another family. It was never the same and she was never quite as happy, but the security of a job was paramount. It was Edmund who couldn't forget, even though he continued at school on a scholarship. He spent hours of afternoons and evenings curled in a tight ball, rocking himself back and forth.

'Do your homework,' his mother would say. 'Come, read me your book.'

But Edmund had looked at her blankly at first and then shaken his head. The space had gone and in its place was a great cavernous hole into which he would fall. There was no floor, no carpet, no end, just this terrifying freefall through nothingness. He felt the hole open up again now with Mrs Whitstable's words and moved anxiously towards the window.

'You remind me of someone,' he said eventually. 'Two people really.'

'Your mother's former employers? Yes, I guessed that much.'

There didn't seem to be any more words to say after that. Edmund watched an eddy of wind pick up the dust outside. The cracked fountain, the empty pond, all spoke of some other time when life was good and things stood tall and new and smart.

'I know what it's like to be lonely.' Mrs Whitstable's voice rang clear, but not unkind.

'I often wish I had never had it, never had the opportunity I was given. I wish they had left me alone.'

Her tone was one of surprise. 'I doubt it. I doubt that's what you really want.'

'Do you?' Edmund was suddenly angry. He turned to her, his eyes full of tears. 'Do you know what it's like to feel different to everyone else, even your own mother – to be *made* to feel different? To be given something and told to make the most of it, to enjoy it because it's going to take you places, to somewhere far, far away. And then to have that something, that something which made you feel safe and secure and loved taken away from you?'

Words, feelings, everything came rushing out of Edmund at that particular moment. He was both man and little boy, a barefoot little boy playing alone in the dust, waiting, just waiting, for so many, many years.

'Do you know what it's like to lie on a mattress on the floor of a tiny khaya every night and dream of Robin Hood and Phileas Fogg? Wishing I could build a balloon and fly away. Around the world in eighty days – except that I wouldn't come back. I'd go on and on and on, far out into space and never come back. That's what I would do. But I never got off the ground, did I? I had my wings most brutally clipped.'

'So you became Robin Hood instead?'

'Robin Hood?' Edmund gaped.

'Of sorts. The good guy, the policeman, making sure the world is put to rights.'

Edmund considered her words. 'Yes,' he said, finally. 'The good guy – and I've failed.'

'No you haven't *failed*. Whatever makes you think that?'

Edmund took a deep breath and sank into a chair, clasping his head in his hands.

'They've arrested Malakai and charged him with unlawful entry and violating a corpse.'

She put her hand up to her mouth in shock. 'Oh no. Just terrible.'

'They won't let me near the case. They say it's a simple case of theft, but...'

'But?'

'Something's not right. Files are missing, I'm not allowed in the records room and I'm told to keep my mouth shut or else.'

'Or else what?'

Edmund shrugged. 'I leave it to your imagination.'

Mrs Whitstable sat quietly in her chair, rubbing her right forefinger and thumb together. It seemed a long time before she finally spoke. 'Well, something has just got to be done about it.'

Edmund was momentarily reminded of his mother and wondered if it weren't an age thing, this belief that the world can just be put to rights with a click of your fingers. There was an attitude of 'Just tell them the truth and all will be well' about the older generation, even when high-level corruption was most obviously involved.

'I feel someone is watching me, every single thing I do. It

really is as though the walls have – not ears – but eyes. I felt it – even when I was the only person in the archives this morning.'

'The archives?'

'I tried to find out... The MacDougals.'

'Sounds interesting.'

'It is – well, it would be if I wasn't so personally involved.'

There was a long pause. Finally, Edmund said: 'I saw Pullman leaving the police station just as I arrived this morning. Confident, self-assured. He's the victim, so to speak, but I can't help wondering what he's hiding. A man with money who goes straight to the top. It happens so many times in this country that I don't know why it surprises me still.'

'You're shocked because you are a good person. It's a sign that you still believe in right and wrong. For others, the boundaries between the two are far more blurred.'

Edmund slumped further down the chair. 'What does it matter about right and wrong here? The Police! The whole thing is a farce. Why do we even bother, why do we pretend we are some moral body looking out for everyone's welfare?'

'Yes,' she said, softly. 'Yes, how very true. But then, if we took it away completely, if there were nothing at all...'

Edmund sat up and leaned towards her. 'I really felt I was getting somewhere.'

'You think it's definitely Pullman?'

He hesitated and then gave in to his need to talk. 'Look, I don't know *how* and I don't know *why*, but he's a man with a past. If I could just get a look inside his premises...'

'Disguise? Look like th'innocent flower, but be the serpent under 't.'

'Shakespeare?'

'Macbeth. Disguise is a form of survival. Do you know how many butterflies mimic the *danaus*?'

Edmund shook his head.

'It's poisonous, you see. Feeds on milkweed as a caterpillar so when it changes into a butterfly, it's pretty lethal. But how many creatures die from eating them? Well, hardly any. The butterflies' bright colours warn them to stay away, they're poisonous – and so they survive. It's such an effective strategy that other non-poisonous butterflies mimic them.'

Edmund snorted scornfully. 'One thing I could never disguise myself as is white.'

'Come here,' she said, wheeling her chair towards the door. 'I want to show you something. Please,' she added, motioning to the handle with a nod of her head.

Edmund obliged and opened the door. It led out on to the small verandah.

'See that plant over there?' she asked without going down the two small steps onto the red polished floor. He looked over at the spindly plant with dark green leaves that grew in a clay pot.

'Yes.'

'That's a Sabi Star. Heard of it?'

'No.'

'It's also called a Desert Rose. Nothing to write home about now as it's winter, but give it a month or so and it produces the most beautiful pink flowers, just like its cousin, *Nerium Oleander*, which has thick green leathery leaves and grows quite profusely when allowed to.'

'It looks like it's dead.'

'It will. It's winter and one thing you mustn't do is water it very often. This is its dormant period; it needs sun and sandy soil, that's all.'

Edmund considered her words. 'What are you saying?'

'It doesn't need a great show of flowers and leaves to prove it's alive. There is a time for everything and whilst this time might not look like the best time in your life–'

' – or feel like it.'

' – or feel like it – there is something going on underneath. Under the soil if you see what I mean. You are getting ready for your time to bloom.'

Edmund swivelled his head up and away from her. He was getting tired of her moralizing everything.

'And let me tell you,' she continued with a meaningful look, 'those Sabi Stars are not to be messed around with. Ask the bushmen.'

Edmund had no intention of doing so and turned back into the room. She spun the chair round with short, frustrated movements and wheeled it back to the centre of the lounge.

'Well, what is it that you think Pullman is up to?'

'That's what I'm not sure of. He supposedly runs a safari business, but it could be a cover. Perhaps he is involved in the illegal shipment of endangered animals or hunting without a licence. Gold dealing.'

'Women?'

'Perhaps,' shrugged Edmund, not convinced.

'Send someone else,' she said, simply. 'To shadow Pullman. I'd go – if things were different. I'd love to do that sort of thing. Put on a wig and invent an accent. I used to be involved in amateur dramatics – did I tell you?' Her blue eyes had lit up and Edmund couldn't help thinking how like a child she looked. Disguises, accents; it was all like something out of a dated crime novel.

'And what would this person do?' asked Edmund, leaning forward over the arm of the chair. 'You go in and in your best Russian accent, you ask to be shown the Matopos. How does it help me find out what Pullman is up to?'

'Well, what you do is to ask a friend to go in – a *man* – and after he's looked through the hotel guide or whatever it is he is shown, he must ask if there is *anything else*. You know.' She nodded her head and gave a very large, obvious wink.

Edmund's heart sank. He managed a very non-committal 'yes' and sat back in the chair. Anything as obvious as that would have Pullman on high alert immediately.

'Or,' she said, wagging her finger, 'or you could get someone to watch the place. Sit outside in a car. Note who goes in and who goes out.'

'Hmm,' Edmund agreed tentatively. 'Except it's probably unlikely that anything will happen in broad daylight.'

'You'd be amazed at what happens in broad daylight, Chief Inspector. My husband always used to say that if you want to get away with doing something, do it in the most *obvious* way possible because no one will believe you're doing it.'

Edmund nodded his head somewhat sceptically.

'Now what else? We still haven't worked out why Pullman killed his wife. Murder, in my experience, Chief Inspector, always springs from very personal motives.'

Edmund smiled at the inclusion of herself in the investigation – you had changed to we.

'And what *is* your experience, Mrs Whitstable?' he asked with a smile. He was beginning to feel a little more positive and was glad for her input, however extraordinary it was at times.

'My husband, as I told you, was a doctor, out in the bush. He dealt with a number of murders in his time. Yes, he was often called out by the Native Commissioner to give his opinion or do an autopsy. I remember one case in particular. There was a fellow called Dhlamini who had a slightly bigger plot than the others in the area and this caused some consternation every year because he always got a bigger harvest than everyone else. Dhlamini had three wives, the last of whom was a very beautiful young lady by the name of Dalubuhle – *born beautiful* – and she most certainly was. She bore her husband the three most beautiful little boys as well.

'One day, after the harvest, there was much drinking and celebrating and the next day Dhlamini was found dead amongst the reeds in the river. My husband was called and his first impression was that the man had got so drunk, he had wandered into the river and drowned. But then he began to think about how everyone had disliked Dhlamini because of his unfair advantage over them and he wondered if there hadn't been some sort of foul play involved. Well, an investigation ensued and they did an autopsy.'

'They could do then what they can't do now,' said Edmund, wistful for the past.

Mrs Whitstable appeared to drift off into a reverie. Edmund looked across at her and saw she was years away.

'What did they find?' he said at last. She snapped back into the present and shook her head.

'So sorry, Chief Inspector. I was lost down memory lane for a second.' She smiled. 'Well, they found that his beer had been poisoned with powder from the roots of the Umfufu tree. You know it, Chief Inspector? *Securidaca Longepedunculata* is the Latin name. Much easier to call it the Umfufu tree.'

'And did they find out who had put it in his beer?'

'Oh yes, but it wasn't who they thought. Various people were brought in for questioning and then released. But then someone reported that they had seen Dalubuhle visiting the n'ganga two days before Dhlamini's death. She was brought in and so was the n'ganga, who refused to speak. Well, to cut a long story short, she had had enough of the old man Dhlamini, however good his crop was, and she wanted to marry his brother.' She smacked her lips together in conclusion, but Edmund didn't see the connection between Dhlamini and Marcia Pullman.

'Which means?'

'Well, what I'm saying is that you have to dig around a bit. You have to go *back*. It was nothing to do with the fact that he had a bigger plot than everyone else that caused Dhlamini's death and he didn't die from drinking too much at the party.'

'So...?'

'Pullman may be involved in illegal gold dealing, but why kill his wife? She must know about it and she's hardly going to tell on him if she's involved. No. One of them was having an affair. I'll bet my bottom dollar on it.'

'He killed her to be free? All right, how? Everything points to her having kidney failure.'

'Yes, that's true. The question is why did she suffer from kidney failure?'

Edmund raised his eyebrows in question.

'Perhaps she was poisoned over time.'

'But then why stab her? Why draw attention to her death?'

'Because... you want to pin it on someone else?' she cried, as though a light had just switched on. 'You want to get someone else into trouble.'

'Again, why?

'Revenge?'

'Mrs Pullman was stabbed sometime between about two and four. Pullman has an alibi for that time.'

'Check the alibi. Is it a woman?'

'His secretary.'

'Ah! Bingo! I'd say you've got your man, Chief Inspector. Now all you have to do is catch him.'

They sat in silence for a while, Edmund with a growing sense of embarrassment for showing his private self to a relative stranger. Mrs Whitstable, on the other hand, was brimming with a sense of excitement.

'You'll get him, Chief Inspector. I just *feel* it. I *know*. Now, how about we have an early celebration with a nice cup of tea. We'll use the tea set again, shall we? I'm sure we've got a packet of ginger biscuits somewhere too.' She wheeled herself towards the door.

Edmund ran his hand over his face and closed his eyes. He opened them when he heard her re-entering the room. No one spoke as she poured the tea.

'A long time ago,' he said at last, 'when I was at school – my first year of school to be exact – I was accused of stealing money out of my teacher's purse.'

'But you were innocent?'

'Some of the boys hated me. They didn't want me in the class. Because I was black. The teacher was very angry. Took me to the headmaster. She was hoping I'd be expelled.'

'And?'

'He was a good man. He refused to give in to the teacher's demands. Two boys were suspended. When the MacDougals left, I was given a scholarship for a year. Then I left. Went to another school.'

'The bad guys don't always win.' Her voice was soft, encouraging.

'Perhaps not,' he conceded. 'Perhaps...'

Emotionally exhausted, Edmund sank back in the chair and pushed Mr Pullman into a remote corner of his mind, or at least he tried to.

Craig, he thought. Mr Martin, you may become useful after all.

Chapter Twenty-nine

'Yep,' said Craig Martin, answering his cell phone. It was stuck together with red tape and he had to press the two halves together to get a connection free of fuzzy static. He scraped the last bits of cappuccino froth out of his cup with a spoon. Three dollars fifty for an oversized tea cup full of fluff, and not much else, all because it was *Italian* and therefore *cool*. These people must be making a mint, thought Craig, who had greeted the waitress's over-friendly gushiness with hardened hostility. He had looked rather disdainfully at the minute biscuit that accompanied his coffee and which appeared to serve little purpose being so small.

'That's a biscotti,' the waitress had answered cheerfully when asked. 'It's made with almonds and cinnamon with just a splash of amaretto.' When she said the word splash, she splayed her hands out like a star. Craig stared grimly back at her, wondering how much of the three dollars fifty the biscotti accounted for.

Sandra had ordered some sort of vegetable cocktail called a Jamaican Sunset, which, he had to admit, looked very appealing in its four layers of orangey-red, but that had set him back a cool five dollars. Five dollars without alcohol. How many carrots could he have bought with that? Jamaican Sunset. Why was it that anything exotic was always named after somewhere faraway? What did people in Jamaica drink, a Zimbabwean Sunset? A slight feeling of panic had stirred in his chest when Sandra had taken a sip and sat back with relish.

'I just love these,' she had gushed. 'I could have at least another three.'

He had smiled benevolently and inwardly hoped she was the feminist type who would insist on paying her share or at least buying a round.

'Craig? Mr Martin, is that you?' asked the voice on the other end of the line.

'Why? Who's asking?' It was perhaps not the best way to greet a prospective customer, but Craig's free fall through nothingness had already begun and he was still enjoying the initial letting go of all restraints, including obligatory manners.

'It's Chief Inspector Dube. Edmund.'

What did he want now? He wasn't going to arrest him, was he? Well, he'd hardly phone him beforehand if he was. Unless he was kind enough to give him a tip off and therefore a head start. *You have at least fifteen minutes to get that Renault 4 warmed up and your worldly belongings thrown in the back, before I come after you.* The Renault 4 – that was it, wasn't it? He wanted to buy it. Craig knew it, he knew the procedure. Investigate a crime, interview him, butter him up a little and then – the phone call. How much? Could he have it on credit? He'd pay at the end of the month. Promise. Craig sucked in his lips and readied himself for the question.

'Yes, Inspector. What can I do for you?' He couldn't help but let a touch of sarcasm enter his voice. He looked over at Sandra, who was looking away.

'I need your help. You said you'd like to be an investigator.'

'Mmm, did I?' replied Craig, puzzled. 'In what sense exactly?'

'I want you to watch a building.'

'Watch a building?' Craig repeated. 'Why, what's this building been doing that's against the law?'

He looked over at Sandra again, this time catching her eye as she took another sip of the vegetable cocktail. He felt a sudden sense of confidence, as though he could actually feel his shoulders grow wider and his jaw lengthen and become more rugged. This is what it felt like to be Manning in a D.P. Radley novel. A beautiful woman on hand while requests to save the world flooded in on his cell phone. Not that Manning had a cell phone; he was usually relaxing by the side of a swimming pool in a floral open-necked shirt (surrounded by bikini-clad women) when a waiter would come across and tell him that there was a call for him at the bar and then Manning would saunter over (still surrounded by bikini-clad women) and pick up the heavy Bakelite receiver handed to him by the barman. 'Manning, you're needed. Two p.m. The docks.'

'Hello? Are you still there?' Edmund's voice brought Craig back into the present moment.

'Yes, you were saying?'

'It's not the building. It's the people in it. Mrs Pullman's husband runs a safari company. I need you to watch and tell me who goes in and out.'

'Isn't that your job? You are a policeman after all.'

'Yes, but he knows me. If he sees me, I will have lost him.'

'Doesn't he know me?' Craig said slowly, wondering how inconspicuous he would be, sitting all day in a car.

'No. He didn't see you.'

Craig lit a cigarette. Sandra immediately pointed to a 'Thank You For Not Smoking' sign on the table. Craig rolled his eyes and stubbed the cigarette out on the leg of the chair. 'But are you sure you can afford me?'

'You'll do it?' Edmund's voice sounded surprised.

'With conditions.'

'What conditions? I can't afford to pay you, I'm sorry.'

'Didn't think you could. No, I want to know what's going on.'

There was a pause.

'I'm not sure,' said Edmund. 'I mean I'm not sure what's going on.'

'Are you going to tell me or not?'

'It's just a feeling, you understand? This is not something to rush to the papers with.'

Craig snorted.

'I can't talk now but... if you agree...'

'All right,' Craig gave in. 'How do you want to do this?'

Edmund gave him some instructions and then repeated

them while Craig nodded his head now and then and uttered the odd 'yes' or 'right'.

Eventually, Craig rang off and looked across at Sandra, feeling rather satisfied with himself. He even considered another round of Jamaican Sunsets and overpriced cappuccinos, but the place was about to close for the day.

'Well,' said Craig, putting his phone in his pocket. 'That was interesting.'

Sandra looked at him, smiling. 'Good news?'

'Ye-es,' said Craig hesitantly, for he wasn't quite sure a request constituted news at all.

'Positive thinking.'

He wasn't quite sure what brought about that comment. In an attempt to sound more certain of himself than he was, Craig said: 'That was the police. They need my help.'

'Oh?'

'Yes. Undercover stuff.'

'Really? You're kidding.'

'No, no, really. That was Edmund, that police officer from yesterday. He wants me to watch Nigel Pullman's safari business in town. See what's going on.'

'Nigel Pullman? You mean Marcia's husband?'

'Yes. How did you know her, by the way?'

She looked away from him then and Craig noticed a slight hesitancy enter her manner.

'I was booked to do some work with her. Aromatherapy, colour therapy. I was very shocked to discover she was dead – and stabbed.'

Craig inadvertently made a strange noise like a snort and she looked at him sharply. 'I'm just amazed it didn't happen earlier.'

'You don't sound as if you liked her much? How did you know her?'

It was Craig's turn to look away. 'I did a few repairs for her at her maid agency.' Not quite a lie, Craig thought, crossing his fingers under the table.

'Why didn't you like her?'

'Oh... er... she seemed like quite a bully. It's the type I don't like.'

She stared at him as though trying to work him out. Craig shifted uncomfortably.

'So you came back to Bulawayo just recently, you were saying?' He tried to steer the conversation back to where it had been before Edmund rang.

'Yes. A few months ago.'

'People don't usually come *back* to Bulawayo. They normally leave in droves.' Craig laughed, but she didn't smile.

'I had a link. I wanted to come back and re-establish contact...'

'Re-establish contact? With a person or just the place?'

She looked down at her hands and picked at her nails. 'A person.'

Craig looked curiously at her. 'And this person doesn't want contact?'

She paused. 'It's a little more complicated than that. It's... well... I haven't found them yet.'

Craig shook his head. 'Okay. You've lost me now.'

She took a deep breath and then spoke slowly. 'I was adopted at birth. I found out when I was twenty-one. I didn't do anything at first. I was more devastated that the people I thought were my parents weren't. About two years ago, my father died. My parents had moved by then to Durban. I was upset, of course, but somewhere in the back of my mind was this thought that my real parents might still be alive somewhere. It was as though I could have a go at a second childhood. I did some research. I had a letter, you see, from my birth mother, in which she explained why she had given me up.'

'Why had she given you up?' asked Craig, realising a little too late the indelicacy of the question.

Sandra didn't seem to mind. 'She was young. He was a married man who already had a family of his own. I don't blame her. In those days the stigma of being an unmarried

310

mother was quite great. Life would have been hard for me as well and she wanted to give me the best start in life that she could. The letter gave me some clues, not a lot, but a few things to go on. That brought me back here.'

'And? What have you found out?'

'My real father is dead. In fact, he died some time ago. My mother, well, every clue leads to a dead end.'

'Maybe she doesn't want to be found.'

'Maybe. But I want to find her – and I will. I do mantras every day and I meditate and visualise our meeting. I know, I just *know* one day I'll find her.'

'Mantras? *Visualisation?*'

'It works, believe me.'

Craig refrained from commenting on the fact that it hadn't worked so far.

'Well,' said Craig. 'Maybe I can help you. After I've done this job for the police.' He couldn't help the swagger in his voice.

'Ye-es,' she said, uncertainly. 'Perhaps.'

He wanted to ask her when he would see her again. Maybe even suggest coming back to his house, although perhaps that was a little presumptuous and anyway he didn't have green tea or any of the ingredients with which to make a Jamaican Sunset.

'So, why do you think Edmund wants you to watch Mr Pullman's business?' she said in what appeared to be a deliberate change of subject as they walked out of the café.

'Stuff going on,' said Craig, hoping that he sounded suitably mysterious. 'You think Bulawayo is a sleepy little town but beneath the surface... well, there's more to it than meets the eye.' He gave her a knowing look and sucked his breath in as though he knew far more than she did.

They stood a little awkwardly next to their respective cars. Craig swung a bunch of keys around his finger, dropped them and then twirled them again. And then dropped them again.

'Well, that was very nice,' he said at last.

'Yes, it was, wasn't it?'

'We should do it again sometime?' He tried to keep his voice level and not sound desperate.

'Yes, we should.'

'Perhaps next week?' He may be able to find a couple of jobs, bring in some money.

'Yes. Perhaps.'

'So, goodbye.' Craig stretched out his hand rather formally.

'Goodbye... but... if you need any help with the detective work, just give me a call, won't you? Perhaps I could watch the house? I've always wanted to be a detective.'

'Yes, yes, great idea' enthused Craig, suddenly. 'Well, duty calls,' he added nodding towards his car with a knowing look.

He watched her drive off first and sat in his car for a few minutes before starting his. That was the first date in a long time that hadn't required huge amounts of alcohol to survive either beforehand, during or after. Feeling buoyed up, he thought perhaps he would stop at the supermarket on the way home and buy some green tea. Then he thought ruefully of his sorry state of financial affairs and decided against it. But a good old cup of tea was a start and he did have a couple of teabags knocking around in the cupboard at home. Feeling less like Manning and more like his neighbour, Craig drove home.

Chapter Thirty

For three days, Craig sat in the Renault 4 across the road from Pullman's Safaris. It was warm in the car and the lack of room made it a rather cramped experience. As he sat there, he found himself thinking back to his school days when they were told that Bulawayo's roads were so wide because they needed to be able to turn a span of oxen and a wagon. Thinking about it now, it raised two questions in his mind. One, why turning an ox wagon was so important that it affected the width of the roads. It seemed a rather clumsy thing to attempt in the middle of town; you got tickets for doing U-turns nowadays. Imagine riding into town with your cart and twenty oxen and saying, 'Oops! Missed the turning. Let me just go back and do a quick turn here. Whoa there! Excuse me! Excuse me! Out of the way, please!'

The other question was why other towns in Zimbabwe didn't have the same wide roads. Did they not need ox wagons? Or maybe the powers that be had decided that ox wagons shouldn't have such sway and mastery over town planning? Such are the philosophical questions that occupied Craig while he sat and waited.

He also people watched. He looked at clothes and fashions and faces and at shoes and hairstyles and what someone carried in their hands. Not many people actually went into Pullman's Safaris. Craig was there early and saw Mr Pullman arrive in his uniform khaki. He stepped out of his khaki Land Cruiser wearing his khaki hat at approximately a quarter to seven every morning and he left at five every afternoon. He was the one who opened and locked up the office every day and there he was, on time every day. He appeared to carry some sort of miniature cooler bag, a newspaper and a large bunch of keys and he left with all but the newspaper, which didn't surprise Craig as there was not much reason to hang onto the *Chronicle* after the five minutes it took one to read it from cover to cover. The news was generally a couple of days late, or wrong or just plain strange: stories about giant snakes who swallowed people whole while they slept or a man in the city of Shenzhen, who kept a thousand cats and knew each one by name. Most of the news in the *Chronicle* seemed to take place in Shenzhen for some reason, probably because news was cheaper from China than other parts of the world.

By the end of the first morning, Craig was bored; by the end of the third day, Craig was very bored. Spending your days watching a building is not much fun; from the comfort of a Renault 4, it is *really* not much fun. The driver's window was stuck and wouldn't open and, as the sun got hotter during the morning, the car turned into a small oven. Winter was in retreat. Perhaps they may have one last cold snap before it finally beat its wings and left them in the throes of the usual short-lived and extremely windy spring.

Hungry, Craig looked despondently at his packed lunch: processed cheese on white bread and something euphemistically referred to as a muffin in the supermarket. It appeared to be something between a dry roll and a fairy cake without the sugar. Across the road from where he was parked was a takeaway. Craig felt his eyes dragged almost hypnotically towards it. He felt in his pocket and pulled out his threadbare wallet, opening it hopefully in case the Poverty Fairy had left money in it overnight. There were a couple of dollars and his bank card, which he wouldn't bother to stick in a machine for fear a hand would come out, grab him by the neck and give him a good telling off for letting his funds get so low. Craig felt a sudden urge of carpe diem; after all, it was Friday and wasn't this what Sandra would have advised him to do – grab life by the horns and live for the moment? He ignored the voice that told him that buying the Friday Special at a greasy takeaway wasn't quite what was meant by seizing the day, and locked his car and crossed the road.

The Special was predictably disappointing. Craig decided that anything that appeared in a gold star on an advertising board usually was. The photo was always bigger than reality and its promise exaggerated and short-lived. The pie he bought was flaky and messy and was a bit like trying to eat an ice cream cone on a hot day when it seems to disappear before your eyes without a morsel passing your lips. He decided to stand outside the car to eat it and let the loose bits fall onto the ground.

Near the car on the edge of the pavement sat an airtime vendor who watched him eat with curious fascination.

'You are wasting it,' he admonished Craig, his eyes looking hungrily at the mess on the ground.

'It's difficult to eat,' Craig replied, feeling a little self-conscious when the man gave a short, incredulous laugh.

Craig didn't know if he should respond so he turned and contented himself with eating a few of the measly over-cooked chips that constituted a king size packet.

'This is the first time you are eating,' stated the man after a minute or so of silence.

Craig turned. 'What do you mean?'

'You have sat in your car for three days. This is the first time you are eating.'

Foiled, thought Craig. He gave up his struggle with the pie for a moment and turned to face the vendor.

'You've been watching me, I gather?'

'I am not watching you. I just see you sitting in your car for three days.'

Craig felt slightly disappointed that someone had spotted him. Sitting in a car for three days wasn't the best disguise in the world, but even if he had worn a trilby pulled down low, a long grey raincoat with the collar turned up and pretended to read an exceedingly large newspaper, nothing would be any different. Nobody sat in their car for three days.

Craig gave a cynical laugh, opened the car door and reached into the back. He pulled out his packed lunch; the cheese in the sandwiches was melting and stuck to the plastic bag.

'Here,' he said, throwing them over to the vendor who sprang up with an outstretched hand.

'Thank you! Thank you! God bless you!' he exclaimed and opened the bag with great anticipation. Craig guessed he wouldn't mind melted processed cheese.

'Are you in this spot every day?' he asked the man who nodded in answer, his mouth full of food.

'What do you know about that place there? Pullman's Safaris.'

He was met with a shrug, but then what did he expect the man to say – that they dealt in armaments to the Middle East or that they were developing nuclear warheads?

The man finished the sandwich, licked the strings of melted cheese off the packet and wiped his mouth with the back of his hand.

'Safari business,' he said with an air of knowledge. 'They take tourists out to see places.'

Craig bit his tongue to refrain from being sarcastic. 'Right. Thanks,' he replied, finding it hard to keep despondency from his tone. He ate the last chip, put all the rubbish in a plastic bag and threw it on the back seat of the car. He brushed off his clothes and pulled the tab on the can of Coke that had come with the meal. It was the least disappointing item in the Friday special. At least you knew what you were getting with a Coke.

Craig decided to call it a day. He would phone Edmund and admit defeat. There was nothing going on here besides what was supposed to be going on. Craig wanted to go home and sleep. It was Friday, but it was a long time since he had felt 'that Friday feeling'. He didn't have enough work to feel it. Or money. Or friends. A girlfriend.

Craig opened the door of the car and got inside. He hoped he had enough petrol to get home. The fuel indicator had ceased to work a long time ago and Craig generally worked on ten dollars a week. It seemed to keep him going. However, he couldn't remember if he had put money in this week or not.

The engine sparked into life, Craig revved the accelerator a couple of times and was just about to reverse when he found the airtime vendor at his window. Not money, thought Craig, despondently. Why was everything reduced to money? I'm driving the oldest car in town but, because I am white, I am supposed to have money just lying around, spilling out of the cubbyhole and used to stuff the seats.

The vendor signalled for Craig to open his window, but Craig had to open the door instead.

'Yes? What is it?' Craig prepared himself to hear the sob story of the day. Family stranded in Esigodini, blind mother and five siblings to support in Luveve, seven children to put through school. Why people didn't go to the *Chronicle* with their stories, Craig didn't know. They were much more exciting than tales from Shenzhen.

'Come back after eight o'clock. You will see something then.'

'What...?' Craig began and then stopped. He looked back towards the office. 'You mean...' He didn't really know what *he* meant. He turned back, confused.

'Come again at eight o'clock,' said the vendor and began to walk away.

'Hey!' cried Craig, jumping out of the car. 'What do you mean? Tell me.'

The vendor, however, seemed to have become dumb and it dawned on Craig that the man's reticence may be born of fear. He watched him arrange his phone cards into neat little piles, eyes deliberately not meeting Craig's.

'Okay. Right,' thought Craig and walked slowly back to the car. 'Tonight at eight.' He felt a surge of excitement and couldn't help a smile creep upon his lips. *Manning leapt into his convertible with one spring. He pushed his sleek dark hair out of his eyes and lit a cigarette. As he reversed, his lip curled up in a grin. Tonight at eight.*

Chapter Thirty-one

It was half past seven and dark. None of the street lights worked and Craig was very aware of his car being the only one on the street. He had locked the car and he and Edmund crouched rather uncomfortably on the back seat. Craig had bought a pair of binoculars, although he wasn't sure why; at home, they just seemed like the kind of apparatus one needed in this situation; now, in the darkness, they looked ridiculous. He also had a navy blue balaclava and a heavy spanner. Again, he wasn't quite sure where all these things fitted in, but they made him feel confident and prepared.

The Famous Five, Craig's earliest blueprint of crime-busters, always seemed to have room for a torch, various bits of string and an endless supply of peppermints in their pockets, all of which came in useful when dealing with the criminal underworld. Manning, on the other hand, generally relied on his wits, a number of karate moves and, in extreme cases, a small revolver. In this instance, Craig decided to emulate the resourcefulness of the younger investigators. Edmund had a camera, which Craig had viewed with great disdain at first. Shouldn't he have a gun? A baton, at least, and numerous pairs of handcuffs. It wasn't as though Edmund was the most intimidating of figures and he was unlikely to instil fear in any criminal.

Craig's thinking was that if they arrived before eight, they would not rouse any suspicion. What happened at eight was anybody's guess. Did someone arrive or did someone leave? When Craig had briefed Edmund on the situation, Edmund had nodded his head in that way that suggested 'the jigsaw is at last falling into place', to borrow a cliché from a D.P. Radley novel.

Eight o'clock came. Craig felt a surge of excitement as he saw the hands on his watch show the hour. He half expected to hear some sort of explosion, but nothing happened. Five past, ten past, a quarter past. Nothing happened. African time, thought Craig, turning to the front of the car.

He wished he had brought something to eat. Stocks were very low at home but he had managed to find a tin of spaghetti in tomato sauce. Instead of eating the whole thing, he had decided to keep half for the next day, a decision that now left him feeling quite peckish. He took a quarter jack of whisky out of the cubbyhole and took a large gulp. Then he held the bottle up in front of Edmund and tapped it. Edmund shook his head. Religious, thought Craig.

'God doesn't mind the odd drink here and there, you know. Jesus most certainly would not have changed water into wine if it had been the case.'

Edmund continued staring out of the back window, not saying a word.

'Monks, they have the right idea. Brew their own.'

'Yes, you told me,' replied Edmund.

There was a long pause in which all that could be heard was Craig swallowing his whisky noisily.

Edmund broke the silence. 'You a Catholic?'

'Yep, you got it in one. Is it the look of eternal suffering that gave you the clue?'

Edmund half turned and faced Craig and shook his head. 'Not at all.'

'Sure? The hair shirt then? The welts across my back?'

Edmund raised his eyebrows and gave another shake of his head.

'Well then, it must be the drink. Ever known a sober Catholic priest?'

'Are you from Bulawayo?'

'Harare. I've lived here for a couple of years.'

'Why did you move?'

'I had this romantic idea of Bulawayo. Roads wide enough to turn a span of oxen, jacarandas, nice people – salt of the earth types.'

'You sound disappointed.'

'Yeah, well. That's life.'

'You have family?'

'My dad. He's in Harare.'

In the darkness, Edmund nodded.

'In a home.'

There was a pause in the conversation.

'Should go and see him more often, I suppose.'

Again, there was a silence. Craig shifted uncomfortably on the seat and looked out of the side window. One hand fiddled with the broken window winder.

'You promised to tell me what this is all about.'

Edmund coughed. 'I did.'

'And, well?'

'I also said it's just a feeling.' Edmund filled Craig in on the details of Malakai's arrest.

'Do you mean to say there hasn't actually been a murder? Mrs Pullman was dead already when she was stabbed?' The disappointment was palpable in Craig's voice. 'All we're looking for is someone who stabbed her after her death?'

Edmund didn't answer, leaving Craig with the distinct feeling that he had missed some vital information. He wished the policeman would just come out with the facts, instead of merely alluding to them.

'And you don't think it's him? The gardener with an axe to grind – literally.'

'There's other things. Who, for example, called in Dr Ndhlovu, the forensic pathologist? I was the first policeman on the scene and I certainly didn't.'

'Pullman?'

'He has no authority to do such a thing.'

'Connections.'

'But *why*? Even if Ndhlovu is a personal friend of his, why should Pullman call him in?'

'In case... there was something he didn't want to be discovered?' Craig said slowly as enlightenment dawned.

'Or so he can hide something.'

'Or he can pay someone to overlook something.'

'Why am I not allowed access to the file on the case? Why was I removed so forcibly from the investigation?'

'You are not corrupt – or corruptible.'

'Mr Pullman initially said he very much doubted Malakai's hand in the affair and then does a complete turn around and supports the findings.'

'Do you think he has access to information you have not been given?'

'No, I feel someone has told him something. Told him to go along with a story.'

'Why?'

'To protect himself?'

'Or someone else?'

'Or to implicate someone?'

'Hmm, interesting,' commented Craig, feeling a tingle of excitement.

'Or to disguise the fact that he really did murder her?'

'Murder? And what's the motivation? Why kill his wife?'

'It seems she was the source of the money and, as he is the sole beneficiary of her will – well, money is always good enough motivation, isn't it?'

'What about a woman? They are usually the source of the rot.'

'Yes, another possibility. A number of books went missing from the book club run by Mrs Pullman and I don't think it's any coincidence at all that one of the women in the office was reading a book by the same author of the missing books.'

Suddenly, there was a knock on the window and the two men jumped. Craig backed away from it as though a hand were about to come through and in the process spilt most of the rest of the whisky down his front.

'Open the door!' came a hard whisper. 'It is me! Open the door!'

Craig looked closer at the window and recognised the airtime vendor from earlier in the day. He opened the door and looked gingerly out. The man was dressed in dark clothes and wore a woollen hat pulled down low. He knelt down in the shelter of the door, rubbing his hands together for warmth.

'You are in the wrong place.'

'You told me to be here at eight o'clock.'

'No. Not here. Down the road at the back.'

'Ah, the sanitary lane?' asked Edmund, looking over from the back seat.

Seeing him for the first time, the man eyed him with distrust. 'Yes,' he said sullenly. 'Go round the back. Be quick!'

Feeling a mixture of excitement and complete fear, Craig got quietly out of the car, pulled on his balaclava, and waited for his orders from Edmund.

'You go that way,' he pointed to the left side of the road, 'and I'll come in down the other way. If anything happens and you are in trouble, try and get back here. Don't bother about me if you have to go quickly.'

Craig nodded. The spanner in his trouser pocket was large, heavy and unwieldy. He hesitated as to whether to take it or not. He decided to leave it as it would probably slow him down if he had to run away and it might make a noise if he dropped it. The vendor made no movement to come with him, instead sitting next to Craig's car as though he intended to guard it.

The sanitary lane was dark and smelly. Craig stepped in a puddle and grimaced. He didn't like to think of what he had just stood in. He walked as close to the wall as possible, without touching it. It seemed impossible not to make a noise with all the rubbish he inevitably walked into or kicked and every so often he would stand still and wait to hear footsteps.

What appeared to be a large removal lorry was parked half way up the sanitary lane outside the back of Pullman's Safaris. The tailgate was down and a ramp had been placed outside. No one was there though, so Craig squeezed into the space between the wall and the lorry and crouched down. From his vantage point, he could see the open back gate of the safari company. A light was on, illuminating some steps and part of a room.

Soon he heard footsteps. His heart beat loudly and his throat clenched. How he wished he had brought the spanner. A man came out and seemed to check the back of the lorry. Then he gave a long, low whistle and a dark mass moved outside the gate and came towards the lorry. Craig stared hard, trying to work out what it was. Then he realised it was people, a group of people huddled together, some with blankets round their shoulders, some with their heads bowed down, but all moving together as one silent, sorry mass. Craig crouched lower and watched from under the lorry. Women, he thought as they walked up the ramp, women's legs. Another group came out, similarly huddled together. Six, eight, ten, twelve, Craig tried desperately to count how many people there were.

After the last scramblings up the ramp and the heavy movement of feet in the back of the lorry, there was a long silence. Craig could not hear a single voice, only a few creaks and groans from the lorry itself, which soon settled down into nothing. The man had followed the women into the lorry and then came out and jumped to the ground. He disappeared back inside the building. A while later, two men came out of the back of the building carrying a desk, which they loaded into the back of the lorry. Another two men came out with what looked like a chest of drawers. This was followed by a sideboard, a large mirror, a very large table and eight chairs and various boxes. Then there were more chairs and a sofa and more boxes.

The men disappeared and no one came out again. The initial sensation of his heart beating fast and a tight, breathless feeling in his chest had dissipated somewhat, leaving Craig feeling a little braver and in control. Perhaps spurred a little dangerously on by movies and books in which the investigator always finds an opportune place to hide, Craig stuck his head out and squeezed the rest of himself round the side of the lorry. He peered cautiously into the

323

open back and tried to make out the strange cargo. If any of the women saw him, it was likely they would assume he was one of the men rather than a stranger and somehow he had the feeling they would say nothing anyway. Feeling even more like a character from *The Famous Five*, Craig climbed into the back of the lorry and took out his phone. It provided a light, which he shone rather gingerly around, expecting to see a dozen petrified eyeballs looking back at him, but there was nothing of the sort. Craig focused the beam towards the front of the lorry, but there wasn't a single person there. He stood still for a moment and listened. There was a creak, a slow creak from the front of the lorry, but he couldn't see anyone.

He turned his attention to the furniture. Old is the first word that came to mind. Old furniture. Some beautiful pieces though. He felt the smooth curves of the table legs. There was one of those old writing desks as well, like the one his grandmother had had. Craig wondered what was in the boxes, but they were sealed up and he couldn't look inside them.

With a sudden sense that the men would in all likelihood be returning soon, Craig jumped lightly out of the back of the lorry and made his way back down into the gloom of the sanitary lane and crouched next to a dustbin to see what would happen next. The stench of rotting food was overwhelming and he had to put his hand over his mouth and nose. He couldn't help cursing the council for not collecting the rubbish on time and letting it putrefy here in the alleyway.

Then he heard a voice, a white man's voice, giving orders.

'Same as usual. Manje, manje now. You're going to need to put foot. No messing about, no stopping on the way. Get through the border as soon as possible.'

'Yes, baas,' came another voice and, about half a minute later, the engine started. Craig, who was down on his haunches, gripped the side of the dustbin. He wanted to be sick. He hated the darkness and the lack of clean air and the feeling of being alone. He heard a noise beside him and turned – just in time to see the dustbin lid come crashing down on his head.

'Here he is, I've got him!' a voice said as Craig was hauled up onto his feet and pushed roughly towards the back gate of the safari office.

Due to the fact that Craig's head was being pushed firmly down onto his chest, he hadn't a clue what his captors looked like. This was the point, wasn't it, when *The Famous Five* were gagged and bound by big surly men wearing stripy blue T-shirts with scars down their left cheeks? They were always buffoons, of course, and the children always outwitted them. A penknife, thought Craig, ruefully, as he stumbled along. The one thing every boy must carry in his pocket. A penknife and string and a torch and a few biscuits to keep everyone going until they had been found and Mother or cook could whip up a glorious tea.

'Sir, I think we may have found who we've been looking for.'

Another voice said: 'What do you think you're doing? What's your game? Who are you spying for?'

'Where was he?' Craig heard the white man's voice again.

'We caught him sitting by a dustbin back there. Is he the one?'

Craig's head was yanked back at that point by a hand, which pulled on his long hair. He looked into the pudgy eyes of Nigel Pullman.

'Who are you working for?' Pullman's face was so close that Craig felt little drops of spit hit his face. He resisted the urge to wipe them away by rubbing his face on his shoulder and continued to stare as blankly as possible at his captor.

'Nkala, you know him?'

Craig opened his mouth slightly and let his tongue roll forward hoping to effect a drunken daze.

'You want a whithky?' He let the words roll out thick and misshapen. 'I got a bottle in my pocketh.' He made a show of fumbling in his pocket and then fell sideways as though the effort were all too much. His sudden movement unnerved his captors, one of whom put a gun to his head. At that point, Craig's bravado deserted him and he felt a warm trickle run down his trouser leg.

Death, thought Craig, suddenly. This is how my life will end. In a rotten, stinking alleyway in the middle of the night. It was true; death gave you no warning. It was a game, just a game and you were never the winner.

'Hold on a minute, you're not that guy from the other day, are you?' Pullman brought his face right up to Craig's and appeared to sniff him. Craig wondered frantically if he hadn't overdone the drunken bit. He tried to maintain a blank squint, but couldn't help thinking he looked as petrified as he felt. Pullman then looked him up and down. 'Nah. Looks like some kind of bum,' he said finally. 'Doesn't look like he'd know what to do with a phone if it landed on his head. I wouldn't worry too much about him. Stinks of booze. He's one of those white whinos from the street.' The man let go of Craig and he fell sideways. 'Drunk as a skunk,' said Pullman, giving him a kick. 'But get rid of him just in case. We don't know what he's seen.'

Craig's heart lurched. In fact, not only did his heart lurch, his stomach did too. His mouth was suddenly full of a mixture of spaghetti in tomato sauce and whisky as a wave of vomit spewed to the ground in front of him. Did Pullman mean what Craig thought he meant? It was like being in a film, without, of course, the reassurance that a director would suddenly shout 'Cut!' and they would all relax and have a cup of coffee.

'Sis!' snarled Pullman, backing off as the mass of sick frothed towards his feet. 'White scum! Bloody insult to the rest of us!' With that, he walked off back into his office.

Although initially relieved that Pullman viewed him as a harmless bum, Craig now realised his position: he was dispensable; a nothing whom no one would miss or even realise wasn't there anymore.

Craig's hands were tied behind his back with a piece of

cord and then he was thrown in the open back of a small truck and told to lie down. What about Edmund? Where was he? Would he arrive in a police car with flashing lights and sirens and decree with the help of a megaphone that Pullman must 'give himself up'?

What about the airtime vendor? What about his car? A vision arose in his mind of the car being stripped for parts or the windows smashed so that the vandals could get at the money stuffed in the seats. The floor of the truck smelt of oil and diesel and dirt. He could taste it in his mouth. The truck hit a bump and Craig knocked his face against the floor; his teeth hurt and he had a sudden urge to cry like a little boy.

What did Pullman mean by get rid of him? Was he just going to be dropped somewhere or... he swallowed hard. Who would know where he had gone? Who was going to rescue him? Craig then did something that completely surprised him: he prayed. He prayed in the only way he knew how, with a great sense of hopelessness and black despair. At the back of his mind, he remembered a bumper sticker he had once seen: If you're waiting for the eleventh hour, make sure you don't die at 10.45.

If there was a God, Craig thought, this was his way of getting revenge. Revenge for Craig's cynicism and disbelief, for his cigarettes and his alcohol, for being sad and lonely and pathetic and trying to fondle an innocent's girl's breasts. Revenge for rejecting the Catholics, with all their incense and humming and hawing, and then the Born Agains, with their tambourines and endless, repetitive mantras. What did Craig want? His own religion? God wasn't finished with him yet, Craig knew that as a fact. The *wrath* of God. Other people got angry, but only God experienced *wrath* and that entitled him to inflict all sorts of punishment.

He had a picture in his mind suddenly of an ancient city with high walls and men pouring hot oil on the people below and the people writhing in pain, their faces distorted in agony. The siege of Jericho, he thought, remembering the

327

page belonging to a children's Bible his grandmother had given him as a child. Or was it? Was it from a history book? Even in his heightened state of fear, he tried to place the picture correctly. It was a medieval favourite, wasn't it, hot oil? People didn't do that anymore, did they? Did they? He began to panic as all types of torture sprang to mind. Not in Zimbabwe, surely not...

He felt sick and pathetic, completely unable to defend himself. *Please God, please God, please God,* he prayed. *Don't let me die. Don't let me die.* He couldn't be a devout atheist; despite all the scientific theories he had read and thought he believed, always there was this doubt and a feeling he shouldn't be too smug. When he rolled his eyes in exasperation with the religious or laughed cynically at them, he was one day going to be proved wrong. Perhaps the sky would turn black and Jesus would arrive on clouds of fire or maybe when he died he'd discover there was a heaven filled with angels and beautiful cherubs playing harps – but there was a gate of entry and it was closed to him.

Edmund, Edmund would go to heaven. He believed. Craig thought of his next-door neighbours, how they were probably in bed and fast asleep, the alarm clock set and placed beside the bed, the curtains drawn, clothes neatly laid out for the next day. How he wished he could have lived his life in this way. No questioning, no fight, no sense of loss and powerlessness. But now, now it was too late. He was going to die.

'Oh, God, what would Manning do?' he thought wildly. Manning would be calm. He would use the situation to his advantage. He would karate kick both men – or was it four men? – and take command of the vehicle. Think logically, think logically, thought Craig in anguish.

'Jump!' he thought suddenly. 'Jump!' Craig lifted his head and looked around. The truck was going fast and not stopping for traffic lights or stop signs, but he could do it, couldn't he? It's what Manning would do. He would jump onto a lorry coming in the opposite direction and get home in time for a whisky and soda.

Craig knew he had to stand and jump in one swift motion. If he dithered, the men in the front would see him and stop immediately and that would be tickets. The problem was how to stand up without falling over. He took a deep breath and pushed himself up onto his knees, looking wildly around. It was dark, completely dark; there was not a street light or traffic light to be seen. They were no longer on the main road; instead they seemed to be hurtling down a narrow track. Nowhere, thought Craig. He was going to die on a lonely bit of wasteland in the middle of nowhere. At that thought, he hurled himself over the side of the truck.

Craig felt himself fly through the air; he almost seemed to be suspended in it. His legs and even his arms, bound as they were, flayed frantically as he snatched at the darkness for something solid and then he hit the ground with an almighty crack. Everything went white suddenly and fuzzy, like that sound the television makes when it's not tuned in. Then it was dark and there was no sound at all. Craig was overwhelmed by a great sense of peace and quiet as his eyes closed.

Somewhere, far away, was a feeling that he should be fighting this delicious sense of abandonment, but he couldn't, he just couldn't. 'Oh, God,' he thought, feeling himself slipping away. 'I've died.'

Chapter Thirty-two

1980

It was a beautiful late September afternoon. The air shimmered with a clear yellow light; he could feel the warmth on his back as he stood on the edge of the swimming pool, knees bent, arms akimbo, toes curled over the side of the pool, ready to jump. Sunlight glinted off the water, making him squint slightly so all he could see was a mass of glimmering blue. He could hear voices though, the voice of his mother in the water.

'Jump, Craig! I'll catch you. Jump!'

He looked at the beautiful creature in front of him, feeling an overwhelming sense of love and security. She had long, thick, dark brown hair with a parting down the middle and large sunglasses shielding her eyes. She was beautiful in a 1950s Ava Gardner way, with a warm gentle rotundity that later generations would eschew as unfashionable. Her costume was a medley of squares in shades of brown, black and cream with a plunging neckline that revealed two creamy half-moons of breast, which quivered slightly in the breeze off the water. There she stood, waist deep in the water, with her arms held out to him, and an encouraging smile egging him on.

Callie sat on a towel on the grass with Dad. He looked so young, so carefree in his black speedo, his tanned chest tight with muscles.

'Jump, Craig!'

Craig, jump!

Mom, she was there. She was smiling, holding out her arms to him. 'Jump, Craig! I'll catch you!'

Craig, jump!

The picture faded and Craig found himself lying on the side of the road in the darkness. All he was aware of was a stabbing pain in his head and the uncomfortable feeling of lying on gravel. It took him a while to remember where he was and what he was doing there. He rolled over, feeling his body ache with pain and exhaustion. His head throbbed and something sticky ran down the side of his face.

'God,' he thought suddenly, 'they'll be back any minute. They'll be looking for me.'

It seemed to take an age to pull himself to his feet. Panic-stricken, he fell over twice and took a minute or so to recover his breath. When he was eventually on two feet, he looked about him wildly, not knowing in which direction he should go. Trying as best he could to shut out the pulsing throb in his head, he went over the last memories he had of being on the back of the truck. Eventually he decided which way to go and set off at a loping run.

His head hurt worse than his worst babalas, but luckily Craig was adept at functioning with sore heads. Running was more difficult with his arms tied behind his back, but fear and hope spurred him on. The truck hadn't stopped; they had not realised he had gone, but how soon would it be before they did?

His legs felt like lead, like those dreams he sometimes had that he was running, but he wasn't moving. He stumbled numerous times and fell once, cutting his lip and hitting his chin. Pain coursed through his body, but eventually he managed to achieve a rhythm to his movements.

Although he was afraid, he also had a strong feeling that he would be all right. He kept the image of his mother at the forefront of his thoughts as he ran.

I must get home, I must get home he repeated over and over to himself. Then he stopped himself. Positive thinking, positive thinking: *I will get home, I will get home, I will get home.* The road that brought him here must take him back. *I will get home, I will get home, I will get home,* he chanted as he ran. *I will, I will, I will.*

Suddenly from out of the blackness behind him came a pair of headlights and a car hurtled towards him, two wheels on the verge, with the horn blaring. At first he stood stock still, frozen by an overwhelming sense of fear. His chest tightened and he tried frantically to rally his thoughts. Then it slowly dawned on him that he recognised the hooter's rather croaky squawk. It was his car.

The door opened as if of its own volition and Craig peered gingerly inside. At the wheel sat the airtime vendor who urged him to get in hurriedly. Craig sank into the passenger seat, never so happy to see someone he hardly knew.

'Thank you,' he breathed. 'Thank you!'

'No problem,' said the vendor, steering the car onto the road again and putting his foot flat on the accelerator. Craig didn't think he had ever been so fast before in the Renault 4, even when he got himself a speeding ticket that fateful day of Marcia Pullman's death. 'I was watching you. I saw what they did, but it was difficult to keep up with them. I had to run back and get the car so I lost them at first, but a security guard outside a shop a road or two down told me in which direction the truck had gone. It was going so fast it was noticeable.'

'How did you get the car to start?' asked Craig, feeling his keys in his pocket.

'Oh, I just hot-wired it. That wasn't such a problem. The biggest problem was getting the door open. Do you know your window doesn't work?'

Craig rolled his eyes with what little energy he had left. 'Yes, I should think so.'

'I couldn't get too close, especially after they left the main road, in case they were suspicious. I was worried, too, because the tank was on empty.'

'Oh, it's not empty, it's just the gauge doesn't work. Well, actually, it probably *is* empty.'

'I couldn't keep up with them and the next thing I saw them coming the other way. I thought I must have been too late and they had already killed you. I went further along the road but it only led to a deserted farmhouse on the left and then the road petered out. I thought if they had taken you anywhere, it was probably to the farmhouse, but it was all in darkness and the gate was locked with such a rusty padlock, I doubted anyone had been in. I turned around and was driving back and I saw you running along the road.'

'Great,' said Craig, feeling genuine thankfulness that the vendor had followed him and found him. 'I'm very grateful that you bothered to come after me.' They had just re-entered the city and Craig caught the man's profile in the fluorescent light of a petrol station. 'I just don't understand why you did it.'

For a long time, the man didn't answer. Craig didn't know whether he had heard him or not and, after a minute or two of not receiving a reply, he turned to face the road in front and settled back into the seat. His arms ached from being tied behind his back, but his sense of exhaustion was greater. He contented himself with watching broken street lights pass by.

'Six months ago, my daughter died. She was eighteen. She was a very beautiful young girl. Her name was Thembi.'

'I'm sorry,' said Craig, turning towards him. 'What happened?'

'She went to school. She did her 'A' levels. But when she left, she couldn't find a job. She thought it would be easy, but jobs are so hard to find.'

Craig nodded. 'I know.'

'She got a job as a maid. We were disappointed; she was capable of so much more, but she said it wasn't just cleaning, it was looking after old people. Bathing, dressing them. Doing some cooking. She had joined an agency that offered training and could find her a good placement. The money wasn't very much though. She had to pay a percentage back – to cover the costs of the training. But then one day, she came home with some new clothes. The following week it was makeup. Then a phone. My wife asked her where she got these things, but she wouldn't answer. Not properly, you know. She said a friend had given them to her. We thought it must be a man and we worried about it. We tried to talk to her, but she wouldn't tell us anything. She would come home late; sometimes she was gone the whole night. It was like she was slipping away. Do you know what I mean?'

'Yes,' said Craig, his voice soft. 'I do.'

'Then one day, she just didn't come back. Some of her clothes were missing – the new stuff – and some personal items. Two days passed. A week. Nothing. I asked her friends, but no one knew anything. I went through her things over and over again and finally I found a card with a phone number on it. At this point I still thought she had gone off with a man. I thought he is not going to want to speak to me so I gave the number to my other daughter and I told her to phone it.'

'What happened?'

'A woman answered. Lydia did not know what to say but she was very quick thinking and said that she was looking for a job. The woman asked her to meet her at a place in town. It was an office.'

'I see,' nodded Craig. 'Did she ever find out what this woman's name was?'

'Yes, she did. She called herself Dorothy, but I don't think that was her real name. She offered the same training in being a carer and explained that my daughter would have to pay back forty-five per cent of what she earned for the first three months and then thirty-five for the following three.'

'Sheez like. Why so much?'

'Specialist training. Because it involved looking after elderly people. I told her to take the job. One day when she went to pick up her payslip, another lady who works in the office called her aside and said she heard she was looking for ways to earn a little more money. I am sure you can guess the nature of her business.'

'Yes, yes, definitely,' said Craig. 'Absolutely. It didn't involve a dating group did it?'

'Light entertainment is what it was referred to. My

daughter began to feel scared. She said she didn't want to do what the woman suggested. It wasn't right. It wasn't moral.'

'Did Shant- the woman get angry?'

'No, she sat her down and talked to her and said that if she was really good and lots of men liked her, it could be arranged for her to go to South Africa.'

'South Africa? Really?'

'She promised a modelling contract and accommodation.'

'In return for?'

'A thousand dollars upfront.'

Craig gave a low whistle. 'How would she earn that amount of money?'

'By working in Bulawayo first.'

'Cunning.'

'Yes. To cut a long story short, I watched all the comings and goings at the office. I followed Dorothy back to her house one day. I watched the house for three days and discovered a white man and woman lived there; Dorothy lived in the khaya. The white woman owned the employment agency, but she wasn't there very often.'

'So the white lady was in charge of the whole operation?

'No, I don't think so. My daughter was told very specifically not to mention anything to her. It was the mixed race lady who organised everything.'

'How far was Dorothy involved?'

'She knew what was going on, definitely, but she had nothing to do with getting the girls jobs in South Africa. I followed the white man, too.'

'Why did you think he had anything to do with it?'

'He appeared at the office a number of times in the late afternoon when it was closed. Always when his wife wasn't there. He and the receptionist left together a couple of times. I felt he was worth keeping a check on.'

'You were on foot?'

'No, on my bike, but in the early morning he was easy to spot and keep track of. I watched him in the day and I watched him at night. Eventually I discovered what he was doing.'

'How was he involved?'

'The girls were put in the back of a lorry and furniture was loaded in afterwards. Old stuff, second hand. It probably wouldn't raise much of an eyebrow going through the border.'

'How did your daughter die?'

'She suffocated. She was found dead in some bush near Beitbridge. There were others. I think the lorry may have sat for a number of days at the border, right out in the sun.'

'It probably has a secret compartment, a container built into the lorry itself, which is why I didn't see anything when I looked inside. Why didn't you go to the police?'

'The police?' The man burst into a bitter, ironic laughter. 'No, my friend. The police are as corrupt as this Pullman man, perhaps worse because Mr Pullman doesn't pretend to protect the public. I was waiting, waiting for the right time, the right way.'

'Then you saw me and you thought...?'

'Well, I thought, a white man...'

'Don't tell me, you thought "a white man who drives a 1975 Renault 4 – he must have loads of money!"'

'No, I thought you might be from Interpol, or South Africa. I thought you might be able to help.'

Craig laughed softly. 'Craig Martin, FBI!'

'There's nothing wrong with your car. If you ever want to sell it...'

It was on the tip of Craig's tongue to put the man in his place concerning his car, but he asked: 'What's your name?'

'Charles. Charles Mathe.'

'Pleased to meet you, Charles. I'm Craig Martin.'

Craig felt his head droop forward with exhaustion. He looked up again at the string of broken lights. His head ached as did his arms. He was tired, so tired. As his eyes closed, he remembered a time so long ago now: he was a child, a little boy of five maybe, and his parents had taken him and his sister to the drive-in. When they got home, Craig had pretended to have fallen asleep and his Dad carried him inside to bed. He remembered the feeling of being lifted slowly and the sensation of being laid in his bed and the blankets laid over him. His mother's kiss on his forehead.

Craig sank lower into the car seat. Wouldn't it be nice to be carried? Just for one day to be looked after? He slept.

Chapter Thirty-three

1979

The bedroom was cool and dark. Edmund sat gingerly on the bed, feeling the springs expand beneath him. He looked up at the picture on the wall. The caption read Loch Morar. It was of a grey and misty lake with a grey and misty sky. On another wall was a mirror in a faded gilt frame and on the wall next to the door was a picture of a prize highland bull and another of Prince's Street in Edinburgh. Underneath the mirror was a small dressing table with a mat embroidered with dark red roses and a small china figurine of a long thin lady raising one end of her long dress with one hand and holding out the other as though accepting the offer of a dance from an invisible suitor. Heavy floral curtains hung closed at the window, making the room dark.

His mother had already put his shorts and T-shirt on the back of a chair. He remembered her instructions to take off his uniform as soon as he got home so it was clean for the next day. Edmund looked down at his shoes and considered undoing his laces. He was reluctant to do so yet, afraid to break the spell.

That night, Mrs MacDougal ran him a bath. He watched as she plunged her arm elbow-deep into the water, swirling it round so that the hot mixed well with the cold. The plug looked miles away, as though he would need a snorkel and goggles to reach it. A big fat pink cake of Palmolive lay in the soap dish and a warm dry towel hung over the rail. Edmund felt a thrill of excitement and yet he was afraid, too. He imagined his mother. What would she say?

But she had phoned and said she would be away another night. Edmund had tried to look suitably sad at the news, but his heart had almost burst with excitement. Perhaps she would stay away another day. And yet another. And another. Perhaps he could live here forever. Edmund pulled his thoughts into line quickly. It was wrong. God would punish him for even thinking that, for wanting his mother to go away forever.

Edmund knocked on Craig's door for the fourth time that day. There had been no answer and each time he had left feeling desperately worried. Where was Craig? Was he alive? Edmund's stomach lurched every time he thought of Craig lying dead somewhere.

This time, however, he had arrived to find Sandra's car parked in the drive. She opened the door to him with her characteristically wide smile.

'Edmund!' she enthused and he felt his heart do a pirouette. 'What have you been doing to Craig?'

'He's alive? Oh, thank goodness.'

'Well, he was very nearly not,' she said, leading the way upstairs to where Craig lay on his bed. He could hardly open his right eye, which was purple and blue and badly swollen. The right side of his face was a mass of scratches and cuts and a big white bandage covered his right ear.

'Edmund!' said Craig, trying to manage a smile. 'You old bugger! What happened to you, hey? Where are the cops when you need them most?'

'I'm so sorry, my friend,' said Edmund, sitting softly on the edge of the bed. 'I didn't know where you were. I didn't know what happened to you. You seemed to have disappeared.'

'I did! In the back of a truck!'

'Ah, I saw it leave.'

'That's nice,' said Craig to Sandra, nodding his head towards Edmund. '*I saw it leave.* Cheers, Edmund!'

'I didn't know you were in it. I waited until Pullman left and I looked for you and couldn't find you and then I saw that your car had gone.'

'And you thought I'd done a runner?

'No, not exactly. I asked a security guard a few shops down if he had seen your car and he said another man had just asked him a similar question about a truck, but it wasn't you, it was a black man in a small white car. I was worried, really worried. I thought you might have gone and tried to be a hero. I got a taxi here and waited an hour, but you didn't return. What happened?'

Craig recounted his story. It was the second time that day that he had told it and now in front of his audience of two, one a beautiful woman and the other a police officer, it ballooned somewhat into a life of its own.

'Well, I had to think quickly and I knew that if I didn't jump I'd be dead meat so I just threw myself off the back and managed to roll to the side as I did so.'

'You're lucky they didn't see you.'

Craig shrugged as though it were all in a day's work.

'Do you know where they were taking you?'

'Somewhere out of town definitely. It was dark and the road was a single track.'

'And then? How did you get home?'

'Ran.'

'Ran the whole way?'

'Ye-ah. Quite a bit of it.' He nodded his head slowly to suggest the distance he had covered. 'With my hands tied. Lucky I'm so fit.' He broke into a racking cough at that moment and Sandra and Edmund shared a smile. 'Then Charles picked me up.'

'Charles?'

'The airtime vendor. He at least *made the effort* to rescue me, unlike some people!'

Edmund smiled apologetically.

'Did you get any photos?'

'No, nothing came out. It was too dark and I couldn't use a flash. What time did you get home?'

'I don't know. All I know is that it was dark and cold.'

Edmund thought hard. 'And they didn't come back to look for you?'

'What are you thinking?'

'I wonder what they meant by "he wouldn't know what to do with a phone if it landed on his head."'

'It's an expression. It means that–'

I know what it means, I just wonder why they said it. Why mention a phone? And why did they say "I think we've found who we've been looking for"? Who were they looking for?'

'The plot thickens,' said Craig with a raise of his eyebrows towards Sandra.

'They obviously don't see you as much of a threat. They didn't make much of an effort to find you.'

'Well, I wouldn't say that. I think I've probably made them reconsider their security arrangements–'

'Have you been to the hospital? Have you been examined?' interrupted Edmund, not wishing to waste any more time on conjecture.

Craig looked a little too lovingly up at Sandra. 'I don't need to. I have my nurse right here.'

Sandra looked away, embarrassed. 'I haven't done much,' she said, folding a cloth on the bed. 'Just cleaned the wound and put a dressing on it. You're lucky it's not deep.'

'You didn't answer the door earlier. I thought you were dead.'

'Just asleep. Man, I was tired when I got home.'

'And this man, Charles, where does he fit in?'

Craig explained.

Edmund nodded his head as he listened. 'That all makes sense. About six months ago, a number of bodies, all of women, were found in the bush near the Beitbridge border. The police had received a tip-off about a possible trafficking operation. Women were being transported to Johannesburg hidden in the back of a lorry. There was a massive computer glitch in the customs' system and the whole system was down for over a week. Hundreds of lorries were stranded at Beitbridge and, as usual, not enough police were assigned to the task of searching them. By the time the women were found, whatever lorry they had been in was gone as well as driver and any accomplices.'

'They got scared and jumped ship?'

'Either that or they too had received a tip-off.'

'And? Was anyone prosecuted?'

'No. The case is still classed as unsolved.'

Craig shook his head.

'To go back to what you saw,' said Edmund, 'You say you think they were all women?'

'Yes. It was so strange. They seemed to disappear into the depths of the lorry.'

Edmund nodded his head thoughtfully.

'Then these guys got on and loaded the lorry with old furniture.'

'Old furniture? Old furniture.' Edmund repeated to himself.

Craig shot him a puzzled look.

'I keep seeing it, that's all, old furniture. Old things.' He thought of the letter-opener used to stab Marcia Pullman.

'You must have seen a lot round this place.' Craig laughed, indicating his house.

Edmund smiled absently and then stood up. 'I must go. I have to find an internet café.'

'An internet café? I know a nice dingy one on 5th Street.'

'I am so glad you are alive,' interjected Edmund, not wishing to hear any of Craig's stories. 'I will call you later and see how you are doing. I wish you would go to the hospital though and get yourself examined.'

Craig rubbed his thumb and middle finger together with a rueful smile to suggest money, or rather the lack of it.

'You've got him now, haven't you, Edmund? This Pullman guy. You can arrest him for this, can't you?' I mean, I don't know what he's up to, but he is definitely a crook – and a murderer.'

Edmund smiled sadly and raised his eyebrows as if to say yes. 'So many people,' he thought as he went downstairs, 'live in a fantasy world.'

Edmund arrived at Twice Loved just as it closed. The door

was locked and there was a big 'closed' sign in the window, but Edmund could see Mrs Reilly at the back of the shop, tidying up. He knocked loudly on the glass and she came bustling over, looking annoyed.

She pointed at the notice. 'Closed.' He put his hand in his pocket and brought out his police i.d.

She pulled a face to suggest 'typical' and opened the door.

'Chief Inspector Edmund Dube, CID,' he said as assertively as possible.

Her face softened slightly although she still looked annoyed. 'Oh, I remember you. What do you want now? We're closed and I'm about to go home.'

'I need to ask you some more questions.'

'Not about Janet Peters? Surely not! I really don't know the woman very well.'

'You told me a story the last time I was here. About a painting that Marcia Pullman had bought here for a few dollars and resold for ten thousand.'

'Ye-es... look, you'd better come in,' she said, standing aside and letting him inside the shop. 'What about it? '

'You said it had belonged to an elderly lady and that she had got no money from the sale of it?'

'Yes, that's right. She had had it for years and never known what it was worth. I think it had been in the family for a long time and she was loath to give it away but she was desperate for money and in a home somewhere and couldn't afford to pay her way anymore. It's very common these days, unfortunately. That's the way this country has gone with the government we have.' She gave Edmund a sideways glance then and once again he was back in Mrs Fourie's class and everything was his fault: Independence, a decline in standards, having to let black children into government schools.

'You said Janet *wasn't* angry about this, only disappointed.'

'From what I gather, Marcia persuaded her that she hadn't bought the picture from the old lady, she had bought it from the shop and the shop had sold it for ten dollars. What she did agree to do though is to see what else the old dear had for sale. If she had one valuable picture, perhaps she had a heap of them. She said that if she saw anything of value, she would make sure the woman knew and could make a decision from there.'

'Do you happen to know who this woman is?'

Another suspicious glance.

'I'm a police officer,' said Edmund suddenly, not quite knowing where his voice was coming from. 'I'm investigating a crime. I need that information.'

'Her name's Elaine Parkinson. You'll find her at Percy Thredwell Home for the Aged. You know the place, out on Third Street?'

'Yes, yes, I do. Thank you very much for your time.' Edmund flashed her a sudden smile and received a hesitant, but warming one in reply.

'You're not like other policemen are you?' she said, letting him out of the door.

'I hope not,' was Edmund's response.

Chapter Thirty-four

With rue my heart is laden
For golden friends I had,
For many a rose-lipt maiden
And many a lightfoot lad.

By brooks too broad for leaping
The lightfoot lads are laid;
The rose-lipt girls are sleeping
In fields where roses fade.

Edmund couldn't help the verses springing to mind as he entered the Percy Thredwell Home for the Aged. He remembered reciting them to Mrs MacDougal and stumbling over the alliteration. *The lightfoot lads are laid.*

'Enunciation is everything, Edmund!' Mrs MacDougal would say sternly. 'Lightfoot lads, lightfoot lads. Light foot lads.'

I was young once, Chief Inspector. He remembered Mrs Whitstable's words. That was the problem, wasn't it? In the eyes of the young, you were old and always had been. Edmund sometimes thought of his own death. He imagined he would be old and respected. A retired police officer. Babamkhulu. A wise old man. Yet it could come so much sooner, as it did so often in Zimbabwe. Living to old age was beyond the expectations of so many. But, thought Edmund, looking gloomily round the entrance hall to the home, was it really such a bonus?

White people, of course, put their parents in homes and didn't like looking after them themselves. He had often heard his mother tut-tut when she spoke about it. It was criminal the way they treated old folk.

He looked around at the threadbare carpet and the faded pictures on the wall. A framed piece of cross-stitch urged the

345

reader to Take It To the Lord in Prayer whilst another bore a picture of a dog with the words Man's Best Friend. A certain staleness pervaded the air, partly disguised by a pungent smell of disinfectant mixed with that of meat cooking.

The nurse at the reception desk greeted Edmund with deep suspicion, looking him up and down disdainfully. She was reading a magazine, the type that specialises in the highs and lows of celebrity life, and obviously didn't want to be interrupted. In her hand she held a half-eaten doughnut.

'Mrs Parkinson? Yes, she is in. And you are?'

'Chief Inspector Edmund Dube.' He left off the CID in case it should sound too intimidating.

'Well, Chief Inspector, is Mrs Parkinson expecting you? Our residents are very old, you know, and they don't like surprises.' She gave him a look that suggested that he might be more of a bombshell than a surprise.

'No, she's not, but she will be happy to speak to me.'

She sighed as though the situation was out of her hands and took another bite of her jam doughnut. 'Number nine,' she said, waving her hand towards the corridor of rooms and then looking back at her magazine.

Edmund knocked gingerly on the door and then listened carefully.

'Yes. Who is it?'

Edmund hesitated. He was a little boy outside the headmaster's door.

'Edmund,' he said softly. 'Edmund Dube.'

There was a pause and then: 'Come in!' He entered to find a tiny, shrunken woman with a marked stoop perched on the edge of a wooden armchair like an emaciated vulture about to take flight. Her eyes, which were small and bright and intelligent, were the most vibrant part of her.

'Have you come to fix the light?' she asked.

'I'm a police officer,' said Edmund, unsure of his reception. 'I'd like to ask you some questions.'

'Oh? Well, how exciting!' she enthused, smiling amiably at

him. 'Is it about the missing money from Mrs Trent's room? If you ask me, I think she may have just misplaced it. She's not always right. She forgets, you know.' She got up very slowly and manoeuvred herself onto her bed. Her hands were red and swollen and quite useless. She motioned for him to take her chair.

'Oh, please, no. I can stand.'

'No, no, I insist. Anyway, I've moved now and it's far too much trouble to move back again.'

Edmund sat, feeling very uncomfortable.

'I've come about a picture,' he said. 'The one you took to Twice Loved.'

'Oh? Oh yes. That was my favourite. What's that got to do with you?'

'Can you tell me about it?'

She hesitated, looking carefully at him. Then she shook her head and spoke. 'It was a lovely picture, really lovely. I should never have sold it, never. I got absolutely nothing for it, not even enough to live on for a week.' She sighed and the sigh seemed to fill the room with a grey sadness.

'Do you know what happened to it?'

'Yes, they told me it had been sold. Why? Is there a problem? I don't still have the money if that's what you're after.'

'The person who bought the picture was a lady called Marcia Pullman.'

Her face hardened and some of the sadness left the room, replaced by a sense of disquiet. Her voice was quiet, but firm. 'Yes. I know Marcia.'

'You know her? Did a lady called Janet Peters bring her to meet you?'

'Yes, that's right. The lady from the shop. Nice lady. Red hair.'

'That's the one. Did Mrs Pullman offer to buy anything else from you?'

Mrs Parkinson pursed her lips in sudden annoyance. 'I would not touch that woman with a barge pole! I know all

347

about Marcia Pullman. I had some trinkets, necklaces and rings, that sort of thing, that I had taken out to show her, but when I realised it was Marcia that Mrs Peters had brought to see them, I quickly put them away. Oh no, no. I was desperate for money, but I still have my principles.' She looked away as though she were about to cry.

'You mean you'd met Mrs Pullman *before* Mrs Peters introduced her to you?'

'Oh, many years ago now. I must have met her in the '70s. I used to work in a children's home. St. Botolph's Home for Boys. I was there for years. 1952 until 1998. It's closed now, but you may have heard of it?'

'Yes, I have. Did Mrs Pullman work there with you?'

The old lady's lips twisted cynically. She tapped the bedclothes slowly with her swollen hands.

'She was what you might call a go-between. Some of our children came from married couples who, for whatever reason, usually financial, felt that they couldn't keep their child anymore and so decided to put them up for adoption. We also had a few who had been taken away from their parents due to alcoholism, abuse, that sort of thing. By far, though, the majority of our babies came from unmarried mothers. The stigma was great in those days.' She gave a rueful smile as though to say that she missed those days.

'Mrs Pullman was a go-between the home and the mother?' guessed Edmund.

'Yes, you see, the mothers often didn't want anyone to even *know* they had given birth. We got babies from all over the country. The young girl from Gwelo may be sent to stay with an aunt in Bulawayo for a few months. The family would say she was doing a secretarial course or such like. She would come down here and not leave the house until the baby was born. Aunty would bring it in and the young lady would return to Gwelo with no one any the wiser. But some young girls didn't have an aunty in Bulawayo; they didn't have anyone at all. Perhaps their parents didn't even know.'

'So Mrs Pullman...'

'Provided them with somewhere to stay – right up until the birth when she brought the baby to us.'

Edmund sat back. His mind was full of thoughts. He had come here in the hope of following a trail of antiques that would help him solve the mystery of Mrs Pullman's death, yet the investigation seemed to be taking another turn.

'I see,' he said at last, although he wasn't quite sure he did. 'You said you didn't like Mrs Pullman though. Some would say what she did was a noble thing.'

Mrs Parkinson tried to pull herself straight on the bed. Her movements were painful and stiff and Edmund watched her anxiously as though at any moment she would keel over and die.

She didn't answer for a while, seemingly lost in thought.

'Look, Marcia did offer the girls she housed training – usually in the secretarial field and she even helped some of them find jobs. But Marcia never forgot *who* she had helped and *how much* she had helped them – and she never let them forget either.'

'Someone else said that of her.'

'Did they?' She gave a wry smile. 'A leopard never changes its spots, Chief Inspector.' There was another silence where she seemed to be lost back down the years somewhere.

'She played a role. A motherly role, even though she wasn't much older than the girls she looked after. But she had money – and a big house – and influence. All three. Many of the girls were just that – girls. They were naïve. Yes, they had had a baby, but I reckon some of them didn't even know how it had happened! Parents were different then; they were strict; having an unmarried pregnant daughter would have been the end for some of them. Some girls were kicked out of home entirely. Marcia must have seemed like an angel in comparison. Imagine, someone to look after you when others would disown you and pay for your lessons and take away your dirty little secret at the end? Marvellous.'

The air, Edmund felt, had suddenly become charged with something quite indefinable. Was it apprehension or excitement? Or was it the strangeness of this little old lady's knowledge and, once again, a trip into the past from which he seemed to always emerge feeling quite suffocated?

'What happened if you did not repay her favours?'

Mrs Parkinson shrugged. 'I don't know if it ever happened. She knew too much about too many people. They were afraid of her. You see, she kept all the details. Names of the girls, names of the men they'd been involved with, details of the baby.'

'How do you know all this?'

She sighed heavily and seemed to consider whether to tell him something or not. 'We had a young girl come to us one day – with her baby. She was in a terrible state. Wanted to give it up, but didn't really want to. Couldn't support herself, never mind a baby. Her father had thrown her out of the house and she had wandered the streets for a while. Then, somehow or other, she had heard of Marcia and her generosity. She had stayed for a few days, but had been woken in the middle of the night every night by a young woman crying. On the third night, she had gone looking for her and found her sobbing her heart out in an end bedroom. All she could tell her was "get out of here before it's too late. Have your baby anywhere else, even on the street, but get out." At that point Marcia had barged in and hauled the girl off. She wasn't there the next night.'

'What do you think she did to her?'

She thought a moment. 'I don't know. I really don't. But the girl who came to us, I think Ellemarie was her name, wasn't going to wait around to experience the same fate and she ran away. She was convinced, you see, that there was somewhere that the girls were taken at night. Once they'd had their babies and given them up, of course.'

'Do you mean a brothel?'

'Not quite. Nothing as obvious – or as permanent – as that. Let's just say they provided entertainment.'

'Mrs Pullman was never investigated by the police?'

'Investigated? Oh, no. Marcia was very clever. Never left traces.'

Edmund closed his eyes. He felt the rushing sensation of a train hurtling through a tunnel. Something was coming together. It was near, he just knew it. *Marcia Pullman knew too much.*

'Such a dear girl was Ellemarie. She wasn't bad, none of those girls were, but Marcia made them think they were and therefore they were only fit for one thing. We gave Ellemarie a job in the office and she kept her baby. I only wish I could have helped more of them.'

'So when Marcia Pullman walked in here many years later, you remembered her?'

'Remembered her? I could hardly forget. I never forget a face. I may be old but' – she tapped her head – 'I've still got all my marbles. I would certainly never forget her face. It broke my heart to think she had my picture. I knew it was worth far more than she had paid for it. I wasn't going to let her take anything more of mine. I am poor, yes, and not much use to anyone now, but when I die I will die with dignity. That is all I ask for.'

Her words were soft and seemed to float gently in the room, like swirls of smoke, spiralling upwards and outwards.

'Mrs Peters is a nice lady, but I don't think she should have got involved with Mrs Pullman. That woman tainted her reputation, I am sure. I tried to warn Polly but she wouldn't listen.'

'Polly?'

'Yes, Polly Randell. Number 14. Upstairs. Janet sold some things for her – a bit of silver and a lovely cameo of one of her great grandparents. I thought she could have got more, but she was quite happy with what she got so who was I to say anything?'

'Could I perhaps speak to Mrs Randell? Number 14?'

'Oh, she's dead now. Poor thing. Dropped dead a couple of weeks after the sale. And do you know, she had kept that money. Hadn't spent a cent. She was hoping to go to England with it. Poor Polly, she had no idea of money. Her niece donated it to Island Hospice.' She gave a wry smile.

Edmund snapped his notebook shut. He hadn't written a word, but he knew he'd remember it all. He looked momentarily around the tiny room: the single bed, the single chair and the single shelf. A photo, a picture and a small china ornament. The sum of a life.

'I hope that has helped you, Chief Inspector. I read in the newspaper that Marcia had been stabbed, but I thought they discovered it was the gardener.'

Edmund laughed. 'Quality reporting as usual.' He got up to leave and then remembered something he had wanted to ask.

'St. Botolph's took only boys, is that correct?'

'Yes. St. Mary's took the girls. Marcia operated there, too, but the person you'd need to speak to is long dead.'

'Not much help then.'

'It's funny I hadn't seen Marcia since well, I don't know, perhaps 1979, but lately she seems to have reappeared in my life. Lucky me.' She chortled.

'What do you mean?'

'Well, I go through spates when I am contacted by people looking for their birth parents and they think I can help – remember a face or a person or just some little link with the past. I hadn't seen anyone for ages until a woman turned up about two months ago. I told her I only dealt with the boys and the person who ran St. Mary's died about twenty-five years ago. She was terribly disappointed. She had come all the way from South Africa. Nice girl. Pretty, too. I did something I probably shouldn't have and told her to try Marcia. She could well have been one of Marcia's babies, especially as she was, well, what's the term? Mixed race? That was another big no-no at one time. Anyway, I gave her Marcia's name. It was worth a try. Nice girl. Told me she was a pet therapist. I'd never heard of it, have you?'

'No, no I haven't. What exactly did you tell her?'

'Oh, I was suitably vague. I told her that Marcia used to help young women who had found themselves in trouble and she might have kept records of those she had helped. I didn't say anything else of course.' She rubbed her swollen hands together. 'She offered to massage my hands. In fact, she gave me a little pot of something. Wintergreen, I think it is. Thought the nurses could rub it in for me every night, but this lot can't be bothered most of the time.'

'Has she been back at all? Do you know if she managed to find Mrs Pullman?'

She shook her head. 'No, I just assumed she must have. I hope she did.'

Edmund nodded slowly. 'I wonder,' he said, more to himself than to her. 'Thank you for your time, Mrs Parkinson.'

'Thank you for yours, Chief Inspector. You'll excuse me if I don't show you out.'

Edmund gave a little wave and smiled. He took one last look at the frail creature on the bed, was once more reminded of an ancient, weathered bird and closed the door.

Chapter Thirty-five

Inside the kitchen, Dorcas sat on a chair. In her hands, she held a dishtowel, which she twisted into a tight knot and didn't release. This had to be it, didn't it? The end. She just wanted to get up and walk out of the door and out of the gate and down the road. She didn't care where it took her as long as it took her away. On the top of the stove, a pot of isitshwala with the lid on cooked quietly, every now and then emitting a gentle plopping sound like that of a stone hitting the smooth surface of water.

She looked down at her hands and it was as if she saw, written on her palms, her whole existence lying before her. She would always be in the kitchen, on the outside, on a chair. The silent invisible who washed glasses and placed them neatly on a tray; who answered questions as to where the napkins were kept and was there any sugar or salt or mustard to be had. The person who cleaned up spills and vomit and mess. 'Dorcas, some tea please.' 'Dorcas, where is my hat?' 'Dorcas, more salt.' 'Dorcas, Dorcas, Dorcas!' The top of the pan moved gently, pushed upwards by the force building up below it.

At once, Dorcas saw her life slipping away. The rest of her existence was at the mercy of someone's kindness, someone's need for order and dust free shelves. Dorcas felt herself becoming smaller and smaller; the cupboards grew, they widened, they towered above her. The table, the chairs, even the sink were great monsters that swayed precariously, threatening to fall and crush her.

'I've got to do it,' she thought suddenly. 'I've got to.'

'You must be crazy!' Craig sank back into his pillow and reached for his cigarettes on his side table.

'Uh-uh,' Sandra said, swooping down on him and

snatching them out of his hands. 'We said ten today and you've already had eight and it's not quite eleven o'clock. How do you expect to get through the rest of the day?'

'Fifteen?' pleaded Craig.

'Nope.'

'I was on thirty a day. It's a big cut.'

'Forty. It's an even bigger cut.' She sat down in the only chair in the room, a basket weave thing that Craig had once bought from a man in a parking lot. It was now broken on one side so whoever sat in it had to be careful they didn't put their full weight down or they'd find themselves on the floor in no time. Sandra seemed to sit there quite happily with her legs crossed in a version of the lotus position, which she seemed to achieve with great ease.

'Sheez like,' muttered Craig, who had at first enjoyed Sandra's attention but was now beginning to feel the drawbacks of having a woman around. Why were they always like this, he wondered? Always trying to change you and... manage you. Yes, manage was a good word for it. Some biological thing no doubt.

He turned his attention back to Edmund, who was perched on the edge of his bed like some sort of emissary from another world.

'As I was saying, you are mad. You have enough on Pullman to bring him in. I thought you'd have locked him in Chikurubi by now. Why do you need to go and spy on his house?'

'Actually, I don't have enough on Pullman. I haven't any photos or evidence or anything of that sort.'

'What about my experience? I could give evidence.'

'He called you a bum. White trash. Believe me, you will be no match for him. He'll have himself covered and the last thing I want to do is blow my chance of nabbing him by calling in the police.'

'You *are* the police.'

'Ye-es, but let's just say I am operating by myself at the moment. This has to be handled very, very delicately.'

'Right,' said Craig, not quite convinced. 'So you want to watch the Pullman's house to see what goes on there at night? If he's that clever, he's not going to run anything from home.'

'I'm not watching him, I'm watching Dorcas.'

'Dorcas?'

'The maid. The one who recognised you from the agency.'

'The agency?' piped up Sandra. 'What agency is that?'

'Oh, nothing.' Craig wished he did not sound so obviously as though he was keeping something quiet. He saw a little smile on Sandra's face as though she knew.

'Why Dorcas? Why not Shantelle?'

Edmund seemed to hesitate. His eyes flickered over to Sandra's.

'Let's just say, I think she knows more about this business than she might like to admit. Maids know everything, don't they?' He gave a short, unconvincing laugh.

'What are you hoping to see?'

Edmund shrugged. 'What comes and goes. *Who* comes and goes.'

Craig felt Edmund was being a little obscure this morning. There was an aloofness about him that went beyond his usual aloofness.

'So, this watching the house business. How are you going to do that?'

Edmund stood up and clasped his hands together. Craig had a good idea of what was coming.

'I thought it might be a good idea to use a car this time. So you could get away quickly if there were any danger.'

'So *I* could get away quickly? Sheez like, I'm still recovering from the last lot. Where the hell are you going to be? Stirring a martini at Rick's bar?'

'Rick's bar?'

'*Casablanca.*' He waved Edmund's enquiry away with his hand. 'Don't worry about it; it would take too long to explain.'

'You'll be in a car and able to drive away,' insisted Edmund.

'Where will you be?'

'I'll be close, don't worry. I won't be far.'

'I hope you know I'm in no fit state to do this. I can't even see out of one eye. I won't be much of a challenge this time around.'

'I'm not asking you to go into the house. That could get you into serious trouble. I just want you to watch it.'

'I'll go with you,' Sandra said. Her voice was calm. 'We can go in my car if you want.'

'No,' said Edmund at once and Craig turned to him, surprised. 'By all means go with him, but not in your car. It's too new. Someone would call Neighbourhood Watch and report you for loitering with intent. An old car, seemingly broken down on the side of the road, is much more inconspicuous.'

'What if Dorcas recognises it? It's a fairly unusual car these days.'

'Don't park directly opposite the house obviously. It's on a corner so maybe diagonally opposite would be better. Remember that the street lights don't work. I think you'll be safe.'

'And what am I looking for – that is if I do decide to undertake this ridiculous assignment?'

'Just note who goes in and who goes out, if anyone. I doubt it will be dangerous work.'

Craig gave a short, ironic laugh. 'Famous last words?' Automatically, he reached for his packet of cigarettes beside his bed. Sandra waved it at him from the distance of her chair. 'No rest for the wicked,' he sighed, lying back on the pillow. Inwardly he chastised himself for not standing up to Edmund's request. He was hardly intimidating so what was it about the guy that Craig gave in all the time?

'I can't believe I'm doing this,' Craig said eventually. 'This is madness.' Yet it was difficult to suppress a sense of excitement. Sandra would be with him. Even Manning, dear, dear Manning, would be impressed.

Chapter Thirty-six

'Dorcas.'

Dorcas spun round quickly, alert with fear. She was chopping up a bunch of parsley in the kitchen and held a large sharp knife in her hand.

'How did you get in?'

'The gate was not locked. Surely I don't have to tell you that. It isn't locked if someone is at home – or has just popped out momentarily to somewhere close by. Next door, for example.'

'Go away!' she snarled, waving the knife at him. 'I will call the police!'

'Please, Dorcas. I *am* the police. I want to help you.'

She shook her head slowly. 'They told me not to trust you. You are not who you say you are. You are not a policeman.'

'Who said that? Mr Pullman? Is that what he told you?'

She didn't answer. 'Why?' her voice was strained. 'Why are you here? Mr Pullman says Mrs Pullman was not murdered. He says she died of kidney failure.'

'Dorcas, listen. Please. I have to ask you some questions. You *must* help me.'

She shook her head nervously. 'No. I don't know who you are. You said you were a policeman but... I always knew there was something wrong about you.'

'Wrong? Dorcas, *please*. Please you must help me. I am not *wrong*.'

He watched as her eyes darted nervously over his face. She had backed herself closer to the wall and held the knife close at chest level.

'I know what you do.' He hazarded the words, knowing full well he was putting himself in danger.

A cloud fell upon her countenance, pulling the side of her mouth down.

'I know about the girls.'

Dorcas shook her head as though she was shivering.

'What?'

'I know, Dorcas,' he repeated.

'No. No, no, no. You're wrong. You don't know anything.' Her voice was thin and faraway, as though she were talking through a long pipe.

'You got the girls jobs. Mrs Pullman made you find the right type: young, but quite naive, unaware of how she was to exploit them. You didn't like it, did you? You didn't like lying.'

Dorcas looked down at the floor.

'But your job paid well, didn't it? Nice place to live, too.'

Dorcas twisted her head to the side. She wouldn't meet his eyes.

'It was hard, wasn't it, knowing what happened later to some of those girls.'

Her head jerked forwards, her eyes frightened.

'Tell me, did Mrs Pullman know what her husband was doing? Did she know of his affair with Shantelle?'

Dorcas paused, looking him straight in the eye. She shook her head. 'No.'

It had been a guess, but one that worked. It spurred him on to make more suppositions.

'The girls would be dissatisfied with their pay, they'd complain to Shantelle and Shantelle might suggest something a little more lucrative. After all, these girls were young and pretty. They didn't want to be cleaning up after old people. They wanted new shoes and clothes and handbags.'

Holding the knife with one hand, Dorcas rubbed the other over her eyes.

'Why couldn't you have warned them? You of all people.'

'I tried.' Her voice was quiet. 'I was afraid.'

'You tried to leave Mrs Pullman?'

'Yes, but she wouldn't let me go.'

'Her business wasn't really doing so well, was it? Girls were leaving after a couple of months, ironically drawn away by her husband and her secretary. Clients probably weren't happy with the rapid turnaround in staff. She needed you to convince the girls to stay. It wouldn't be very encouraging if you left.

'Did you tell Mr Sherbourne?'

Dorcas remained silent, sucking in her lips. Her body tightened in fear.

'Let's stop pretending. I know about you and Mr Sherbourne. Now what did he suggest?'

Dorcas was silent, as though a silent hand had her by the throat.

'Dorcas, what did he suggest? I need to know what it was.'

Her voice broke. 'Mr Pullman...' Placing the knife on the kitchen counter, she bent over, her face in her hands.

'You went to Mr Pullman? You spoke to him?' Enlightenment dawned. 'You *threatened* him?'

There was a barely perceptible nod from Dorcas in reply. 'Why?'

'I wanted it all to stop. It had to stop.'

'A dangerous move. A very, very dangerous move.' Edmund stared at Dorcas, trying hard to think of her making threats against Mr Pullman. 'You threatened him that if he didn't help you leave, you would tell his wife what was going on. On one hand, you know all about his business and, if you leave, who knows who you might tell. On the other, you might go and tell his wife what he gets up to with Shantelle. It may not be a close marriage, but she's the source of the money.'

A flicker of something indefinable crossed Dorcas's face just then, a softness, a vulnerability, as though something she had been unclear about suddenly made sense. Then she pulled her cheeks in as though to keep back an avalanche of tears and became more resolute. She turned away from him and picked up the knife again. She resumed chopping up the parsley.

'What did he say? Was he angry?'

Dorcas shrugged as though the event was of no interest to her.

'Dorcas! What did he say? He must have said *something*. Was he angry? What?'

Dorcas closed her eyes and slowly shook her head.

'Nothing? He didn't say anything?'

'Nothing.' She wiped her eye with the corner of a tea towel.

'If he didn't say anything it's because he wanted to take his time to plan. He would have discussed it with Shantelle. Did she say anything to you?'

'No. Nothing.'

'And this was how long ago?'

Dorcas swept her head backwards and opened her eyes. 'January.'

'January? Six months ago! You made a threat and they didn't respond and you didn't carry it through?' Edmund had a sudden urge to shake Dorcas by the shoulders. 'Or did you?'

'It stopped. The girls... the ones going to Joburg. It stopped.'

'But *you* were still *here*. *You* were still bringing in girls for Mrs Pullman. *You* were still unhappy.'

Dorcas looked down at the knife in her hands.

'Mrs Pullman found out about you and Mr Sherbourne. *That's* what happened. And you realised you weren't the only one with a trick up your sleeve. You could tell her all about her husband and Shantelle, but that wouldn't set you free. If you were going to humiliate her, she'd make sure she took you with. She'd wreck your life; she'd wreck his.'

Dorcas didn't move an inch; she continued to stare at the knife. Slowly, a single tear rolled down her cheek.

Gently, Edmund took the knife from her and laid it on the chopping board.

'I want to know about the day Mrs Pullman died. What was she like that morning?'

'Bad mood. She wasn't feeling well. She had this stuff on her face. Like sweat. White stuff. She didn't want any breakfast because she said she had a headache.'

'Was it unusual for her to feel unwell?'

Dorcas shook her head. 'She has been like this for some time. On, off, on, off.'

'What did she do?'

'Nothing. She didn't eat, but she took two aspirin. She always took aspirin. She said she had too much to do that day.'

'Did she have any appointments? Does the name Sandra mean anything to you?'

Dorcas shook her head. 'She phoned someone.'

'A different story now.' Edmund couldn't help but feel exasperated. 'Did she say who it was?'

'No. She wanted some mushrooms.'

'But there was a carton of mushrooms in the fridge. Why did she need more?'

'Different mushrooms. Those are button mushrooms. These were different. She said they were very expensive.'

'What did she use them for?'

'Soup. She had served it at bridge club.'

'And everyone drank it?'

'Yes. They said it was delicious. Mrs Pullman was very happy. She wanted to serve it at book club as well. She phoned and started asking about mushrooms and if she could buy some more and then suddenly she said "Oh, it's you. I've got the wrong number."'

'Did she get through eventually?'

'No. I think she dialled the same number again, because as soon as the person answered, she hung up. She was very angry.'

Edmund looked long and hard at Dorcas. 'Do you know anyone with the initials S.P. who came to the house?'

'S.P.?' she shook her head slowly. 'No.'

'How often did Mrs Peters come here?

'Whenever book club was held here.'

'She didn't come any other time?'

Dorcas thought, sucking in her lips as she did so. 'She came round once at the end of last year. Just before Christmas.'

'Do you remember how she seemed? Was she angry or annoyed for instance?'

Dorcas almost smiled. 'With Mrs Pullman? No, Mrs Peters is too shy. But she wasn't happy.'

'How do you know?'

'I had asked her if she had a job for me and she said no. She had finished talking to Mrs Pullman and she was on her way out and I followed her. When I caught up with her at her car, she looked like she wanted to cry. She said she wished she could offer me a job. She said: "I would do anything to get you away from this woman."'

'Do you have any idea what she was upset about?'

Dorcas paused. She ran her tongue over her bottom lip as she seemed to consider whether to say something or not.

'No, but I think... I think... I had the feeling that Mrs Peters had given Mrs Pullman something and she wouldn't give it back.'

'You had "the feeling"?' Mentally, Edmund rolled his eyes and gave an exasperated shake of his head. Dorcas was giving him a lot more information now than she had initially, but it was highly subjective.

'When I had brought in the tea, Mrs Peters was saying, "But you said you'd only have them a couple of weeks." Mrs Pullman looked angry that Mrs Peters had said that while I was there and waited until I had gone out before she answered. She asked me to close the door.'

'Were those the exact words?'

'You don't believe me?'

'I didn't say that.'

'Then why do you ask, ask, ask?'

'Why didn't you tell me all this in the beginning?'

Dorcas crossed her arms. A rain cloud had settled on her countenance.

Edmund decided to push on with questions. 'And that was the only time you remember her coming round when it wasn't book club?'

'Yes.'

'Dorcas, I am your friend. Please know that. I just wished you had told me this information earlier. You kept so much from me.'

Dorcas shrugged and looked at her feet.

'You are a very difficult person to speak to.'

She shrugged again, but Edmund was convinced he saw a small half-smile on her face.

'Tsx,' she exclaimed, straightening up and scraping all the parsley together with the knife. 'I told you who it was. That man. That ikhiwa one who came here.'

'Mr Martin? That was a mix up. He did threaten Mrs Pullman, but it was a stupid mistake.'

'Madam didn't like him.'

'Well, he was angry. That thing he did in the office – remember? You saw what he did.'

He watched her face closely.

'She didn't like him before that.'

'Before that? When?'

'When he came here to the house.'

'You mean she had met him on a previous occasion?'

'He was supposed to be mending a tap in the bathroom and Madam found him looking in her cupboard.'

'Looking in her cupboard? Are you sure?'

'Yes, I am sure. She accused him of looking for money. She told him to leave.'

'And what did he do?'

Dorcas shrugged. 'He said he was very sorry but he had dropped a screw while carrying his tools into the bathroom and he thought it had rolled under the cupboard door.'

'Was she very angry?'

Dorcas opened her eyes wide and nodded. 'As he was leaving, she called him white trash.'

'White trash?'

She nodded. 'Yes. He turned around. He said, "Excuse me?" She said, "That's what you are. White trash."'

'What did he do?'

'Nothing at first. But I could see he was very, very angry.

364

He put all his things in his car. Then he came back. He said, "I know what you did. Don't you call me trash, when what you did is not even human."'

Edmund hesitated. He had taken out his notebook but his pencil hovered on top of the page, unable to write anything. 'You are sure he said that?'

Dorcas turned away, clearly annoyed. 'You think I made it up? Okay, fine.'

'I didn't say that. I just need to know... I need to know the truth. Time, you know, changes our memory of what happened.'

Like a flower closing up for the night, Dorcas had retreated back into herself and was obviously not going to tell Edmund any more. He felt a twang of conscience for he didn't want her to feel he doubted her.

'So that's how you knew who he was when he came here to the house.'

Dorcas gave a slight shrug of her shoulders and a look that said that he could make of the information what he wanted. She pushed the knife down hard on the chopping board. The bunch of parsley turned quickly into a heap of shredded green.

'What happened that morning? Why were you at the office?'

'The agency wasn't doing well. She wanted to go through the records and see who could be phoned up. To try and get them interested again.'

'Why did she give you the afternoon off?'

Dorcas paused for a second, then scraped the parsley to a corner of the chopping board and wiped the knife on a tea towel. She turned and faced him, her lips set in a thin, determined line.

'She wanted me to go out and look for more people to join the agency.'

'Even though it was book club that evening?'

Dorcas clicked her tongue. 'Everything was ready. Everything was cleaned. I told you this. I had cleaned everything the day before.'

'On a Sunday?'

'Yes, on a Sunday. She said it was my fault because I wasn't bringing enough people in. Mrs Peters was coming round to help her with the books. She didn't need me. I was just about to leave when that man came in and shouted at Shantelle. She came running into the kitchen.'

'Where you and Mrs Pullman were?'

'Yes. Mrs Pullman asked Shantelle, "What is wrong? What is wrong?" Shantelle says, "That man who came to do some work fixing things is here. He is shouting." Mrs Pullman says, "Let me deal with this. I will sort it out." She goes outside. She shouts at him. He tells her he is going to kill her.'

'He suggested it. He didn't actually say it?'

Ignoring the comment, Dorcas carried on.

'When he left, she was very angry with me.'

'With you? Why?'

'She thought we were working together.'

'You and Mr Martin?'

'She thought it was me who told him where she works so he could come and make threats. She said I was trying to drive her mad so that I could leave.'

'But he had done some work in the office. Why would he shout at Shantelle if he was after Mrs Pullman?'

'She wasn't thinking properly. She was not feeling well, I told you. She was in a very bad temper and told me to get out. Go, she said. Just go away. Go to your white man. I don't want to see you.'

'She fired you?'

'No. Not fired. She was just angry. She would expect me back at four o'clock.'

'Why would she think you were involved with Mr Martin? She knew about you and Mr Sherbourne.'

'You and Mrs Johnson! You are asking me the same questions.'

'You spoke to Shantelle? When was that?'

Dorcas pushed out her lower lip in a fat sulk. 'Today. She was asking me questions about that man in the office.'

'Craig? Mr Martin?'

'Did I know him before he joined the dating group? What did I know about him? She got angry when I said I don't know anything. She didn't believe me. She said why was Mrs Pullman angry with me? Why did she say those things about him?'

'Did you tell her that Mrs Pullman found him looking in her drawers?'

'Yes. She asked me lots of questions about him. I said I don't know him. I don't know who he is, but she didn't believe me.'

'Thank you,' said Edmund, putting his notebook and pencil away in his coat pocket. 'I appreciate all the help you have given me. And I won't say I have spoken to you. I won't mention your name.'

Dorcas picked up the knife with sudden vehemence. 'Please go. Just go!' she cried. 'They told me you are bad. That you are *mad*! Please just get out of here!'

Chapter Thirty-seven

1979

'Edmund. Buya!'

Edmund turned to see a man standing behind one of the jacarandas. He backed away, clutching his satchel. The figure moved into the open.

'Edmund, come here.'

Edmund stood still. He was afraid to move. Afraid to speak.

'Hey, you! I said come here. I am your father. I even speak to you in English and you do not listen.'

'I don't want to. I will be late.'

His father walked slowly closer.

'Late for what, heh? You have finished school. What will you be late for?'

Edmund shifted his feet. 'I need to do my homework.'

Stopping in front of him, his father snorted with contempt. 'You think you are white, hey? Doing your work with the old white policeman? You think you can go to school and learn to read and write and be like them, eh? You think you're going to have some smart job in an office one day?'

Edmund didn't answer. His father leant over and took Edmund by the collar. Edmund tried to back away, but his father held him in a tight grip.

'Let me tell you something. We're going to drive the white man from our land. We're going to rid ourselves of this pest. You understand? They think they've come to educate us, but really they've come to take over our minds... to subjugate... to control. Your Mr MacDougal, the good policeman, he's going to go. We're going to kick his butt all the way back to England—'

'He's not from England,' interrupted Edmund, remembering how Mr MacDougal didn't like being referred to as English.

'Huh?'

'He's from Scotland. You'd have to kick him back to Scotland.'

Edmund's father loosened his grip and Edmund fell back a step. He rolled his head from side to side and smoothed down his shirt. His father laughed, a horrible toothless squawk. He dropped to his haunches.

'Okay, my boy, we kick his *Scottish* butt all the way back to *Scotland*.' He stretched out his hand.

Edmund started walking. 'I'm going to be late.'

His father stood up. His smile had disappeared.

'You – you are being changed by the white man's ways,' he shouted.

Edmund carried on walking faster and faster, until he broke into a run.

'I'm going to get you, Edmund!' his father shouted. 'I am going to get you and keep you. You are my son! Do you hear me?'

The street was dark with the absolute blackness of a power cut. A couple of lights could be seen in the houses along the road: dim squares of yellow accompanied by the dull whirr of generators. The Pullman's house was shrouded in darkness; not even the light at the gate was on. It was evident that Pullman wasn't there.

Craig's right arm throbbed with pain. He hadn't been to see a doctor because he didn't believe it was broken. He'd have bones sticking out if that were the case, he was sure. What did the doctors give you anyway? Painkillers. He had enough of those already. What he really wished for was a strong drink. He imagined pouring a double whisky, the rich amber spilling out over the ice. He didn't know why he imagined ice as he didn't have it usually; it seemed more sophisticated somehow, more Manning.

Sandra had a little silver flask with her and two cups.

'Green tea,' she said, offering him one. He sipped it and grimaced. How on earth did anyone get used to drinking this stuff, he wondered. It tasted so awful it must be good for you.

'You drink too much,' she said to him, suddenly. He was surprised at her openness.

'Do I?' He would usually have got angry at such a statement, but he didn't think he could ever get angry with Sandra.

'Why?'

'*Why?* Why's the sky blue?' He felt backed into a corner by her frankness.

'You have to find your original experience. If you drink to run away from the world, ask yourself why. When did you first feel like escaping? That's the thing you have to deal with. Whenever you go through something traumatic, your body remembers how you felt. Certain situations can trigger the same feeling. The situation itself may not necessarily be a problem, it's the reliving of the feelings.'

'You sound like a textbook.'

'I'll give you an example from my own life. I told you, didn't I, that I was adopted? Well, throughout my younger years, I suffered from a feeling of abandonment. I didn't know why because I didn't know I was adopted. I also didn't have the wherewithal to identify it as such. Even when I was told about my adoption, I didn't make the connection. It was only later, much, much later, that I was able to find a reason for that feeling. By that time, I had made a huge mess of my life. Been anorexic, been married, had a child.'

Craig looked quickly at her. *A child*. She had never said anything about a child before. Or being married.

'I had also been a drinker. It was spirits in particular that I was attracted to: I binged on anything. I moved from obsession to obsession. I bought things I didn't need and made meals with fancy ingredients and then couldn't eat them. I got into debt. I got divorced.'

'And then you found Jesus! Amen!' said Craig rather cynically. He wished immediately that he hadn't said anything.

She was quiet for a long time. Finally, she said: 'I've never told anyone what I've just told you.'

They sat in silence for some time. The pain in Craig's arm was dulled considerably by the voice that shouted over and over again: 'Idiot! You're such a bloody idiot!' He wanted to tell her about the other night; about how he'd thought he'd died and how a memory he thought was long hidden had surfaced again. His mother, he wanted to tell her about his mother.

'My mother died when I was six.'

'I'm sorry to hear that. What happened?'

'She drove her car off a completely straight road. Rolled it three times.'

She took his hand and squeezed it.

'It was a Monday morning.' He gave a short laugh. 'Who dies on a Monday morning on a completely straight road?'

'Accidents happen when we least expect them to.'

'Except it wasn't an accident.'

'Oh, I'm sure it was–'

'She was an alcoholic. She'd been in hospital – a special hospital for mad, bad alcoholics. They wanted her to talk, *discuss* her *feelings*.'

'And now you drink because she did. You drink to justify her actions, so you yourself won't feel angry with her. Because you did, didn't you? You felt very angry with your mother.'

Craig was surprised at the wave of feelings that washed over him then. Pain, anger, remorse – and a need to cry out, to kick something, to hurt himself again and again. The picture of his mother in her bathing suit, her hair pulled back, her shoulders glistening with tiny drops of water, her arms outstretched, was still fresh in his mind. Her smile, her joy, her exuberance; and the feeling of security, of being loved and looked after, how it wrapped itself around him, held him up in a bubble above the world. *Jump, Craig! I'll catch you!*

'I'm sorry–' he began, but she held up her hand to stop him.

'Ssh!' she whispered. 'Look!'

A red car had drawn up in front of the Pullmans' house. It didn't hoot, but flashed its lights. A few seconds later, a figure slid the gate open and got into the car. It reversed and drove off down the road.

Sandra and Craig looked at each other.

'Follow that car!' commanded Sandra, the most animated he had seen her since they met.

Craig turned the key in the ignition. The car started and then conked out. He tried it again three or four times, but it wasn't going anywhere.

'Petrol!' exclaimed Craig, hitting the steering wheel in frustration. 'Bugger!'

'Quick, call Edmund. Tell him it's turning right into town.

Craig reached into the pocket of his jeans for his phone. Typical, he thought. This wouldn't have happened to Manning.

Suddenly, Sandra opened the door and got out. 'I'll be back,' she said softly, looking through the window at him. 'Don't worry about me. You stay here. Okay? Promise.' She raised her hand to her mouth and blew him a kiss and then, without a sideways glance, she was gone off down the road and into the inky blackness of the night.

Chapter Thirty-eight

The house was heavy with the darkness of abandonment. There was no sound of a generator and Pullman's Land Cruiser wasn't there. Edmund trod softly up the drive, aware of the soft crunch of his feet on the gravel. A sudden fluttering of wings from a large tree startled him momentarily; shapes, grey and black seemed to loom towards him, reaching, touching and then slowly easing back into the shadows as he realised they were large flowerpots or bushes.

Edmund tried the handle of the back door, easing it down slowly and then giving a gentle push. It opened. He stood still for a moment and listened. He heard the rushing sound again. He had been here before. He stopped. Of course he had – just the other night. He steadied himself. There was nothing, not a sound. He carefully placed one foot in front of the other, gingerly feeling the space in front of him lest he should knock against a table or chair. In the passageway, the floorboards gave a little creak. He stood still and listened again. He thought he could hear the rustle of paper and a drawer being shut.

The end of the passage seemed miles away, a place immersed in a forbidding, haunting darkness. He made his way forward in what seemed an eternity, careful not to knock against the pictures on the wall. Then Marcia Pullman's bedroom door opened and a shadow emerged.

'Are you aware that you are guilty of breaking and entering?' His voice, though level, was cold, absent of fear. Sandra stood there, wide-eyed. She dropped her head forward and then rolled it back.

'I haven't stolen anything, if that's what you mean.'

'You don't need to. Not in the eyes of a court of law. What's in your hand?' Even in the gloomy darkness he could see that she held something in her hand behind her back.

'These? Oh, nothing. Just papers.'

He switched a torch on and shone it straight in her eyes. 'Belonging to Mrs Pullman?'

She didn't reply, but looked away from him, squinting.

'Are you going to report me?' she asked at last, her voice wavering.

'No, I'm going to arrest you.'

The response was immediate. She swung round on him and for the first time he saw her anger.

'*What?* Whatever for? I told you, I haven't stolen anything!'

Edmund shrugged. 'Depends what you're after. Not jewellery, perhaps, but other things.'

'*Things?* What things?' Her voice rose angrily.

'Calm down,' he said, quietly. 'I think you'd better tell me what is going on.'

She stared at him, her face like marble: cool and smooth and devoid of emotion.

'All right,' he said, eventually. 'I'll tell you what I think. You came to Bulawayo to look for your birth parents. You were put in touch with Marcia Pullman by a lady called Mrs Parkinson who used to work at St. Botolph's Home for Boys. She told you that Marcia might have been the lady who arranged your admittance to St. Mary's Children's Home. Marcia, it seems, was a 'go-between' for young, unmarried mothers and these two children's homes in Bulawayo. You came to see Marcia and you asked her if you were one of 'her children' and, if so, could she provide you with any information whatsoever as to the names and whereabouts of your parents. Now, Marcia Pullman liked being in a position of power and for people to be at her beck and call. I don't know what she got you to do or at least asked you to do in return for the information, but I'd hazard a guess that what you wanted was slow in coming. You got frustrated – and then you decided to take the matter into your own hands.'

'By killing her? How would that help?'

'All you wanted was the information, wasn't it?' Edmund indicated the file. 'You didn't really need Marcia Pullman, you needed the file she had, the list of all the people she had 'helped' over the years and the babies' dates of birth.'

'I wouldn't need to kill her to get those.' Edmund noticed that her usual calm manner had gone and her fingers played nervously with the edge of her jacket.

'No, you wouldn't. But she would have known. She knew everything – and she would have held it against you. You would have paid for it in another way. Instead, you struck up something of a friendship with her. S.P. in Mrs Pullman's diary is you, isn't it? You used a different surname, a maiden name perhaps? You came over for lunch sometimes, became something of a counsellor for her. She hadn't been feeling well, had she? As you massaged her ankles, she talked. Perhaps she told you that she thought her husband was having an affair. Gradually, over time, you devised a plan.'

Sandra stood stock-still, shaking her head slowly. She looked like a little doll, Edmund thought as he spoke. On his part, he had little idea where his conjecture was going. He didn't know where Sandra fitted in at all with Pullman and Shantelle, but if he pushed and sounded confident, she may give herself away.

'One morning she phoned you up. She'd had a terrible time: there'd been an incident at the office. She was in a fluster; book club was on that evening. She asked you to come round as she was desperate for one of your treatments, your treatments that made her feel *so* much better.'

Sandra rolled her head back and laughed. When she looked back at Edmund her face was dark and sneering. His confidence wavered.

'I thought Mrs Pullman was stabbed.' She said it in such a way that it suggested he was a complete buffoon who had forgotten the basic details of the case he was investigating.

'Yes, she was, but that isn't what killed her. She was already dead. There wasn't enough blood, you see. Just not enough blood.' He added the last words for effect in an effort to suggest he knew something she thought he didn't.

'Why stab her at all then?'

'So that's what it looked like – a stabbing.'

'And exactly how did I actually kill her, *Chief Inspector*?'

Edmund paused. He was out of his depth and he knew it, but he took the plunge anyway.

'Mrs Pullman suffered from varicose veins, a redness and swelling in the legs.'

Sandra shrugged. 'So?'

'Thrombophlebitis.' Edmund pronounced the word with a certain confidence. He was glad he had pronounced it correctly. 'Blood clots in the legs.'

Sandra looked sideways as though this was news to her. 'And?'

'Reflexology. It's good, isn't it? But not for everyone. Pregnant women, for example. Press the wrong pressure point and you could have an early labour on your hands.'

'Where are you going with this?'

Feeling a little unnerved, he ploughed on.

'People with thrombophlebitis should not have reflexology.'

'Are you saying–?'

'You knew what to do. You knew she was unwell and you also knew what could speed up her demise.'

'What?' Sandra burst into laughter shaking her head. 'Giving someone reflexology is not tantamount to murder!'

'You came round to give her another of your treatments,' Edmund continued, knowing that he was getting deeper into water that was both murky and unfamiliar. If he could just make her snap, make her say something that she regretted. 'Marcia had had quite a morning, not a very nice morning. She didn't feel well. You offered to come to her house because she could then have a relaxing afternoon before book club without having to drive home. She agreed and you came over. You could see that Marcia was in pain and struggling. After the treatment, you left, perhaps advising her to go and have a lie down. You knew Dorcas had the afternoon off and that Janet Peters would be around at four o'clock because Marcia told you so. Perhaps she was hoping

376

to feel better by then. When you left, you took the spare key so that you could re-enter a while later, which you did – and found Mrs Pullman dead on the bed.'

Sandra started laughing, a slow intermittent yelp that gathered momentum until it was a full-scale raging river.

In vain, Edmund tried to talk over her, but he had lost confidence in his words.

'You looked for the file – but you couldn't find it. Eventually you had to leave, but you had the key so were safe in the knowledge you could return. A couple of days later you were back. You rang the buzzer. If Dorcas had been there you'd have some story to tell her about something you left behind. You opened the gate. There was no one around. You looked in through the lounge window to see if anyone was there and that's when you saw me – whom you definitely weren't expecting.'

'Go on, this is all sounding good.'

'And to make matters worse, you found out Mrs Pullman had been stabbed. Well, now you were a little worried. The police, it seemed, were actually investigating. What if information was found that linked you to her and gave you a motive for murder?'

Sandra gave a brief snort of contempt. 'This is like some sort of book.'

Edmund ploughed on. 'You offered me a lift – and you took my phone – so you had to bring it to Mr Martin's house. You tried to find out how much I knew and how much he knew and you discovered that Pullman is a questionable character and the police are watching him. Now you thought: what if he's caught? What if he goes away to prison? What will you do then? You had to think fast. And then there it was, your opportunity. I asked Craig to watch the house. You saw Dorcas leave and you knew this was your chance. You knew in all probability Craig wouldn't follow you. He's had a bad time, he's injured and he's scared of being recognised. When you get back to the car, you'll pretend you went and looked in the khaya. You have a story already prepared.'

As Edmund had spoken, his voice had got louder and louder and he now ended the explanation of his hypothesis on a higher note than he had begun. Sandra had stopped laughing and looked away, down at her hands, which trembled in the darting beam of Edmund's torch.

'I had to know!'

Edmund's chest tightened. Was this it – a confession?

'You don't know what it is like not to know who your real parents are! I've longed to meet them, *dreamed* of meeting them. Then I found my father was dead, but I didn't know about my mother. I *had* to find her. I just *had to.*'

'Is this true?' Craig's voice was small and dry.

'Craig?'

Edmund spun round.

'Craig, I didn't do it! I didn't, I promise. It sounds like a great story but that is all it is. *I did not murder Marcia Pullman.*'

'Is any of what Edmund said true? Did you use me?'

She looked away and the file fell from under her armpit. 'It's the wrong file. I can't find anything!' She ran her hand through her hair and took a step towards him. 'I had to find out what you knew. I had to find a way to get back into the house. I didn't have a key. If I had, I wouldn't have bothered with you. I would have gone round when Dorcas was out and let myself in. I didn't kill her, I *didn't.* She didn't know who I was and what I was looking for. I never told her I was looking for my birth mother. It's true that I befriended her, but she always came to my house. She hadn't been well, but she wouldn't take the doctor's advice. I did some karmic cleansing and colour therapy.'

Edmund stared long and hard at Sandra who looked away, embarrassed.

'What about the key? How did you get in tonight?'

She looked down at her feet while she spoke. 'Craig's tool box.'

'You took my screwdriver?'

'A screwdriver and piece of wire, that's all you need. The

gate lock was more difficult because of the position more than anything. I'm a thief, yes,' she said with sudden determination. She pushed her head back so that her chin jutted out defiantly. 'And I haven't been very honest. But I'm not a murderer. I promise. Anyway, she got what she believed she deserved.'

'What she believed she deserved...' Edmund repeated, wondering where he had heard those words before.

Craig looked across at Edmund who was deep in thought. 'What do you want to do?' he asked him. 'Take her into custody?'

Sandra rolled her eyes in exasperation.

Edmund's phone rang just then and he put his hand in his pocket and pulled it out.

'Yes?'

Craig watched Edmund's face intently. The person on the other end was doing all the talking; Edmund said a couple of words before ringing off. He stood still for a few minutes, deep in thought, before he turned to Craig.

'Could you give me a lift? Just back to the station?'

Sandra eyed Edmund suspiciously, as though waiting for the catch.

'Right away,' said Craig. 'The car's outside. I got it going. It's not empty; carburettor problems that's all.'

Taking Edmund by the elbow, Craig led Edmund aside.

'What about Sandra? Are you taking her into custody?'

Edmund seemed quiet; distracted. 'Would you mind dropping her at home? Thank you.'

'But–?'

'Thank you,' said Edmund, walking down the passageway. 'I think that will be all.'

Chapter Thirty-nine

1979

'Do you want to come back to my house today?' Edmund had been contemplating asking his friend all morning and now the words tumbled out as though he had no control over them. His heart beat fast and his palms were damp. He prepared himself to be turned down.

The two boys were lying reading on a small square of grass near the school kitchen. Jasper had been unable to find them at break for a week.

Rupert sat up, leaning back on his elbows.

'I'll ask my mom.'

Edmund's heart beat even faster and he felt a surge of pain cut through his chest. They had never been to each other's houses before; his mother would never have allowed it. On his part, he had never told Rupert what his mother did, not because he lied, but simply because the subject had never come up between the two boys. With his mother away, he imagined the MacDougals would be more than hospitable.

'Rupert, pleased to meet you. I'm Mrs MacDougal,' she said, greeting Rupert at the door. 'Come in. We're so glad you could join us this afternoon. We're so happy to meet one of Edmund's friends.'

Edmund was excited to share the experience of doing his homework with someone else.

'Right, Edmund, let's get out all your books. Where's your ruler and pencil.'

Edmund looked eagerly at Rupert to see if he was as excited as he was. But Rupert's face was blank, if not a little bored. Edmund laid his ruler above his book and then placed his pencil above that. He sat very straight, sucking his chest in and feeling the back of the chair dig into him.

'When can we go and play?' asked Rupert, eyeing his homework with a bored, forlorn look.

'All in good time, young man. Work first, play later.'

Rupert duly completed all his sums and handed Mr MacDougal his book.

'Hmm,' said the older man, running his eyes over the workings, gently nodding his head and pulling in his mouth at the corner. 'You've a couple of errors here, my boy. Now, you come and sit right here next to me and we'll have a look at them. All right?'

Rupert nodded and stood up with his chair still affixed to his bottom and waddled round to Mr MacDougal's side of the table.

'And you, Edmund, you get on with some subtraction, okay?'

Edmund nodded from his side of the table. He stuck his pencil in his mouth and sucked hard. Mr MacDougal's soft voice blended into the measured tick of the clock as they worked. Just after finishing his maths homework, Edmund dropped his rubber on the carpet and went under the table to get it. As he rose, his eye caught sight of Mr MacDougal's hand resting carelessly on Rupert's knee. He got back on his chair and ruled off his homework. He sat quietly for Rupert was still working. Mr MacDougal's head bent over him, nodding every now and again.

'Very good, lad,' he said at last, looking up. 'Very good. He's clever, your friend, Edmund. He just needed a bit of help. You don't need help, do you, Edmund?'

Edmund watched as Mr MacDougal patted Rupert on the head. Rupert looked up at him with a shy smile on his lips. He looked away when he saw Edmund watching him.

'You keep that,' said Mr MacDougal as Rupert handed him his ruler back. 'It's a little present for being top of the class.'

You see, Edmund wanted to say. I told you you would

have fun here. I told you you would love it, but he couldn't help feeling something else, too, a dark burn somewhere in his chest, accompanied by the quickening of his pulse. The bestowment of the ruler was too easy, flippant, even. He had had to wait for his birthday for his. Here was Rupert given a ruler, Mr MacDougal's ruler, without much effort on his part. Rupert who was bored and didn't like sums. Rupert who just wanted to play outside. Part of him wished he'd never invited Rupert back at all.

'This is my room,' said Edmund, quietly opening the door to the spare room where he had slept the night before. His uniform was hanging on the back of the chair, his schoolbooks piled on the little table.

Rupert nodded.

'Do you want to see inside?'

Rupert shook his head. 'I can see from here.'

'This,' said Edmund, ignoring him and opening the door wide and entering the room, 'is Loch Morar in Scotland.' He pointed up at the picture and Rupert nodded. 'And this is a highland cow and this is Prince's Street in Edinburgh.'

Rupert nodded, but wasn't interested. 'Where are your toys?'

'In another room,' said Edmund, delighted with himself that he answered without a pause. 'But I don't like playing with them all the time.'

Rupert looked around the sparse room, taking in the brown candlewick bedcover and the heavy floral curtains.

'Is that lady your mother?' asked Rupert. 'The old lady.'

Edmund laughed; a short, nervous laugh. 'Oh, no, no. My mother is away. She's gone to Salisbury.'

'Who is that lady then? And that man?'

'*Come*, let's go play. Let's go outside.'

Rupert rushed down the corridor while Edmund closed the door quietly. 'No running,' he called after him. He found Rupert waiting outside for him.

'Slowcoach,' he said.

Edmund shrugged. He was eager to play, but he wasn't used to having the run of the garden.

'What do you want to play?' he asked with a certain note of hesitation in his voice.

'Don't know. Do you have a bike or anything?'

Edmund shook his head.

'A cricket bat?'

Again, Edmund shook his head.

'What about catching butterflies? said Mrs MacDougal, coming up behind them. 'Have you ever done that?' The boys shook their heads.

'You haven't? What's the world coming to? I'll show you. Give me five minutes to take the biscuits out of the oven.'

Edmund looked at Rupert but he didn't seem to mind Mrs MacDougal's input. She came bustling out of the kitchen, undoing her apron, a butterfly net under her arm.

'Right, watch and learn,' she joked. 'Watch and learn. There's plenty of these lovely creatures around at the moment.'

'The brown-veined African Migrant,' said Edmund, bursting with self-importance.

'Oh, who's a clever chops, then?' said Mrs MacDougal.

'That's what Mr MacDougal says.'

'Well, if he says it, it must be true,' laughed Mrs MacDougal, swiping the air with a net and nearly falling backwards. 'Oh my, I nearly lost my balance.'

Soon the boys were running all over the front lawn, one holding the net, the other running alongside him.

'Over here! Over here!'

'I've got it! Oh no... I haven't!'

At teatime, Mrs MacDougal brought out a small tray on which was placed a teapot and two blue enamel mugs and a plate of biscuits. Rupert ran up on the verandah, ahead of Edmund who still circled the flowerbeds with manic speed. Mrs MacDougal held out her arms and Rupert stopped suddenly, holding his own arms behind his back. She caught him in an awkward half-hug, then she tousled his hair and let him go.

'Edmund, catch them, Edmund! Catch them!' she called.

Edmund leapt, spun, twisted wildly in the air. He let his happiness take over, let it spill out and sweep behind him on the grass; let it lift him up above the flowers and the trees and the verandah, until Rupert and Mrs MacDougal were faint spots beneath him.

'Edmund!' called Mrs MacDougal. She was big and fluffy and soft and powdery. 'Edmund!'

He ran up the steps, his arms wide. She was showing Rupert something.

'Beautiful, isn't it?' she said, holding out her palm and revealing a soft, powdery white butterfly. 'Watch out, Edmund,' she warned as he careered up the steps. 'You'll damage it.'

Edmund backed off, breathing hard.

'Now, get that down you,' she said, motioning to the tea table with her head. 'When Mr MacDougal gets home he said he'll take you for ice creams, too.'

Edmund and Rupert exchanged excited looks.

'We often have ice creams,' said Edmund once Mrs MacDougal was out of earshot.

'We don't,' said Rupert. 'You're lucky.'

By the time five o'clock came, Rupert was anxious to go home. Although usually quiet, a change had come over him. He picked up his bag and waited next to the driveway.

'Perhaps he's never been to someone's house before,' said Mrs MacDougal to Edmund as she looked at Rupert out of the kitchen window. 'That's a shame.'

'Who's for an ice cream?' said Mr MacDougal, getting into the car.

'Me!' shouted Edmund, his hand shooting up in the air.

'I just want to go home,' said Rupert from the backseat. 'I don't want an ice cream.'

Mr MacDougal and Edmund exchanged looks.

'Won't be two ticks,' said Mr MacDougal. 'We'll get them from the ice cream man at the park.'

Rupert shrugged and rolled his head. He sat silently all the way there, with his arms folded across his chest.

Edmund felt a growing distance between them. His voice got louder, more excited, to compensate for his friend's lack of talk.

'Can I run down the path to the fountain,' he asked Mr MacDougal, hoping Rupert would want to come.

'Yes, laddie, you go do that. I'll wait here with your friend.'

Edmund shot off, the pace of running kept all thoughts of Rupert from his mind. At the fountain he looked back towards the car. Rupert's sad little face stared out of the window. Mr MacDougal stood next to the car, looking in. At one point he seemed to bend over like he was going to climb in the window but then he stood straight again and waved to Edmund.

'Time to go,' Mr MacDougal said as Edmund ran up to the car. 'Time to go home.'

Edmund stared through the window at Rupert's dejected form. What had he done? What had he done wrong? He sat quietly in the back of the car and when they got to Rupert's house, Mr MacDougal took him to the gate.

'It's all right, laddie,' said Mr MacDougal, easing himself into the car. 'These things happen. He's still your friend, you know. He'll be all right tomorrow.'

But Rupert wasn't all right. He didn't want to speak, he shrugged off Edmund like he was a heavy coat he didn't want to wear. He no longer waited at break time for Edmund to get his lunch box and hat. Edmund searched the playground for him after he failed to find him in their favourite spot near the kitchen. He told himself that the short answers he received in response to his questions was just Rupert being shy and he took to hanging back in the shadows, watching his silent, lonely friend from afar. He wanted to make things right again, but one day when he asked Rupert if he could borrow his rubber, he noticed how the boy deliberated for a second or so before giving it to him and how Edmund's thanks received the briefest nod of his head. A week later, Edmund came into the playground and found him playing with Jasper Meyer.

Somehow Edmund always knew this day would come. Every night for the last ten years, he had gone to sleep with the thought that it hadn't happened that day, but it could happen the next. This was it, his day of reckoning. It had bided its time; he had seen it waiting in shadows and corridors and out in the market square. It was in a child's smile and the sly, sideways glances of the women on the bus, their heads wrapped in doeks and their produce for sale piled high on their laps. It was in the hunchbacked shuffles of old men and the wary aggression of stray dogs. It was in the call of the minibus conductors and the rev of the engines: your day will come.

And so it had. The sky was alive with the blaze of orange from the fire. People ran all over the place like ants that have had scalding hot water poured into their nest, screaming and shouting and wailing. The fire boiled and spat and raged, burning with the confidence that came from knowing controlling it was beyond the power of any there. Some rushed foolishly at it with buckets of water, tins of water, mouthfuls of water. By the time the sirens of the fire engine could be heard, clanging wearily nearer, the fire had beaten its antagonists back and they ran, no longer people, but shadows flitting fearfully through the darkness.

Amidst the noise and the chaos, Edmund saw his neighbour, Ma Ndlondlo, standing speechless, looking up at the huge flames engulfing his house and seemingly unaware that they could reach out and lick her up with their long, red tongues. She had her arms crossed over her chest and she rocked backwards and forwards on the balls of her feet. Only when Edmund got closer did he see that she was crying.

'Go away! Go away!' she wailed as he came closer. 'You! You are the one who has brought this about. Get away from me!'

Edmund reeled in anguish. Her words stung like a whip across his face. Was it true? Was he the one who had brought this about? He remembered another night some years previously and another fire. He wasn't Chief Inspector then and he had been ordered to jump on the back of the truck with all the other policemen. They had truncheons with them and helmets and they had roared off into the western suburbs of Bulawayo to search and destroy.

Many houses had tumbled that night. They fell so quickly it was almost like playing a game of dominoes. Asbestos walls and tin roofs caved in under the blows and kicks. Belongings scattered easily in the rush. He remembered a picture of Jesus, his finger raised in blessing – or was it admonishment – curling and twisting in the flames of the fire. Plastic bowls, aluminium cups and plates rolled down into the ditch, mothers ran with babies on their backs and children in their arms while men stood and watched helplessly.

'Mama! MAMA!' he remembered the screaming child, walking in slow motion out of the shack like a zombie, her arms and legs on fire. As she burned, she illuminated the whole street, a great red angel of fire, turning softly in the night. He had run towards her but had met with an angry fist in his face and had fallen and lain in the dirt while people rushed past him and over him. The next day, when he heard that she had died, he was strangely surprised, so alive she had been.

Now here he was facing his day of reckoning. *Fear God and give him glory, for the hour of his judgement has come.* Mary, he thought, beautiful Mary has gone. He had been so nasty and so dismissive and despised all that was good about her, never valuing what she had to offer. She couldn't possibly have survived, could she? Could she have got out? Would Pullman's men have made sure she was securely locked inside before throwing the first match?

Suddenly someone was at his elbow; he could feel their warm sweet breath before he made out a shape. It was one of the firemen. Sweat trickled down the side of his face and his voice was punctuated by short gasps of breath. He put his hand on Edmund's shoulder, gripping it hard.

387

'I am so sorry,' he began. 'So sorry! We have found a body, a body of a woman. Please, I will need you to come with me.' The man took a step back and waited deferentially behind him. Edmund tried to steady himself as the world swayed around him. He grappled to hold onto the moment, the present moment as though it were the last moment in his existence. For indeed it was: he knew that from now on, his life would change and that the first half of his life was already cut asunder, floating away from him over the rim of the world and into the darkness beyond. He took a deep breath and turned to follow the man.

A shape lay on the ground, covered by a blanket, a shape Edmund had seen so many times before at accident and murder scenes. A group of people stood around it and a fireman was doing his best to push them back and give him room. People stared at him with the morbid longing to witness tears and desolation and grief. Even those who averted their eyes would be disappointed if Edmund showed no emotion at all.

'Are you ready?' asked the first fireman and Edmund nodded. He gripped his hands into fists and let out a deep breath. *Be strong. Be strong.*

Although the face was disfigured beyond recognition, Edmund knew at once that the body in front of him was not that of his wife. He dropped to his knees and stared blankly at it, running his eyes over the shape and form. Although it wasn't Mary's, it seemed vaguely familiar. Eventually, his eyes rested on the hands, which, despite the ferocity of the fire, were almost gruesomely intact. He picked up one in his own and held it, recognising then the small half-moons of pink nail varnish.

'Dorcas...' he whispered. 'Oh God, Dorcas!'

He looked back at the burning house. A group of people crowded into a circle around someone. Mary. She was alive. He felt anxiety leave his body, but something else entered, a strange dark grief. Why wasn't she at home? He couldn't approach her. She was surrounded by people who protected her, who *knew* her. They stood either side of a great divide. A cavern opened up, a darkness that increased at an exhilarating speed, until she was a shadow, then just a shape; then nothing: no laughing eyes or smiling mouth. He was alone.

Chapter Forty

Edmund had a fitful night's sleep. His desk did not make the best of places to lay his head and he was tired and cranky when he awoke. His clothes were heavy with the stench of smoke and death but he lacked the will to refresh himself. It was five o'clock and still dark, and he was very hungry.

He made himself a mug of grey tea and sat back down behind his desk. The police station was the last place he wanted to be, but it was the only place he could think of going to in the middle of the night where no questions would be asked. He had known, hadn't he, that Dorcas was in danger? It was why he had asked Craig to watch the house. He had wanted to protect her; to find her and save her before any harm could be done. But he had followed the wrong lead, for he had set up Sandra, knowing – wanting – her to try to enter the house. He wanted to follow her in and catch her red-handed, as he had done. He wanted to be the good cop, the all-knowing Chief Inspector and, in doing so, he had let a good woman die. Sandra, whom he had no reason to suspect was looking for anything besides her identity documents, could have been challenged at another time.

Desperately trying to push all thoughts of Dorcas from his mind, he flicked gloomily through his notebook. He stopped at a word he had circled. He remembered Pullman's habit of putting his words in boxes. Boxes, thought Edmund, his eyes heavy with sleep, boxes. Everything in boxes. Books packed in boxes in a house. People in boxes in the back of a lorry. *Don't put people into boxes.* Who had said that? Mrs Ncube or Mrs Whitstable?

Edmund sat up suddenly and tapped his pencil on his notebook. *Don't put people into boxes. Just because he's a gardener, doesn't make him a murderer.* If there had been one thing that had played on his mind since he began investigating the case, it was the gardener. Everyone had said it was the gardener – and he hadn't believed them. Yet, why had he been fired? Why? He had never believed the story about the Vim.

He washed his face and hands in the sink in the toilets and then drank another two cups of tea and wrote copious notes in his diary. He arranged names on a piece of paper and connected them to each other with dark blue lines and arrows. The sky began to lighten and, looking outside, Edmund was suddenly aware of what he had to do. The front office was dead at this time of day. Soon there would be a change of shifts, the hustle and bustle of the start of the day and the more important police officers would arrive at work.

Next door to Khumalo was his secretary's office; an adjoining door linked the two rooms. Edmund knew she arrived at work at about half past seven, a full half an hour at least before Khumalo did. It was her routine to open the office and then go and make tea in the kitchen at the end of the corridor. Standing in the entrance to the police station, Edmund saw her arrive and waited five minutes before following her upstairs. Just as he turned into the corridor, he saw her come out of her office and make her way to the kitchen, tray in hand.

Quickly, Edmund darted inside and opened the adjoining door to Khumalo's office. He had about three minutes to get what he wanted and leave. He opened Khumalo's drawers, but couldn't find what he was looking for. He tried a cupboard but that too yielded nothing as did a shelf containing box files. Finally, Edmund opened a filing cabinet and, searching behind the files, at last found the small bag. He slipped it into his pocket and closed the cabinet quietly. Carefully he peered into the secretary's office, but it was still empty. From the end of the corridor he could hear laughter and hoped she was having an extra long gossip with someone. As he turned to leave Khumalo's office, his eye caught sight of the file on Marcia Pullman. He flicked through it quickly, noting the forensic report and an interview with Malakai.

Aware that time was not on his side, he placed it back on the table. It was then that he noticed another file, that concerning the case of the dead women found at the Beitbridge border post. His eyes scanned the pages, hardly seeing anything at all; he was in such a panic. He tried to steady himself, letting his eyes come to rest on the opening line. It concerned the tip-off from a man by the name of Albert Zeke. It struck Edmund immediately as strange that anyone would give their name when informing on such a type of operation. But he didn't have time to think too hard. He could hear the officious clip-clop of heels along the corridor. He closed the file and darted out of the office, closing the door behind him. He tried to get out into the corridor and bumped into the secretary returning with the tray. Hot tea sloshed over the side of the mug.

She looked at him as though he were the office cleaner.

'Yes, Chief Inspector. What can I do for you so early in the morning?' Her mouth curled up into a narrow smile as she passed him and put the tray down on the table. Her eyes flickered over to the adjoining door, but it was closed.

'I was looking for Khumalo, that's all.' Edmund's voice was dry and clipped. 'I'll come back later.'

Again, the eyes moved towards the door and this time held a question. Edmund dived out of the room, walking quickly, far too quickly down the corridor and down the stairs. He flew down the steps of the police station and out into the cold of the morning. Still walking quickly, he crossed the road and hailed the first taxi he saw.

Burnside was far and no doubt the taxi fare would be a large one, but Edmund didn't care. He wanted to be away from the prying eyes of anyone who knew him. He didn't want anyone to recognise him and point and laugh or sneer or say that he had got what he deserved. Instead, he relaxed into the air-conditioned luxury of the taxi and enjoyed the ride.

'How's business?' he asked the driver, deciding a little light conversation would help pass time.

'Ah, bad, very bad.'

Edmund smiled. 'You guys always say that. Show me a taxi driver who's happy with life.'

They lapsed into silence until the taxi arrived at its destination. A little fluffy white dog came rushing to the gate, barking in the high-pitched yappy way that characterises little, fluffy dogs, and then a lady came out shouting 'Beano! Who is it? Stop barking! Such a noise!'

She looked quizzically at the car and Edmund hurriedly got out. When she saw who it was she rolled her eyes, but opened the gate anyway which Edmund saw as a good sign. At least she wasn't going to speak to him through the bars.

Edmund stuck his head back inside the taxi window. 'Can you wait?' asked Edmund suddenly feeling very flush. 'Give me fifteen minutes.'

'Two dollars waiting time,' said the driver and switched off the engine. He picked up the newspaper and began to read.

Lydia Ncube showed Edmund onto the verandah where she offered him a chair.

'I hope you've come to tell me that Malakai is to be released.' Her voice was one of strained politeness.

'I'm trying,' said Edmund. He wanted to tell her what he was up against and that he couldn't be sure that Malakai would be released should he solve the crime in its entirety. 'I need to ask you some more questions though.'

'Ask away.'

'Malakai worked for you for about a week?'

'That's right. Not a long time at all.'

'Can you tell me then why you are so convinced he is innocent?'

She pursed her lips and leaned forward suddenly as though she were a cobra ready to plunge its fangs into him. He stopped her.

'You can understand my predicament, Mrs Ncube. A lot of people have an innate mistrust of gardeners. Something's broken, it's the gardener, something's missing, it's the gardener, someone's murdered, it's the gardener. Why then are you so convinced it's *not*, especially as he hasn't even worked for you for a whole month?'

Mrs Ncube took a deep breath and leaned back in her chair.

'I've known him ever since I joined book club. I always told him there was a job with me waiting. I wanted to get him two years ago when he was looking for a job, but Marcia jumped in first and offered him a salary he couldn't refuse. I was delighted when I heard he had been fired.'

'He was fired for cleaning the car with Vim?'

She laughed. 'A man with that much experience should know better.'

'You think he wanted to be fired?'

'I think there's a good possibility. She paid him well, but he was there all hours. Half a day off on a Sunday to see his family and no time off if the Pullmans went away when he acted as a security guard. Yes, I think there's a strong possibility he wanted out, but on her part I don't think she meant to fire him for good.'

'What do you mean?'

'Well, she phoned him over the weekend and asked him to come back.'

'She did? But why didn't you tell me this before. It shows Malakai had no reason to attack Mrs Pullman.'

'But I did – well, I didn't tell you, but that other policeman, Khumalo. I told him.'

Edmund sat for half a minute, letting the information sink in. He squeezed his eyes shut and then opened them again.

'You didn't like Mrs Pullman?'

'Not particularly.'

'Do you mind me asking why?'

Lydia settled herself back in her chair. 'There is a type of white person here in Zimbabwe: they complain about the government and corruption, they say they want change. But they make sure they benefit from the situation. They'll bribe the police, they'll charge exorbitant prices, they'll make sure they are well and truly looked after: that was the Pullmans. Marcia was bossy and controlling. She was okay as long as you kept your distance and didn't let her do anything for you.'

'Didn't let her do anything for you? What do you mean?'

'She called in favours. I'll do this for you, but don't ever forget it. I don't operate that way. I lived in London – I don't have time for small town bullying. That's why I left. Poor old Janet Peters got roped in though and couldn't get out at all.'

'What had she done for Janet?'

'That I don't know. Something to do with money, probably. It always is in this world.'

'How well do you know Mrs Peters?'

'Fairly well. Lives with her elderly mother who is now in a wheelchair, I believe. Zimbabwe has become a very hard place for people like them, Chief Inspector. It's sink or swim nowadays and you won't believe the number of people who are sinking.'

'Yet she survives without having a paid job?'

Mrs Ncube shrugged.

'Then again,' said Edmund, 'she has a son in the UK who probably sends her money every month.'

Mrs Ncube looked down at the ground and then back up at Edmund. She seemed to hesitate over whether to tell him something or not.

'Mrs Whitstable gets a British pension every month. Her husband's war pension. It's not a lot. Not enough to live on. Really, it isn't. I change it for her – I give her the money here and she transfers it into my account in the UK. I try and give her a good rate. I know things are not easy for them.'

'Not enough to live on. I see. She and Janet still need another source of income.'

'Zimbabwe is a very hard place and people have ended up doing things they would never have dreamed of doing. I suppose in some rather harsh way it has been a good learning experience for the white people here. Brought them down to earth a bit.'

'Go on,' urged Edmund.

'Janet has an agreement with her maid. From what I understand, it got to the point where they couldn't afford a maid or gardener anymore. The gardener went, but the maid was anxious to stay on. To be honest, I think she has it good. The house doesn't require that much work and the accommodation is more than adequate. Loveness, I think her name is, put it to Janet that if she could stay there and accept a lower wage, she would continue doing the housework and looking after Granny when needs be. But she wanted to have the afternoons off. If Janet could provide the initial capital, Loveness would buy a few packets of sweets and tomatoes and cigarettes, you know the sort of thing, and sell them on the street corner. Janet told me that not only did Loveness manage to pay the loan back, but she made three or four times her salary in this manner.'

'Sounds like a good idea,' said Edmund who had half expected to hear that it was Janet who was running a prostitution ring with the large and unwieldy Loveness as her madam.

'Ye-es, a good idea in many ways, but then Janet began to see that *she* could make some money. She gave Loveness more money, even sent her to Botswana, I think, and they branched out a little – cheap wigs, cosmetics, body lotion. Well, it wasn't just an overturned cardboard box on the side of the road any more, it was a regular stall.'

'Whereabouts?'

'Fife Street flea market, I think.'

'I take it that Janet takes a cut from all this?'

'Oh, absolutely. I think she really enjoys it. She went down to Francistown about a week or so ago with Loveness.'

'They left Mrs Whitstable on her own? I'm very surprised.'

'I'm sure they will have sorted something out. Janet also needs a break and it's a bit of an outing for her and they actually make a bit of money. Well, enough. It's interesting, too, how little you really need to live on. You don't need so much as you get older.'

'But Mrs Peters isn't that old. Sixty, sixty-one perhaps. Still time to want more from life.'

'Oh, I agree, but you do get used to not having certain things. Take the garden, for instance. There's nothing there now, but it used to be absolutely beautiful. She ran the Horticultural Society, you know, Janet's mother? She was very, very proud of her garden, but they couldn't have a gardener *and* a maid and that's when Malakai got a job with Marcia.'

Edmund sat up and leant forward. 'Malakai used to work for Janet Peters?'

'Yes. Didn't I say? He worked for them since he was sixteen and Mrs Whitstable taught him all she knew about the garden. On his part, I think he saw her as a mother figure, someone who looked after him. She was the one who phoned me and asked if I was looking for someone to work in the garden and would I still be interested in him.'

'Mrs Whitstable? When did she phone?'

Lydia thought for a moment. 'The Sunday before last I think it was. A week before Marcia died.'

'Are you sure? She phoned you *before* Malakai was fired?'

'Like I said, I think he was looking to go. He'd obviously got to breaking point and I was more than happy to take him on. He's the real thing, Chief Inspector, a proper gardener, not one of these fly by nights who come and cause more damage than anything else. You can see why I wanted him so much.'

The taxi drew up at the market in Fife Street and Edmund alighted with a certain spring in his step. 'Keep the engine running!' he wanted to say, but was content with asking the driver to wait. The market was big and he had no idea where to begin looking. Being the morning, the stall wouldn't be operating now and Loveness would not be around to raise the alarm if she saw him.

Edmund wandered around, looking for a friendly face who liked to talk. He stopped at a stall selling baby clothes and smiled at the woman behind the table.

'Yes, what is it?' she asked him after they had exchanged greetings.

'I'm looking for a stall run by someone called Loveness. She sells wigs and body lotion.'

The woman looked him up and down with a little smile on her face.

'All the wigs are over there,' she said, gesturing behind him with her hand. 'You want it for yourself or for someone else?'

Edmund laughed a little nervously. 'Not the wife, the girlfriend,' he joked. 'Wives know you don't have any money. Girlfriends don't want to believe it.'

The woman laughed and said something to her friend in the adjoining stall, which Edmund didn't quite catch. Both women laughed and raised their hands in a high five.

'She is your girlfriend, this Loveness?'

Edmund looked embarrassed, but tried to laugh away the suggestion. 'Ah, no, no. But I hear she has nice things from Botswana on her stall. Which one is it?'

There was more laughter this time. One of them said something to the other behind her hand and they both fell forward in a hearty cackle.

After much more laughing and high five-ing, they were able to point Edmund in the right direction and he left them feeling relieved. The stall was closed, covered with a heavy green tarpaulin. Edmund looked at the woman in the stall next to it. She was tall and thin, dressed in a long red halter neck dress that clung to her every curve. She stretched languidly back in a broken chair, a long thin hand resting under her chin. Her hair, which was short, was orange in colour.

'Hey, Sunshine!' she greeted him in a fake American accent. 'What can I do for you today?'

Edmund smiled, more than a little overwhelmed by her confident personality.

'I'm looking,' he began and then had to stop and clear his throat. 'I'm looking for the woman who runs this stall.'

'Yeah? She'll be here this afternoon.'

'Can you remember if she was here on Monday afternoon?'

The woman eyed Edmund through slightly slanted eyelids. 'Hmm. Can't remember. She's been shut up a couple of times recently.'

'Can you remember when exactly?'

The woman shrugged, a soft, liquid movement for her, very different from Dorcas's short sharp shrugs.

'About a week ago maybe.'

'Any particular day?'

'Thursday. Yeah, maybe Thursday.'

'Thursday?' He wondered if the woman was lying. 'Do you know where she went?'

'Well, don't quote me, honey, but I'd hazard a guess at Francistown.'

'Francistown?'

'Stock. She picked up some cool gear. She sure puts a mark up on it though. I said you gotta be kiddin' me, darlin'. You ain't gonna make no money that way.'

'Did she go by herself?'

'Who knows, honey? Who knows?'

'Do you ever see a white lady here?'

'Yeah, we have a few come in from time to time.'

'An older lady. Red hair?'

'Oh yeah, I've seen her a couple of times.'

'At Loveness's stall?'

'Yeah, I think so. I've seen her lookin'.'

'Do you remember the last time you saw her?'

'Monday, I think. Yeah, Monday.'

'Loveness wasn't here on Monday.'

Looking coquettishly at Edmund, she said, 'Well, there's plenty of other stalls to look at. She was here, looking at the underwear.' She picked up a gaudy red g-string and pulled it taut. 'Some people were like laughing and like, you know, sniggering, but I'm like if the lady wants to buy something, let her do it. What's the big deal?'

'She was looking to buy some?'

399

'No. She looked very nervous, y'know. Like somethin' was wrong.'

'There was something she couldn't find?'

'It was more like she was trying to hide. She kept looking around. At first I thought she was just embarrassed, you know. She was the only white here.'

'Trying to hide?'

'Yeah. As though she had seen someone. Someone who made her afraid.'

'She left on her own?'

'Yeah. I don't know what she saw, but it certainly put the wind up her.'

Chapter Forty-one

Craig drove slowly down George Silundika and out towards Bradfield. The road suddenly seemed much wider than it usually did and his car much smaller. Bulawayo felt empty, empty of people and life and happiness: all had retreated into their little brown burrows and stayed there, afraid to come out. The sky stretched wide and blue above town, a deep blue: the blue before the dust really whipped up and the heat was ushered in.

He hadn't felt such desolation in years. Not since the school holidays after his mother died. With his father at work, he was left in the care of Wilson, the cook. Every day stretched interminably into the next; each one a long strip of nothingness punctuated by three meals and two tea times. Craig had taken to passing the day according to what was served to him. His father had usually left by the time he awoke and he ate his bowl of cornflakes alone at the large table in the dining room. Wilson would enter half way through, a dishcloth over his arm and put his hand under the tea cosy to feel if the teapot was still hot enough, holding it there like a doctor checking a pulse. He then ran through a rudimentary checklist, straightening Craig's place mat if it was askew and ramming a teaspoon into the sugar bowl over and over again to break up any lumps.

Tea was brought to him on a tray at ten o'clock. He hardly ever drank it, choosing only to eat the biscuit that accompanied it. After tea was lunch, alone again at the dining room table. It was usually a sandwich of polony on white bread. Wilson always placed a small bottle of mustard next to it, checking it beforehand to see if there was enough; there always was. It seemed to Craig now, looking back, that that same bottle of mustard must have survived his entire childhood. He didn't think it was ever replaced; it was never full and never empty. Like school holidays that ran on and on and provided an infinite source of amusement for other children, it, too, represented a time of limitless sun-filled days that stretched on and on like an endless migraine.

Wilson was left money every week with which to do the shopping. He'd set off on his big black bike and return an hour or two later with a cardboard box strapped to his carrier. Sometimes Craig went with him, perched on the cross bar. The shops were at the bottom of a hill that they'd whizz down. Wilson would tell him to hold tight whilst Craig closed his eyes and gripped the handlebars in sheer terror. Wilson always had a list of required groceries and Craig would tick off the items they found as they were placed in the shopping basket. Mazoe orange juice, a packet of Rich Tea biscuits, white bread and Vegex were staples on the list. Sometimes, Craig persuaded Wilson to buy him a Freddo with the change, but those days were few and far between.

At four o'clock, Wilson would bring in the tea tray again. It was always an anxious time: waiting for his Dad to come back from work and knowing that the day was coming to an end, that soon Wilson would be going. Craig and his father made an awkward pair, neither knowing how to behave in the other's company. His father tried to be jovial, but it just wasn't him, the hand ruffling the head, the hearty hug. He attempted to take an interest in his son's day, but Craig had little to say. Each day was the same; it was like being in a prison without bars.

On his part, Craig, too, attempted to be jolly, waving away his dad's concerns that he was too much on his own and pretending he enjoyed his solitude. Really, he longed for normality, whatever that was. He dreamt of going away somewhere on holiday; wanted his dad to come home one day and say they were leaving the next day and needed to pack the car. He wanted to go on a long road trip at the end of which would be the sea. He would swim into that sea and swim and swim until he found the end. He would pass dolphins and whales and mermaids and pirates and shipwrecks and then he would find a desert island and stay there for the rest of his life. He would never come home. That was his dream.

Craig had returned home the previous night to find that his house had been ransacked. The door had been kicked open and what little furniture he had lay scattered around the house. His clothes had been pulled out and trampled upon the floor along with the contents of his medicine cabinet and that of his bedside drawer. When Edmund failed to answer his phone, Craig had taken his duvet and a three quarter empty bottle of whisky, which he kept under his bed, and driven to the police station. He parked outside and made himself comfortable in the back seat. If anyone were to come after him, help should be near at hand. He had finished the whisky and settled down for the night.

When he had finally managed to get in touch with Edmund, he found the police officer unusually impatient and was surprised that he didn't come round at once, only arranging to meet him later in the day. What had he expected? Sympathy? But he had thought, hadn't he, that they were in this together, joined by some invisible thread; that they were friends, real friends, not Facebook buddies or cyber pals, but something real and tangible and, for some reason, Edmund's response left Craig feeling lonelier than he had for a long, long time, which was saying something for someone as accustomed to loneliness as he was.

It got him thinking and, as usual, that thinking took him down a long, winding, morbid route. Would anyone have missed him that night, only a couple of nights ago now, if he had been coshed on the head and left somewhere for dead? His dad might have wondered why he didn't call, for a bit at least, although he was now used to hearing from Craig once every so often rather than once a week. What about Edmund? Would Edmund have really worried? Yes, perhaps.

Craig imagined his funeral. A couple of people, besides

Edmund, would come, surely? The neighbours? He hadn't ever really spoken to them; they might just think he'd moved somewhere and they might be quite glad of a change of tenant: someone who wouldn't plant empty beer bottles like a hedge along the path or play loud, crazy eighties music at unsociable hours. Would anyone know what his favourite hymn was or whether he wanted a religious ceremony or not? Would he be buried somewhere in a pauper's grave with not even a withered bunch of flowers to mark his passing?

The memorial service for the late Marcia Pullman will be held at the Church of the Ascension in Hillside at three o'clock. This is to be followed by refreshments at 274 Clark Road, Suburbs.

The notice only served to exacerbate Craig's wretched mood. In death, as in life, Marcia had somehow escaped hardship. The service would be well-attended; the priest would speak highly of her: generous, warm-hearted, giving, life and soul of the party, centre of the community. There would be prayers, hymns, no expense spared on the arrangements of flowers. Tea and coffee afterwards. Biscuits and a range of exquisite gateaux; canapés, vol-au-vents, mini-quiches, chipolata sausages on toothpicks and little squares of cheese. Wine, red and white, and an array of spirits. Whiskies and liqueurs and imported brandy for those who stayed on. Good friends. *She'll never be forgotten. Always in our hearts. Looking down on us now and smiling.*

Marcia was someone. Craig was nothing, a no one. Craig shook his head as though that would make the thoughts go away. He had had such hope. Just yesterday, just last night. 'Sandra,' he was going to say in the tradition of all the best clichés, 'You know we make a great team.' She would smile and kiss him and that would be the end, the happily ever after – or was it perhaps just the beginning? Perhaps they could have become private investigators and lived a life of daring and adventure, a modern day Tommy and Tuppence? But all those dreams were shattered now. All gone. She had never been interested in him, rather in some mother she had never seen and who may or may not be alive.

Where was she now, he wondered? He had dropped her at home without a word and didn't wait to see her enter her house safely. Instead, he had driven away at speed, all his anger brewing up again.

Craig drew up outside Bradfield shops and Edmund got in.

'Hello,' Craig said, a little stiffly, for he still smarted after what he believed was Edmund's abandoning of him after discovering Sandra in the Pullmans' house.

'Hi,' answered Edmund, not looking at Craig. 'I need you to do something for me.'

'Not again! Look, shamwari, I'm thinking I've had enough of this. Don't you have a police force or something that can help you? I'm just a poor white guy in a Renault 4 who has just had their house broken into, in case you'd forgotten. Some help may be in order, *Chief Inspector.*'

Edmund ignored him. 'I need you to get into Sandra's house.'

Craig stared. 'You want *me* to *break into* Sandra's house? Look, this is just too weird. I don't even know – are you a policeman? A proper one? Because proper policemen don't usually ask members of the public to break into other people's houses.'

'I told you, I'm working on my own from now on. I need you to have a look around. I need anything – something – that will help – give me concrete evidence. Paperwork, messages, emails, a diary. If there's a link between Sandra and Pullman, I need to find it.'

Craig didn't respond. Although angry with Sandra, he couldn't think of her as a killer. Surely she would have run away by now – perhaps she had. Being a gentleman at heart, he had dropped her at home after Edmund's departure without much hope of ever seeing her again. Much to his chagrin, he admitted his heart sank to think of her gone. Eventually he said, 'And how am I expected to *break into* her house? Should I use my cat burglar training or my ex-Marine skills? Which one do you think?'

Again, Edmund ignored the sarcastic barrage. 'It's easy. You're a handyman. You know very well how to pick locks.'

Craig burst into laughter. 'Pick locks! I *change* locks, I don't *pick them*.'

'But you know how to do it.'

'Ye-ah,' agreed Craig uncertainly. 'Look Edmund, you're a nice guy and I've got a couple of kicks out of all this, but what are you doing, really? Sandra didn't do it. She's a liar – and probably a thief – and all that inner child stuff was a load of the proverbial, but she's not a murderer. Pullman's your man. I don't know why he killed his wife, or how he killed his wife, but in all likelihood he killed her, right? He exports people in the back of furniture vans to South Africa. His wife ran a dodgy employment agency. Let's not feel sorry for her. She's dead, you've got enough on him to put him away for a few years. Let it go.'

Edmund was silent for a long time. 'No,' he said at last, scrambling out of the car. 'No, you don't understand. You, all of you white people, you live in your own little world, a lovely white-washed world. You still believe in good. You still think the police can help. You may criticise us, you may think we're pretty rubbish, but you still think that you can walk into a police station anywhere in this country and say, 'Officer! Please, I need help!' and it will be given. You *don't* understand. You just *don't understand!* I can't let this go, Craig! I can't.'

'Hey! Hey!' shouted Craig, jumping out of the car and following Edmund. 'Don't do all that I'm better than you stuff just because you're black and you've "suffered".' Craig encapsulated the word in imaginary quotation marks with his fingers. 'I've suffered too. Being *white* doesn't make me immune from suffering. *Stop* being a martyr, all right.'

'Dorcas is dead,' cried Edmund, spinning around. 'Dead.'

'What? Dorcas the maid?'

'Dorcas Hlabangana was her name. She was a person, not just a maid.'

'I'm sorry. I didn't mean... how?'

'She burnt to death last night in a house fire. My house fire.'

'Your house...? I don't get it. I...'

'It's obvious, isn't it?' snapped Edmund. 'It's a warning. Stay out. Keep away.'

'But why...?'

'Why?' Edmund was incredulous.

'You're a policeman.'

'*But I'm not one of them.*' Edmund sniffed contemptuously and shook his head. 'Everything was wrong right from the beginning. *I was wrong.*'

Craig frowned and ran his hand through his hair, scratching his scalp in exasperation.

'Look, Pullman is not the type to work with the police, but who does he fraternise with? The police. Who is called in to examine his wife's body? Not the family doctor, but a government medical officer who is also very conveniently the chief pathologist. Why? Why is it specifically Khumalo who he wants to investigate this case?'

'We've been through this. Because he's crooked. He wants to be able to pay them off. He murdered his wife and so he pays off the police.'

'But that's just it. *Did* he murder his wife?'

Craig drew up his shoulders. 'Yes. He's having an affair. He wants to leave his wife but she's got the bucks–'

'No, no, no,' said Edmund, throwing up his hands in exasperation. 'Don't you see? It's not him, *but he knows who it is.*'

'He knows?'

'Yes. Absolutely. And he's just waiting for that person to relax a little and then he'll strike.'

'What do you mean? Who will he strike?'

'Do you remember what you told me those guys said when they found you hiding the other night?'

'White whino? Stinks of booze? A disgrace? Which one?'

'No, no. About the phone. What did they say about the phone.'

Craig screwed up his forehead and tried to think.

'They said you wouldn't know what to do with a phone if it landed on your head. That's what you told me, remember?'

'Ye-es.'

'Well, does that not strike you as a strange thing to say. What's the relevance of the phone?'

Craig slowly shook his head.

'And they also said "we've found who we've been looking for." Remember?'

'They had just found me hiding by the bin.'

'But they weren't *looking for you*!' Edmund was almost shouting at Craig. A couple of people turned to stare at them.

'Keep your voice down!' commanded Craig. 'I see what you mean – I think. You mean they thought I was somebody else.'

'Exactly!'

'Who?'

'Whoever it is must also be white and I'd bet that whoever that person is was the one who informed the police at Beitbridge about the lorry. Someone who had inside information.'

'Someone who works for Pullman in the office?' began Craig.

'The person who informed the police was someone called Albert Zeke, but it's likely to be a pseudonym.'

'Zeke?'

'I googled it. It sounds a likely Zimbabwean name, doesn't it? But Zeke is also the surname of the man who played the lion in *The Wizard of Oz*. And guess what his first name was?'

Craig shook his head.

'Bert.'

Craig shook his head. 'I'm sorry... I just don't get it.'

'Dorcas's favourite film is *The Wizard of Oz*. She often watches it with Mr Sherbourne.'

'Who is he?'

'The Pullmans' neighbour. He and Dorcas were in a relationship.'

Craig rolled his eyes. 'This is like living in a soap opera! Right. I see. I think. So you mean... it was Dorcas and Lover Boy, the neighbour, who informed on Pullman?'

'Yes. Obviously, they wanted to bring the whole thing to a halt and by doing so hopefully expose what was going on to Mrs Pullman.'

'But–'

'But there was a computer problem and the whole system was down. Cross-border traffic was backed up for days. The truck drivers were either informed that the police were after them or they panicked, not knowing what to do with all the women in the back. Either way they ran. The women are in a secret compartment in the lorry and they can't get out and, if they shout, no one can hear them. Remember, you said you couldn't hear them when you were in the back of the lorry, but they had just got in and they would be settling themselves down. You would be bound to hear something. They die of dehydration or heat stroke or both but Pullman's connections with the police help him out; the bodies are moved, dumped in a bush somewhere. But it costs, it costs a lot and he is forced to lie low for a while. I imagine his operation the other night was the first one in a while. Plans were made, but then his wife was stabbed. It's a challenge but from who?'

'And then I turn up.' Craig breathed out heavily. 'And he let me go.'

'Did he?'

'Well, of course... he said...'

'He said for you to be got rid of. I wouldn't call that being let go.'

'No,' conceded Craig.

'And when you got away, he panicked. He must have realised your drunken act was just that, an act. He describes you to Shantelle and she confirms you as Craig Martin, the person who threatened his wife the day she died.'

'But... but...' began Craig. 'No... I mean... you mean they thought *I* was working with Dorcas and this boyfriend of hers?'

'No. I think they thought *you* were the boyfriend.'

'No, wait!' cried Craig. He stood still as he frantically rubbed his forehead hard with his fingertips as though it would help the information sink in. 'No, that doesn't make sense. Dorcas ran after me. She shouted that I was the person who threatened Mrs Pullman. How does that fit in?'

Edmund looked momentarily stumped but then he pointed his finger at Craig and said: 'Simple. They assume there has been a fall out between the two of you. She wasn't expecting you at the house and suddenly you arrive in the company of a police officer. She's the one who stabbed Mrs Pullman and you know it's her. Perhaps you've come to turn her in. She's a maid, you're a white man. Who is more likely to be believed. She panicked and you change your mind and run away.'

'I don't sound very brave or much of a threat. It's very far-fetched.'

'No, it isn't. Listen,' commanded Edmund. 'I got it all wrong. Dorcas was being used by both Mr and Mrs Pullman for unethical but different ends. Dorcas is desperate to leave their employment, but neither of them will let go: she simply knows too much. Now, my mistake was in believing that Dorcas had threatened Pullman, but it's highly unlikely she would have done so. He would have laughed in her face. No, a much better plan would be to expose the illegal trafficking and get Pullman into trouble. Not only would it cause trouble for Pullman legally, it would also reveal to his wife what has been going on behind her back.'

'So?'

'So, somebody – Alfred Zeke aka Roland Sherbourne – informs on their operation but it doesn't go to plan. Pullman pays the police and his wife is none the wiser. However, what is clear is that they have a leak and they guess rightly that that leak is Dorcas.'

'How do they know that?'

'She knows everything – and she's tried to leave, hasn't she? Mrs Pullman *must* have mentioned to her husband that

Dorcas wanted to resign. He think she's in cahoots with a white guy and–'

'Wait, wait, wait.' Craig held up his hand as a signal for Edmund to slow down. 'How do they know he's white. Come to that, how do they know she's working with anyone at all?'

'Mr Sherbourne no doubt tried to hide his accent on the phone, but he's the kind of guy who wouldn't be able to help sounding white however hard he tried. Then you come along. At first, despite running away from the house, you are not much of a suspect. Pullman asks Dorcas about you and she relates the story which Shantelle corroborates. You were angry with Shantelle. You may have not known Mrs Pullman was even there until she came out of the back room so it is really unlikely that you came there to threaten her. Maybe you heard she was dead and you had some morbid fascination with the fact and you got caught and ran when spotted. But then I start asking questions about you–'

'Did you? Who did you ask?'

'Shantelle. Now,' Edmund carried on swiftly, leaving Craig no opportunity to delve deeper, 'I'm told I'm off the case and Pullman thinks I'm an idiot anyway so any questions I may have asked are discarded as irrelevant, but maybe, *maybe*, I've planted a possible seed there. You appear for the second time, this time as a drunken bum. Pullman doesn't know what you look like but he's not going to let you go without a few questions being asked. The problem is that you escape before he is able to get any further. Shantelle confirms the description of the bum as you and they are now on full alert. Perhaps you joined the agency to see how things worked. To see what offers you would get. Shantelle remembers how you threatened Mrs Pullman *and* now she thinks that perhaps it wasn't as random a gesture as it once appeared. *And* she remembers Mrs Pullman's comment to Dorcas when you had just left the office: "Go to your white man." What if that man is you?'

'Me?'

'And so,' continued Edmund, ignoring Craig's question, 'they ransack your house. It's a warning. A dire warning. They know you're alive and they know where you live – and they'll be back.'

'The million dollar question is why would they think Dorcas would stab Mrs Pullman?'

'A warning. She found Mrs Pullman dead. She took advantage of the situation to make it look like she'd been murdered. She doesn't know, of course, that to a doctor or a pathologist, or even a policeman such as myself, it would be obvious that she had died before she was stabbed.'

'But a warning from whom?'

'A rival gang. They mentioned Nkala, didn't they? Robert Nkala is currently in Chikurubi doing fifteen years for people trafficking, but some say he still manages to run his business from behind bars. Perhaps Dorcas and Mr Sherbourne wanted to scare Pullman? Make him give up. They wouldn't need Dorcas anymore then, would they?'

Craig stood shaking his head for half a minute. 'Unbelievable,' he muttered. 'Unbelievable.' He rocked back on his heels and stared up at the sky. 'So they killed Dorcas because...'

'It was probably a mistake. They just wanted the information about who she was working with; they didn't mean to kill her. There was an injury to the back of her head which is suggestive of a fall. She may have been pushed and hit her head against a wall.'

'Pullman...'

'No, not Pullman. One of his men. Pullman is not the type to get blood on his hands. She was picked up from the house, taken somewhere else and continually questioned as to who you were and what was going on. She denied the story was true, and it wasn't and as they didn't ask about Roland Sherbourne, she did not mention him.'

'OK. Someone pushes her and she hits her head and dies. They want to get rid of the body. Why your house? Why not mine if I'm the one who is in cahoots with her?'

Edmund smirked. 'I could suggest a number of reasons, but let's stick with the most practical. You live two blocks from the fire station. If they want to get rid of a body in a fire, chances are that that fire would be put out pretty soon.'

'The same could be said for your house. Somebody could have called the fire brigade as soon as it started.'

Edmund didn't answer. He had no wish to tell Craig that most people where he lived would delight in any misfortune that befell him.

'Your neighbours are more likely to notice something amiss if a strange car arrived and a body was carried into a house.'

'I don't agree. All neighbours are nosy, wherever you live. Besides, I don't think mine even look in my direction.'

Edmund was quiet.

'Perhaps it's you they want to warn, not me?' Craig suddenly burst out. 'But why? Where do they think you come in?'

'Oh, I'm just the accidental policeman. A man just trying to do his job. I ask too many questions and I poke my nose where I'm not wanted.'

'And Sandra?'

'That's what I don't know. Is she perhaps a connection of theirs in South Africa?'

'Oh come on, Edmund. Does she really strike you as being involved with those two, Pullman and Shantelle?'

'That's what we have to find out.' Edmund's voice was calm now and his form relaxed. 'Please. Trust me that I know what I'm doing. Just one last thing for me.' He gave Craig a long, pleading look. Finally, Craig turned away, shaking his head.

'I... I don't know how you do it... all right, one last thing.'

'Thank you.'

'The funeral is today.'

'Yes. Yes, I know.' Edmund looked away and then back at Craig. 'Do what you can. Please, Craig. You're a good man. You want justice.'

'Whatever that means,' said Craig, getting back in the car. He shook his head. 'I just hope it's worth it.'

Edmund was right. Picking a lock was easy and Craig was able to enter the house without much ado. The previous night was the first time he had been to her house, but he had once or twice, all right seven times, driven past it when he had first met her. What he had been hoping to see, he didn't know: a heart shaped hedge or a banner hanging out of the window with the words: 'Forgive me Craig' emblazoned on them. Whatever he had hoped, he had seen nothing. Her car was gone so he presumed she had as well and it was a weekday morning so he imagined her child would be at school.

He looked around the sparsely decorated lounge with the white Buddha in the corner and the clear glass bowls full of smooth, unpolished pebbles and the linen throws, all in soft shades of white and blue, and he saw an emptiness; the kind of emptiness that remains when the pain has gone. He had seen it in her eyes the night before. She wasn't sorry, she was angry she had been caught. How dare something, anything, stand in her way? The kitchen was neat, but sparse. A small pantry revealed a couple of boxes of herbal tea, a packet of quinoa and a jar of coconut oil. A vegetable rack in the corner held a cauliflower and a dozen potatoes. There wasn't a wine bottle or beer can in sight: she was true to her word in that sense at least.

He looked in on the little boy's room with all its pictures of dolphins jumping over the waves and horses running along the beach and the accompanying maxims: 'Go into the world and do well, but more importantly go into the world and do good' and 'What you think, you become.' A little Buddha sat on a table next to the bed but someone had given him green eyes with plasticine.

In the small bathroom, the only signs of habitation were two toothbrushes in a glass and a half-used tube of toothpaste. In her bedroom, he opened the drawers of her bedside table. He had hesitated before doing so, expecting underwear or strips of birth control pills or giant packets of condoms. Instead, he found it empty of everything but a book of mantras. He picked it up and flicked through it and then threw it back in the drawer and closed it. He had to give her credit: if she was a con artist, she was a good one.

Feeling more than a pang of guilt, he cautiously opened her cupboard, but at one glance it was obvious she wasn't hiding anything. There was a small pile of mainly white T-shirts and what might be termed 'yoga gear' – loose calf-length trousers in bland shades of washed blue and beige. A couple of smarter outfits hung in the wardrobe and a straw hat lay on a top shelf. She certainly travelled light. Craig couldn't help feel a vague sense of comfort that he hadn't found anything incriminating as he took one look around the room, thinking sadly that this would be the only time he'd ever see it, and went down the passageway and out through the kitchen door. He walked quickly up the road, and turned the corner into the next road where he'd left his car and threw himself on the seat with relief.

The fun had gone, he thought. Manning would have shrugged his shoulders at the cunning of the woman. Manning never lost his heart, did he? At the traffic lights on the Hillside Road, his was the only car in sight, but he couldn't be bothered to jump the red light. No doubt some happy little policeman would be sitting somewhere, ready to book him if he did. Instead, he sat and hungrily eyed the bottle store across the road. He had five dollars. He could probably pick up a half jack of Don something or other sherry or Count someone or other's vodka.

Loneliness and despair washed over him. For the first time in a long, long time, Craig sat and cried. His were the tears of exhaustion and mental fatigue. His freefall ended here in a glare of sunshine on an empty road with him slumped over the steering wheel, his face wet, his eyesight blurred and every iota of hope gone. *Nobody knew how the accident happened. She drove off a straight road.*

He saw the body at the bottom of the pool, such a tiny body. He heard people shouting, someone ran, there was a great splash of water. Nobody saw him on the side, his toes curled over the edge of the pool, watching. There was a man, it was his father, bending over the body, blowing air into the mouth. *Come on, Callie. Come on! Don't do this to me, don't go.* Don't go. Don't go. And his mother running, screaming, his father holding her back, his arms around her, pulling her to the ground. And then the sound, that terrifying sound that broke from his dad's throat like a roar. The pain that ripped through the world threatened to engulf all there. Come, someone had said and they had picked him up and taken him back into the clubhouse and given him ice cream. People had been nice, too nice. Patting his head and hugging him and giving him things. And all he thought about was his father, his father who never cried, not even in the saddest part of *Watership Down* when everyone cried, or when Socks died or when he cut his finger with the saw; his father sobbing like a little boy.

The lights changed to green and then changed back to red, but still Craig sat, his body racked with sobs. Years of loneliness, sadness and despair peeled off him; all the layers he had used to cover and protect his small inner core, that bit that longed to be held and loved and soothed.

He thought of his mother's funeral. There were six people in all. The priest had hummed and hawed; his dull voice heavy with admonishment as he plodded through the mass. There had been no love, no kindness in his eyes when he shook hands with him and his father outside the church. Craig remembered the cold clamminess of his hands and the way his eyes looked over Craig's head into the hibiscus hedge behind him. What his mother had done was wrong, was shameful. She had sinned and all sinners must pay the price. Craig had felt her disgrace settle on him like a bird arranging itself in the nest.

'Move out of the way! Idiot! Loser!' Craig looked to the left and saw the Fixit Brothers overtake him with a screech of wheels. One of them stuck his middle finger out of the window and made a stupid face as he passed.

Craig stared over the steering wheel as they disappeared down the road. Wiping his face with the back of his hand, he sat back and put his car into first. He knew what he had to do.

Chapter Forty-two

Craig looked around the office, feeling a knot of apprehension turn inside him.

When he had asked at the front office if he could see Chief Inspector Edmund Dube, he had noticed a definite shared glance between the two policemen behind the counter. One of them had asked him numerous questions, most of which Craig did not feel were any of his business, while stapling various forms together and never looking him in the eye.

The other officer had scuttled off and then returned and asked Craig to follow him down a corridor and up some stairs and down another corridor. Craig had followed with some trepidation. He couldn't help feeling as though he were being led to a private cell or an interrogation room in which his teeth would be extracted one by one followed by each and every fingernail and toenail, and finally his eyeballs.

Instead, he was led into a typical government service office with dated, somewhat battered furniture and filing cabinets, curtains that were too short for the windows and missing numerous curtain hooks, and various notices stuck to the wall with sticky tape.

He had been shown a seat and then left on his own for what seemed an age. The office smelt of greasy takeaways; it was obvious that the windows, which were thick with dust, had not been opened for a long time, adding to the claustrophobic feeling of the room. Eventually, a tall, rather suave policeman entered, looking far smarter and superior to the minions Craig had seen earlier.

'Detective Inspector Joseph Khumalo,' he introduced himself with a cold handshake and a fleeting smile before settling himself behind the desk, taking out his phone, scrolling down the messages and finally turning his attention to Craig.

'What happened to your face?' he asked, his face smooth and free of all emotion.

'Walked into a wall.'

He didn't laugh. 'Walls can be dangerous.' Craig looked away. The man seemed to stare right through him.

'So, you are looking for Edmund Dube?'

'Chief Inspector Dube. That's right.'

The policeman sucked in his lips and shook his head. 'Chief Inspector. Hmm.' He sat back in his chair, picked up his pen and drew invisible circles on a clean white pad of paper. Craig watched his face, wondering what was going to come next.

'Tell me, how do you know *Chief Inspector* Dube?'

'He–' Craig stopped, not knowing how to go on. 'He's a friend, a good friend of mine.'

The policeman ran his eyes over Craig. 'Well, if so, you will be aware of your friend's shortcomings.'

Craig hesitated, not quite sure what to say. 'You mean his...?'

The man didn't respond to his prompt. Craig shifted uneasily in his seat. All that could be heard was the soft movement of the pen on the paper.

'Look,' began Craig. 'All I want to know is where my friend is. I'm not sure why I have been brought in here. I think it must have been some mistake. I'll call him, all right? I'll see him later.'

Craig got up and made for the door.

'Sit down, Mr Martin.' The voice was calm, but firm.

Craig sat.

'I'm not sure how you know Edmund Dube, but I believe that he has involved you in his latest – what shall we call it? Adventure?'

'What do you mean?'

'It might help for me to give you a little background history.' He leaned forward, 'Then you may make up your own mind about your good friend.'

'I'm listening.'

'Good.' Detective Inspector Khumalo balanced the pen

horizontally between the tips of his two forefingers. 'Edmund Dube came to us as a new recruit. He was doing very well. He is perhaps not the most forceful of people, but he was good – conscientious. You know what I mean?'

Craig nodded.

'A number of years ago, about ten or so, he was involved in a police operation to remove illegal squatters and vendors–'

'Operation Murambatsvina. I remember. You burned down people's houses and market stalls.'

As the pen fell, the policeman snatched at it and caught it with one hand and put up the other in protest. 'That is neither here nor there. The fact of the matter is that Edmund was one of the police officers involved. He didn't want to be, he wanted to stay inside the police station all the time. He was consumed by paperwork.'

'I can imagine.'

'Well, I wasn't having that. He had to be involved; we all did. I ordered that he go out with the rest.'

'And he did?'

'He did. But he had a bad experience.' The man leant back into his chair, throwing his pen down on the desk as he did so. 'There was a child who died. Nobody knew she was still in the shack when it was set alight.'

Craig shook his head. 'Nobody knew! Nobody cared.'

The policeman ignored the comment and pushed on. 'It affected Edmund very badly. He would sit for hours at his desk doing nothing, staring at the wall, not speaking. One day, someone found him in the toilets, sitting on the floor, rocking himself backwards and forwards. We persuaded him to take time off; he didn't want it, but he took it. When he came back, he was asked if he would like to leave the force. Perhaps there was something else he could make a career out of. I remember he just smiled at me, this big funny smile and he said that all he wanted to be was Chief Inspector.'

The policeman stared hard at Craig as though waiting for the information to sink in. Craig nodded.

'He had got it from a book or a film, some such place.'

He waved his hand in the air above his head. 'He had this idea it was his title. You see what I am saying?'

'Mmm,' said Craig, not knowing which way to respond. 'What did you do then?'

'Well, we joked about it. We still do. You'll hear the officers refer to him as Chief Inspector, but it's a nickname.' The policeman now leaned forward over his desk, clasping his hands in front of him. 'Edmund wasn't worried about money. He wanted – and this is very difficult to explain – he wanted to organise us, to organise the police force. He wanted every single paper, every single document to be correct. Sign here, sign there. That was how he could put the world to rights. That suited us. Many of our officers don't want to do paperwork. I felt sorry for him. Life in Zimbabwe is harsh. Where was he going to get a job? I let him do what he was good at.'

There was a note of arrogance in the man's voice that was difficult to ignore. Craig studied his face. He could detect no emotion.

'What about the investigation into the death of Marcia Pullman? Is that also part of your plan to humour him?'

Again, the policeman looked directly at Craig. His mouth had hardened and there was a clear note of warning in his tone.

'Let me make what I am going to say absolutely categorically clear. Edmund Dube is not part of the investigation into Mrs Pullman's death and he never has been.'

'But... I gave him a lift. From the police station that day of the murder... to the Pullmans' house.'

The man shrugged. 'So, you gave him a lift. Was there anyone with him? Any other officers?'

'N-no. No, there weren't.'

'It didn't occur to you that this was unusual?'

Craig hesitated. The truth was, it had.

'Have you ever seen him work with anyone else?'

Craig thought and then shook his head. 'No. No, I haven't.' He felt his heart sink lower.

'While in your presence, has he ever been in touch with the station or another policeman?'

'I think he made a call... once.'

'A call.' The sarcasm in the man's voice was palpable. 'He usually stays stuck in his little room typing up traffic offences, but something made him latch onto this case.'

'But he came to my house... he asked questions. He asked me to do some work for him...'

The policeman's eyes narrowed. 'What sort of work?'

Craig regretted his words before he could stop himself saying them. 'He... I... nothing really. Just watching somebody, their movements, that's all.'

The policeman shook his head as though he had just heard the most outrageous story.

'Have you not thought it would be easier for a policeman, a *trained* policeman to undertake the observations of this person, this... er... whoever it was that he asked you to watch rather than you, a stranger to the profession?'

Craig had thought exactly that on numerous occasions, but he didn't want to admit it. 'Perhaps Edmund didn't feel he had your support?'

Khumalo made a loud rasping noise signifying disbelief, waving away Craig's comment with the back of his hand.

'And you think you are so special, hey? So special.'

Perhaps I am, Craig wanted to say, but he was out of his depth and he knew it. He realised, too, that he had been right on all the occasions when he had asked Edmund who he really was or scoffed at his friend's assertions that he was a police officer. He was more like a fictional character than anything; not a Manning P.I. by any stretch of the imagination – more like P.C. Plod, the kind, dependable copper.

Khumalo unlocked his top drawer and pulled out a large file that he passed over to Craig. 'There is more to this case than meets the eye.'

Momentarily taken aback by the size and official-looking nature of the file, Craig hesitated before gingerly opening it. He was confronted by a wodge of papers. On top, was a yellowing police employment record.

'Archibald Balfour MacDougal,' Craig read, his eyebrows

raised in puzzlement. Not much about the conversation had helped make sense of the last few days and the addition of a Scottish policeman into the bargain was not helping him achieve clarity.

'Chief Inspector MacDougal was Edmund's mother's employer. A long time ago. Late seventies.'

Craig slowly scanned the page and then turned it over. The next piece of paper was from a photocopy from a newspaper. Again, he scanned it.

"Chief Inspector MacDougal had charges of child abuse laid against him by the complainant's father. When asked to confirm the allegations, the child agreed that he had been inappropriately touched by the police officer."

'Edmund? The child was Edmund?' Craig sat back in the chair. He felt uneasy. Ill-prepared for this revelation. He was aware of the police officer's eyes watching him slyly, like a crocodile's just above the water of a murky river.

'That's not all,' said Khumalo, picking up an article he had deliberately kept to one side and passing it to Craig with a certain sense of triumph. 'This had taken place a couple of months previously.'

"Local businessman, Nigel Pullman, said he would be suing the police over a recent raid on his home in Suburbs. Pullman, who runs a local safari business, said that his house had suffered damage during the raid on Tuesday. Chief Inspector Archibald MacDougal said they were acting on a tip off from a member of the public that he was meeting wanted arms dealer, Rick Bernadie, but when the police arrived, they found Mr Pullman alone and watching television."

Craig felt a tingle down his spine. 'Edmund knows this. He knows.'

'A few months before her death, Mrs Pullman had reported a man watching the house every day for about two weeks.'

'No, that was...' began Craig. He stopped, torn between telling Khumalo about Charles, the airtime vendor, and protecting the man.

'The file was found in his office,' said Khumalo, watching Craig's face carefully. 'It was obviously something of an obsession. Mrs Pullman's death – from natural causes – offered him an opportunity and he took his chance.'

'Chance to do what?' asked Craig, looking up.

Khumalo merely tilted his head gently to one side as though that were up to Craig to decide.

Craig looked down again at the papers. 'And was MacDougal right about Pullman?'

Khumalo passed him a large, old brown envelope.

'What's this?'

'MacDougal's case notes concerning Pullman. Edmund no doubt feels that the man was justified in what he did, but he was acting on very little evidence.'

Craig withdrew a sheaf of papers from the envelope. He studied the small, neat handwriting carefully, but wasn't sure what he should be looking at.

'Ultimately, he acted on one person's testimony. You will see there what she said.'

Craig read. 'Mrs Hera Amoris.' He shrugged. The name meant nothing to him. 'Sounds Greek. Who was she?'

'It seems she didn't exist. A further investigation couldn't trace her at all.'

'She was made up? She certainly sounds made up.'

Khumalo shrugged. 'It was a long time ago. Who knows. Please, Mr Martin, do not get involved any more with this man. We have warned him. We have tried to tell him. Unfortunately, we have pandered to his whims once too often. We cannot entertain the likes of him in the police force. We have every reason to believe he is a very dangerous man.'

Chapter Forty-three

1979

'*This* boy has taken money from my purse.'

Edmund's cheeks smouldered as the noise of the class evaporated, retreating out of windows and into corners. All eyes were on him. Mrs Fourie was livid: her purple cheeks shook with rage, making her eyes sink back into her sockets until they were two thin slits of hate. Her chest, which had turned a bright crimson, heaved with emotion.

'After all I've done! All I've done for this child.'

The headmaster stood next to her; his face was one of serious contemplation. He was not prone to violent outbursts of rage, preferring to deal with matters behind doors. He was known to be fair; he would investigate, ask questions, write notes in his small sloping handwriting with his fountain pen.

'Come to my office immediately,' was all he said.

They were ushered into the suffocating heat of the office with its wooden panelled walls and long sash windows kept firmly shut and the heavy green curtains which, although not drawn, blocked out the glare of the sun, absorbing its heat in its every fold and radiating it back into the room.

Mrs Fourie was offered a chair and a glass of water. About five minutes into the interview, a secretary brought in a tray of tea with two ginger biscuits on a plate. Mr Smithson waited until she had poured the tea and then gave her a nod and she disappeared out of the door, shutting it softly behind her.

Mrs Fourie gave vent to her side of the story.

'It was at the end of break. I had spent most of it in the classroom with Edmund – *this* boy – showing him how to conjugate sentences correctly. I went to get a glass of water

– I was only going to be a couple of minutes.' She snorted with disdain. 'They're quick, aren't they? It's so inbred it comes naturally.'

'What happened?'

'I returned to find *him* taking money out of my purse. Money! Can you believe it? From his own teacher.'

'How much?'

'Two dollars.' Mrs Fourie lay the offending note on the headmaster's desk with a certain flourish and sat back with her arms crossed.

The head continued to write in his notebook without looking up at Edmund. Edmund shifted uneasily on the carpet, staring up at the bust of Plato whose blank eyes looked both unseeingly and directly at him. His lips were parted slightly as though he were taking a breath before his words of admonishment billowed out.

At last the headmaster spoke.

'What do you have to say for yourself, Edmund?'

Edmund's throat contracted. He looked at the carpet as he spoke.

'I was putting the money back.'

'Speak up. We can't hear you.'

'I was–'

'Look at me when I'm talking to you! Am I lying prostrate on the floor?'

'No, Sir.'

'No. Well, look this way then.'

'Yes, Sir.'

'Well, come on. Let's have it. What were you doing in Mrs Fourie's bag?

'I was putting the money back, Sir.'

'Putting it back?'

'I found it in my desk.'

'I don't understand. What are you saying?'

'Before break, Mrs Fourie was explaining to us about currency. She showed us the note.'

The headmaster nodded. 'Yes.'

426

'At break time, Mrs Fourie was going to help me with my English. I went to use the toilet and when I came back, the note was in my desk. It was definitely not my money. I knew it was hers.'

Mr Smithson looked at him carefully over the tops of his glasses.

'What are you suggesting?'

Edmund moved his feet.

'That is what happened. I didn't put it there.'

'Are you saying someone else did?'

Edmund squirmed. 'Maybe.'

'Are you saying they did it deliberately?'

'Perhaps.'

'And why would they do that?'

Edmund looked down at his feet.

'And why would they do that?' Mr Smithson repeated with a slight note of irritation in his voice.

'I don't know.'

'You *don't* know?'

'No.'

Mr Smithson shook his head as though Edmund was beyond salvation. He wrote a few more notes in his book.

'Do you know who might have done this?'

Edmund began to shake his head again and Mrs Fourie burst out: 'He's a liar. Which boy would do that? No one. No one would. You're a liar and you know it.'

Mr Smithson held up his hand with more patience than he had shown to Edmund. 'Mrs Fourie, please. A minute.'

Mrs Fourie's mouth opened and shut. She took an angry gulp of tea.

'Edmund, has someone been bullying you?'

Edmund thought before answering. Mr MacDougal's words came back to him. *Everyone has a weapon, Edmund. You need to find out what yours is and use it.*

'Edmund, I repeat, has someone been bullying you?'

There was no air. He couldn't breathe. It was as though a hand were at his neck, pressing harder and harder. The

427

blank eyes watched him, urged him on. He felt eyes everywhere, hot, angry eyes. A wisp of steam rose from Mrs Fourie's cup, curling slowly upwards before dissolving into the unmoving air.

'No,' he answered. 'No one.'

Looking quickly from side to side, Edmund walked through the open gate of 274 Clark Road, trying his best to affect a casual air. There was a marquee up in the garden and employees from a catering firm were busy setting up a bar table and arranging chairs. Flowers were arranged on tablecloths that swept to the ground in huge swathes of white; a barman in a smart black waistcoat polished glasses, holding them up to the light to ensure they were free of marks and smudges; someone else arranged napkins; yet a third made sure the sprigs of parsley adorning the tray of canapés were placed just right; bottles of wine stood in rows, some red, some white, some open, allowing their contents to breathe correctly, for this was not just any farewell: this was Marcia Pullman's.

Not wishing to draw attention to himself in any way, Edmund had dressed casually in a pair of jeans, belt, white shirt, trainers and a cap that he had picked up at the market. He carried a clipboard with him, the reasoning being that if anyone saw him in the house, they would assume he was there in some official capacity. Clipboards were designed to have that effect. The kitchen door was open. He trod softly up the steps.

The funeral had just finished when Craig arrived. The church doors were open and mourners streamed out, shaking hands with the priest and Mr Pullman before moving slowly off to congregate in small groups or get into their cars. Craig sat for a full five minutes in the church car park, gripping the steering wheel tightly and staring at Mr Pullman's profile. He watched the confident way the man clasped each proffered hand in his, the heave of his shoulders as he stood back to talk, the nod of his head, the smile. Despite his dark suit, he was still very recognizable as the man he had seen a couple of nights previously overseeing the loading of furniture, and people, into the back of a lorry.

Craig looked down at his own clothes and wondered how recognizable he would be. He had gone home and sorted through the clothes littered across his bedroom floor. He had decided on his chinos with the slightly worn patches, a long-sleeved white shirt, a black tie and a white jacket. The jacket, although hardly worn, had been bought for a wedding twelve years previously, and was a little tight under the armpits and across the back. It was all right as long as he did not bend his arms. Craig had washed his hair and tied it back into a ponytail and, looking at himself in the mirror before leaving, couldn't help but think that, except for his facial injuries, he was looking quite debonair.

He started the car and drove slowly out of the church car park and then out towards Suburbs. There were already a number of cars parked outside the Pullmans' house and people were congregating on the lawn. Craig parked a fair way down the road so that he could leave easily without the danger of someone blocking him in. He took a small piece of paper out of his pocket, clasped his hands in front of him in prayer, cleared his throat and spoke aloud.

'Vengeance... vengeance...' He stopped and cleared his throat again, looking a little self-consciously out of the window to see if anyone was watching and then back at the piece of paper. 'Vengeance is Mine, and retribution. In due time their foot will slip; For the day of their calamity is near, And the impending things are hastening upon them.'

Aware that he had said the words a little too quickly, he squeezed his eyes shut, sucked in his lips, looked at himself once more in the rearview mirror and nodded his head.

Aloud, he said: 'Let's do this thing.'

Sandra Smith had woken early that morning to meditate and recite affirmations and now felt especially positive as she smiled and nodded her way through the crowd of people in the tent, gently pushing her way to the food table. She asked for a bottle of sparkling water, unscrewed the lid and stood back to survey the scene.

'Can I get you a drink?' asked a voice at her side. She turned to see Nigel Pullman standing next to her. 'Whisky. Double. Quick.' He said to the barman. He turned back to Sandra, looking her up and down approvingly.

'I have one,' she answered, holding up her bottle of water.

'Let me ask you again. Can I get you a drink? A real one.'

She laughed as she poured the water into a tall glass. 'No thank you.'

'So,' he said, taking a large swig of whisky. 'I haven't seen you around before.'

Sandra smiled, trying not to show any hint of nervousness. 'I knew your wife. I'm so sorry...' she began.

He shrugged. 'Yeah, well. Shit happens.'

'What are you going to do now? Will you stay here?'

Pullman shrugged and took a swig of his drink. 'Maybe, maybe not. No hurry.'

A waiter appeared at that point with a tray of snacks.

'No thank you,' said Sandra.

'Go on,' urged Pullman. 'You gonna make me think there's something wrong with everything just now.'

Sandra ran her eyes over the array of food. She shook her head again. 'I'm sorry. It's just that I don't eat certain things. I have my own.' She reached into her bag and brought out a plastic container. Taking off the lid, she offered it to Mr Pullman. 'I don't mean to be rude, but I don't eat dairy or wheat so I tend to fend for myself.'

Pullman's small, pudgy eyes looked down at the container.

'I can't eat half the stuff here either,' he said with a short laugh. 'It's bad for my arthritis. I'm supposed to be gluten free.'

'Have one.' She proffered the container a little closer to him. 'No wheat, I promise. I wouldn't think the whisky helps.'

Pullman took one of the biscuits and shoved it in his mouth. He crunched it for a couple of seconds before swallowing it down.

'Not bad,' he conceded with a nod of his head.

'They're made with almond flour.'

'What about the cheese? Thought you said you couldn't have it?'

'I can't. It's sesame cheese.'

Pullman raised his eyebrows. She offered him the box again. He took another, biting it in half this time.

'You not having one?' He gestured towards the box.

'I will, just not now,' she smiled.

'Nigel, Nigel you're wanted over here,' called a voice and Shantelle appeared in a silky black skirt suit. She looked Sandra up and down, her brows drawn together in a frown. 'Nigel, you're neglecting your guests.'

'Shantelle,' said Nigel, touching her lightly on the arm. 'Meet... sorry, I didn't get your name.'

'Sandra.'

'Meet Sandra.'

Shantelle gave Sandra the briefest of glances, the corners of her mouth twitched curtly in a smile and then she turned back to Nigel. 'Really, Nigel. Come on. Get a drink and come over here.'

Pullman rolled his eyes. 'We'll speak later,' he said to Sandra. Then he downed his drink, got another and followed behind Shantelle.

In the kitchen, Janet took a quiche out of a basket and set it on the table.

'This is for Mr Pullman. I'm sorry, who are you? What is your name?'

'Buhle. I'm with the agency.'

'I see. Well, Buhle. It's not to go out with the rest of the food, you understand?'

Buhle nodded.

'Just for Mr Pullman, because of his problem.' She mouthed

the word problem as though it were of an unseemly nature. Buhle looked confused.

'He can't eat certain things – you'll learn soon enough. There's no crust. I'm sure he'll be hungry later on and the last thing he'll want to do is go out and buy something. Where is Dorcas? She should be here, not having the day off.'

Buhle shrugged and smiled and then took the dish and placed it in the fridge.

'You'll need to warm it up. A couple of minutes in the microwave should be enough. Perhaps you could make a salad to go with it?'

Buhle stared at Janet, who appeared to be waiting for some response. When she didn't get it, she folded up the cloth she had used to cover the quiche and placed it carefully back in the basket.

Janet imagined Marcia looking scornfully at the quiche.

'Oh, how nice,' she would enthuse, but her smile would be false, her eyes too quick to move onto something else. 'All by yourself, Janet. How clever.'

Janet turned away from Buhle. 'It's gluten-free and all that.' She paused, seemed to want something but wasn't sure how to say it. 'It's been years since I cooked for a man. It's different, you know, to cooking for your mother.'

From a place at the back of the tent, Edmund surveyed the crowd. He was surprised to see so many people for he had been under the impression that white people didn't have big funerals. He saw Ndhlovu in his dark brown suit, overfilling a small plate with numerous snacks and taking large gulps of white wine from a glass in his hand. Edmund pulled his cap down and huddled into the shadows.

Shantelle stayed as close to Pullman as possible without raising eyebrows, remembering every so often that she shouldn't be laughing too loudly or too long and assuming a face of quiet mourning. Pullman himself was the life and soul of the party, telling anecdotes and knocking back whisky.

Sandra Smith was making her way through the crowd, water in hand. Edmund watched her stop at the edge of the marquee, look around and then walk quietly towards the house. She obviously had other business to attend to.

Janet Peters wandered down the path from the house. She pulled her jacket closer and patted down her hair. Edmund was surprised at how much lighter and younger she looked. A bit of makeup, perhaps. Or was it something else? Relief. Marcia really had gone.

Sandra walked quietly through the house. Everyone was outside, except for a couple of people in the kitchen washing glasses or clearing empty trays of snacks. If anyone asked what she was doing, she would say she was looking for the toilet. It was the kind of thing one could get away with at this type of event. She would clasp her hand to her chest, utter 'Silly me, just having a blonde moment' and then scuttle out of the room.

She got to the end of the corridor and quietly turned the handle of the door. Quickly, she let herself in and closed the door behind her. The last time she had come in here, she had managed to look in one of the wardrobes but it was dark and she hadn't had time to look through everything. She opened it again now and looked inside. There were clothes hanging on a rail and clothes folded in neat piles on the shelves. At the bottom of the wardrobe was a long drawer, which she had looked into on her previous foray. She opened it again now and looked briefly over the contents, which were surprisingly few. She shut it and looked around. There was a chest of drawers in the corner that she now opened. One drawer was underwear, the next scarves, the next jerseys. She was just bending down to open the bottom drawer when a voice behind her made her jump.

'What are you doing?'

Sandra spun round to find Shantelle standing near the door, arms akimbo and a look of anger on her face.

'Oh, er... hi!' She tried a voice of friendly surprise.

Shantelle didn't say a word, but took a step forwards.

'I was, er, just looking for the... for something warm to wear. It's quite chilly outside.'

'So you go through a dead woman's things on the day of her funeral?' Shantelle approached Sandra, her arms folded across her chest. She stopped when she was a footstep away. 'I wasn't born yesterday. I know what you're doing. You're a thief.'

'No, no, no. You've got it wrong. Look, I know what it looks like, but I'm not stealing anything.'

'I don't know who you are, but I knew you were trouble when I saw you all over Nigel.' She came right up to Sandra's face now and ran her red fingertips over Sandra's cheeks. One skimmed the bottom of her eye. 'Baby eyes, soft skin, nice booty.' She grabbed Sandra's buttocks and pulled her close. Sandra pulled away sharply, but Shantelle was quick. In one swift movement, she had Sandra up against the wall, a hand around her throat. Sandra gasped wildly, struggling for breath.

'If I see your cute little ass here again, I'm going to kill you. Understand? Keep your hands off what's not yours.'

Sandra nodded as best she could. She felt the grip tighten. Shantelle smiled, then let her go.

Sandra grabbed her bag and made for the door, clutching her throat. In the passageway, she leant against the wall, trying to recover her breath and then stumbled back down to the kitchen. Going out of the back door, she almost fell over Craig who was sitting on the top step. He had a full glass of whisky in his hands.

'Where ya goin' pretty lay-day?' he laughed, but he wasn't smiling. He dropped his head into his hands.

'Out. Away from here,' she sneered.

'So soon? And the night's so young?'

She sniffed contemptuously at him, trying to get past.

'Looking for Nefarious Nigel?'

She ignored him and started walking away.

'You're all the same, aren't you?'

She stopped.

'Women I mean. You, with all your inner child and talking to animals and all that crap. You just want money. That's all it's about, isn't it? Well, he's buxed up to the hilt, I'm sure. But not so keen on the lotus position – although I'm sure you can teach him how to reap the benefits.'

She started walking again and then stopped. 'It's not true,' she said, marching back towards Craig. Her voice was a warble, somewhere between anger and tears.

'What's not true? You were all over him with your lettuce surprises.'

'Lettuce...?' She stopped and turned. 'OK, look, admittedly, I would not usually be in the habit of offering my food to just anyone–'

'Well, that's good to know. We wouldn't like to get the wrong idea about you.'

'Let me finish!' she snapped, lording over him, hands on her hips. 'I wouldn't *do anything* with the man. He's horrible!'

'So what were you doing?'

'To be perfectly honest, *I don't know.*'

Craig raised his eyebrows as if to suggest he knew that all along. She started walking away again.

'Oh well, Craig, you never were much good with the ladies.'

She looked back. 'It's not all about you.'

He shook his head sadly. 'Yep. In fact, it's never about me, is it? Nothing is ever about me.'

Sandra wiped her eyes and looked away.

'Turn off the sprinklers. You don't pull the wool over my eyes.'

She took a few steps up the path, still stumbling a little as she did so.

'Don't go now; you'll miss the end and I can assure you it's going to be a good one.'

She carried on walking, ignoring him.

'Vengeance is mine, and retribution.'

She stopped and looked back. 'What do you mean?'

'I mean what I mean. Someone's going to get what's coming to him. And soon.'

Sandra shook her head and carried on walking.

'Don't say I didn't tell you,' called Craig. 'This is one party you don't want to miss.'

In the kitchen, Nigel Pullman gave directions.

'Where's the quiche Mrs Peters brought? The quiche. The pie, you know. Where is it?'

Buhle scampered around the kitchen in a tense, skittish manner.

'It's frigging cold. Warm it up.'

Sandra was nearly at the gate when a voice spoke from the shadows.

'Going home?'

She jumped. 'Edmund? Is that you? What are you doing here?'

'I could ask you the same question.'

'I had to go in there,' she gestured to the Pullmans' with her head. 'I needed to find that file.'

'Did you?'

'I just wanted to get inside the house. I don't really know what my plan was.'

She looked at him beseechingly. He looked away; he still found her attractive.

'I can't help you,' he answered. 'I'm sorry.'

She shook her head and made her way through the gate, deflated.

'Vengeance is mine and retribution,' called Craig. 'Remember what I said. The party ain't over yet.'

'Your mother is all right by herself, Mrs Peters?' Edmund approached Janet, who was standing alone on the edge of the throng of people. She was lost in thought and jumped when Edmund spoke.

'Inspector. You gave me a fright. I... didn't recognise you at all.' She passed her glass from one hand to the other with a furtive nervousness. She tried a smile. 'Yes, Loveness is back home and will stay with her.'

'Back home from?'

'The hospital. Her granddaughter has been sick.' She took a hesitant sip of her glass of wine.

'Oh, the hospital? She's not been out managing the stall today?'

Janet went a little pale and then a little pink. 'The stall?' She laughed in a high-pitched, artificial manner.

'Yes, the stall that you finance. The stall that keeps you all going. Your income, in other words. Well, one source of it at least.'

The glass of wine wobbled precariously in her hand. Janet took another frantic sip.

'I don't know what you mean, Chief Inspector.'

'I think you do, Mrs Peters.'

Janet was silent.

'Mrs Pullman was not a nice lady. We all know that. She liked to have power over people. This power began disguised as helpfulness. She gave Dorcas a well-paid job, for example. But then she liked to find out things, weak spots let's call them and that's when her kindness mutated into something else, something quite cruel, quite vile. What did she know about you, Mrs Peters?'

Janet's face had slipped into a grim stare. 'I... I don't know what you're talking about. I... I must mingle. Good evening, Chief Inspector.'

Craig knocked back his drink, drawing his lips back in response to the unusual taste. He felt a flame of fire shoot through him. The world he saw was in bright, bold colours; everything seemed larger than life. People lunged towards him, holding out glasses, their faces big and wide and laughing; their smiles long and red, their teeth grinning. More and more people seemed to be arriving. The noise of

437

glasses clinked loudly, ice cubes tinkled. He backed away from the bar, working his way through the horde of people. Some turned, annoyed at being pushed past; a man said 'excuse me!' in a loud voice and a number glared at him as he stood on their feet.

'Watch it!' shouted a voice as Craig stumbled sideways, his drink sloshing over the side of the glass and onto someone's arm.

'He's drunk,' said another voice. 'Drunk as a skunk. That's what free booze does for you.'

Craig wanted to reply, but he was aware of a hand at his elbow and being led firmly out of the tent and into the garden behind the house. It was dark and safe.

'Edmund! What you doing here, buddy?' Craig fell against a statue of a small angel on the edge of a tall concrete flowerpot. Edmund caught him.

'You've had enough. Let me take you home.'

Craig laughed, a dark, bitter laugh. 'Enough? The party's only just beginning.'

'Come on. Give me your car keys? I'll take you home.'

'*You'll* take *me* home?' He laughed again and lifted the glass to his lips. 'The nectar of the gods – cheers!' Edmund snatched at it and took it away. He poured the contents into the flower pot.

'What a waste of a good coke,' Craig protested in mock horror. 'I don't know what you're worried about. I'm perfectly sober.'

Edmund looked sceptically at him.

'Seriously. I haven't had a drop. I just wanted to see what it is like for everyone else when I'm drunk. I can never remember.'

'What are you doing here? If Pullman sees you–'

'If Pullman sees me? Buddy, if Pullman sees *you*, you're dead. He burnt your house down. *Shit!* He only ransacked mine.' Craig spluttered into laughter.

Edmund grabbed Craig's arm. 'I'm a policeman–'

Craig started laughing. 'A policeman? Oh, yes, Chief

438

Inspector Dube, *C.I.D.*' He began laughing a little too hysterically for Edmund's liking. 'Thing is no one wants you around, Chief Inspector. You said it yourself, you're working on your own. One good cop amongst the bad. *My hero!* What you going to do, hey? How are you going to solve the mystery? Dun dun dun! Tune in next week to another exciting episode of... The Mystery of Murdered Marcia.'

Edmund let go of Craig's arm. In that moment, he saw that Craig was not talking from the depths of a drunken delusion. He was clear-headed, perfectly honest. His eyes stared straight into Edmund's.

'Look, Edmund, let's just call it quits, shall we? All this stalking around, high espionage, Famous Five stuff. If you won't do something about him, I will. Do you want to know why I've come here? I've come to grind his face into the mud. I hate him as I hated her. She deserved to die; she deserved worse than death. I hope she burns in hell for what she's done.'

Edmund chose his words carefully. 'And what exactly did she do?

'Those girls – exploiting them. They were so young, so naïve.'

'Which girls?'

'And him, making money out of the rubbish country that we live in.'

'What do you mean about her and the girls?'

Craig came up to Edmund's face. His hands were gesticulating wildly. 'All everybody wants is a normal life. A *normal* life. A job and a wife and a couple of kids. A dog and a cat and a nice little house.' Craig took Edmund by the shoulders and shook him. 'How did we get here, Edmund? How?'

But Edmund wasn't listening. Besides those of the kitchen, the passageway and the toilets, the lights in the house were all off. Mr Pullman had obviously wanted to keep everyone in one place and preferably outside. Looking towards the back of the house, Edmund was certain he saw the dull flash of a torch every now and then. It wasn't in Mrs Pullman's bedroom, but in a room on the other side of the corridor. He thought he heard the sound of something falling and breaking. Perhaps it was a drunken guest who had dropped a glass or someone had lost their way to the toilet, turned into the wrong room and knocked something over in the dark. He thought of Sandra. Was she back inside looking for her papers?

He touched Craig's arm. 'I'll be back,' he said. 'Wait a minute.'

'Go on, Magnum, P.I.'

'Please, Craig, wait for me.'

Craig shrugged.

'Please.'

'All right,' conceded Craig. 'I'll wait for you.'

Chapter Forty-four

1979

The sun had gone and the silver sky was darkening into twilight. Edmund was standing on the top step leading up to the front door, which was closed.

After his meeting with the headmaster, Mr MacDougal had been very quiet. Sad, even. He hadn't said much to Edmund, just leaned over to unlock the door for him, giving him a brief, wan smile as he did so. He didn't say a word: not a single comment. He didn't even hum a ditty as he usually did.

When they got to the house in Suburbs, Mr MacDougal had told him to wait in the car and there was something about the way he said it that made Edmund afraid. He had sat, twiddling his thumbs, wondering what it was the headmaster had said and what the verdict was, but after what seemed a long time of sitting and staring at nothing, he had got out and gone to look for Mr MacDougal.

Slowly, he pushed the handle down and eased it open. Although it was heavy, it opened easily without even the tiniest of squeaks. Beyond the hallway, a passage led off into the darkness of the house. Edmund could hear voices; abrupt, firm, male voices. He crept slowly along, one foot in front of the other, afraid of the dark, but glad that it kept him hidden.

On the left a gleam of light came through an open doorway; the voices came from inside. They were arguing. Edmund could hear a distinct note of protest in one voice as he tried to keep it calm. The other voice was harder, the speaker punching his words out like he was reinforcing each one with the jab of a pitchfork.

'There is a completely innocent explanation. This has been taken completely out of context and you know it.'

'Let's ask a jury to decide.'

'A jury?'

'If it comes to it.'

Edmund's chest contracted. Was this about him? About the money? Was he going to jail?

'I was trying to help the boy, that's all. He needs a father. This story won't stand up in court. You need *evidence*, man.'

Rupert, thought Edmund. Rupert and his dead father. He remembered Mr MacDougal helping him with his maths, buying him an ice-cream, taking him home, his arm round the boy's shoulder. There was a long pause. Edmund strained to hear anything. There was nothing except the faint clink of ice cubes in a glass.

'Times are changing, my friend. Soon the black man will be in power. He's not going to want your type. Your paternalism, your education, hmm? He's going to want to do things on his own. It's what you and your ilk don't get. You think you're treating them like equals? A pat on the head here and there. Well done, boy. Good work. Soon you'll be chief police officer like me. But is that what you want, what you really, really want, hey? No. You're a hypocrite. All you want is the "yes, baas", "thank you, baas", but you as sure as hell don't want him wearing your hat.'

'What do you mean? I don't know what you mean.'

'Control. You can't control them. The puppet has a mind of its own.'

There was another pause. Edmund heard a click, like the sound of a briefcase being opened and then the sound of paper being unfolded.

'This can't be true. I don't believe it.' Mr MacDougal's voice caught in his throat.

Edmund started. What had Rupert said? What did he say Mr MacDougal had done? What had happened? There must be a mistake. They could go to Rupert's house. Edmund knew where they lived. They could speak to his mother. It could all be sorted out.

Anger rose like a flame in Edmund's heart towards

Rupert. He knew something had changed that day. He remembered his face when he had returned to the car; the look of desolation as Edmund approached.

'There it is in black and white.'

'No...'

Edmund clenched his fists. His cheeks were hot with indignation. How dare Rupert do this? How dare he? Edmund would sort it out. He'd give him a real good punch in the face, knock him to the ground, get him in the stomach. He crept as close as he could to the doorway. The darkness was complete now. He felt some strange force pulling him closer and closer as though the air itself was alive with his rage.

'I don't believe the boy would say this. I don't.' The voice was little more than a whisper. 'Not after all I've done for him.'

Edmund stood on the top step leading up to the front door, his hand paused on the handle. A bead of sweat ran down his temple; his heart was beating fast. He turned frantically one way and then the other. It was the same place. A few different pot plants; a new gate; the driveway had been paved and a number of shrubs had been planted, but it was *the same place*. He checked again and again, until the plants and the drive and the flowerpots swung by in manic succession. His head dropped into his hands and he staggered down the steps and back down the path that led to the front garden.

It was Rupert's fault. What had he said? What did he think Mr MacDougal had done to him? He was sitting in the car, his small thin face staring out. Edmund saw the tears; small, slow rivulets making their way down his face. He wanted to take his friend's pain away; he wanted to open up his arms and hug him and hug him until all the longing and sadness oozed out and he could let his body go again. But instead he had just watched. Just stared at him through the glass of the window. He shoved his hands into his pockets and looked away. Mr MacDougal stood next to the car, his hands folded across his chest.

'He doesn't want to talk about it, Edmund. Today's the anniversary of his father's death. He's just a bit down in the dumps. Let's go and drop him at home.'

Edmund nodded and climbed in the back seat. Rupert continued to look out of the window until they got to his house.

'I'll see you at school,' said Edmund. 'Tomorrow.'

Rupert nodded and slid off the seat onto the ground. Mr MacDougal took him into the house, his hand lightly touching the boy's shoulder. Edmund watched Rupert's mother come to the gate, could see a short exchange between her and Mr MacDougal, how her face changed to one of concern, how she dropped down beside her son and gathered him in her arms, how Mr MacDougal ran his hand through the boy's hair and patted his back. And Edmund felt a rage he had never felt before; a thick, dark jealous rage and drove his nails into his palms.

How he hated Rupert then. Rupert who was short and fair, who had a silly parting and who was bad at maths and cried all the time.

Edmund stumbled out into the garden. The amount of people seemed to have multiplied, or was it just the voices?

Rupert who had a mother who loved him and a house and a car and a dog called Spot and a sister called Sally and a hero for a father, a father who was never going to come home from work again, walking in and taking off his hat and swinging his son in the air while his white teeth flashed in the light.

He felt drunk, although he hadn't drunk a drop of alcohol in his life, and with the feeling came confidence, a brazenness that poured through his body and pounded in his veins.

Rupert with his dead father he wore like a medal round his neck, wallowing in the sadness and loss.

He felt himself fill and swell and grow until he was very tall and wide, a great towering figure making his way through the tent.

'There it is in black and white.'

'Hey, you! What are you doing here? Get out! Get out now!'
    Pullman was upon him, so close their chests touched. Edmund could feel a spray of spit on his face. He wiped it off and looked Pullman in the eye.
    'I know what you did,' he said, holding his stare.

'I don't believe the boy would say this.'

Pullman laughed, a short nasty cackle. Then his face snapped back into a snarl. '*I said*, get out!'

'After all I've done for him.'

By now, the talking had stopped and everyone was looking at them. Edmund watched the bulbous features of the man redden and wobble. His mouth opened slowly and Edmund steadied himself for the blast. But it didn't happen. Instead, the large man turned purple, his eyes almost bursting from their sockets. He was gasping, holding his throat, loosening his tie. Then he fell forward, knocking Edmund to the side as he collapsed on the ground.

Rupert, a boy whom a policeman would rescue and take home to his mother, running his fingers through his hair, patting his back. *It's all right, Sonny. It's all right.*

There was a scream, a high-pitched woman's scream and Shantelle was upon Pullman, slapping his cheeks, her long red fingernails scratching his face.

Rupert who got to have and keep things, not just borrow them and give them back.

'Oh my God, oh my God,' she screamed. 'Get an ambulance someone!'

And so later, when he sat in the room that his father had taken him to and the man in the uniform asked him: 'Edmund, has Mr MacDougal ever touched you?' Edmund had thought of Rupert and Mr MacDougal. He thought of the ruler and the ice cream and the hand on Rupert's back. He thought of the butterfly he had chased across the garden. He had swiped this way and that, bringing the net down clumsily on clumps of grass and bushes while it fluttered on ahead. Now on the flowers, now on the rock, now on the wall, now hovering above the lawn. 'Catch them, Edmund. Catch them!' Yes, Mr MacDougal had put his hand on his back, around his shoulders, between his legs. Edmund had nodded compliantly as he did with all the other questions the policeman asked, wanting desperately to claim Mr MacDougal for his very own.

'Too late,' said Ndhlovu dropping down beside the body and feeling for a pulse, careful not to spill his full glass of wine as he did so. 'He's dead.'

Chapter Forty-five

Edmund felt himself sway forwards as though he were being sucked into a large hole. People swarmed in front of him, all trying to get to Mr Pullman. Someone was shouting, 'Everybody back, please. Everybody back.' Edmund stepped backwards as a tremor of faces and voices thronged forward. He felt a hand on his arm and suddenly he was being pulled through the crowd and out down the driveway and through the gate.

'Get out of here,' said Craig. 'Just get out. Get in my car and I'll give you a lift to wherever you want to go. You need to make yourself very scarce.'

Edmund closed his eyes, hoping that the world would slow down to a stop.

'Something is going on,' he managed at last, his breath shallow and painful. 'Something's not right.'

'I'll say! But it's not for us to sort out, Edmund. Not this time. Look,' he paused, hesitating to say his next words. 'We need to get out of here. Let's *go*!'

Edmund stopped. He stared at Craig. 'What have you done?'

'What do you mean what have *I* done? What are you suggesting? That I've killed Pullman?'

'Why are you here?'

'I could ask you the same question.'

'I'm a...'

'Yeah, right. You're a policeman and I'm Manning, P.I. Give it a break, Edmund. The party's over. I'm going home.'

'What was your plan?' Edmund's voice was harsh and accusing.

'My plan? Let's see. Electrocute his testicles. Slit his throat. Chop him into little pieces and then dissolve him in acid. I am a handyman after all. I've got all the gear.'

Edmund rolled his eyes in exasperation.

Craig dug his hands into his jacket pocket, rolled his head back and let out a harsh guttural sigh. 'Look, I wanted to challenge him, humiliate him, grind his fat face into a tray of mushroom vol-au-vents. That's all.'

'You didn't.'

'I know. I didn't have time. *Somebody* got there first.

'What was Pullman drinking?'

'Ambrosia.'

'What?'

'The nectar of the gods? Whisky. Imported doubles. Well, he won't be having many of those now.'

'Easy to slip something in.'

'Is it? The barman poured the drinks and I couldn't have got near him. Anyway, I would have made sure he suffered. Death is too good a punishment for that son of a bitch.'

'What about food? What did he eat?'

'Listen, I'm not the guy's right-hand man if you hadn't noticed. I'm sure he ate what everyone else did. How do you poison one guy and not everyone at a party?'

'He didn't,' shouted Edmund, suddenly. 'He didn't eat the same as everyone else did. He didn't eat wheat. Something to do with arthritis.'

'Really? I didn't know that.'

'Didn't you? Why were you in the kitchen earlier?'

'When?'

'When you were sitting out on the step. Talking about revenge and the wrath of God.'

'Revenge and the... oh, for the last time, will you get in the car? They are going to come for you. You *will be* arrested.'

'No,' declared Edmund, stopping short of the car. 'I need to know what he drank and ate this evening. Somebody's murdered him.'

'The guy was fat and unhealthy. He probably had a heart attack. You didn't see how many drinks he knocked back.'

'No,' said Edmund, quietly. 'I wasn't watching.'

'He had those lettuce surprises that Sandra made him.'

'Lettuce surprises?'

'And the new maid was warming something up for him in the kitchen. Something Mrs Peters bought him.'

Edmund was silent, as though waiting for the information to sink in. Then he said: 'Meet me next door in about ten minutes.'

'Next door?'

'With Sandra.'

'Sandra? How? She's left.'

'Phone her. Tell her I have what she wants. I have the papers.'

'Edmund–'

'I'm going to get Mrs Peters to join us, too. Please, Craig. Just do as I ask.'

Chapter Forty-six

Edmund cut the padlock on Roland's gate and unwound the chain, letting it fall to the ground. He tried to throw the gates open, but they were stiff with lack of use so he had to push them to their maximum capacity. The lounge lights, which were on as he walked up the drive, went off immediately he knocked on the door. Edmund knocked louder. Finally, he banged over and over again with the flat of his hand until he heard a voice shouting.

'I have a gun! And it's loaded. And... and I'm not afraid to use it.'

'It's me. Edmund Dube. Let me in, please.'

There was a short pause before he heard the locks being opened and the bolt slid back.

'I've had just about enough of this–'

Edmund pushed past him and strode down the passageway into the lounge. Before Roland could say anything, Edmund sat on his favourite chair.

'Pullman's dead.'

A nerve twitched in Roland's left eye. Otherwise, his face was expressionless.

'There's a good chance he was murdered.'

'Would you mind leaving?'

'Not until I know who did it.'

'Oh, *come on!* Please can we make an end to this Inspector Clouseau routine. I've had enough. Please would you leave my house at once.'

The knock on the door dissolved Roland's composure. He looked frantically at Edmund.

'Who on earth– ?' he began, but Edmund interrupted him.

'It's all right. I'm expecting them.'

'*You're expecting them?* Them who? The police?'

'Acquaintances.'

'Oh, that's nice, isn't it? Bring your friends over! Tea, anyone? A slice of cake perhaps?'

'Yes, please,' said Edmund. 'Tea would be great. I for one need a really strong cup. Two sugars please.'

Roland blew noisily out of his nose but went off to the kitchen anyway, mumbling and shaking his head. Edmund opened the front door to Craig. Behind him, standing rather gingerly on a step was Janet Peters. Behind her, looking particularly apprehensive, was Sandra.

'Mrs Peters,' nodded Edmund. 'Sandra.'

Janet looked rather nervously at him, her little bird eyes taking in the hallway and the rooms going off to the left and right. It was as though she were seeing if there were an easy way out should she get boxed in.

'Come in,' commanded Edmund with a great sweep of his arm. 'Come in and sit down.'

'Right,' said Janet, looking around and stepping over the threshold as though she were taking her life in her hands by doing so.

'Another tea,' said Edmund to Roland, just as he entered with a tray of cups and a teapot. 'I assume you're a tea drinker, Mrs Peters? Milk, no sugar? Am I right?'

She smiled uncertainly, clutching her handbag with both hands. 'Yes, that's right. Thank you.'

'Craig, Sandra, tea?'

'Green or jasmine for me, thank you,' said Sandra, sitting down.

'Tequila for me,' said Craig. 'Double.'

Roland ignored him.

'Oh, all right, I'll have tea. But just this once. It's not good for my health,' conceded Craig. 'Darjeeling if you have it.'

An awkward silence reigned whilst Roland busied himself in the kitchen. Edmund waited for the tea to brew before he poured it. He closed his eyes momentarily, imagining the tea leaves swirling in the dark depths of the teapot, watching them rise up and up, like tiny fireflies lifting into the night.

When Roland returned, Edmund poured the tea. He took

a sip and placed his cup on a side table. Roland immediately picked up his cup and put a coaster underneath. Edmund stood up and walked over to the fireplace where he stood for a few moments before turning to address the others. This was how they did it in books, those detectives who, having reached their 'Aha!' moment, gathered all the suspects into one room and proceeded to unravel the most ingenious of plots. He turned around with what he hoped was a look of deep gravity. He took a deep breath.

'Could you pass the sugar, please?' said Craig, taking his moment from him.

'It's not good for you. You do know that?' said Sandra who sat with her arms folded across her chest.

'We're all going to die one day. May as well die happy,' said Craig with a forced smile. 'Better than dying of oh, let's see, poisoned canapés. Gluten-free, of course.'

Sandra picked up the sugar bowl and placed it squarely in front of Craig who, a little surprised at the bluntness of this gesture, turned his attention back to Edmund. Edmund tried again. He cleared his throat.

'Look around the room, please.'

Everyone obeyed dutifully.

'Mrs Pullman had something on each of you here.'

'Not me!' said Craig, sitting up indignantly.

'Yes, you too, Mr Martin. I'll come to you just now.'

Craig reddened and sank back into his chair.

'Let's start with you, Mr Sherbourne.'

Roland's chin wobbled up and down as though it had a life entirely of its own.

'I need to know the truth,' Edmund said as he approached Roland Sherbourne, his voice calm and clear. 'The truth about Dorcas Hlabangana.'

Roland backed up against the wall of his sitting room. He was dressed in his black silk dressing gown and brown leather slippers. He felt like he had been caught in a state of undress and that made him feel even weaker than he usually did. Here he was, stripped to nothing, or nearly nothing, by this policeman who refused to go away and refused to stop asking questions.

Like a rabbit drawn to the ever-encroaching headlights of an oncoming car, Roland seemed unable to run, unable to resist the man who was a terrible nemesis to which the only response was surrender.

'Sit down,' he said, at last. 'Please just sit.' He couldn't stand the way the policeman walked round the room, like some sort of comic book avenger.

Edmund sat. Roland sat opposite him, his pasty face distorted with grief. His hands were folded on his lap and his head was lowered ever so slightly, his eyes fixed on some indeterminate place on the carpet, away from Edmund. He curled his feet under the chair: it was a mannerism he had adopted as a child when his mother was angry with him.

'What do you want to know exactly?' he asked as innocently as possible, hoping against hope that Edmund might ask something innocuous.

'Everything. I want to know how you met and what the nature of your relationship was; what she did for a living – not the maid bit. You know what I'm talking about. And what part she played in the life and death of Marcia Pullman.'

Roland's mouth opened and closed like a goldfish.

'Marcia...? No, no, you've got it all wrong. Dorcas had *nothing* to do with that at all.'

'Oh, yeah right?' interjected Craig. 'Lie number one.'

Edmund held up his hand to Craig, a gesture that asked him to refrain from comment. From Roland there was no response. The policeman sat quietly, staring at him.

Eventually, he asked, 'Why was Dorcas in the office of Top Notch the day Marcia died?'

'Cleaning...'

'Don't lie to me. She was involved in a prostitution racket run by Nigel Pullman.'

'Trust Edmund to go *straight* to the heart of things. Good old Chief Inspector Dube!' Craig slapped his thigh in mock awe of the policeman.

Roland had gone completely white.

'No... no... no, no.' Roland took a deep breath. His voice was barely audible. 'She... She would never do that. Never.'

'Could you please explain your relationship with her?'

Roland swallowed hard. 'It's not what you think.'

Craig sniggered. 'Famous last words.' Sandra dug him hard in the ribs with her elbow.

'We don't... we didn't...' Roland continued. 'It's not what you think. We used to watch old movies and talk. Sometimes... we would cuddle.'

Craig laughed again. This time, both Edmund and Sandra glared at him in response.

'Is that why she didn't stay the night?' continued Edmund. 'You'd sit and watch *The Wizard of Oz*?'.

'*The Wizard of* what?' spluttered Craig. Roland went red.

'And how long has this... *cuddling* been going on?' asked Craig. His voice was hard and unfeeling. Roland felt each word as a lash across his back.

'About a year, maybe.'

'About a year, *maybe*. And Mrs Pullman knew about it?'

Roland shook his head emphatically. 'Oh, no. Absolutely not.'

'You're lying.'

'I'm not.'

'Yes, you are. It's the way you say things that gives you away. You're too definite.'

Edmund hushed Craig with his hand again.

Roland played with the frayed cuff of his dressing gown. His face was one of tortured anguish. 'She found out about six months ago.'

'What did she do?' asked Edmund, trying to regain his position as the one in charge.

Roland bowed his head again.

'She wanted money. Pounds sterling.'

'Woah!' cried Craig. 'Talk about going for the jugular.'

'Otherwise?' asked Edmund.

'Otherwise she would tell everyone.'

'Everyone being?'

'Everyone she knew, everyone she met. *Book club* and her *bridge parties*. It didn't bother me too much; those people who know I exist probably think I am a bit odd anyway.'

'Really? It didn't bother you?'

'No... but Mother...'

'Your mother is dead.'

Roland rubbed his forehand with a hard, frantic movement. 'She – Marcia – said she'd make sure Dorcas would never have got a job anywhere else. She'd make sure she suffered, that she went to jail. At one time I imagined we could both live here. In this house. An island in the sea of controversy. But... it wouldn't have worked. She was a young girl; she needed a life. A life beyond me. So, I paid the money.'

'It must have been expensive.'

Roland shrugged. 'If you think I killed her, you're wrong. Look at me, I couldn't kill a fly.'

'It must have been tempting though. I mean, how long was it going to go on?'

'I... I don't know. I was hoping to make a plan. If... if I could just leave the house.'

'Leave the house?' echoed Craig.

'When did you last leave it?' asked Edmund, determined to keep control of the questioning.

'I'm not sure... a while ago. I'm afraid.'

'Afraid of what?'

'That I'll drown.'

'In the *garden*?' cried Craig.

'I've never heard of anyone doing that,' said Janet who had been quiet throughout. 'Especially not in Bulawayo. I mean we just don't get the rain.'

'Of course... I know... the logical argument.' Roland ran his hands through his hair so it stood on end. 'It sounds crazy, but I've always had a fear of water. I nearly drowned in a swimming pool as a child. I was about six and at school and the master was showing us how to dive. We all jumped in together, except that I didn't come up to the top. I felt

455

myself going down, down, down. Then suddenly I was pulled up by another boy, a great hulking brute of a boy called Roberts. He pulled me up – and then pushed me down again. He did it twice, as though I were a yo-yo. Eventually, he let me go and threw me out. I could hardly breathe. The worst thing was that no one else had noticed. The master, the other boys: they were just carrying on with the lesson – while I nearly died. My father didn't help matters. He would tease me. He was a very good swimmer.'

Edmund looked over at the framed medal on the wall. 'He had saved three men from drowning.'

'Exactly. But he lost his own leg in the process and it made him bitter. It made him a bully. He had to have a wooden leg. He couldn't swim properly again. He was never satisfied with anything, least of all me. My mother tried hard to make me *acceptable* to him, but I never was. Never.'

'I still don't see how this stops you going outside?' said Craig, narrowing his eyes.

'I was fine for a long time. Years. I didn't swim, of course, never have. I had a job, went to work every day. Then my mother died. My father had died some years previously and my mother had been unwell. She lived with me here. When she died, I developed this fear of going outside.'

'Because you'd drown?'

'Because I'd drown.'

Craig made a spluttering, snorting noise, but Sandra leaned forward with a look of concern on her face.

'I feel... I'm not sure of course... but I feel this has something to do with your relationship with your mother,' began Sandra.

'Here speaks your intuitive guide,' nodded Craig.

Embarrassed, Sandra curled back up in her chair, but not before adding: 'I think that's the key to your healing process.'

'His healing process!' scoffed Craig. 'Oh my giddy aunt. Do you make this stuff up or do you get it from a book?'

'Then how did you meet Dorcas?' pursued Edmund, determined to keep the questioning on track.

Roland stood up and went to the window. 'I'd watch her from here. So beautiful and graceful – even in her maid's outfit. Like a gazelle. She was so happy at first. She would hum a tune as she walked along; sometimes she would even sing. I used to wonder where she went on her afternoon off. Mentally, I would follow her, walk alongside her, sniffing the air, feeling a spring in my step, embracing every little moment of the day. One day, I called out of here, out of the window. I asked her if she could get me some groceries. I'd pay her, of course. She agreed.'

He turned to the policeman with a soppy smile on his face.

'And?'

'And the rest, as they say, is history.'

'Tell me about Top Notch.'

Roland's face, from whence the cloud of despair had cleared momentarily and brightened as he had spoken about Dorcas, darkened again. He sat back down in his chair.

'She didn't *want* to do it, Chief Inspector! Marcia made her!'

'Didn't want to do what?'

Roland hesitated, searching the faces in front of him for some sign of pity. 'She found people for Marcia – women who were hard up, but young and often attractive and had the ability to learn. They were trained to be carers and companions to the elderly. They would cook and clean and keep house and watch television with the old dears. Some of them even read to them. The old people were fine: they were more than well looked after. Their relatives in Australia or the UK or wherever they were, paid Marcia, who was supposed to pay the carers, which she did. After all her deductions it was an absolute pittance. She claimed back a large percentage and said it was to cover training expenses. *Training expenses!* What a load of rubbish. Inevitably, the girls' interest would wane and they'd often leave before they had paid off these so-called expenses. There were always plenty more willing to sign up. Dorcas hated it. She hated the lying. She hated seeing the girls so excited about finding a well-paid job and working so hard for nothing.'

Roland's words held a sense of finality that Edmund didn't buy into.

'That's it. That's why she didn't like Marcia and wanted to leave her employment?'

'Yes, absolutely.'

Edmund walked towards the window and then turned around. 'It's just not enough to get so upset about.'

'It *is*! I assure you–'

Edmund waved him away with his hand. 'Do you know anything about a lady called Shantelle who works at the agency?'

Roland shook his head. 'Never heard of her.'

'Really? Are you sure? You don't know anything about girls at the agency being offered work as prostitutes?'

Roland's breath was short and raspy. 'No, absolutely not. Ab-so-lute-ly not. No, no.'

'And what about the truck full of girls going to South Africa, hmm? What about them?'

'Girls? What truck?' Roland sat up now and stared at Edmund.

'Don't pretend you don't know about it. People trafficking it's called. Each one pays a thousand dollars – earned by being a *prostitute* – to get them across the border. They're crammed into the back of a removals lorry behind a false back and, if they're lucky, they get there without too much hassle. Some may die of suffocation or exhaustion, some may be raped along the way as part of the 'payment', but ultimately, for those who get there, it's worth it, isn't it? They'll easily get a job with the skills they've learnt.'

'Really!' cried Sandra. 'That's terrible.'

'Horrendous,' agreed Janet.

'No, Dorcas... no.' breathed Roland.

'Let's see, here are the facts,' said Edmund, enjoying the effect his words were having. 'The employment agency is run by Mrs Pullman. According to you, she made money out of the sweat of young girls. She promises jobs and training, but the girls themselves get very little out of it. Mrs Pullman's assistant, working with Mr Pullman, then promises greater things if the girls would like to go to South Africa. They are told they could be models and so they are forced to work as escorts, *prostitutes*, to raise the money for the trip to Johannesburg. They are loaded onto the back of a removals lorry and taken off. Whether they get to South Africa or not is anyone's guess.'

'Look here–' began Roland, but Edmund silenced him with a hand.

'But in order for operations to run well, the police had to be in the pay of Mr Pullman. I'm not talking about a couple of twenty-dollar bills here and there; this is high-level corruption. Do you understand?' Edmund stopped in front of Roland and glared down at him. Roland nodded.

'I was a mistake right from the beginning, you see? It should have been Khumalo who was called and it would've been had Pullman made the call to the police – but Dorcas did and so good old Chief Inspector Dube was called out. Yet that was all right, wasn't it, because people like me are stupid and incompetent. We're the laughing stock of Bulawayo. But then I start asking questions – too many questions – questions people don't like. I get too close to the truth and, let's face it, Mr Sherbourne, who likes the truth? Do you?'

Roland squirmed in his chair, swivelling away from Edmund who bent his head down until his face was in Roland's.

'Now I ask myself, if Mrs Pullman died under suspicious circumstances and Nigel Pullman is involved then it is obvious that he does not want the case investigated. Surely that is the reason he is not the most helpful of people. Don't you agree, Mr Sherbourne?'

Roland was silent.

'I said, don't you agree, Mr Sherbourne?' Edmund did not raise his voice, but a note of menace had entered it, which unnerved Roland even more. He nodded. Edmund straightened himself and took his notebook out of his pocket. He did not open it though.

'Tell me, Mr Sherbourne, what's your opinion of Mr Pullman?'

Roland swallowed hard. 'Thick.' His voice was a barely audible squeak. He cleared his throat and tried again. 'Typical of his kind – big bully beefy men.'

Craig laughed. 'Yep, I agree.'

'Really? You think he's thick?' asked Edmund. 'I think he's quite clever. Devious, don't you think?'

'Well, he tried to kill me. Didn't succeed, of course. Got more than he bargained for when he took me on.'

Roland's forehead folded into a frown.

Edmund ignored Craig as much as possible, but he found himself increasingly irritated with the number of interruptions he was experiencing. He ploughed on. 'Pullman is a man who is to all appearances respectable.' He raised his hands in quotation marks around the word respectable. 'He runs a safari business. He has a nice house and garden. His wife is queen of the book club. Nobody would ever think he deals in people trafficking, would they?'

'No,' conceded Roland, tilting his head slightly in agreement.

'So now, if he was to decide to murder his wife, let's face it, he would have done a better job. The last thing he wants is bad publicity and gossip. An accidental fall down stairs, gradual poisoning over a period of time; these are methods he may have used and no one would have been any the wiser – so why then stab her? It doesn't make sense.'

'So he could pin it on the gardener?'

'But *why?* Why? He doesn't need to pin it on anyone.'

'So...?'

'The fact is – Mrs Pullman wasn't murdered was she? She suffered kidney failure. To all intents and purposes, she died naturally. She was stabbed *after* she had died.'

'Really?' Roland asked, tilting his head in a question.

'Yes, really. And you would know that from talking to Dorcas,' continued Edmund. 'So why bother to stab her?'

Roland puckered his lips as he thought, shaking his head slightly from side to side. 'He didn't know she was dead?' he ventured. 'He thought perhaps she was asleep.'

Craig laughed.

Edmund shook his head. 'Unlikely.'

'Maybe he was going to kill her and found that she had died already?'

Edmund laughed. 'So he thought he would stab her anyway? No, no. It just doesn't make sense. You want to kill her, you find her dead. Why stab her? Why was it so important that her death look like a murder?' Edmund stopped in front of a watercolour picture of a windmill in the middle of a cornfield. He gently pushed the left-hand corner down a fraction and took a step back to see if it was now straight. 'Who could get inside the house?'

'A passing chancer? A maniac...'

'No, no, Mr Sherbourne. I'm talking *hatred*. To hate someone, you have to know them. Most murders are committed by someone the victim knew. Don't you of all people know the statistics? Let's look a little closer to home.'

'Malakai...'

'And Dorcas.'

'Dorcas? No...' Roland sat motionless, his pasty face distorted with fear and his head lowered ever so slightly.

'Now let's go back to our friend, Pullman. Let's assume that he *didn't* stab his wife. Let's assume he's just as surprised as everyone else. But,' Edmund drew in a deep breath and said very deliberately so that the impact of each word resounded in the room, 'what if he knows who stabbed her and why?'

Roland sat watching Edmund, wide-eyed. Despite the chill in the room, a little line of perspiration ran down his jaw from his temple. Even Craig was silent.

'What if he's waiting, biding his time...'

Roland ran a finger down his right temple, wiping away the trickle of sweat.

'Do you know what I think, Mr Sherbourne. Do you really want to know?'

Roland's nod was almost imperceptible.

'I don't think Mrs Pullman's death was natural at all.'

Roland swallowed hard. Another bead of sweat snaked its way down his cheek. 'Don't you?' he wheezed.

'No, not at all.' Edmund bent down and stared hard at Roland before pulling himself upright again and taking a step back. 'I think whoever stabbed Mrs Pullman may have been protecting someone else.'

Roland nodded in a slow, rhythmic fashion, as though he were being gradually hypnotised.

'How old are you, Mr Sherbourne?'

'Fifty-nine.'

'Fifty-nine? Edmund paced the room, with quick, restless energy, attempting to slow down in an effort to calm himself. 'Well, let's see. Say you're in prison for fifteen years? That means you'll be seventy-four when you come out. That's not bad – if you survive. You might still have a couple of years left. Still, you've had a good life, haven't you?'

'Fifteen years?' cried Craig, astounded.

'Fifteen years!' echoed Roland in disbelief. 'But–'

'But if you'd like a lighter sentence. Ten years, perhaps, you need to start talking.' Edmund sucked in his chest and crossed his arms.

'Ten years,' breathed Roland. He wet his lips and drew breath as though he were about to jump into a deep pool of water. 'Look, how much will it cost? I have money... I can pay. How much?'

'A bribe, Mr Sherbourne? Whatever would your father say?'

Roland's cheeks grew pink and his eyes filled with tears. 'I'm sorry, I should have stopped it. I should have stopped it a long time ago. I shouldn't have let her!'

'No, you shouldn't. But then, she wasn't your servant, was she?'

Roland gulped and looked away, his hand stroking his chin.

'What's this, Mr Sherbourne?' asked Edmund, pulling a piece of paper from his pocket. 'July 19th – 223 – violence in Nigeria; 29 – small plane crash in Andes; 1004 – died of starvation; 2,000,000 AIDS. Total 2,001,256.' Edmund held up his hands as though it were a complete conundrum.

Roland was almost beetroot by now. He looked away, shaking his head. 'Where did you find that?' His voice was a dry wheeze.

'Never mind where or how I got it. I want to know what it is. Come on, Mr Sherbourne. You can tell me.'

'It's a list, if you really want to know, of the number of people reported dead on that day.'

'All of them?'

'As reported by the BBC.'

'Oh, *the BBC*! Of course. A *reliable* news service. What's it for?'

'There are too many people in this world, Chief Inspector. Far too many.'

'So you tick them off as they die?' cried Craig. 'For Pete's sake, just as I thought you couldn't get any more weird.'

Roland rubbed his face in his hands and looked desperately up at Edmund. 'Thomas Malthus,' he said, anger creeping into his voice. 'The Malthusian theory of population is that we need famines and droughts and epidemics to keep the world's population down. Without them, we would be overrun with people.'

'I see,' said Edmund, staring down at the paper. 'Interesting. So this acts as some sort of reassurance for you to know that there is that little more space in the world for you because two million, one thousand, two hundred and fifty-six people have kindly given up their places.'

'Not just for me! For everyone!'

'For everyone else? Until *they* die. But never you, Mr Sherbourne, never you. A boat capsizes in Thailand. What a relief for you sitting here in Clark Road! You weren't on the boat. Chances are you'll never be on the boat. It's all right, isn't it, for other people to die? But what about you, Mr

Sherbourne, what about you? What do you give to this life that is so important?'

Roland was pale again now and his hands shook so violently he had to hold on to the arms of the chair.

'What was your plan?' Edmund's voice was low but angry.

'There was no...' began Roland, shaking his head.

'Tell me!' shouted Edmund, towering above the man. 'You're in the boat now, Mr Sherbourne, and it's sinking fast. Speak to me.'

'Dorcas wanted to leave, but Pullman wasn't having any of it.'

'Pullman? What about his wife? Surely it was her who wanted Dorcas to stay?'

Roland shrugged. 'She wasn't happy about it, but I think she would have gone along with it in the end. No, it was Pullman and Shantelle who protested and told Dorcas to shut up.'

'Because she knew too much.'

'Exactly.'

'Go on,' prompted Edmund, making a rolling motion with his forefinger.

'One day when she came over, she said she had an idea. She said that she had overheard Shantelle on the phone to Pullman: a truck of Pullman's carrying women in secret to South Africa had left the previous evening, but was held up at the border due to some computer problem. She said why didn't I phone the police and tell them.'

Roland stopped and looked meekly at Edmund. 'I didn't know what they had paid and how they had earned the money. I didn't know anything about the conditions.'

Edmund raised his eyebrows in disbelief.

'I was nervous, but she said no one would know if I used a different name, a pseudonym. Rather ironically, I chose Zeke, not only because it sounded Zimbabwean, but because it was the real name of the actor who played the lion in *The Wizard of Oz*. The lion wanted courage.'

Edmund nodded.

'I phoned the police. I spoke to the top man. I told him everything we knew, and then I put the phone down. We just wanted them to stop, that's all, and if them going to prison was the only way Dorcas would be allowed to go free, then I was prepared to make sure they did.'

'It was a daring plan. Dorcas was a clever woman.'

'To be honest, I was quite surprised at what she suggested. I loved Dorcas, but she was – at least she could be – very defeatist. She didn't often take control of her life. I was the nervous one, but she even instructed me what to say: she picked up the phone and pretended to be speaking. Told me what to say and what to leave out. She had rehearsed it well. I felt almost as if–'

'As if what?'

'Well, I know it sounds strange, but I almost felt someone had put her up to it. Told her what to do, what to say. It was the first – and only – time I wondered if she was faithful.'

Edmund watched Roland's face carefully. 'What happened after you made the call?'

'I'm not sure what happened. Dorcas didn't know either. Everything went very quiet. I read about some bodies being found in the bush near Beitbridge and that was it. Dorcas said everything stopped. She wasn't told why, but that side of the agency didn't appear to be operating any more.'

'But Dorcas was still not able to leave?'

Roland took a deep breath. 'She lay low for a long time. We didn't want any connection made with the tip-off. The agency wasn't doing very well, but Marcia couldn't see that it was largely her fault. She was continually in a bad mood, always complaining, always nasty. I think she would have let Dorcas go, but then she found out.'

'About you?'

Blushing, Roland chewed his lip. He tore off a sliver of skin and it bled.

'Yes, about me. And she loved it. It gave her a new lease on life; there would be no fun in letting Dorcas go.'

'So what did you do?'

'I didn't know *what to do*. Marcia was making all sorts of demands. She wanted money. She was out of control! Dorcas wanted to run away, but she didn't want to leave me and I couldn't go with her. One day when Dorcas came over, she seemed a lot happier than she had been, as though a cloud had lifted. I commented on it, but she refused to tell me any more. All she said was that she was going to sort things out. The next thing I heard, Malakai had been fired. Dorcas was upset – very upset. She said it was all her fault.'

'Do you know what she meant by that?'

Roland hesitated, the fingers of his right hand tapped his knee in a hard, manic rhythm.

'She had been stealing things,' he blurted out. He started crying in a noisy childish way. 'She stole food, she spoilt Marcia's tablecloth, she lied outrageously. Marcia went mad, absolutely mad. She phoned me. She made all sorts of accusations and threats. She told me we wouldn't get away that easily. I couldn't believe Dorcas when she said Marcia was right – she had done these things. Why on earth would you think that would be a good idea, I asked her.'

'And what did she say?'

Roland looked away, ashamed. 'She got angry. We had an argument and she stormed out. You white people, she said. I thought you had all the answers.'

'You white people? What did she mean by that?'

'I don't know, except that maybe she thought I had wanted her to do it.'

'Or that somebody else had told her to do it?' Edmund mused.

Roland looked up at Edmund, as though expecting some sort of understanding from the man. 'What were we to do? What were we to do?' he cried weakly, throwing up his hands in despair.

'You were in a difficult predicament. Dorcas was in a job she could never leave, not even through dishonesty and theft, and you were being blackmailed by a woman who wouldn't leave you alone, even if you had given up your relationship with Dorcas. Both of you were bound forever to Mrs Pullman unless she died.'

Suddenly Roland pitched forward slowly and slipped to the floor, staring up in horror as Edmund squared round on him. 'Did you or Dorcas kill Mrs Marcia Pullman?'

At that point, Roland burst into tears and bent over, his bony frame racked with sobs.

'No. We didn't! I promise you we didn't! It was someone else.'

'Did either of you stab her?'

'Absolutely not! Absolutely not.'

'Did you kill Mr Pullman in revenge for Dorcas' death?'

'No, no! I would like to have done, but I couldn't. I just couldn't. Please, please believe me. Please!' His was a small, pathetic voice from the heap on the floor.

Edmund stood over the snivelling mess of Roland Sherbourne and touched his shoulder gently, noticing how he flinched as he did so. 'I believe you,' he said gently, dropping down on his haunches and looking him in the eye. 'I do believe you.'

Chapter Forty-seven

'You believe that guy?' While Roland went out of the room to blow his nose, Craig took Edmund to a corner of the room, looking over his shoulder to see if anyone could hear him.

'Yes, I do.'

'You actually believe that story about him not leaving his house since his mother died?'

Edmund nodded.

Craig shook his head in disbelief.

'I don't get you. Here's a guy with motive and opportunity and you believe some crazy story of his that he'll drown in *the garden* if he goes outside.'

'Everyone has a crazy story.'

'And what's yours, Chief Inspector?'

Edmund turned back to the room where Roland had reappeared and sat hunched up in a chair.

'Back to business,' he said, walking away from Craig. 'Mr Martin, please, if you could return to your seat.'

'Certainly, Monsieur Poirot,' said Craig, talking loudly and affecting a French accent. 'Let us hear what ze little grey cells have to say. Was it Professor Plum in ze conservatory with ze lead piping or was it ze beautiful Miss Scarlet in ze kitchen with ze gluten free sesame seed bon bons?'

'You sound like some sort of Nazi,' smirked Sandra.

'No, no, not a Nazi, just a mass murderer, my dear. How did I do it? Vell, vell. Ze truth is a curious thing, n'est ce pas?'

Sandra rolled her eyes at Craig but refrained from answering him. Roland glared at him. Only Janet Peters seemed unaware of what he was saying. She was staring at Edmund as an accused criminal might stare at the judge about to pass sentence.

Before Craig had an opportunity to say anything more, Edmund launched himself back into his denouement.

'Mrs Peters. Now we come to you.'

'Ze most hardened of criminals,' began Craig, but a collective groan shut him up.

'All along I've wondered how you've survived, you and your mother? You work in a charity shop that doesn't pay a penny. Your lives are frugal, yes, but you survive still. In your own house. With a maid. It doesn't make sense. You had to have an income from elsewhere.'

'What you saw in the house just now... it's not what you think. I'm not a thief.'

'I know. I know that. But I know what you did.'

Janet swallowed hard and continued to stare at Edmund with a strange fascination.

'I know about the stall. Frankly, I couldn't care less. I'm not going to ask to see your tax records or anything like that. No, I'm more interested in your other work. The work you did for Mrs Pullman.'

Craig caught Edmund's eye; he was numb with shock. Surely, Janet Peters wasn't involved in a prostitution ring?

Janet shook her head, slowly. 'I see,' she said, her voice barely audible.

'You put people, elderly people, in touch with her, didn't you? What happened after the episode with Mrs Parkinson's picture? You took Marcia to see her. You genuinely wanted to help her, I am sure. But the old lady wasn't having any of it, was she, and she turned you both away? Was that when it started?'

Janet stared ahead, her face a distortion of embarrassed anguish. 'She said... Marcia said she felt Mrs Parkinson would have shown me her jewellery if she hadn't been there. She was confident and people like confidence; they feel safe with someone who knows their mind. But many older people can feel intimidated by it. I began to think. I worked in a place where people brought in all sorts of old things all day long. A lot of it is rubbish, of course, but other stuff... it was worth a try. If there was no one else there in the shop, I would

469

approach them. I'd tell them that I could get a better deal for their things. I was the soft touch, the go-between. They trusted me so they trusted her. Sometimes they went with it but not all the time. Often, they'd show me other things they wanted to sell. I saw it is a win-win situation. Marcia paid them better than the shop would have.'

'Did you go to their houses or did they come to you?'

'I went to them. Despite appearances, Chief Inspector, I have an eye for what will sell and what won't. Often, I'd go and inspect a necklace and leave with a writing desk or a set of chairs.'

'Ah, the furniture,' said Edmund. 'It goes out of the country?'

'Yes, antiques are in great demand in South Africa, and in the UK as well. Some of the old people here have some beautiful things. People would pay a fortune for them overseas. When I'd see something of interest, I'd call Marcia and tell her I had an S.P.'

'An S.P.?'

'Sales Possibility. Once I had seen the item for sale, she'd come in and make an offer.'

'There and then?'

'Most of the time. Sometimes I took a photo to show her before she would make a decision and some of them wanted a valuation first, especially where jewellery was concerned. She'd fly down to Joburg every couple of months and take them to a valuer if she thought they were really worth something.'

'What happened?'

'She paid me a commission. It was enough to live on, but there was something underhand about the whole thing and that's what I disliked. I wanted it to all be above board and honest. I wanted Mrs Riley to know and for the shop to receive some sort of commission perhaps. The money from the shop does go towards helping the elderly in general after all. I told Marcia, but she said it wouldn't be worth her time. She said the tax man would then want a cut and then no one would benefit.' She paused, fiddling again with the big gold button on her cardigan. 'Then... then I discovered she was giving false valuations. She was making a lot of money and only giving back to the owner a fraction of what the item was worth. Fifty dollars is a lot of money to some people. It broke my heart to see their faces so lit up and relieved that they could now live another month on tins of baked beans and corned beef, while Marcia Pullman made canapés and gave bridge parties.'

'You tried to stop?'

'Yes. I told her I didn't want any more to do with it. If she wanted to go that route, she could do it by herself.'

'And she wouldn't let you?'

Janet took a deep breath and sighed. 'No. She said I was in too deep, that she would tell Mrs Riley, that I would lose my job.'

'Would it matter? It wasn't a paid job?'

Janet smiled a sad tired smile. 'It's all I have, Chief Inspector. It's what gets me out of bed in the morning. It's what gives my life a purpose. Besides, I couldn't bear the shame. Making money out of the vulnerable is the lowest of the low.'

'Where were you on the afternoon of Marcia Pullman's death?'

'I told you, I was at home until four. My mother can vouch for me.'

'Can she? Your elderly mother confined to a wheelchair who sleeps every afternoon?'

'Yes! Look, she was asleep... but so was I.'

'You weren't out canvassing for any more S.P.s?'

'No. I'd done that in the morning. I was exhausted. Emotionally drained. I wanted out of the whole thing.'

'Who was the person Marcia Pullman was going to meet for lunch? S.P. was booked in for lunch in her diary.'

Janet cocked her head to the side in a question. 'I'm not sure. I wasn't aware of anyone meeting her. I usually arrange the appointments. None of my clients ever went to her house.'

'Had there been any trouble? Had anyone ever found out they had been shortchanged?'

Janet shook her head slowly. 'I don't think so. I don't know how they would have. Most of the people we dealt with are on their own with no family close by to investigate on their behalf. Most have no access to the Internet either and they probably wouldn't use it anyway. They belong to a different generation.'

'One with ethics,' sneered Roland.

Janet looked at him as though she had just noticed him. 'Please don't think I lack ethics because I don't. You don't know what it's like to be poor, really poor, to rely on your own maid for an income! I thought I was being clever. I thought I was helping some of these people.'

'And yet all you were is her slave. I hope you can sleep at night!'

Edmund turned and glared at Roland who scuttled back into himself again, pulling his dressing gown close and settled on glaring at Janet from the distance of his armchair.

'Anger,' began Edmund, feeling suddenly like a priest in a church, 'is a great burden to live with. Day after day. Anger, loss of livelihood and standard of living; loss of self.'

Janet, who was about to blow her nose, stopped as he spoke, her handkerchief covering her mouth instead. Her eyes darted left and right.

'You were a doctor's daughter, weren't you, and although your father was a frugal man in general, you were used to a certain way of life. Status, even? A lovely house – a lovely garden. It must have been hard to see that all go.'

Janet sat motionless, rather like a mouse that knows it's cornered and waits anxiously to see which way the cat's paw will swipe.

'On the afternoon of Mrs Pullman's death, you went to the market, didn't you? You were going to run the stall yourself.'

Edmund smacked his lips with what he hoped would suggest a worldly authority.

Craig looked across at Edmund, his face one of disbelief. He shook his head at him, but Edmund ignored him.

Janet stared. 'How... how do you know?'

'Bulawayo is a small town.'

Janet seemed to accept this rather generalised proclamation as proof enough. Her head hung low as she twisted her handkerchief in her hands.

'So, let me get this straight,' said Craig, confused. 'You mean to say you left your mother at home by herself? I thought she was elderly and in need of care?'

'She is, she is!' Janet moaned. 'She knew I was at the market. I had to do it. We couldn't miss a day of business. She sleeps most of the afternoon. She promised not to get up until I got back. She has a cell phone for emergencies that I don't think she has ever used, but at least it's there if needs be. It sounds terrible, horrendous, but what were we to do? My mother's medical bill took all our savings. I got into debt, massive debt. What could I do? People would stop and stare. Crazy old white lady running a stall, but I have nothing to lose. I am neither young nor attractive. I am not well off. All the things that prevent us from making ourselves a figure of fun did not apply to me.'

'But you didn't open up, did you?' Edmund's voice was soft and kind.

'I meant to, but I couldn't. I just couldn't,' cried Janet, looking up, her lined face flushed with red.

'Because you saw Dorcas at the market.'

'Yes. I don't think she even saw me, but I wasn't prepared to take the chance. I was afraid she would tell Marcia; maybe not deliberately, but somehow it might come up in conversation. Marcia would love it – I mean, she would have loved it. She would have let it drop that she knew. Or she would have held it over me. I didn't speak to Dorcas. I don't think she even saw me. But it made me think that if Dorcas was there, then Marcia was on her own. I wanted to talk to her. I needed to talk to her – alone!'

'About the missing ornaments?' asked Edmund.

'Ornaments?' chorused Roland and Craig.

Janet shook her head gently. 'You know everything, don't you? Everything.' She stared up at him, wide-eyed and pale.

'Let me tell you what I think I know,' said Edmund slowly. 'I think you took a chance. Yes, you were making a little money here and there and yes, it covered the bills. But you knew it wouldn't last. Even Bulawayo is not an infinite source of elderly people with antiques for sale.' He reached into his coat pocket and pulled out a little leather drawstring bag from which he took two small ornamental elephants, which he placed onto the coffee table in front of her.

'A navratna,' breathed Sandra, reaching forwards to pick up one of them. 'Do you know how valuable this is?'

'At last! They're safe,' breathed Janet, sinking back into the chair.

'Poor and struggling!' scoffed Roland. 'It's always the same with your sort. Pleading poverty on one hand and–'

'Quiet!' ordered Edmund, annoyed at being interrupted by Roland who wasn't quite such a snivelling worm now it wasn't him being questioned. 'You can hardly talk.'

'You had some things of value,' persisted Edmund. 'Perhaps these are your mother's? Perhaps she does not even know they are missing? Everything was going well. Marcia was to all intents and purposes helping people: she was taking the time to go to the valuer whenever she went to Joburg; people were being paid out for their belongings and getting far more than the shop would have paid them. You felt you were doing some good. You gave these to Marcia and asked her to take them to South Africa on her next trip and sell them on your behalf.'

Janet's eyes filled with tears as she twiddled the gold button on her cardigan. She shook her head. 'You're not quite right. In October last year, my mum had a bad fall out of the bath. She broke her hip and had to stay in hospital for six weeks.' She paused for a moment. 'About six months previously, I stopped paying our medical aid. I couldn't keep up the payments, but I didn't tell Mum. I made sure she went to a private hospital; it took all our savings. Everything we had. I started to sell things.'

Edmund nodded.

474

'It was Marcia's dishonesty that gave her away. There are not many people here in Bulawayo who could have afforded to buy the elephants, not at their true value and I wasn't going to sell them to Marcia. They would need to be sold elsewhere, but I also needed to know how much to ask for. When I showed them to her, I could see she was interested in them. She offered to pay for the valuation herself; she said she wanted to help me out. But when she returned from Joburg she said she had sold them on my behalf. I was devastated, bereft, especially as the money she gave me was next to nothing. It was an insult. She said they were nothing special, that we had it all wrong. I didn't believe her. I knew the elephants were worth much, much more than she said they were. Moreover, she couldn't provide any proper paperwork, not even a receipt. It was then that I realised that if she had lied to me, she had probably lied to everyone.'

A change came over Janet then, a wave of hardness which set into all the crevices of her face: eyes and mouth and all the lines between. She raised her chin and looked, completely dry-eyed, at Edmund.

'She made fun of me, she mocked me and everything I did and said. I was just a joke, a poor, lonely sad joke. And what did I do about it? What did I do? Nothing! I was nice. I thought nice would work. I was always at her beck and call. Janet do this, Janet do that. Well, nice doesn't work. Nice has no power and no voice. Nice made me a slave! The elephants belonged to my father. I didn't *want* to sell them. I would *never* have sold them. But I was desperate. *Desperate!*'

They all stared at her.

'And your mother, did she know what had happened?' continued Edmund.

'Eventually, I had to tell her. She knew something was wrong and I couldn't keep it from her anymore.'

'How did she take the news?'

'She was upset, naturally, although she was never angry with me. She blamed herself for falling out of the bath. She felt guilty that she had brought this all on.'

'She has a good heart.'

'My mother, Chief Inspector, is the dearest person to me. We had always been close and when my marriage fell apart she took me in with open arms. She was always so strong, she always knew what to do, but this time – after her fall – she became very depressed and withdrawn. I saw in her a look I had seen in the eyes of so many elderly people. It was a longing. A longing to go. A feeling that life has run its course.'

Janet stopped as her voice wavered. Her hand moved to her scarf, which she loosened as though it were a noose grown tight.

'It's the spirit, you see. It's a knowing. And they don't fight it. They don't fight it like you and I would fight for *our* lives.' She turned to him, her eyes bright with tears. 'It's like an old dog that knows its time is up and finds a corner in which to curl up and go to sleep. The same is true of people; they look for that corner. They want to go back to some place they really loved; perhaps the place from where they began life. One old lady I met wanted to go back to England, a place she had left in 1948. She was saving for a place to die peacefully. And I couldn't... I wouldn't let Mum do that.'

A tear rolled down Janet's cheek that she patted dry with her handkerchief before pushing it up her cardigan sleeve.

'One day she told me she wanted to go to Shangani. Where we used to live. I tried to put it off simply because we couldn't afford it, although I didn't tell her that. Then one morning at breakfast she put some money down on the table and said: 'Please, take me home.' We went to the old house. I had hoped she would feel some sort of joy, that she would find something to live for. But it was so dilapidated, it was awful. Everything was rusty and broken. And filthy. Home to four families who lived in absolute squalor. There was no sign of the garden she had planted; it was just a big bare brown patch. But we had made the journey and I was desperate to find something good in the experience. We drove down a dusty road and found a place to stop. She sat in the car, with the door open, and we had a picnic lunch. She asked me to find some things for her. Flowers and roots and leaves. She was always interested in natural remedies and she knew what would help with pain. When I came back she was sitting with her eyes closed and she had a lovely smile on her face and... and I thought she had died and a part of me wished she had. No more pain, no more suffering. Peace.'

'Did the trip help?'

'Yes, yes it did. She came back to life, got that twinkle in her eye again, but she won't live forever. I know that and I accept that, just as I accept that one day I will be on my own.'

They sat in silence for a moment or two until Janet said: 'All that money. She had all that money and all the time she wanted more. She was protected, looked after, untouchable.'

Edmund walked to the door and then turned and faced Janet.

'Janet Peters, did you stab Marcia Pullman?'

There was a silence whilst Janet stared into the distance. The others in the room all leaned in a little closer.

'I envy you, Chief Inspector.'

'Me? Why?'

'Because you're black. You belong to a community, a race. Living here, being white is such a burden. We've been cut adrift from wherever we came from, amputated like a gangrenous leg that no longer works. We have no roots, no base. Everything we aspire to is a lie. Our lives are one long farce, one long struggle to keep up appearances. We don't *do* charity, not for our own people. Oh, yes, I know what you're thinking. How can I say that when I work in a charity shop? Well, there the irony! It's all right to help the elderly; the people living in one room in a home somewhere who have no one else to look after them. These we refer to as *our precious senior citizens*. But my mother and I? Oh, no. Enid and Janet have a home, they have a car, they have a maid. They have things they could sell. *They* don't count. White people here *don't like* poor whites. We sit quietly and watch as someone struggles to keep their head above water. Bob...

477

bob... bob. Then we watch as they silently slip beneath the waves, never once throwing a lifeline. Down... down... down. Then we laugh.'

She looked around at the small group gathered around her and then down at her hands. Her voice was quiet but clear as she spoke.

'I came round early wanting to talk to her. The gate was unlocked. It is if she is at home. I knocked on the door, but no one answered. Her car was there, but I couldn't find her. I looked everywhere she could possibly be in the garden and then I thought she must be out. I tried the front door and it was open. I... thought I'd look in her bedroom for the ornaments. I went in and there she was. At first I thought she was asleep, but then I realised she was dead. She looked so normal except for a white sheen on her face and her eyes – they were wide open with this terrifying wild, startled look in them. My first instinct was to call for an ambulance or the police. But then I stopped. I realised that here was my opportunity to look for the ornaments.'

'You went through the cupboards?'

'Yes. I was stupid really, I left fingerprints everywhere. I went through the drawers and the wardrobe. There was nothing. I looked down at her, lying there and suddenly I felt so angry. *So angry!* And then I thought how vulnerable she was. Death was the only thing that made her vulnerable. And me, so powerful. When they don't eat, the gods lie down breathless and sleep. They lose all their power.'

'She wasn't a god.'

Janet gave a rueful laugh. 'Wasn't she? The gods don't have blood, not like us mere mortals. She didn't bleed.'

'You stabbed her.'

'Yes. Of all things, I had a letter opener in my bag. I had just got it that morning from an elderly lady in Sauerstown. I took it out and I stabbed her. So stupid and yet it's the best thing I ever did in my entire life. Is that sad? Maybe.' She looked around at all the faces watching her, a small hunched figure, her tired eyes drooping.

'I thought I was being quite clever coming back later and pretending to find the body. I wouldn't have thought anyone would've guessed. I knew where Marcia hung the keys. I locked the door so that I *would have* to ask Dorcas for her key and if anyone asked she'd say I only went in when she gave it to me. I put the key back when I returned later.'

She paused for a long time and then turned to Edmund with what could almost be termed a smile. 'I suppose you have to take me away soon. Don't tell my mother, will you? Tell her something else. Speeding, perhaps? Drunk driving?' She gave a high-pitched squeal and immediately put her hand over her mouth. 'Could you give me some time? Let me finish my tea? Just let me pretend a little longer?'

Edmund smiled sadly at her and nodded.

'Let me get you another cup,' Edmund said, going towards the door. Turning back, his heart was moved to see Janet slumped in the chair, her handbag on her lap, her feet turned inwards. Her dejection overwhelmed him and he walked back to her, dropped to his knees and took her hand in his.

'It's going to be all right, Mrs Peters. It is. Please don't worry about anything.'

Chapter Forty-eight

'Get Mrs Peters another cup of tea,' Edmund commanded Roland. 'This one has gone cold.'

Roland obeyed, if not particularly willingly.

'What about Mr Pullman? Do you know anything about him?'

Janet shook her head. 'I didn't know any of what you just said about him. I hadn't a clue. He was hardly the brow-beaten husband and I don't think it would have been long before he had remarried. That seems to be the way life goes. The bullies win every time.'

'A bully? Yet you made him something to eat because you knew he couldn't eat the snacks.'

Janet pulled in a corner of her mouth. 'I suppose it gave me a very petty feeling of one-upmanship that this big confident man was reliant on me. Me, who could never do anything right.'

While Janet took a sip of her tea, Edmund turned to look out of the window at the house next door in the gathering darkness. Sandra came up to him and whispered softly.

'Have you got it? The file? Please.'

Edmund reached inside his jacket pocket and took out some folded papers. He made as though he were about to give them to her and then withdrew them. 'How did you know who your father was? Who told you?'

Sandra threw back her head and glared at Edmund. 'It was in the letter my mother left me. My real mother, that is.'

'Why do you think she would do that? She doesn't leave her own name, but she leaves the name of your father?'

Sandra shrugged. 'I don't know.'

'Don't you? Don't you think she hoped you'd go and find him? Embarrass him, maybe. Let me make an educated guess and say he was married?'

Another shrug. 'Maybe.'

'And did you track him down?'

Sandra turned away, annoyed. 'Yes, I did. At least not him, but his wife.'

'He had died?'

'Yes. He was much older than my mother.'

'And how did this woman take the news?'

'All right, considering. She wasn't particularly surprised let's say.'

'But she didn't know who your mother was?'

'No, no, she didn't.'

Edmund looked down at the papers in his hands, unfolding them and smoothing them down. He handed them to her. 'Good luck with the rest of your life,' he said and then turned back to looking out of the window.

'Where did you get them?' she asked.

'From the house this evening.'

There was a pause as she considered saying something and decided against it. 'Thank you,' she said, eventually. 'Thank you very much.' She walked slowly back to the chair she'd been sitting on, holding the papers close to her chest.

Now Craig, who had been hovering nearby, watching the exchange, stood next to Edmund.

'A bit of a turn up for the books. Mrs Peters, I mean. Well done.'

Edmund remained silent, looking out into the dark.

'Who would've thought it? Always the dark horses, isn't it?' He gave an uncertain laugh, unnerved by Edmund's silence. 'And what about Pullman? She must have bumped him off as well. I've heard murder gets easier the more people you kill.'

'Mrs Peters did not murder anyone.'

'Yes, but... well, I mean stabbing her like that. It's a start, isn't it?'

'Why didn't you tell me you knew Mrs Pullman?'

Craig moved restlessly, thought a moment and then said: 'Was it important?'

Edmund lowered his head in exasperation. He took a deep breath and looked up again.

'You told me you had only seen her once, the morning of her murder, in the office.'

Craig was silent.

'I need the truth.'

'The truth!' exclaimed Craig. 'The truth! That's rich coming from you.'

Edmund didn't move or say a word.

Craig turned to him, exasperated. 'What's going on, hey? I'm breaking into houses and watching buildings and risking *my life*. Where are you, hey? Where are you? And while I'm asking questions, *who* are you exactly? Just *who the hell are you*, roaming around like Sherlock Holmes on the track of some great criminal mind who turns out to be a poor soul who, in my mind, had every right to do what she did? Well done, full marks to you for working it all out, but it isn't even a proper murder.'

'I asked you for the truth,' demanded Edmund, battling to keep his temper. His mouth set into a hard line.

'The truth is that I went to the police station. I spoke to some big nob called Khumalo. Creepy guy, but well, I think he knows his stuff.'

Edmund didn't move an inch. Nor did he say anything.

'Do you know what he told me, this Khumalo dude? He told me a strange story. Let's see, how did it go now? Oh, I remember. You're not a Chief Inspector.'

Roland Sherbourne, who had heard the beginning of the argument, moved closer to the pair.

'And not only are you not a Chief Inspector, you're not a real policeman either.' Craig was aware of the blunt cruelty of his words, but he had no intention of letting up. He turned to the others and with an exaggerated sweep of his arm, declared: 'The show's over, everyone. You may all go home. Yes, even you, Mrs Peters. We won't tell anyone if you don't.'

'*What?*' The tips of Roland's ears went red.

'But–' began Janet.

'Listen to me carefully. This – man – is – not – a – real – policeman. Go home!'

'Tell me when you first knew Mrs Pullman,' growled Edmund, who had gone an ashen grey.

'It seems you're the office typist.'

'Tell me!'

'Employed out of charity to keep the filing up to date.'

'I said tell me!' Edmund's voice was so loud that Craig lost his composure and took a step backwards. Roland visibly cowered. No one said a word.

'I need to go back to the house,' Edmund said, turning on his heel. Exasperated, Craig kicked the wall.

'My mother died when I was six. She drove a car off a straight road. Everyone wondered how it happened.'

Edmund stood completely still, not moving an inch.

'A completely straight road in broad daylight.' An angry wobble entered his voice. 'Who does that?'

Edmund turned to face Craig.

'She had been put in a home, some nice little cosy place where they keep all the crazies and lunatics and alcoholics and anyone else who feels the truth of this broken world too keenly. Where they shut them away from the world that has given them so much pain, so much grief. Where they give them pills so they won't feel, they won't hurt, they won't long for what they no longer have.' As he spoke, little flecks of spittle flew out of his mouth, like fireworks illuminating his words. 'All she wanted was *to feel*, to feel joy again, not to be removed from it. Not to carry this large, heavy, *numb* burden around with her everywhere.' Craig's eyes filled with tears. 'Not to be punished. She wanted *me*. She didn't want to lose me as well. *Not me as well.*' Suddenly, he wanted his mother as he had never wanted her before. The wall that had earlier given way inside of him, now allowed a tsunami of emotion to sweep out of him. He was crying again, running his hands over his face in a vain attempt to recover his angry composure. Roland looked at his feet, embarrassed, but Sandra's face softened.

483

Craig was aware of a hand on his shoulder and someone helping him to sit in a chair. When his tears subsided, he blew his nose noisily and rolled his head back. When he opened his eyes, Edmund was sitting beside him. He offered Craig an extra handkerchief. They sat in silence for a while, Craig wiping his face and Edmund looking down at his hands.

'Tell me about your mother,' Edmund said eventually. 'What happened?'

'Edmund, I don't know who you are... I don't know how I got caught up in this mess.'

'Tell me about your mother.'

A part of Craig wanted to stand up and laugh in Edmund's face. The man was mad, a lunatic who believed he was an important police officer. Another part of him wanted to talk and be listened to. For someone to hear his crazy story.

'She gave up a baby for adoption when she was sixteen. Her father would have disowned her had he known she was pregnant, but she told her mother who arranged for her to go away to someone she knew in Bulawayo and do a secretarial course. She lived in Mutare, the other end of the country, far enough away for her not to come back for a while. She did the course, but she also gave birth to a baby. It was a little girl; she called her Callie. At the last minute, she didn't want to give her up, but the woman she was staying with persuaded her it was the best thing for all.'

'Was it?'

'She gained some qualifications, she got a job, she met my father and got married. She had two children. Some would say it was the best decision.'

'But?'

'When my sister was born, it was as though a ghost had reappeared. Here was her daughter she had given up. Here was her chance to look after her again, to get back all that lost time. She even gave her the same name. Callie. She adored her, she spent every minute of every day with her. Yes, her life was complete.'

'And then?'

Craig paused. 'Callie died when she was three.'

'I'm sorry.'

'It all happened so quickly. We had been at the pool at a sports' club. While my dad played snooker, we went to the bar with Mom to buy some crisps, but when we got there she discovered she didn't have her purse so she told us to wait while she went to the car to get it. She stopped on the way to talk to somebody and for us it seemed like she had been gone a long time. I said I'd go and find her, and when I got back with Mom, Callie had gone. She must have wandered off back to the pool. It was my dad who found her.'

The two sat in silence for a while. Eventually, Edmund spoke.

'It was Marcia who had persuaded your mother to give up her first child?'

Craig nodded. 'Yes. When my dad decided to move into a nursing home, I helped him sort out the house. He had never dealt with anything, never thrown anything away, but now he suddenly decided that he didn't want any of it any more. He kept giving me stuff – books, photographs, lots of bits of chipped crockery. I didn't want any of it. I didn't want any of the past. We gave a lot of it away, but in one of the boxes I found letters. Letters from my mother to her unborn child. She didn't want to give her up. She was prepared to withstand her father's anger and her mother's shame. She was prepared to be alone, to fight for both of them. But then she gave up. She said that Marcia had said she was selfish, she wasn't thinking of the child, of her parents. All she was thinking of was herself. "You're unfit to be a mother," is what Marcia told her. "You wouldn't stand a chance."'

Craig paused, wincing for his eye still hurt.

'And so when Callie 'reappeared' so to speak, she felt as though she was bound to lose her. That she didn't deserve her.'

'You came to Bulawayo to find Marcia?'

'I'm not a stalker or a psychotic weirdo or anything like that. I'd had enough of Harare, enough of not getting anywhere. I don't know what I was looking for. Whatever it was, I never found it. I suppose I had some morbid fascination with finding out who Marcia was. I did a bit of detective work and found out that she owned the agency, Top Notch, or whatever it is called. I did some work there, but she didn't come in. Shantelle ran the show. I went to her house and said I was looking for maintenance work. She happened to have a few jobs for me to do. I considered wiring the lights wrongly in her room so she might get a judder or two when she switched them on. But really, what was I going to do? Confront her? No.'

'She found you going through her things?'

Craig looked surprised.

'Dorcas told me. You recognised each other from the time you came to the house and from Shantelle's dating parties. You made sure to tell me that you'd seen her at a party in case she claimed to have seen you at the house.'

'Good detective work.'

'I realise now why you said you hated Marcia even though it was Shantelle who had arranged your date.'

Craig laughed, a small, sad half-laugh. 'It was her shoes that riled me most of all. Those horrible black shoes. Like the witch's in *The Wizard of Oz*. She disappeared just as quickly as well. Respectable shoes. But she was less than respectable.' He let out a deep sigh. 'It's been a strange couple of weeks; it's like we're all connected. It really is a small world, isn't it?'

'Connections or vibrations?' Edmund posed the question to himself more than Craig. 'A butterfly flaps its wings in Brazil and a tornado hits Bulawayo.'

'I don't follow you,' said Craig, looking sideways at Edmund with great perplexity.

'Now would the same happen if a butterfly had flapped its wings in 1975?'

'You've *completely* lost me now.'

'The chaos theory. A butterfly flapping its wings in Brazil could cause a tornado in Bulawayo. That's chaos over distance, but what about chaos over time.'

'You mean?'

'I mean, a man smiling at a woman in 1975 causes the death of another woman forty years later.'

'I see... I think.'

'Every moment is the accumulation of a lifetime of moments.'

Craig nodded slowly. 'Right...'

'You called the whisky the nectar of the gods? Why did you do that?'

'*Imported* whisky. Not just any whisky. The drink of the gods – that's what it is in Zimbabwe where we can't afford the good stuff. At least mere mortals can't, that's for sure – and the immortals keep it to themselves and so it is that they confer longevity upon their businesses and their homes and their families. I suppose it's been that way for centuries in every culture. Do you know that in ancient Egypt, commoners weren't even allowed to *pick* mushrooms; they were the complete preserve of the pharaohs.'

Edmund did not appear to be listening.

'And in Ancient Greece, they told everyone not to eat anything red. Not even strawberries or lobster. They said all red food was poisonous. And do you know why?'

'Hmm?' Edmund was staring at the ground, his lips moving silently as though he was trying to work out a difficult sum.

'Because the mushrooms were red and they were afraid of them being picked by the average person. We wouldn't want them to achieve immortality now, would we? Life has never been fair, has it?'

As though something of Craig's wonderings was beginning to seep into Edmund's bubble of self-absorption, he turned to Craig with sudden interest.

'Sorry. What is the connection there? Between the mushrooms and immortality?'

'Ambrosia – the nectar of the gods – was made from mushrooms. Small red magic mushrooms that enabled whoever ate them to have visions and hallucinogenic dreams. Who would want to share those with the common man? Rather use them to make yourself appear magic.'

'On the day she died, Mrs Pullman was upset as she had run out of mushrooms for book club. Dorcas said they were special mushrooms – they were expensive – and she had used them the previous week for food for her bridge club.'

'Yeeaah. What's your point?'

Edmund rolled his head from side to side. 'I don't know. I just don't know. If the mushrooms were poisonous, more people would have died or at least been ill. And anyway, the day Mrs Pullman died, she was told the mushrooms had finished.'

'So she went and bought them somewhere else and they were dodgy and she died.'

'And yet we haven't heard of anyone else dying? If she bought mushrooms from someone selling them, then surely other people would be affected?'

'Unless she's the only one who bought them...' began Craig.

'– or the only one offered them,' cried Edmund, leaping up. 'Someone knew she was looking for mushrooms.'

'But I thought she died of kidney failure?'

Edmund ignored Craig's question. 'Where did you get that information about mushrooms and ambrosia?'

'An old lady I did some work for. An interesting old duck – I could have spoken to her all day long – and drunk tea. Unfortunately, the work she asked me to do was a two-minute job – and even then she didn't pay me. Well, she tried but I told her to forget it, it wasn't worth it. She seemed to want to give me advice – told me to cut my hair and spruce myself up a bit. All very well if you have the cash.'

'Can you remember her name?'

'Funny name. Greek, I think. Amoris. Lives about a road up from here. In a wheelchair, husband's long dead. Quite sad.'

'I need your car.'

'Not again! This is ridiculous. Where are we going to this time?'

'You stay here. Look after Mrs Peters. She is not fit to go anywhere at the moment.'

'Mrs Peters? Why on earth should I stay with her?'

'Because I need you to. Don't let her go home.'

'Let me come with.'

'No. No. Absolutely not. I know what I'm doing. Please.'

Craig shook his head in surrender and handed him the car keys. 'Take care,' he said, giving Edmund a sudden awkward hug. 'We want you back.'

Chapter Forty-nine

1979

It is hot, sticky hot. That hot before the first rains of the season when sweat sticks to you like a second skin and each day unfolds a menacing blue migraine and the thought of rain clouds is beyond imagining. When the short-lived cool of the dawn burns off the tarmac and evaporates off roofs and pathways and even the shade is a glare that brings little relief to those who seek its solace.

Mrs MacDougal usually spends the early afternoon sleeping; Edmund hears the creak of her bed while he sits under the jacaranda and waits for the afternoon to pass. But today, she stands in the garden, on the paving where they sometimes take chairs and poetry and read aloud after lunch. She is standing on a small stepladder which she moves round with unusual speed, pruning a miniature climbing rose that covers the wall right round to the sitting room, where their little white heads can sometimes be seen bobbing happily at the window.

Her pride and joy.

'It's taken us years,' she says. 'Years to get this right.' Dead heads snap and fall in a pile at her feet.

'Years, years, years,' she says, each word accompanied by a firm snip. Edmund sits on a rock. He doesn't know why he doesn't sit on the chair, but today there is no poetry book, no teapot with the funny knitted cover. Today there is nothing. He detects a certain anger in Mrs MacDougal's movements. It is his fault, he knows. They think he has stolen the money.

'Anyway,' she says, stopping suddenly with a sigh. 'It'll all be here long after I'm dead and gone.'

Edmund pushes his big toe in a hole in the rock then tries

to stand up and falls over. He looks at Mrs MacDougal, but she isn't laughing. It is then that he sees them, the pile of white heads lying with the brown dead ones. They are whole, soft still, perfect. He can smell the blossom; imagine their warm, faintly beating hearts. Mrs MacDougal is crying. Her face is distorted into a grimace of agony as she swipes blindly at her wet face. The secateurs fall to the ground, like a drunken metal angel, sending a shiver of white rose petals into the air.

'Edmund! Oh, Edmund!' she gasps. 'How could you?'

The house was quiet as Edmund entered. Quiet and dark and he bumped into a small table in the passageway. The gate had been easy to jump over and the key easily accessible under the back door mat. He could see light under the door of a room at the end of the corridor and it was this he approached with growing trepidation. He opened the door slowly and stepped back. The room was dark except for the wavering light of two candles, one of which was nearly out. A figure in the corner of the room moved and looked round at him.

'Chief Inspector, I thought you'd never come.'

'Mrs Whitstable...' He stared hard at her before turning slowly and closing the door behind him. 'You know.'

'Yes, of course I do. Always have.'

He walked slowly towards her and sank into a chair. He sat quietly for a few minutes, lost in thought, his hands neatly splayed on the arms of the chair. Then he sat forwards and reached into his coat. He took the drawstring bag from his pocket and handed it to her.

She took the elephants out, marvelling at their existence as though seeing them for the first time.

'Oh, thank you! Thank you! They belonged to my husband. It looks like they belong together, but they are from two completely different sources.' She held the white one up to the light as though inspecting it for damage. 'This ivory ele belonged to my father. He spent two years in India at the beginning of the last century. It was given to him by a very dear friend who was later killed in the First World War.' She put it back in the bag and took the other elephant out, holding it like a pet hamster in her hands. 'This one was my husband's and is much, much more valuable. It's jadeite jade, you know. A very precious form of the stone; and the stones around the elephant's belly form what is called navratna. Nine gems from a diamond to a blue and a yellow sapphire to an emerald and in the middle is a ruby. It's worth an awful lot of money and it could have solved our problems a long time ago.'

Edmund watched her hold the elephant to her chest, clasping it with a mixture of appreciation and awe.

'It was given to my husband in the camp. He also had a dear friend who died, a man called Kenneth Mattison. They came for him early one day, the guards that is, and took him outside. Left him in the sun all day tied to a stake. It's a terrible punishment: you go bonkers in a short space of time. Heat stroke. When they took him down, he was in a bad way, a very bad way. Ted saw to it at once that he was bathed with warm water and given as much to drink as possible, but he knew dear Kenneth would not survive. Just before the end came, he whispered to Ted the words, 'in my left boot'. It was the elephant. Ted believed Kenneth wanted him to have it so he kept it.'

Edmund didn't say a word. In his mind's eye, he saw a dying man in a far-off country so many, many years ago giving his doctor friend his only possession in life.

The light of the candle caught the stones; they glittered like a Christmas tree.

'Hatred. "The longer it runs, the deeper it digs." Heard that one?'

Edmund didn't answer.

'And you waited a long time, didn't you, my boy? All the taunting, all the jibes, the snide remarks. Who wouldn't have hated?'

Agitated, Edmund let out a deep breath and ran his hand through his hair. He stood up and paced the room.

'Once a bully, always a bully and sometimes bullies need to be put in their places, don't they?' she continued.

Edmund shook his head repeatedly. He was mumbling to himself as he strode across the room, mumbling and shaking his head.

'And, of course, they underestimate us, don't they, bullies? If you're quiet, you must be thick. If you don't say anything, if you *accept* everything they do and say, they have no respect. It's not simply a case of lying low, is it? Keeping your head down, making sure you're never in the wrong... never provoking anyone.'

Edmund leaned against the wall, resting his head on his arm.

She rolled the larger of the elephants in her hand. 'The navratna is supposed to protect one from demons, snakes, poisons, a whole list of dangers. Rather ironically, it failed on that point.' She gave one of her half-twisted smiles then a short laugh. 'What are things after all? One day we shall all die and come to dust?'

He turned so his back now leaned against the wall. 'I can understand why you wanted them back.'

'I'm so glad you found them. It's made my day.'

'But I imagine you already knew I had them.'

Her head twitched towards him in a question.

'Dorcas came to see you the day before yesterday after I'd been to see her. She told you I had them. Although she denied ever seeing them before, she knew perfectly well what they were.'

She ran her tongue over her bottom lip, watching his face carefully before she spoke.

'You're quick, Chief Inspector.'

'You used Dorcas. All along you've used her.'

'Not at all. *I* was *of use.*'

'If it makes you feel better.'

Annoyed, Mrs Whitstable snapped, 'She had once spoken to Janet and said that she was unhappy in her job so I phoned her. I suggested she come and see me. I told her that the only

493

way she could leave Marcia's employment was to be suspected of being a thief. Don't go for anything big, I said. You don't want the police called in. She was afraid of what Marcia might do though – spread the word she had stolen things, destroy her reputation. I promised her that, should she ever leave Marcia, I would give her a reference, saying that she had worked for me for the past five years and that the only reason she had left my employment was because I couldn't afford her anymore.'

'And in return?'

'In return, I asked her to look for the ornaments Marcia refused to give back to Janet.'

'Did you also ask Malakai to look for the missing ornaments?'

'He used to work for me, you know. He's a wonderful gardener and one never appreciated by Marcia Pullman!' She shook her head in indignation at the thought of such wasted talent. 'Well, to be honest, I wasn't a hundred per cent sure of Dorcas. Not that I thought she'd keep the things herself or tell Marcia anything. I just felt she was a little too much under Marcia's power. I wondered how hard she'd looked for them or whether she would be too scared to take them if she did find them, so I recruited Malakai to have a look round as well.'

'Malakai found them and kept them?'

'Yes, the morning before he was fired, he phoned me and said he had found them. Marcia had been in a temper looking for a key she had lost to the writing desk. It was a very small key that she kept with a bunch of other keys. She had both Malakai and Dorcas searching the premises for them, and when they didn't surface she thought she must have left them somewhere when she went to town. She ordered Malakai to search the car and he found them under the seat where she had obviously dropped them. The clever man kept them to himself and told her he hadn't found anything. Later, when she had gone out, he tried the keys in the writing desk and opened it.'

'He found the elephants.'

'But he didn't take them. Not then.'

'He phoned you and you told him what to do.'

'He had to leave before she found out.'

'You told him to use Vim to wash the car.'

'We had to make sure he would be fired.'

'We.' Edmund's laugh was dark and sarcastic.

'She flipped – and fired him just as we hoped she would. A resignation would never have worked.'

'And you made sure he had a job to go to.'

'Of course. It would have been stupid not to have done.'

Edmund was silent a moment whilst he digested the information.

'You are saying that Malakai was prepared to lose his job and perhaps even go to prison so that you could get your ornaments back? A very dedicated ex-gardener.'

'I see you find that hard to believe.'

'Yes, I do.'

'I trained him. I taught him everything he knows. I made him one of the most sought after gardeners in Bulawayo. He could get a job anywhere.'

Edmund still wasn't convinced.

'You had already found him a job. With Lydia Ncube.'

'Is there anything wrong with that? Malakai told me how she had told him she would take him on anytime.'

'But she couldn't offer him the same salary. He was prepared to take a pay cut to help you out?'

'To get away from Marcia, yes. He hardly had any time off. Wasn't allowed to take leave over Christmas or Easter. You cannot underestimate these considerations.'

Edmund shook his head. 'Let's talk money.'

She laughed. 'Money, Chief Inspector. Money? I haven't got a cent. You know that. Take a look around.'

'Maybe not now, but you were planning on having some.'

She laughed again. 'How? When?'

'Your pension wasn't being paid into an account here. It never has been. It's paid into an account in the UK. You changed money with Mrs Ncube on a regular basis.'

'Oh, all right, officer. You've nabbed me there.' She tried to joke, but it fell flat.

'How else would Janet be able to afford to go to Francistown to buy goods for her stall?'

'Is there anything wrong with that, I ask you? Using my own money to survive?'

Edmund shook his head. 'No, none at all. None at all.'

'If I wanted to give Malakai a little *bonus*, have I breached the law in any way?'

'Paying him to steal something might not look good in a court of law.'

'It wasn't theft. I cannot steal what belongs to me.'

'It's a grey area.'

'Most of life is.'

'But tell me, why didn't he give the ornaments back to you right away? You live very close by.'

'Oh, he did come round – but it was a Monday and we weren't here. We go shopping on a Monday. Then he started his new job, which was in Burnside, quite a distance from here.'

'And then unfortunately, Malakai got caught with the ornaments in his possession.'

She ground her thumb into the palm of her hand. 'Yes, that wasn't part of the plan.'

A silence sprang up between them. Edmund felt tired, weary of the world.

She laughed, a thin, grey cackle that made the flame of the candle swell and then waver and die back down again.

'Bullies, eh? You certainly have to be on your toes with them. But then you'd know all about it, wouldn't you, Edmund. Got to have a plan. Got to have a plan.'

The sweat came on him again. A rush of heat that swept up his body, along his arms, spreading out through his fingers. He felt emboldened yet dizzy with an overwhelming nausea. He stood up. He needed to walk. He wanted to be outside on the road, under the canopy of jacarandas that lined the road, feeling the crunch of tar, making his way by the light of the stars. He stopped and tried to breathe.

'Pullman's dead. Died this evening. He saw me at his house. He got angry and shouted. The next thing he was dead.' The words came, thin and rasping, as though a grip of bony fingers clutched at his throat.

She didn't answer. Her mouth set into a thin straight line, her eyes stared ahead. Then the corners of her mouth curled slightly like those of a macabre mannequin.

'Good job.'

Edmund's throat ached with tears. He shook his head slowly backwards and forwards.

'What's wrong? I told you, mimicry is a form of survival. It's a hard life. In order to safeguard ourselves, we watch who wins, who loses; we adopt methods of survival.'

'No, no!' He ran his fingers through his hair feeling the damp sweat of his fear. His mouth filled with a sour saltiness. He was back in the headmaster's office, standing with his hands behind his back, feeling the eyes boring down on him; the empty, hollow eyes of Socrates. A butterfly fluttered out of his cold, marble mouth and on to the top of a picture. Then another. And another. One after the other, they shook themselves out of their stone cocoon and hovered upwards. Edmund shook his head, trying to gain control, to remember clearly. *This boy is a liar! This boy is a thief!*

'No, no!' he said again, his voice a low moan in the darkness. Mrs MacDougal was there, hugging herself as she rocked backwards and forwards. *Edmund, how could you?*

'It worked. *You* got away with it.'

The tears came fast now as Edmund shook his head from side to side. He stopped walking and stood by the window. It was a relief, a strange relief to allow himself the privilege of weeping. There would be time later for accusations and explanations, but now was his time. He did little to stem the tide of emotion and tears, instead rubbing his hands across his face and into his hair. He felt the phlegm run from his nose, but ignored the impulse to wipe it away. In great, racking sobs, a long-concealed, dark misery leaked out of him and into the grey heaviness of the room.

When she spoke, her voice was calm and quiet. 'I know what it's like. The hatred, how it builds up. How it simmers like a pot of water on the stove. How it stirs, gently at first, getting stronger and darker, so that soon it is black and thick like treacle. But no one sees it, do they? No one sees the hate bubbling away beneath the surface, no one else feels how it spits and rages.'

Edmund paced the room again. He turned his head from side to side. He could feel the heat now. There was another wave coming. Up through his chest, which was hard and tight, up to his throat; even his ears tingled.

'Murder...' he began, but the words caught in his throat.

'Murder, I told you, springs from very personal motives.'

'The beautiful Dalubuhle,' he murmured, still rolling his head sideways.

'The umufufu tree. You remember the story I told you?'

'Two murders...' His voice trailed off.

'Yes, there were two murders, if you count the stabbing as murder. The first murder was a quiet one, done by someone who didn't want to cause any particular harm or pain. Someone clever, too. Someone who could plot a murder that could go undetected as such.'

He nodded his head backwards and forwards, backwards and forwards.

'The stabbing was less well thought out. In fact, it showed little forethought or planning. It was done on the spur of the moment by someone who acted on impulse; someone far more emotional than the first murderer.' She was sad now and her face dropped.

Edmund listened hard to catch the words. In his mind he was catching butterflies with a large net. He was running over the garden, along the velvety, cool green grass. Powdery white butterflies blossomed and soared into the air whenever he swiped his net downwards.

'Catch them, Edmund, catch them.' Mrs MacDougal was standing on the verandah, her hands on her hips. He could see a 'v' of red where her chest plunged into her dress. She was hot, a little breathless, happy. 'You're a good lad, Edmund,' she said as he rushed up to her. She stretched out her hands and he thought she was going to hug him. He opened his arms wide. He was a butterfly, soft and white and gentle. He could fly where he wanted, soar the heavens, plummet the depths.

'Careful!' she commanded and he stopped suddenly. 'Butterflies die if you touch them.' She had something in her hand. It was one of them, a butterfly caught in the curl of her palm. His arms dropped limply beside him, like the propeller of a plane coming to a stop. He looked up uncertainly, struggling with her rejection of him, which stung like a slap across the face. Her eyes were on the butterfly that jerked spasmodically in her hand, its tiny legs drawn to its chest, gasping for life, for pity, for mercy, for one more chance. Gently, she lifted her hand and let it go. She watched it flutter away and then turned back to Edmund. 'You'll be wanting your tea soon,' she smiled. 'How about some toast and soup?'

'All I wanted,' he managed to say at last, 'was a simple life. A job and a wife and a couple of kids. A house and a cat and dog. What could be simpler than being a policeman? All the rules are laid out, the forms just have to be completed and orders carried out. Someone is either innocent or guilty and justice is fulfilled.'

She laughed. 'But life isn't like that, is it? We have *feelings*. We live, we breathe. We don't always know what the rules are. Edmund, *I understand*. I know why you did it. *I know*. Bullies have to be put in their places. It's as simple as that.'

'Stop!' snapped Edmund, suddenly. She was momentarily taken aback. 'Stop. I haven't done anything. I *didn't do anything wrong!*'

Her mouth curved into an ironic smile. 'You may like to see it like that–'

'It was *you* who reported Pullman,' Edmund interrupted

her. Another wave took over his body. He felt its warmth shoot up through his fingers and cover his face. 'Mr MacDougal was following *your* tip-off. Mrs Hera Amoris.'

She stopped talking. Her eyes narrowed and she looked quickly at him.

'Yes, yes it was me,' she said finally. 'Hera is the–'

'I know who Hera is,' interjected Edmund. 'The wife of Zeus. The Queen of the gods.'

'The protector of married women. She presides over weddings and blesses nuptials. She hates anything that threatens the sanctity of marriage.'

'Amoris for love.'

'Pure love, real love. Not cheap... *sex.*'

'Your allegations were baseless.'

She sighed deeply, her finger tracing light circles on the armrest of her wheelchair. '*Something* going on and I knew it involved Pullman. I took an educated guess. I was wrong.'

Edmund sniffed scornfully. '*Something* going on *somewhere.*'

'Yes, yes. I knew that something was going on. Something untoward. I had to do something about it.'

'Why?'

'*Why?*'

'Why should it concern you? Why did it matter so much?'

She pulled up her shoulders as though to suggest she didn't see what the problem was. 'Such things going on in our neighbourhood. We were respectable people then...'

Edmund turned and faced her.

'How did you know?'

'How?'

'Yes, *how?* How did you know about this... this place?' Edmund's voice was firm and loud. He took a step towards her and she backed into her chair.

'The maid...' she began.

'No!' insisted Edmund, 'You're lying!'

She swallowed hard. 'The maid told me–'

'*No, no, no!*' shouted Edmund, grabbing her by the shoulders and shaking her. 'The truth! I want the truth!' He was trembling, shaking uncontrollably, aware of her tiny fragile frame, how easily he could compress it, snap it, break it. He knew then that everything she had represented to him: comfort, nostalgia, the unchanging stability of the past was nothing, all a hoax. He had let himself be led down a beautiful flower-strewn lane only to find an overgrown stagnant pond at the end. He released her with a rough jerk. She rubbed her arms, pulling her bony shoulders away from him and turned to the wall.

Edmund fumbled in his coat. He took some folded papers out of his pocket and laid them before her, holding them flat a moment with his fingers splayed.

'Sandra Smith is your husband's illegitimate daughter.' He took his hand away and the papers concertinaed together softly.

There was a silence. A moth flew into the candle wax, crackled alight and burnt to nothing. She spoke at last, her voice sad and soft. 'Yes, that's right.'

'She appeared one day and revealed to you that she was the product of your husband's affair with a mixed race woman.'

'*Affair?*' she tossed her head backwards. The long line of her face was scornful at his suggestion. 'I would hesitate to call it that. His *dalliance* maybe. Affair is too grand a word.'

'Dalliance, then. She showed you the letter her mother had written as proof.'

'Oh, I didn't need proof. I could see it all there in the eyes. It was like looking at him all over again.'

'She wanted to know who her mother was, didn't she, but you didn't know.'

She looked down at her hands, which were folded neatly on the blanket across her knees. 'No, I didn't. There were more than a few. Once or twice in the beginning it was the maid. Dear Violet; the accident with the bleach was just a cry for help.' She shook her head with a wry smile. 'Later, he... well, let's just say that he found a place to be entertained away from our house.'

Edmund softened. 'Pullman?'

She rapped her knuckles hard on the arm of the wheelchair. 'Nigel Pullman was young and wealthy. He was one of a number of people involved in sanctions busting during the Rhodesian war. It was important for him to keep in with certain people, but he didn't just restrict himself to the police or government officials. His net included a few lawyers and doctors. His reasoning, I suppose, was that you never knew when someone would come in useful. He was clever. He found one's weakness and he fed it, whether it was booze, or cards, or women. There was nothing he could not arrange. It all began with an innocent invitation to his house for a drink after work. Then dinner. Wives were discouraged. I was told it was not my thing. I'd be bored. After all, how could I with my mere female brain understand what intelligent men may discuss? The next day he would recount the evening in vague descriptions that focused on the food. I began to feel that Ted made a show of being bored. However much he said he didn't want to go, he went whenever he was invited.'

'Did he ever say who else was there?'

'No. I think that was part of the deal, not to mention who you had seen or spoken to. It was high level. It was important to keep quiet.'

'How often did your husband go?'

'About once every couple of weeks at first, but then the invitations became more regular. He'd come back late. He hadn't been drinking, but there was this feeling. It is very hard to describe, but it was a feeling of separation. He was never nasty to me, but he became very secretive, which is in many ways worse.'

'Did you ever confront him?'

'About what? About the feeling? No, I didn't. I suppose I hoped it would blow over.'

'But it didn't.'

'One night, I decided I'd had enough. If he was going to treat me like a dumb wife, I would play the part to my own advantage. I knew where the house was so I went round. There were a number of cars parked in the driveway but otherwise nothing seemed out of order. When I knocked on the door, a man in a standard khaki house servant's uniform opened it, but was reluctant to let me in. He said he would call my husband, but instead of asking me to wait inside, he closed the door and left me standing on the step. When Ted appeared, it was all I could do to hide my rage. I gave him his jacket. I said he forgotten it and I didn't want him getting cold.'

'And, how did he seem?'

'Annoyed. For the first time ever with me, he was annoyed.'

Mrs Whitstable sat in silence for a few moments.

'He knew, you see, what I was up to. He knew I did not trust him and, whether I was justified or not in what I had done, it marked a turning point for us in our relationship.'

'What happened?'

'I was just leaving. We had said an awkward good-bye in which he had kissed me reluctantly on the cheek and as I turned, I saw someone come out of a room at the far end of the left hand side of the corridor, and go into another, closer room on the right hand side. It was a young woman in a cocktail dress. Almost immediately she went into the room, a man came out and went into the room she had left. I assumed one room was the bathroom and the other was the dining room.

'When I got outside, I did not leave immediately. I crept around the side of the house, making sure to keep below the windows to where I had worked out the dining room was. My guess was confirmed by a lot of laughter and chatter.'

She looked at Edmund as though expecting a reaction.

'Did you see or hear anything else?'

She shook her head.

'*That* was it? That was your evidence?'

Mrs Whitstable shrugged. 'I *knew*. I just knew. As soon as I saw the girl.'

'In an evening dress?'

'What else could account for the time spent away from home, the secrecy? Why wasn't I allowed, but another woman was?'

'Maybe she was somebody's wife?'

'Instinct, Edmund, instinct.'

Edmund remembered what Mrs Parkinson had said. *Some of the girls went out at night.*

'You reported the matter to the police. And then what happened?'

'It has always been my belief that there was a leak, an informant.'

Edmund rolled his head back as though he were in physical agony. After a deep breath, he continued. 'I see. A conspiracy theory.'

'You don't believe me, Chief Inspector?'

'Maybe not.'

'The man I saw cross the corridor, he was a police officer.'

'He was in uniform?'

'No. But he had a limp. A very specific limp. When I first decided to inform the police, I went in person. The Chief Superintendent also had a very specific limp.'

'Mr Sherbourne,' breathed Edmund.

'I'm not sure what his name was, but I left without making a report. Later I phoned in. I spoke to your friend, MacDougal. He was very interested, if ineffective.'

'Ineffective?'

'He was determined. I'll give him that, but it was beyond his capabilities. There was a reason that Pullman kept certain people happy: so they would protect him. He always kept a contact or two in the police.'

A sudden image of two police officers standing outside the khaya rose into Edmund's mind. *We would like to ask your son a few questions. He will need to come to the station.*

'Let me get this straight. You took this story of going to Pullman's house and seeing a woman in an evening dress and a man with a limp to Mr MacDougal and he agreed to investigate on your behalf?'

'Yes.'

Edmund rubbed his forehead with his hand. 'I don't believe you.'

'What don't you believe?'

'Evidence. I keep coming back to it. You think something untoward is going on in your suburb and you call someone of high rank in the police force and, as a result of your testimony, they rush out and raid the place. It's unlikely, highly unlikely, that any police officer would act on so little information.'

She tapped her hand rhythmically on the handle of her wheelchair.

'You're clever. Do you know that?'

'It's common sense.'

'All right. I phoned him. MacDougal. He was interested in my story. Pullman, you see, was at the centre of more than one sanctions busting affair: smuggling arms into Rhodesia and gold out to China, but nothing could ever be proven. Pullman was always on the periphery, but made sure to distance himself from events. My story gave MacDougal another way in. Al Capone, you may have heard, was arrested on tax evasion, not for being a Mafia leader.'

Edmund raised his eyebrows.

'In particular, MacDougal was looking for any evidence that pointed to a connection between Pullman and a man called Bernadie, a South African arms dealer. I was impressed with MacDougal; I think, in all honesty, he was a fair man. He didn't like bullies and he didn't like the system of patronage that existed here, even if it meant that he himself would never be promoted beyond his current station. He sent someone round during the day to check on the place, ask a few questions. Made up some excuse to have a look around the house. Nothing seemed out of order. He himself had watched the house one evening. He had seen a couple of men go in and then, a few hours later, come out again, but there was nothing unusual in that. Eventually, he left it to me. He asked me to get more evidence.'

505

A dark, ominous feeling crept up Edmund's spine. 'What did you do?'

'It was my birthday. Ted got a phone call. I went into the kitchen, but then came out again. His back was turned so he didn't see me in the doorway. I was incensed, furious. I made up my mind to confront him there and then. But then I heard him say "not tonight". Instead of being angry with him, I wanted to save him. Yes, save him – us – from this awful path of destruction. I couldn't bear it anymore. All the lies, the subterfuge. I wanted an end to it all.'

'So you?'

'So when he had gone out, I picked up the phone and called MacDougal. I told him that I had overheard a conversation in which it was mentioned that Bernadie would be at Pullman's house that evening. He must have asked me three or four times about the reliability of my information. I assured him he would not be disappointed if a police raid were to be arranged.'

'But you didn't know–'

'No, I didn't. But I thought the raid would turn somebody or something up. There was definitely something going on. If he didn't get Bernadie, he would get someone else.'

'There was nobody there.'

'Nobody at all. Just Pullman watching tv.'

'Was Bernadie ever caught?'

'Not that I know of.'

'Pullman had to make sure MacDougal was put in his place.'

'Somebody, even a policeman, can be accused of theft, bribery, murder, corruption and survive the allegations, but mention child abuse and they're finished.'

'Pullman did his own investigations,' said Edmund slowly as enlightenment dawned on him. 'He must have spoken to Simeon Nyathi, that horrible piece of humanity, who told him how often I went inside the house, how I had stayed there whilst my mother was away!'

'Oh dear!'

Edmund ran his hands through his hair again and again. 'And then there was my father who was looking for a way to get me back.'

'It saved my husband,' Mrs Whitstable carried on as though she had not heard Edmund. 'He never went back.'

Edmund shook his head in disbelief.

'You saved one broken person. You pretended your marriage wasn't a lie–'

'It wasn't,' she snarled. 'How dare you–'

'How dare I? How *dare* I?' he leaned over her again, desperate to shake some sense into her. 'All these years after his death, you continue to protect him.'

'I protect Janet, not him.'

Edmund paced the room, trying to breathe deeply, trying to remember what he had read about the importance of keeping calm. *Anger gives your opponent the upper hand. Remain calm by counting slowly to ten.*

'When Sandra appeared, you pushed her in the direction of a Mrs Parkinson? You thought if she found her mother, she wouldn't be so interested in her father's side of the family or meeting Janet.'

'No, I pushed her in the direction of the children's home, St. Mary's, but it had closed down and the person who had worked there who could have helped her had died. Sandra did speak to her daughter though who referred her to Mrs Parkinson.'

'And Mrs Parkinson referred her to Marcia Pullman.'

There was another silence. 'I couldn't believe it when Sandra told me. I phoned her to see how she was getting on. She was so happy she could find this person who could help her.'

'Did Mrs Parkinson explain to Sandra why Marcia would be able to help her?'

'Yes, she did. It didn't surprise me.'

'Marcia Pullman was the last person you wanted to know about your husband's indiscretion.'

'Exactly. Janet was in a sticky enough situation with her

over the elephants she had given to Marcia to have valued. I also knew what Marcia was all about. If Sandra were to show her the letter or just mention to her that she knew who her father was, Marcia would make our lives even more miserable than they already were.'

'Does Janet know about her father's indiscretion?'

'No, not at all. I loved my husband very much, Chief Inspector. Perhaps that comes as a surprise, but there is more to a relationship than sex, and I knew he loved me. He was a good man, but he was a damaged soul. He spent the best part of four years in a Japanese prisoner of war camp and what he witnessed was horrific, simply horrific. He couldn't speak about it; he was tormented. In nightmares, he'd wake and stalk the house. He thought he was back at the camp, walking up and down the fence, looking for a way out. He was haunted; a deeply, deeply troubled man. But there was one person he loved more than anything in the world.'

'Janet?'

She nodded her head. 'Yes, his little Janet. When she was a baby, he would sit with her for hours, looking at her little fingers and toes, marvelling at her innocence. A clean page, he said. No scars, no marks, no hurt. How he'd like to start all over again. Janet, too, adored her father. She thought the world of him. He was everything she wanted in a father and I am only sorry she didn't find that in a husband. If she had found out she had a half-sister, she would have been devastated. Life has been too cruel to her already. I couldn't let that happen. I made sure that Janet knew nothing of Sandra and Sandra knew nothing of Janet.'

'What did you do?'

'I persuaded Sandra not to approach Marcia. I told her what she was like and that it was unlikely she would yield the information without wanting something in return. I said it was better that she tried to find the information in a less indirect way.'

'How?'

'Well, she was in the perfect position really, doing all that

508

counselling or whatever she calls it. Karmic cleansing.' She raised her eyebrows as though to say she didn't believe a word of it. 'Luckily, Marcia was unwell; too much of the good life if you ask me. It provided a perfect opportunity for Sandra to introduce herself. She put a flyer in the post box offering foot massages and the like and Marcia called her. That bit was quite easy.'

'Did you really think someone like Mrs Pullman would reveal to her who her mother was while receiving a foot massage?'

'No. What I was hoping was that Marcia would invite Sandra to her house and that might provide the opportunity to snoop around. Unfortunately, Marcia didn't want anybody to come to the house. You would have thought she would have preferred to be in the comfort of her own home, but Marcia was the type who didn't like the maid to see anything. The madam having a treatment – it was a sign of weakness.'

'So what did you do?'

'It all began to run away from me a little. Sandra was getting desperate and, well, I also began to think that she actually *liked* Marcia. The last thing I wanted was a friendship springing up between those two. Janet was unhappy and I feared her doing something silly like going to the police. When Malakai found the elephants, I was happy, of course, but then I realised that Dorcas might be implicated in their disappearance. I was afraid that Marcia might be true to her word and get the girl locked up for something she didn't do.' She stopped and clenched her fists into tight balls. 'You have no idea how frustrating it is to be stuck in *this!* This thing!' she banged her fists down hard on the arms of the wheelchair and tears filled her eyes, turning them a liquid blue. *'I can't do anything! Nothing! Nothing at all!'*

A silence followed, in which Edmund considered putting his hand on her shoulder in sympathy. Then he hesitated and looked away. Only one candle was burning now.

'You had to get rid of her,' said Edmund at last.

'I'm not a doctor, just a doctor's wife. When Ted worked out in the bush, I was his right-hand woman. I was his secretary and his assistant and even a midwife on occasion. Well, going on the description of Marcia that Janet gave me, I knew she was not well. Marcia's high blood pressure was well known, but I knew it was more than that. She was overweight, but ate all the wrong things, often got breathless and tired. Ah, I thought, here's someone with a possible risk of kidney failure. The best way to maintain her condition would be through drinking lots of water and healthy eating, but if a doctor ever did advise this, she certainly never heeded them. Too much at variance with her social life, but it gave me an idea.'

'So you...?'

'Ah, you haven't worked this bit out have you?' she said with great glee. 'Oh, I'm so glad. I'd hate to have been outwitted on every score.'

She wheeled her chair a little closer to the table. From her dressing gown pocket, she pulled out a small tin that had once contained fruit gums and prised the top off. She shook the contents gently and handed it to Edmund.

'Dried mushrooms?'

She nodded her head. 'After my fall, I got very down. I suppose I thought it was the end.' She looked up at Edmund with a rueful smile. 'There are disadvantages to living to old age. If you die young, you probably don't expect it, but when you're my age you think of it more and more. Every ache, every pain – you wonder, is this the one that will finish me off?'

Edmund nodded.

'There's nothing more rewarding than taking control of one's destiny.'

'Suicide?'

'It's an act looked down upon by so many, but really it's very much underestimated. Of course, I'm not referring to throwing oneself off a bridge because of a lover's tiff. I'm

510

referring to it being an honourable way out. The Japanese knew it and that's what made them a force to be reckoned with.'

'Not the Greeks?'

She stared hard at him. 'No, not the Greeks. Unless you include Socrates, forced to commit suicide by drinking hemlock.' She turned on Edmund with sudden vehemence. 'He knew too much, you see. Far too much. Same old story, isn't it? Perhaps that's the secret of a long life – keeping ignorant.'

'You were telling me about the mushrooms,' prompted Edmund.

'So I was.' Her head dropped and she was silent for a moment. 'Things were on a low financially. The elephants had always been our back up plan. We had decided we would try and not sell them; we would weather the storm, but if we really *had to* sell them, we would. We managed – until I had had the fall, which cost us more money that we could afford. The costs were just phenomenal. Janet tried to get an evaluation of the elephants and very stupidly gave them to Marcia who refused to give them back. It was, perhaps, the worst time of my life. I felt like such a burden, a millstone. I longed for Death to take me. Janet was worried. She offered to take me back to Shangani. She had this idea I suppose, bless her, that it would make me feel better. Memory lane, the good old days and any other cliché you can think of. I had other plans.'

Edmund looked sideways at her.

'Let's just say I went out with the intention of finding something that would allow me an honourable discharge from life – the bush provides plenty of answers – and I came back invigorated.'

'You found something beneficial – a plant?'

She laughed and then leant forward. 'I found a way to murder someone.' Her lips parted in a hideous grin and Edmund shrunk back.

'The mushrooms!' she exclaimed. 'Come on, now. The mushrooms.'

'You picked poisonous mushrooms, which you served to Marcia Pullman six months later?'

'I didn't pick them: Janet did. Just a couple by mistake, poor thing. *Inkowankowane* looks so much like *nedza*, especially after it's rained and the warts wash off. Exactly the same, just like the butterflies that mimic the monarch. *Look like th'innocent flower, but be the serpent under 't*. Of course, I know the difference. I told Janet about it and we had a bit of a laugh. "I know who I'd like to give those to," she joked. It gave me an idea and instead of throwing them away as I said I would do, I dried them and kept them.'

'Do you mean to say that you planned to kill Marcia six months ago?'

'No, I'm not saying that at all. I just felt so helpless, so completely helpless. And having them, having the mushrooms, made me feel so incredibly powerful. I hadn't a clue how I'd use them or if at all, but I needed a weapon, a secret weapon. I wasn't going to fade away. I wasn't going to be one of these old dears that everyone speaks of as having "a good innings" or describes as "slipping away peacefully in their sleep". Oh no, I was going to fight back. I might not have had a plan, but I had plenty of time on my side. *Plenty* of time to sit and think.'

'But how did you do it? You dried the mushrooms and then?'

She smiled like a child who has managed to do something her mother has sworn she would be unable to.

'It was almost... *poetic*. Yes, poetic. She was such a snob, such a complete and utter snob that I was delighted to do what I did. She phoned about the book club stocktake and asked Janet if she knew where to get some mushrooms. Only because she took such a delight in putting her down. Janet tried to be helpful and mentioned a supermarket where she'd seen them for sale, but Marcia was scornful. 'I didn't expect you to know,' she said. And that was when I decided to carry my plan through. She deserved it. Ooh yes, she deserved it.'

Edmund noticed how she seemed to make herself more

comfortable in her seat and how her face brightened as she talked.

'The problem was, if I was to poison her, how was I to give it to her? I couldn't get to her so she would have to come to me. But to do so, both Janet and Loveness had to be out of the house. Then an opportunity came my way.'

She looked hard at Edmund as though deliberating whether to tell him something or not.

'Loveness has a stall at a market–'

'Which Janet pays for. I know.'

She looked surprised. 'You know? Well, you are a clever man.'

Not knowing if she meant the comment as a genuine compliment or if she was being sarcastic, he made no response.

'Janet had to buy new stock and Loveness wanted her to buy it in Francistown. It's cheaper, you see. Cuts out the middleman. They could catch a bus early on the Thursday morning, do their shopping and be back later on in the evening. Of course, Janet was loath to leave me alone, but I insisted I would be okay. She made me lunch and supper and left it in the kitchen. Loveness brought in a granddaughter of hers, a rather gormless young girl of about fourteen who was supposed to heat the food up, but I managed to get rid of her quite easily. Told her I would call her if I needed her help and she was quite content to sit in the sun and do very little. Then I telephoned Marcia on my cellphone and said I had heard she was looking for mushrooms.'

'And she was, of course?'

'Well, actually no. She had found some. But I told her these were porcini mushrooms. They're very expensive. The fact that they are brown and the *inkowankowane* are white didn't matter as I made them up as a soup. As soon as Janet was out of the door, I phoned Marcia. I said I had some porcini mushrooms. She wanted to come right away, but I arranged for her to come at lunch time and when she did I had a little meal prepared.'

'Wait, wait, wait,' began Edmund, holding up his hand. 'This was on the Friday. Marcia died on the Monday.'

'Well, I couldn't have her dropping dead here. The last thing I wanted was a dead body to deal with!' She leaned forward in a conspiratorial manner. 'The best thing about this type of poisoning is not that it is slow working – it takes at least three days to kill you – but that it doesn't happen all at once. After an initial upset stomach, the victim feels fine and then, two days later, they collapse and die of kidney failure.'

She sat back, tilting her head upwards in an expression of triumph.

'Good, eh? I gave her a lovely bowl of soup all for herself – and she lapped it up. She asked where I had got them and I said my son-in-law in Cape Town. I said I loved them but they weren't so good for me any more – you can say those sorts of things when you are old and no one bats an eyelid. She was quite bowled over. She asked if she could buy some from me. Said she would like to make some soup because she was having visitors over to play bridge. Then I said well, lucky for you, I've got some more soup right here and I gave her an old ice-cream container full. Made with *nedza*, totally harmless stuff. I didn't want anyone else bumped off.'

'It was a very tricky business for a number of things could have gone wrong, not least Marcia recognizing the mushrooms as not being porcini. As it is, it all went wonderfully!'

'It was the first time you met her and she had no idea you were Janet's mother?'

'None at all. She asked me how I knew she was looking for mushrooms and I mentioned the name of one of the ladies at book club. Said I knew her and she had told me that Marcia had had difficulty finding them. She was exactly as I imagined – bossy, self-assured, a snob. She came in, looked around and viewed everything with scorn. Except for my decanters, of course. She was interested in them – made an offer of absolutely nothing. Made out she was being incredibly generous.'

'You're lucky Marcia didn't tell anyone where she was going. She didn't even write the address down.'

'Why should she? It's only a road down from where she lives and I made up a name, Mrs–'

'Mrs Hera Amoris.'

She looked sharply at him, like a bird at the water's edge suddenly aware of a crocodile amongst the reeds. 'Anyway, you're forgetting it wasn't supposed to look like a murder. It wasn't *supposed* to be investigated.'

'Marcia knew where you lived. She could have come back at any time.'

'Not if she was dead.'

'You were quite happy to sit there and watch her eat the soup, knowing it could kill her?'

'Correction. Knowing it *would*. And the best thing was it would never be traced back to me, a poor old lady in a wheelchair. She suffered from kidney problems, the doctor would corroborate the facts. No one would think of what happened three days before and if anyone did think about the fact that she had been ill on Friday night, they would also think that she had recovered and the two incidents couldn't possibly be linked. And if anyone had been suspicious of the mushrooms she ate, they would have to ask themselves why the rest of her bridge club ladies hadn't suffered in any way. It was... it could have been... perfect.'

'All along I thought someone met her the day she died at her house. There were two glasses and two plates left next to the sink after lunch.'

'Oh, that'll be her husband coming home for lunch, I expect, and bringing his floozy because he knew his wife was out.'

'He said he was gone all day.'

She rolled her eyes. 'Wouldn't you say that in the circumstances?'

'Where was she?'

'I phoned her. I pretended to be an old duck with a bit of silver to part with and asked her to meet me. Gave her the wrong address. That kept her going round in circles.'

'She didn't recognise your voice as the same as the person who sold mushrooms?'

She smiled slyly and spoke in an Irish accent, 'Butterflies are the souls of those waiting to go through purgatory. Remember?'

Edmund felt a stab of fear in his chest.

'Where are your friends, the MacDougals?' Her accent had changed. 'See, I do Scottish as well. I told you I was involved in amateur dramatics, didn't I?'

Edmund felt his heart quicken; her voice was so much like Mrs MacDougal's.

'Why?' he began. 'Why did you want her out of the house on the Monday?'

'To get her frustrated, annoyed, give her a bit of a run around. Tire her out.'

'You gave me a run around.'

'I keep telling you, her death wasn't supposed to be investigated. You're the one who blew it out of proportion.'

'And you encouraged me!'

'Don't look at me like that. Don't tell me you didn't like the mystery. An appointment in a diary. I gave you clues. I told you you have to look at what happened before.'

'Every moment is an accumulation of all the others,' sighed Edmund with heavy resignation.

'It was just like a story, a perfect story.'

Edmund kept quiet, his pride smarting.

'Until Janet found her.'

Mrs Whitstable's face fell. 'When Janet told me that Marcia had been found stabbed, I couldn't understand what had happened. It didn't take me long to work it out though.' She shrugged and smiled as though Janet had made a cake that had flopped rather than stabbed someone in the heart with a knife. She shook her head. 'Why, *why* did she do it?'

'Because she knew,' said Edmund, softly, watching his words sink in. 'She knew what you had done. Perhaps not all the ins and outs, but looking at the body she may have recognised the signs of kidney failure. She remembered the phone call in the morning. She had answered your phone, hadn't she? She must have wondered how Marcia had phoned you by mistake and why she was asking about mushrooms. Perhaps she remembered your trip into the bush earlier in the year. It was Janet who put two plates and two glasses next to the sink to make it look as though Marcia had had a visitor and it was that mysterious visitor who was responsible for Marcia's death. Your daughter was making sure you were not a suspect.'

'Stop!' Mrs Whitstable cried, putting her hands over her ears. 'Just stop! Stop!'

'Why? Does it irk you that Janet worked it out? That it wasn't the perfect murder?'

She was indignant. 'No, no. Of course not. I'm annoyed that what could've been put down as a sudden death due to a known condition, suddenly became suspicious.'

'Annoyed? You're annoyed?' He scoffed at the understatement. 'Malakai is in prison, Dorcas is dead, my house is burnt to the ground and you're *annoyed*.'

'Dorcas is dead?' She pulled in her lips and gave a little shake of her head. It was evident to Edmund that, at most, she felt embarrassment.

'Unfortunately, your control of her didn't extend to protecting her.'

'My control! What an exaggeration!'

'Is it? She told you what Pullman was doing six months ago, didn't she? She told you about the girls and the prostitution and what did you do about it? You told her to make an anonymous phone call. Then when that plan didn't work, you told her to start stealing things and doing things wrong. All it did was make Pullman highly suspicious of her – and Malakai, especially when the ornaments were found on him. He thought they were working together. You got Malakai into trouble when all he had done was try and help you.'

'I didn't mean for Malakai to get into trouble. As I keep saying, Marcia's death wasn't supposed to be investigated.

When the ornaments were found on him, he was made to look a guilty man. What exactly was I supposed to do? How was I to save any of those girls?'

'You could have told me. Instead, you sent me on a wild goose chase.'

'With the object of achieving the same result. '

'Which is why you pushed the idea with me that Mr Pullman was the guilty party?'

'Yes, exactly. I'm sorry things didn't go as I hoped.'

'Not quite like a book then?'

With a flush of embarrassment, she attempted a conciliatory smile. 'Perhaps not.'

'Although you are like an author, conducting everything from the comfort of your armchair, using innocent characters to commit your crimes, weaving stories, dropping clues.'

The look she gave him was vague and blank. Edmund saw an old, tired woman in front of him, one very different from the perceptive sharp-eyed lady he had initially met. She looked down at her hands and rubbed the wedding ringer on her finger. 'I've never wanted more than I felt was due to me in my life and what was due was what was earned. Marcia took what wasn't hers. That is *wrong*.'

'Yes, but there is the law...' began Edmund. He dropped down beside her and took her hands in his.

'A law that should *protect*. But does it? Does it? We had no proof Marcia had the items and, even if we had, she would have hired a good lawyer. We could never afford anything like that. Once you get past a certain age, Chief Inspector, you are a bit of a joke, not to be taken very seriously.'

'I have never thought that of you.'

'Haven't you? Are you sure?' She looked straight at him and he looked away, embarrassed. 'You would never have discussed the case with me had you thought me a threat, would you?'

He didn't answer.

'And perhaps sometimes you have tired of my talk?'

'I have never not respected you,' insisted Edmund, turning to face her and squirming in the shrewdness of the bright blue eyes. 'Never.'

They sat in silence for a while, him staring at a set of faded flower prints on the wall, and she at the ring on her finger. The smallest candle was now a pool of wax on a saucer, still alight, but flickering. Suddenly, she brightened.

'Tell me, how did I do? Out of ten, what would you say? I'd love to know.'

'Five.'

Her face fell.

'Five and a half.'

'You're far too generous.'

'You lost marks for making other people suffer. Bad planning.'

She didn't answer. His words dropped through the air into an empty silence. They sat for a long time, not saying anything. A cold draught blew down the corridor and the curtains sucked into the window. Something rattled outside and the tin roof clanged.

'And Pullman?' asked Edmund at last. 'Why?'

She sucked in her lips and raised her chin. Then she turned a cheery smile on him as though he was a child who had done something clever. 'Pullman? Pullman was your doing.'

'I don't know what you mean...' His voice was rough, his tongue heavy in his mouth.

'Oh, yes, you do, Chief Inspector. Oh, yes you do.'

Suddenly, she slapped her hand down on the arm of her wheelchair. 'You see, we're the same, you and I. We have to work behind the scenes, get what we want in less conventional ways. But we do get what we want, don't we? You're part of this, Chief Inspector. You and I, we're like two peas in a pod.'

'No...' he began, shaking his head. 'No.'

'I remember the MacDougal abuse case so well. The charges were so unusual back then. Elizabeth MacDougal was the W.I. treasurer. Lovely lady. It was you who drove him away, Chief Inspector. You destroyed them. Saying all those nasty, nasty things. I'd also pack my bags and run.'

Edmund backed away, horror, like a stream of vomit, rising hotly up his throat. Her face loomed in front of him, the skin so white it was almost luminescent and her hair drawn back so her cheekbones rose high and sharp, almost skeletal under her skin. He stared at her, his eyes wide with fear. His voice came thin and raspy as though someone held his throat in a claw-like grip.

'I did it,' he whispered. 'I did it.'

She stared at him, her thin lips set into a line of triumph.

'I took the money. Meyer got expelled not suspended. His dad beat him so badly he couldn't walk for three days.'

She nodded, still smiling.

'Mr MacDougal had already made a complaint about the bullying. It was racism, he said, and he was right, but nothing was done. I knew if I was accused of stealing, the head would be forced to investigate. I made a point of denying I knew who it was, which only confirmed suspicions that I feared the repercussions of getting someone into trouble.'

'The headmaster was a good man.'

'A fair man. He was only trying to do what was right.'

'It was a difficult time, 1979. So many people were trying to do the right thing.'

Edmund pulled himself back into the present. 'Janet has admitted to stabbing Marcia.' He watched as his words drove hard into her. 'Pullman...'

'Pullman... was you. I thought you were never going to stand up to the man. But you did!'

'Liar!' shouted Edmund. 'Liar, liar, liar!'

She looked away from him, one hand smoothing down the arm of her threadbare cardigan.

Edmund felt his hands tingle with frustration.

The roof clanged again as the wind beat round the house. Car lights on the road caused shadows to stretch up the walls.

The smile disappeared. Her voice was tight, controlled, as

though she were talking through clenched teeth. 'I didn't do a thing. Not a thing. You made him angry. He saw red. He collapsed. He died. It's karma; what goes around, comes around. He deserved it. He deserved everything that came to him. They both did.'

'Karma?' Edmund realised now that he had never believed her words on the subject. 'You *murdered* Marcia Pullman.'

'Karma, Chief inspector, is for those who *can* wait. I've run out of time. I believe in justice.'

He laughed, his voice rich with scorn.

'You believe in it too, Chief Inspector.'

'Justice?'

'Pass me my tea, would you?' She motioned to her bedside table on which was placed one of her special rose cups and saucers.

'No,' said Edmund as the meaning of her words sunk in. 'No.'

'I told you. Everyone is called one day to settle their karmic account.'

'No, not you.'

'For Janet's sake. I'm not long for this world, Chief Inspector, but Janet has a life to live. She still has time. Don't let her to go to prison, please. Don't let her go.'

He backed off, suddenly afraid, not of her, but of her request and the great cavern of darkness it opened up. He felt he had taken a detour somewhere and, in trying to stick on the straight and narrow, he was being led further and further away down a road he didn't know and in a direction he could not turn from.

'My tea, Chief Inspector.'

Edmund breathed out deeply and walked slowly over to the bedside table. He paused a moment, remembering his earlier admiration of the pattern on the cups. Then he took another deep breath, picked up the cup and saucer and carried it carefully to Mrs Whitstable, who took it from him with a trembling hand.

'Did I ever tell you the story of Hero and Leander?'

Edmund shook his head.

'Poor dear Leander was so in love that, every night, he swam the Hellespont to see his sweetheart, Hero. One terrible night, he was drowned in a storm, his body crushed against the rocks.' She winced and looked down at the teacup. 'The next day, Hero looked for him. "O Leander! O Leander!" she called. When she found him washed up on the sand, his dead hand clutched a beautiful flower which she kept and nurtured and it grew into a marvellous bush, a symbol of their love.'

Exhausted, he sank beside her.

She placed her hand gently on his head as though he were a little boy. She paused and then spoke in a quiet voice heavy with the weariness of the world: '"Fear no more the heat o' the sun, Nor the furious winter's rages." Karma? Did you really want to wait another lifetime to get revenge?' Suddenly her hand gripped his head tightly.

'Why did you bring me here?' he breathed, as the room descended into cold black shadows.

'You came of your own volition. You know you did. You've never stopped searching, never stopped looking. Tell me, did you find them, Chief Inspector? Did you find who you were looking for?' Her voice had become a whisper, a hard, dry whisper that spoke to him out of the encroaching darkness. 'Did you find the truth?'

The candle went out.

Chapter Fifty

Edmund walked slowly down Clark Road. It was early August and a warmth had entered the air. The earth was alive with the promise of spring as sprays ticked gently in the background of gardens where the shoots of new flowers pushed their heads through the soft soil with a youthful insistency and where buds swelled with the promise of new life. A better life or the same adorned in new garments?

The August wind lifted eddies of dust and spun them along the road. There was a smell in the air of blossom and water on dry earth. Edmund stopped to breathe deeply the heady scent of Yesterday, Today and Tomorrow, letting memories wash over him as he did. In a month or so the jacaranda would be out, painting the suburbs with their bursts of purple flowers. November would see them lying in indigo pools on the ground. November, before the rain.

But he was jumping ahead now when all he wanted to do was hold onto the moment. How to bottle that particular smell of spring? How to clasp one's hand over the trembling air and put it away for less glorious days? Edmund wanted to do something he hadn't done for a long time. He wanted to run down the road and jump in the air and catch the mites of dust that hung suspended in shafts of sunlight. He could do it. His coat was gone. In fact, he looked very un-Edmund like in a pair of blue jeans and a striped golf shirt. Edmund, no longer the police officer.

Edmund felt a great sense of relief, of the shedding of himself. He was lighter, happier. Alive. That morning he had gone to visit his mother and sat with her while she made tea and held his hand and said how good it was to see him.

'I know what happened, Mama,' he had said. 'The MacDougals. I know what happened that day. Why they left without saying goodbye.'

She was silent for a long time, stirring her tea and watching the little black leaves rise to the surface and then sink again. When she looked back at him, she had a strange hesitant smile on her face.

'Like so many white people, Edmund, the MacDougals left because of Independence.'

'The truth, Mama. Please, I am a man now.'

His mother sat, slowly shaking her head. 'Staying on was not what they wanted. They were old. They wanted to go home.'

'Please, stop persisting with this. You are lying to me. I remember.'

'Please, forget it, Edmund. Forget it.'

'I *know* what happened that day.'

His mother was trembling. She caught hold of his arm with both her hands; her fingers dug into him with a fearful insistency.

'When you didn't remember–' She took a deep breath and let it go with a long sigh. 'We thought it best. It was best to forget.'

'You thought it best...? All these years. All these years, you didn't say anything?'

She nodded sadly. 'How could I tell you, my son? How could I tell you? Your father wanted you so badly, he was prepared to make you lie. Simeon told him how you had slept in the house while I was away, about all the time you spent together. It got his dirty mind going.'

'Simeon, yes. So when Pullman came looking for dirt on Mr MacDougal, he had a ready supply.'

'Who better to introduce your father to?'

His mother shook her head sadly.

'What happened to him? My father.'

'When the MacDougals disappeared, no one was interested in his case any more. He didn't have the money to take it to court. He disappeared soon after.'

'Once a loser, always a loser.'

Her eyes were wet with tears. She ran her hand over his face. 'Now forget again. Forget again, my son.'

Edmund heard a car behind him and moved closer to the side of the road. The car drew up next to him and Craig called out of the passenger window. It had been a couple of weeks since they had met and talked things out. They had parted amicably, but with little sign they would ever meet again.

'Hey, is that you, Ed? Do you want a lift?'

Edmund stopped and looked over at Craig, who was also not instantly recognisable.

'You've cut your hair.'

Craig ran his fingers through his short crop of hair, looked in the rear-view mirror and said, 'Ah, so I have! Good detective work!'

'How's things with Sandra?'

'Who's Sandra?' said Craig, looking down at his hands on the steering wheel. 'Old news. The future before us lies! Jump in. I'll give you a lift.'

Edmund looked up the road with a slightly wistful expression on his face. He had looked forward to walking the length of it that morning.

'What's happening with your job?' asked Edmund. 'You staying with it?'

Craig shrugged. 'I was thinking I might try something different. You?'

Edmund shook his head. 'I have well and truly left.'

'They should have made you Chief of Police after all that.'

Edmund smiled.

'I heard Malakai was released.'

'Yes. Insufficient evidence. Janet phoned the police and told them she had given him the elephants.'

'A likely story.'

Edmund shrugged. 'They were hers. She could do with them what she wanted.'

'And Nigel Pullman?'

'Died of a heart attack. And Marcia Pullman died of kidney failure. They should have heeded their doctor's advice.'

'*Jump in* for crying out loud in a bucket! Listen, I'll make it easy for you. You drive, okay?' Craig got out of the car and came round to the passenger side. 'Go on, get in. You can drive, I remember.'

Edmund stared. He looked at Craig and then at the car and then back at Craig. 'Yes,' he said, eventually. 'I can drive.'

He sat holding the steering wheel for a minute or so before putting the car into first. He looked ahead down the road to where dusty pink bougainvillea petered out into the distance and the air trembled just above the blue road. He thought of all those people who had trodden that road; all the people, now gone, who had felt their hearts miss a beat at the first stirrings of spring. Life, it went on, didn't it?

He pressed his foot on the accelerator, feeling tingles of excitement at the delicious rev of the engine.

'Have you anywhere to go?' He turned to Craig with a smile.

'No, nowhere.'

'Right, let's go to nowhere.'

The car shot forward down the road, lurching a little to the side. A little boy was walking along with his mother. He held her hand, skipping over the shadows of the bare overarching jacaranda branches thrown down on the road. She, a large lady in a brown *doek* and flowery maid's uniform, pulled him close as the car passed. The two stood and stared, catching Edmund's eye for a fleeting second. Then the little boy raised his hand momentarily as though snatching at a mite of dust.

Edmund waved, then accelerated, and the car took the corner of Clark Road on two wheels.

Acknowledgements

The publishers acknowledge the excerpts from 'A Red, Red Rose' by Robert Burns, 'Ozymandias' by Percy Bysshe Shelley and 'A Shropshire Lad' by A.E. Housman.

PARTHIAN Fiction

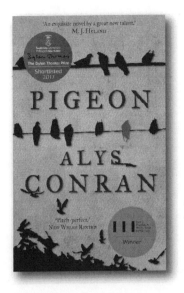

Pigeon

ALYS CONRAN
ISBN 978-1-910901-23-6
£8.99 • Paperback

**Winner of Wales
Book of the Year**

'An exquisite novel by a great
new talent.' – M.J. Hyland

Ironopolis

GLEN JAMES BROWN
ISBN 978-1-912681-09-9
£10.99 • Paperback

**Shortlisted for the Orwell
Award for Political Fiction and
the Portico Prize**

'A triumph' – *The Guardian*

'The most accomplished
working-class novel of the
last few years.' – *Morning Star*

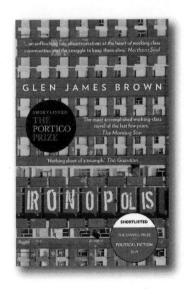

PARTHIAN   Fiction

Martha, Jack & Shanco

CARYL LEWIS
TRANSLATED BY GWEN DAVIES
ISBN 978-1-912681-77-8
£9.99 • Paperback

Winner of the Wales Book of the Year
"Harsh, lyrical, devastating... sings with a
bitter poetry." – *The Independent*

Love and Other Possibilities

LEWIS DAVIES
ISBN 978-1-906998-08-0
£6.99 • Paperback

Winner of the Rhys Davies Award
"Davies's prose is simple and effortless, the
kind of writing that wins competitions."
– *The Independent*

Grace, Tamar and Laszlo the Beautiful

DEBORAH KAY DAVIES
ISBN 978-1-912109-43-2
£8.99 • Paperback

Winner of the Wales Book of the Year
"Davies's writing thrills on all levels."
– Suzy Ceulan Hughes

Hummingbird

TRISTAN HUGHES
ISBN 978-1-91090-90-8
£10 • Hardback
£8.99 • Paperback

Winner of the Stanford Fiction Award
"Superbly accomplished... Hughes's prose is
startling and luminous." – *Financial Times*

PARTHIAN   Fiction

The Web of Belonging
Out 2021

STEVIE DAVIES
ISBN 978-1-912681-16-7
£8.99 • Paperback

"A comic novelist of
the highest order."
– *The Times*

The Cormorant
Out 2021

STEPHEN GREGORY
ISBN 978-1-912681-69-3
£8.99 • Paperback

Winner of the
Somerset Maugham Award
"A first-class terror story with a
relentless focus that would have made
Edgar Allan Poe proud."
– *New York Times*

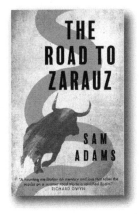

The Road to Zarauz

SAM ADAMS
ISBN 978-1-912681-85-3
£8.99 • Paperback
"A haunting meditation on memory
and loss that takes the reader on a
summer road trip to a vanished Spain."
– Richard Gwyn

PARTHIAN   Fiction

Also by Bryony Rheam:

This September Sun

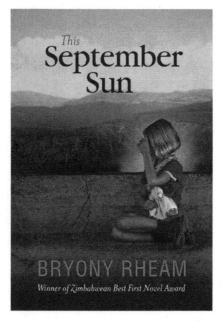

978-1-906998-53-0
£9.99 • Paperback

**Winner of
Zimbabwean Best
First Novel Award**

'Rheam's Africa is not
the Africa of the
media – that is a
continent reduced to
nothing more than
poverty and strife, it
is a place where real
people live with
everyday worries and
regular problems and
the novel strikes an optimistic tone missing in most African
Literature.' – **Tendai Huchu**

'…beautifully crafted. There is drama, an absorbing journey
… a feast for the senses…' – **Gwales.com**

'In *This September Sun* Bryony Rheam takes a bold but
necessary step toward exorcising the ghost of Rhodesia from
the house of Zimbabwean letters.' – *The Warwick Review*